Fierce READS

PRESENTS

KISSES AND CURSES

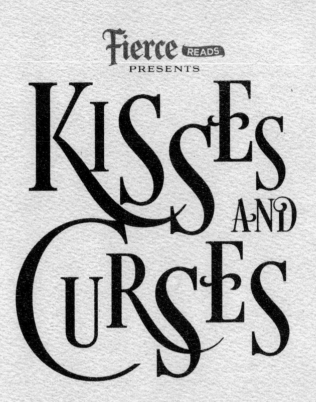

Fierce READS
PRESENTS

KISSES AND CURSES

Ann Aguirre ◆ Gennifer Albin ◆ Courtney Alameda

Anna Banks ◆ Leigh Bardugo ◆ Jessica Brody

Katie Finn ◆ Nikki Kelly ◆ Emmy Laybourne

Jennifer Mathieu ◆ Lish McBride ◆ Marissa Meyer

Caragh O'Brien ◆ Marie Rutkoski ◆ Lindsay Smith

Edited by Lauren Burniac

SQUARE
FISH

New York

SQUARE FISH

An Imprint of Macmillan
175 Fifth Avenue
New York, NY 10010
macteenbooks.com

Square Fish books may be purchased for business or promotional use.
For information on bulk purchases, please contact the Macmillan Corporate
and Premium Sales Department at (800) 221-7945 x5442 or by e-mail at
specialmarkets@macmillan.com.

Library of Congress Cataloging-in-Publication Data

Fierce Reads : kisses and curses / Ann Aguirre, Gennifer Albin,
[and fourteen others].
pages cm
Summary: "With standalone short stories from a handpicked set of Fierce
Reads authors, this collection will include a mix of original content and
popular favorites, and will often feature characters or worlds from existing
Fierce Reads books"—Provided by publisher.
ISBN 978-1-250-06053-2 (paperback) — ISBN 978-1-250-07509-3 (e-book)
1. Short stories, American.   [1. Short stories.]
PZ5.F45 2015
[Fic]—dc23
2015002258

First Edition: 2015
Book designed by Ashley Halsey
Square Fish logo designed by Filomena Tuosto

10 9 8 7 6 5 4 3 2 1

Table of Contents

Marissa Meyer ◆ *Glitches*

1

Marie Rutkoski ◆ *Bridge of Snow*

33

Jennifer Mathieu ◆ *Dynamite Junior*

51

Anna Banks & Emmy Laybourne ◆ *Monster Crush*

75

Courtney Alameda ◆ *Fixer*

127

Jessica Brody ◆ *Unstolen*

151

Ann Aguirre ◆ *Secret Heart*

165

Lish McBride ◆ *Death & Waffles*

179

Lindsay Smith ◆ *Krisis*

203

Table of Contents

Katie Finn ♦ *Deleted Scenes*
227

Caragh M. O'Brien ♦ *Tortured*
251

Nikki Kelly ♦ *Blue Moon*
275

Gennifer Albin ♦ *The Cypress Project*
305

Leigh Bardugo ♦ *The Too-Clever Fox*
365

Fierce READS
PRESENTS

KISSES AND CURSES

GLITCHES

Marissa Meyer

BY MARISSA MEYER

~ The Lunar Chronicles ~

Cinder

Scarlet

Cress

Winter

And don't miss Levana's story in . . .

Fairest

Meet Marissa Meyer

"Glitches" is a prequel to *Cinder,* set about five years before the start of the novel. The story offers a glimpse into some of Cinder's first memories: waking up from the surgery that changed her life forever; moving to a new country; and meeting her adoptive family (including a stepmother who is already worried about caring for her own two daughters, much less an orphaned science experiment). All the while Cinder is trying to come to terms with her new identity as a lowly cyborg. The story also shows the start of the friendship between Cinder and her beloved sidekick, Iko—a beginning that even I didn't know until I was writing it.

Cinder's tale began one night in August 2008, when I awoke with a start after having a peculiar dream. In that dream, I'd seen Cinderella—your typical Cinderella, wearing her lavish ball gown and running away from the palace as the clock began to strike midnight. Only, in my dream, rather than a glass slipper falling off, her whole foot fell off.

My first thought upon waking: It's Cinderella . . . as a *cyborg.*

The concept wasn't quite as unprecedented as it might seem. A few months prior to that dream I'd entered a short-story-writing contest with a science-fiction retelling of "Puss in

Boots," in which the protagonist was a robotic talking cat trying to reunite a lost princess with her kingdom on the moon. I didn't win the contest (full disclosure: out of only two entries, I came in second place), but I did come away from it loving the idea of combining science fiction and fairy tales and imagining an entire series of futuristic retellings. My cyborg Cinderella dream was merely the missing puzzle piece that I needed to start pulling together months' worth of plotting and brainstorming, and I've loved working in Cinder's world ever since.

Though *Cinder* is the first novel I ever completed, I've been an avid reader since I was a child, and I've wanted to be a published author from the time I realized such a job existed. When I was fourteen, my best friend introduced me to the popular Japanese anime *Sailor Moon* and the world of online fan fiction. Instantly immersed in the fandom and a community where I could share my writing and receive valuable feedback, I would go on to complete close to fifty works of fan fiction. They say that every writer has a drawer full of unpublished manuscripts in their desk—for me, my "drawer" is my fanfiction.net page, and I largely credit this experience with helping me learn the craft of storytelling.

After high school I attended Pacific Lutheran University in Tacoma, Washington, where I earned a bachelor's degree in creative writing with an emphasis on children's literature. I also hold a master's in publishing from Pace University. I worked as a managing editor for a publisher of fine-art books in Seattle for five years before becoming a freelance proofreader, all the while working on *Cinder* and dreaming of the day that I could call myself a full-time writer.

At the time of writing this, that dream has come true. With four published novels now bearing my name, I find myself waking up every morning feeling lucky and proud to have made my own little fairy tale a reality, and it continues to amaze me when I hear from readers who have fallen in love with Cinder and her allies as much as I have.

I still live in Tacoma, now with my husband, two beautiful foster daughters, and two demanding cats. Interested readers can follow me on Twitter (@marissa_meyer) or subscribe to my blog and quarterly newsletter at marissameyer.com.

GLITCHES

by Marissa Meyer

"Are you ready to meet your new family?"

She tore her gaze away from the window, where snow was heaped up on bamboo fences and a squat android was clearing a path through the slush, and looked at the man seated opposite her. Though he'd been kind to her throughout their trip, two full days of being passed between a hover, a maglev train, two passenger ships, and yet another hover, he still had a nervous smile that made her fidget.

Plus, she kept forgetting his name.

"I don't remember the old family," she said, adjusting her heavy left leg so that it didn't stick out quite so far between their seats.

His lips twisted awkwardly into an expression that was probably meant to be reassuring, and this ended their conversation. His attention fell down to a device he never stopped looking at, with a screen that cast a greenish glow over his face.

He wasn't a very old man, but his eyes always seemed tired and his clothes didn't fit him right. Though he'd been clean-cut when he first came to claim her, he was now in need of a razor.

She returned her gaze to the snow-covered street. The suburb struck her as crowded and confused. A series of short one-story shacks would be followed by a mansion with a frozen water fountain in its courtyard and red-tiled roofs. After that, a series of clustered town houses and maybe a run-down apartment complex, before more tiny shacks took over. It all looked like someone had taken every kind of residence they could think of and spilled them across a grid of roads, not caring where anything landed.

She suspected that her new home wasn't anything like the rolling farmland they'd left behind in the European Federation, but she'd been in such a foggy-brained daze at the time that she couldn't remember much of anything before the train ride. Except that it had been snowing there, too. She was already sick of the snow and the cold. They made her bones ache where her fleshy parts connected to her steel prosthetics.

She swiveled her gaze back toward the man seated across from her. "Are we almost there?"

He nodded without looking up. "Almost, Cinder."

Enfolding her fingers around the scar tissue on her wrist, she waited, hoping he would say something else to ease her nerves, but he didn't seem the type to notice anyone's anxiety above his own. She imagined calling him *Dad*, but the word was laughably unfamiliar, even inside her head. She couldn't even compare him with her real father, as her memory had been reduced to a blank slate during the intrusive surgeries. All she had left of her parents was their sterile identity profiles, with plain photos that held no recognition and a tag at the top labeling them as DECEASED. They'd been killed in the hover crash that had also claimed her leg and hand.

As confirmed by all official records, there was no one else. Cinder's grandparents were also dead. She had no siblings. No aunts or uncles or friends—at least, none willing to claim her. Perhaps there wasn't a human being in all of Europe who would have taken her in, and that's why they'd had to search as far as New Beijing before they found her a replacement family.

She squinted, straining to remember who *they* were. The faceless people who had pulled her from the wreckage and turned her into *this*. Doctors and surgeons, no doubt. Scientists. Programmers. There must have been a social worker involved, but she couldn't recall for sure. Her memory gave her only dizzy glimpses of the French countryside and this stranger sitting across from her, entranced by the device in his hands.

Her new stepfather.

The hover began to slow, drifting toward the curb. Its nose hit a snowbank and it came to a sudden shuddering stop. Cinder grabbed the bar overhead, but the hover had already settled down, slightly off-kilter in the packed snow.

"Here we are," said the man, eyes twinkling as the hover door slid open.

She stayed plastered to her seat, her hand still gripping the bar, as a gust of icy wind swirled around them. They'd arrived at one of the tiny shack houses, one with peeling paint and a gutter that hung loose beneath the weight of the snow. Still, it was a sweet little house, all white with a red roof and enough dead branches sticking up from the ground that Cinder could almost imagine a garden come springtime.

The man paid the hover with a swipe of his wrist, then stepped out onto a pathway that had been plowed down to a sheet of ice. The door to the house opened before he'd taken a step and two girls about Cinder's own age came barreling down the front steps, squealing. The man crouched down on the pathway, holding out his arms as the girls launched themselves into him.

From her place inside the hover, Cinder heard the man laugh for the first time.

A woman appeared inside the doorway, belting a quilted robe around her waist. "Girls, don't suffocate your father. He's had a long trip."

"Don't listen to your mother, just this once. You can suffocate me all you like." He kissed his daughters on the tops of their heads, then stood, keeping a firm grip on their hands. "Would you like to meet your new sister?" he asked, turning back to face the hover. He seemed surprised at the empty pathway behind him. "Come on out, Cinder."

She shivered and pried her hand away from the safety bar. Sliding toward the door, she tried to be graceful stepping out onto the curb, but the distance to the ground was shorter than she'd expected and her heavy leg was inflexible as it crunched through the compact ice. She cried out and stumbled, barely catching herself on the hover's doorframe.

The man hurried back toward her, holding her up as well as he could by the arm, one hand gripping her metal fingers. "It's all right, perfectly natural. Your muscles are weak right now, and it will take time for your wiring to fully integrate with your nervous system."

Cinder stared hard at the ground, shivering both from cold

and embarrassment. She couldn't help finding irony in the man's words, though she dared not laugh at them—what did integrated wiring have to do with being perfectly natural?

"Cinder," the man continued, coaxing her forward, "this is my eldest daughter, Pearl, and my youngest, Peony. And that is their lovely mother, Adri. Your new stepmother."

She peered up at his two daughters from behind a curtain of fine brown hair.

They were both staring openly at her metal hand.

Cinder tried to shrink away, but then the younger girl, Peony, asked, "Did it hurt when they put it on?"

Steady on her feet again, Cinder pried her hand out of the man's hold and tucked it against her side. "I don't remember."

"She was unconscious for the surgeries, Peony," said the man.

"Can I touch it?" she asked, her hand already inching forward.

"That's enough, Garan. People are watching."

Cinder jumped at the shrill voice, but when she looked up, her stepmother was not looking at them, but at the house across the street.

Garan. That was the man's name. Cinder committed it to memory as she followed Adri's gaze and saw a man staring at her through his front window.

"It's freezing out here," said Adri. "Pearl, go find the android and have her bring in your father's luggage. Peony, you can show Cinder to her room."

"You mean *my* room," said Pearl, her lip curling as she began to shuffle back toward the house. "I'm older. I shouldn't have to share with Peony."

To Cinder's surprise, the younger girl turned and latched on to her arm, tugging her forward. She nearly slipped on the ice and would have been embarrassed again, except she noticed that Peony's feet were slipping around too as she pulled Cinder ahead. "Pearl can take the room," she said. "I don't mind sharing with Cinder."

Adri's face was taut as she looked down at their intertwined elbows. "Don't argue with me, either of you."

Condensation sprang up on Cinder's steel hand as she went from the chilled air to the house's warm entryway, but Peony didn't seem to notice as she led her toward the back of the house.

"I don't know why Pearl's upset," she said, shouldering open a door. "This is the smallest room in the house. Our bedroom is much nicer." Releasing Cinder, she went to pull open the blinds on the single small window. "But, look, you can see the neighbor's cherry tree. It's really pretty when it blooms."

Cinder didn't follow her to the window, instead casting her gaze around the room. It seemed small, but it was larger than the sleeper car on the maglev train and she had no prior bedrooms to compare it with. A mattress sat in the corner with blankets tucked neatly around its sides, and a small dresser stood empty on the nearest wall.

"Pearl used to have a netscreen in here, but Mom moved it into the kitchen. You can come watch mine whenever you want to, though. Do you like *Nightmare Island*? It's my favorite drama."

"*Nightmare Island*?" No sooner had Cinder said it than her brain started streaming data across her vision. `A popular drama aimed at teenage girls that includes a cast of thirty-six young celebrities who are`

caught up in lies, betrayal, romance, and the
scheme of a crazed scientist who—

"Don't tell me you've never heard of it!"

Cinder scrunched her shoulders beside her ears. "I've heard of it," she said, blinking the data away. She wondered whether there was a way to get her brain to stop doing that every time she heard an unfamiliar phrase. It had been happening almost nonstop since she'd woken up from the surgery. "That's the show with the crazed scientist, right? I've never seen it, though."

Peony looked relieved. "That's fine, I have a subscription to the whole feed. We'll watch it together." She bounced on her feet and Cinder had to tear her gaze away from the girl's excitement. Her gaze landed on a box half tucked behind the door. A small pronged hand was hanging over the edge.

"What's this?" she said, leaning forward. She kept her hands locked behind her back.

"Oh, that's Iko." Abandoning the window, Peony crouched down and scooted the box out from the wall. It was filled with random android parts all jumbled together—the spherical body took up most of the space, along with a glossy white head, a sensor lens, a clear bag filled with screws and program chips. "She had some sort of glitch in her personality chip and Mom heard that she could get more money for her if she sold her off in pieces rather than as a whole, but nobody wanted them. Now she just sits here, in a box."

Cinder shuddered, wondering how common glitches were in androids. Or cyborgs.

"I really liked Iko when she was working. She was a lot more fun than that boring garden android." Peony picked up the thin metal arm with the three prongs and held it up so that the fingers clicked together. "We used to play dress-up together." Her eyes lit up. "Hey, do *you* like playing dress-up?"

Adri appeared in the doorway just as Cinder's brain was informing her that "dress-up" was `a game often played by children in which costumes or adult clothes are used to aid in the process of imagination . . .`

Obviously, she thought, sending the message away.

"Well, Cinder?" said Adri, tightening her robe's belt again and surveying the small room with a pinched face. "Garan told me you wouldn't want for much. I hope this meets your expectations?"

She looked around again, at the bed, the dresser, the branches that would someday bloom in the neighbor's yard. "Yes, thank you."

Adri rubbed her hands together. "Good. I hope you'll let me know if you need anything. We're glad to share our home with you, knowing what you've been through."

Cinder licked her lips, thinking to say thank you again, but then a small orange light flickered in her optobionics and she found herself frowning. This was something new and she had no idea what it meant.

Maybe it was a sign of a brain malfunction. Maybe this was a glitch.

"Come along, Peony," said Adri, stepping back into the hall. "I could use some help in the kitchen."

"But, Mom, Cinder and I were going to—"

"*Now*, Peony."

Scowling, Peony thrust the android arm into Cinder's hand and followed after her mother.

Cinder held up the limb and shook it at their backs, making the lifeless fingers wave good-bye.

❧

Six nights after she'd arrived at her new home, Cinder awoke on fire. She cried out, tumbling off the mattress and landing in a heap with a blanket wrapped like a tourniquet around her bionic leg. She lay gasping for a minute, rubbing her hands over her arms to try to smother the flames until she finally realized that they weren't real.

A warning about escalating temperatures flashed in her gaze and she forced herself to lie still long enough to dismiss it from her vision. Her skin was clammy, beads of sweat dripping back into her hair. Even her metal limbs felt warm to the touch.

When her breathing was under control, she pulled herself up onto weak legs and hobbled to the window, thrusting it open and drinking in the winter air. The snow had started to melt, turning into slush in the daytime before hardening into glistening ice at night. Cinder stood for a moment, reveling in the frosty air on her skin and entranced by how a nearly full moon turned the world ghostly yellow. She tried to remember the nightmare, but her memory gave her only fire and, after a minute, the sensation of sandpaper in her mouth.

Shutting the window, she crept toward her bedroom door, careful not to trip on the bag of secondhand clothes Pearl had begrudgingly given to her the day before, after her father had lectured her about charity.

She heard Adri's voice before she reached the kitchen and paused, one hand balancing her on the wall as her body threatened to tip toward its heavier left side.

As she strained to hear, Adri's voice grew steadily louder, and Cinder realized with a jolt that Adri wasn't *speaking* louder, but rather something in her own head was adjusting the volume on her hearing. She rubbed her palm against her ear, feeling like there was a bug in it.

"Four months, Garan," Adri said. "We're behind by four months and Suki-jiĕ has already threatened to start auctioning off our things if we don't pay her soon."

"She's not going to auction off our things," said Garan, his voice a strange combination of soothing and strained. Garan's voice had already become unfamiliar to Cinder's ear. He spent his days out in a one-room shed behind the house, "tinkering," Peony said, though she didn't seem to know what exactly he was tinkering with. He came in to join his family for meals, but hardly ever talked and Cinder wondered how much he heard, either. His expression always suggested his mind was very far away.

"Why *shouldn't* she sell off our things? I'm sure I would in her place!" Adri said. "Whenever I have to leave the house, I come home wondering if this will be the day our things are gone and our locks are changed. We can't keep living on her hospitality."

"It's going to be all right, love. Our luck is changing."

"Our luck!" Adri's voice spiked in Cinder's ear and she flinched at the shrillness, quickly urging the volume to descend again. It obeyed her command, through sheer willpower. She held her breath, wondering what other secrets her brain was keeping from her.

"*How* is our luck changing? Because you won a silver ribbon at that fair in Sydney last month? Your stupid awards aren't going to keep food on this table, and now you've brought home one more mouth—and a *cyborg* at that!"

"We talked about this . . ."

"No, *you* talked about this. I want to support you, Garan, but these schemes of yours are going to cost us everything. We have our own girls to think about. I can't even afford new shoes for Pearl and now there's this creature in the house who's going to need . . . what? A new *foot* every six months?"

Shriveling against the wall, Cinder glanced down at her metal foot, the toes looking awkward and huge beside the fleshy ones—the ones with bone and skin and toenails.

"Of course not. She'll be fine for a year or two," said Garan.

Adri stifled a hysterical laugh.

"And her leg and fingers can be adjusted as she grows," Garan continued. "We shouldn't need replacements for those until she reaches adulthood."

Cinder lifted her hand into the faint light coming down the hallway, inspecting the joints. She hadn't noticed how the knuckles were fitted together before, the digits nestled inside each other. So this hand could grow, just like her human hand did.

Because she would be stuck with these limbs forever. She would be a cyborg forever.

"Well, how *comforting*," said Adri. "I'm glad to see you've given this so much thought."

"Have faith, love."

Cinder heard a chair being pushed back and backed up into the hallway, but all that followed was the sound of running water from the faucet. She pressed her fingers over her mouth, trying to feel the water through psychokinesis, but even *her* brain couldn't quench her thirst on sound alone.

"I have something special to reveal at the Tokyo Fair in March," Garan said. "It's going to change everything. In the meantime, you must be patient with the child. She only wants to belong here. Perhaps she can help you with the housework, until we can get that android replaced?"

Adri scoffed. "Help me? What can she do, dragging that monstrosity around?"

Cinder cringed. She heard a cup being set down, then a kiss. "Give her a chance. Maybe she'll surprise you."

She ducked away at the first hint of a footstep, creeping back into her room and shutting the door. She felt that she could have wept from thirst, but her eyes stayed as dry as her tongue.

⟡

"Here, you put on the green one," said Peony, tossing a bundle of green and gold silk into Cinder's arms. She barely caught it, the thin material slipping like water over her hands. "We don't have any real ball gowns, but these are just as pretty. This is my favorite." Peony held up another garment, a swath of purple-and-red fabric decorated with soaring cranes. She strung her bony arms through the enormous sleeves and pulled the material tight around her waist, holding it in place while she dug through the pile of clothes for a long silver sash and belted it around her middle. "Aren't they beautiful?"

Cinder nodded uncertainly—although the silk kimonos were perhaps the finest things she'd ever felt, Peony looked ridiculous in hers. The hem of the gown dragged a foot on the floor, the sleeves dangled almost to her knees, and street clothes still peeked through at her neck and wrists, ruining the illusion. It almost looked like the gown was trying to eat her.

"Put yours on!" said Peony. "Here, this is the sash I usually put with that one." She pulled out a black-and-violet band.

Cinder tentatively stuck her hands into the sleeves, taking extra care that no screws or joints caught the fine material. "Won't Adri be mad?"

"Pearl and I play dress-up all the time," said Peony, looping the sash around Cinder's waist. "And how are we supposed to go to the ball if we don't have any beautiful dresses to wear?"

Cinder raised her arms, shaking the sleeves back. "I don't think my hand goes with this one."

Peony laughed, though Cinder hadn't meant it to be funny. Peony seemed to find amusement with almost everything she said.

"Just pretend you're wearing gloves," said Peony. "Then no one will know." Grabbing Cinder by the hand, she pulled her across the hall and into the bathroom so they could see themselves in the mirror. Cinder looked no less absurd than Peony, with her fine, mousy hair hanging limp past her shoulders and awkward metal fingers poking out of the left sleeve.

"Perfect," said Peony, beaming. "Now we're at the ball. Iko used to always be the prince, but I guess we'll have to pretend."

"What ball?"

Peony stared back at her in the mirror as if Cinder had sprouted a metal tail. "The ball for the peace festival! It's this huge event we have every year—the festival is down in the city center and then in the evening they have the ball up at the palace. I've never gone for real, but Pearl will be thirteen next year so she'll get to go for the first time." She sighed and spun out into the hallway. Cinder followed, her walking made even more cumbersome than usual with the kimono trailing on the ground.

"When I go for the first time, I want a purple dress with a skirt so big I can hardly fit through the door."

"That sounds uncomfortable."

Peony wrinkled her nose. "Well, it has to be spectacular, or else Prince Kai won't notice me, and then what's the point?"

Cinder was almost hesitant to ask as she followed flouncing Peony back into her bedroom—"Who's Prince Kai?"

Peony spun toward her so fast, she tripped on the skirts of Adri's kimono and fell, screaming, onto her bed. "*Who's Prince Kai?*" she yelled, struggling to sit back up. "Only my future husband! Honestly, don't girls in Europe know about him?"

Cinder teetered between her two feet, unable to answer the question. After twelve whole days living with Peony and her family, she already had more memories of the Eastern Commonwealth than she had of Europe. She hadn't the faintest idea what—or who—the girls in Europe obsessed over.

"Here," said Peony, scrambling across her messy blankets and grabbing a portscreen off the nightstand. "He's my greeter."

She turned on the screen and a boy's voice said, "Hello, Peony." Cinder shuffled forward and took the small device from her. The screen showed a boy of twelve or thirteen years old wearing a tailored suit that seemed ironic with his shaggy black hair. He was waving at someone—Cinder guessed the photo was from some sort of press event.

"Isn't he gorgeous?" said Peony. "Every night I tie a red string around my finger and say his name five times because this girl in my class told me that will tie our destinies together. I know he's my soul mate."

Cinder listed her head, still staring at the boy. Her optobionics were scanning him, finding the picture in some database in her head, and this time she expected the stream of text that began to filter through her brain. His ID number, his birth date, his full name and title. Prince Kaito, Crown Prince of the Eastern Commonwealth.

"His arms are too long for his body," she said after a while, finally picking up on what didn't feel right about the picture. "They're not proportionate."

"What are you talking about?" Peony snatched the port away and stared at it for a minute before tossing it onto her pillow. "Honestly, who cares about his arms?"

Cinder shrugged, unable to smother a slight grin. "I was only saying."

Harrumphing, Peony swung her legs around and hopped off the bed. "Fine, whatever. Our hover is here. We'd better get going or we'll be late for the ball, where *I* am going to dance with His Imperial Highness, and *you* can dance with whoever you would like to. Maybe another prince. We should make one up for you. Do you want Prince Kai to have a brother?"

"What are you two doing?"

Cinder spun around. Adri was looming in the doorway—again her footsteps had gone unnoticed and Cinder was beginning to wonder if Adri was really a ghost that floated through the hallways rather than walked.

"We're going to the ball!" Peony said.

Adri's face flushed as her gaze dropped to the silk kimono hanging off Cinder's shoulders. "Take that off this instant!"

Shrinking back, Cinder instantly began undoing the knot that Peony had tied around her waist.

"Peony, what are you thinking? These garments are expensive and if she got snagged—if the lining—" Stepping forward, she grabbed the collar of the dress, peeling it off Cinder as soon as the sash was free.

"But you used to let Pearl and me—"

"Things are *different* now, and you are to leave my things alone. Both of you!"

Scowling, Peony started unwrapping her own dress. Cinder bit the inside of her cheek, feeling oddly vulnerable without the heavy silk draped around her and sick to her stomach with guilt, though she wasn't sure what she had to be guilty about.

"Cinder."

She dared to meet Adri's gaze.

"I came to tell you that if you are to be a part of this household, I will expect you to take on some responsibilities. You're old enough to help Pearl with her chores."

She nodded, almost eager to have something to do with her time when Peony wasn't around. "Of course. I don't want to be any trouble."

Adri's mouth pursed into a thin line. "I won't ask you to do any dusting until I can trust you to move with a bit of grace. Is that hand water resistant?"

Cinder held out her bionic hand, splaying out the fingers. "I . . . I think so. But it might rust . . . after a while . . ."

"Fine, no dishes or scrubbing, then. Can you at least cook?"

Cinder racked her brain, wondering whether it could feed her recipes as easily as it fed her useless definitions. "I never have before, that I can remember. But I'm sure . . ."

Peony threw her arms into the air. "Why don't we just get Iko fixed and then *she* can do all the housework like she's supposed to?"

Adri's eyes smoldered as she looked between her daughter and Cinder. "Well," she said, finally, snatching up the two kimonos and draping them over her arm. "I'm sure we'll be able to find *some use* for you. In the meantime, why don't you leave my daughter alone so she can get some of her schoolwork accomplished?"

"What?" said Peony. "But we haven't even gotten to the ball yet."

Cinder didn't wait to hear the argument she expected to follow. "Yes, Stepmother," she murmured, ducking her head. She slipped past Adri and made her way to her own room.

Her insides were writhing but she couldn't pinpoint the overruling emotion. Hot anger, because it wasn't her fault that her new leg was awkward and heavy, and how was she to know Adri wouldn't want them playing in her things?

But also mortification because maybe she really was useless. She was eleven years old, but she didn't know anything, other than the bits of data that seemed to serve no purpose other than to keep her from looking like a complete idiot. If she'd had any skills before, she had no idea what they had been. She'd lost them now.

Sighing, she shut her bedroom door and slumped against it.

The room hadn't changed much in the almost two weeks since she'd come to call it home, other than the cast-off clothes that had been put into the dresser drawers, a pair of boots tossed into a corner, the blankets bundled up in a ball at the foot of her bed.

Her eyes landed on the box of android parts that hadn't been moved from their spot behind the door. The dead sensor, the spindly arms.

There was a bar code printed on the back of the torso that she hadn't noticed before. She barely noticed it then, except that her distracted brain was searching for the random numbers, downloading the android's make and model information. Parts list. Estimated value. Maintenance and repair manual.

Something familiar stirred inside her, like she already knew this android. How its parts fit together, how its mechanics and programming all functioned as a whole. Or, no, this wasn't familiarity, but . . . a connectedness. Like she knew the android intimately. Like it was an extension of her.

She pushed herself off the door, her skin tingling.

Perhaps she had one useful skill after all.

⁂

It took three days, during which she emerged from her room only to sit for meals with her new family and, once, to play in the snow with Peony while Adri and Pearl were at the market. Her metal limbs had frosted over with cold by the time they were done, but coming inside to a pot of green tea and the flush of shared laughter had quickly warmed her back up.

Adri had not asked Cinder to take on any household chores again, and Cinder imagined it seemed a lost cause to her stepmother. She stayed hopeful, though, as the jumble of android pieces gradually formed into something recognizable. A hollow plastic body atop wide treads, two skinny arms, a squat head with nothing but a cyclops sensor for a face. The sensor had given her the most trouble and she had to redo the wiring twice, triple-checking the diagram that had downloaded across her eyesight, before she felt confident she'd gotten it right.

If only it worked. If only she could show Adri, and even Garan, that she wasn't a useless addition to their family after all. That she was grateful they'd taken her in when no one else would. That she wanted to belong to them.

She was sitting cross-legged on her bed with the window open behind her, allowing in a chilled but pleasant breeze, when she inserted the final touch. The small personality chip clicked into place and Cinder held her breath, half expecting the android to perk up and swivel around and start talking to her, until she remembered that she would need to be charged before she could function.

Feeling her excitement wane from the anticlimactic finale, Cinder released a slow breath and fell back onto her mattress, mentally exhausted.

A knock thunked against the door.

"Come in," she called, not bothering to move as the door creaked open.

"I was just wondering if you wanted to come watch—" Peony fell silent and Cinder managed to lift her head to see the girl gaping wide-eyed at the android. "Is that . . . Iko?"

Grinning, Cinder braced herself on her elbows. "She still needs to be charged, but I think she'll work."

Jaw still hanging open, Peony crept into the room. Though

only nine years old, she was already well over a foot taller than the squat robot. "How . . . *how?* How did you fix it?"

"I had to borrow some tools from your dad." Cinder gestured to a pile of wrenches and screwdrivers in the corner. She didn't bother to mention that he hadn't been in his workshop behind the house when she'd gone to find them. It almost felt like theft and that thought terrified her, but it wasn't theft. She wasn't going to keep the tools, and she was sure Garan would be delighted when he saw she'd fixed the android.

"That's not . . ." Peony shook her head and finally looked at Cinder. "You fixed her by yourself?"

Cinder shrugged, not sure if she should be proud or uncomfortable by the look of awe Peony was giving her. "It wasn't that hard," she said. "I had . . . I can download . . . information. Instructions. Into my head. And I figured out how to get the android's blueprint to go across my vision so I could . . ." She trailed off, realizing that what she'd been sure was a most useful skill was also one more strange eccentricity her body could claim. One more side effect of being cyborg.

But Peony's eyes were twinkling by the minute. "You're kidding," she said, picking up one of Iko's hands and waggling it around. Cinder had been sure to thoroughly grease it so the joints wouldn't seize up. "What else can you do?"

"Um." Cinder hunched her shoulders, considering. "I can . . . make stuff louder. I mean, not really, but I can adjust my hearing so it seems louder. Or quieter. I could probably mute my hearing if I wanted to."

Peony laughed. "That's brilliant! You'd never have to hear Mom when she's yelling! Aw, I'm so jealous." Beaming, she started to drag Iko toward the door. "Come on, there's a charging station in the hallway."

Cinder hopped off the bed and followed her to a docking station at the end of the hall. Peony plugged Iko in and, instantly, a faint blue light started to glow around the plug.

Peony raised hopeful eyes to Cinder when the front door opened and Garan stumbled into the hallway, his hair dripping. He wasn't wearing his coat.

He started when he saw the girls standing there. "Peony," he said, short of breath. "Where's your mother?"

She glanced over her shoulder. "In the kitchen, I thi—"

"Go fetch her. Quickly, please."

Peony stalled, her face clouding with worry, before hurrying toward the kitchen.

Intertwining her fingers, Cinder slid in closer to the android. It was the first time she'd been alone with Garan since their long trip and she expected him to say something, to ask how she was getting along or if there was anything she needed—he'd certainly asked that plenty of times while they were traveling—but he hardly seemed to notice her standing there.

"I fixed your android," she said finally, her voice squeaking a little. She grabbed the android's limp arm, as if to prove it, though the hand did nothing but droop.

Garan turned his distraught gaze on her and looked for a moment like he was going to ask who she was and what she was doing in his house. He opened his mouth but it took a long time for any words to form.

"Oh, child."

She frowned at the obvious pity. This was not a reaction

she'd expected—he was not impressed, he was not grateful. Thinking he must not have heard her correctly, she went to repeat herself—no, she'd *fixed* the android—when Adri came around the corner, wearing the robe she always wore when she wasn't planning on going out. She had a dish towel in her hand and her two daughters trailing in her wake.

"Garan?"

He stumbled back, slamming his shoulder hard into the wall, and everyone froze.

"D-don't—" he stammered, smiling apologetically as a droplet of water fell onto his nose. "I've called for an emergency hover."

The curiosity hardened on Adri's face. "Whatever for?"

Cinder pressed herself as far as she could into the wall, feeling like she was pinned between two people who hadn't the faintest idea she was standing there.

Garan folded his arms, starting to shiver. "I've caught it," he whispered, his eyes beginning to water.

Cinder glanced back at Peony, wondering if these words meant something to her, but no one was paying Cinder any attention.

"I'm sorry," said Garan, coughing. He shuffled back toward the door. "I shouldn't even have come inside. But I had to say . . . I had to . . ." He covered his mouth and his entire body shook with a cough, or a sob, Cinder couldn't tell which. "I love you all so much. I'm so sorry. I'm so, so sorry."

"Garan." Adri took half a step forward, but her husband was already turning away. The front door shut a second later, and Pearl and Peony cried out at the same time and rushed forward, but Adri caught them both by their arms. "*Garan!* No—you girls, stay here. Both of you." Her voice was trembling as she pulled them back, before chasing after Garan herself, her night robe swishing against Cinder's legs as she passed.

Cinder inched forward so she could see the door being swung open around the corner. Her heart thumped like a drum against her ribs.

"GARAN!" Adri screamed, tears in her voice. "What are you—you can't go!"

Cinder was slammed against the wall as Pearl tore past her, screaming for her father, then Peony, sobbing.

No one paused. No one looked at Cinder or the android in their hurry for the door. Cinder realized after a moment that she was still gripping the android's skeletal arm, listening. Listening to the sobs and pleas, the *No*s, the *Daddy*s. The words echoed off the snow and back into the house.

Releasing the android, Cinder hobbled forward. She reached the threshold that overlooked the blindingly white world and paused, staring at Adri and Pearl and Peony, who were on their knees in the pathway to the street, slush soaking into their clothes. Garan was standing on the curb, his hand still over his mouth as if he'd forgotten it was there. His eyes were red from crying. He looked weak and small, as if the slightest wind would blow him over into the snowdrifts.

Cinder heard sirens.

"What am I supposed to do?" Adri screamed, her arms covered in goose bumps as they gripped her children against her. "What will I do?"

A door slammed and Cinder looked up. The old man across the street was on his doorstep. More neighbors were emerging— at doors and windows—their gazes bright with curiosity.

Adri sobbed louder, and Cinder returned her attention to the family—her new family—and realized that Garan was watching *her*.

She stared back, her throat burning from the cold.

The sirens became louder and Garan glanced down at his huddled wife, his terrified daughters. "My girls," he said, trying to smile, and then a white hover with flashing lights turned the corner, screaming its arrival.

Cinder ducked back into the doorway as the hover slid up behind Garan and settled into the snow. Two androids rolled out of its side door with a gurney hovering between them. Their yellow sensors flashed.

"A comm was received at 1704 this evening regarding a victim of letumosis at this address," said one of the androids in a sterile voice.

"That's me," Garan choked—his words instantly drowned out by Adri's screaming, "NO! Garan! You can't. You can't!"

Garan attempted a shaken smile and held out his arm. He rolled up his sleeve and even from her spot on the doorstep Cinder could see two dark spots on his wrist. "I have it. Adri, love, you must take care of the girl."

Adri pulled back as if he'd struck her. "*The girl?*"

"Pearl, Peony," Garan continued as if she hadn't spoken, "be good for your mother. Never forget that I love you so, so very much." Releasing the hard-won smile, he perched himself uncertainly on the floating gurney.

"Lie back," said one of the androids. "We will input your identification into our records and alert your family immediately of any changes in your condition."

"No, Garan!" Adri clambered to her feet, her thin slippers

sliding on the ice and nearly sending her onto her face as she struggled to rush after her husband. "You can't leave me. Not by myself, not with . . . not with this *thing*."

Cinder shuddered and wrapped her arms around her waist.

"Please stand back from the letumosis victim," said one of the androids, positioning itself between Adri and the hover as Garan was lifted into its belly.

"Garan, no! NO!"

Pearl and Peony latched back on to their mother's sides, both screaming for their father, but perhaps they were too afraid of the androids to go any closer. The androids rolled themselves back up into the hover. The doors shut. The sirens and the lights filled up the quiet suburb before fading slowly away. Adri and her daughters stayed clumped together in the snow, sobbing and clutching one another while the neighbors watched. While Cinder watched, wondering why her eyes stayed so dry—stinging dry—when dread was encompassing her like slush freezing over.

"What's happened?"

Cinder glanced down. The android had woken up and disconnected herself from the charging station and now stood before her with her sensor faintly glowing.

She'd done it. She'd fixed the android. She'd proven her worth.

But her success was drowned out by their sobs and the memory of the sirens. She couldn't quite grasp the unfairness of it.

"They took Garan away," she said, licking her lips. "They called him a letumosis victim."

A series of clicks echoed inside the android's body. "Oh, dear . . . not Garan."

Cinder barely heard her. In saying the words, she realized that her brain had been downloading information for some time, but she'd been too caught up in everything to realize it. Now dozens of useless bits of information were scrolling across her vision. `Letumosis, also called the Blue Fever or the Plague, has claimed thousands of lives since the first known victims of the disease died in northern Africa in May of 114 T.E. . . .` Cinder read faster, scanning until she found the words that she feared, but had somehow known she would find. `To date, there have been no known survivors.`

Iko was speaking again and Cinder shook her head to clear it. "—can't stand to see them cry, especially lovely Peony. Nothing makes an android feel more useless than when a human is crying."

Finding it suddenly hard to breathe, Cinder deserted the doorway and slumped back against the inside wall, unable to listen to the sobs any longer. "You won't have to worry about me, then. I don't think I can cry anymore." She hesitated. "Maybe I never could."

"Is that so? How peculiar. Perhaps it's a programming glitch."

She stared down into Iko's single sensor. "A programming glitch."

"Sure. You have programming, don't you?" She lifted a spindly arm and gestured toward Cinder's steel prosthetic. "I have a glitch, too. Sometimes I forget that I'm not human. I don't think that happens to most androids."

Cinder gaped down at Iko's smooth body, beat-up treads,

three-fingered prongs, and wondered what it would be like to be stuck in such a body and not know whether you were human or robot.

She raised the pad of her finger to the corner of her right eye, searching for wetness that wasn't there.

"Right. A glitch." She feigned a nonchalant smile, hoping the android couldn't detect the grimace that came with it. "Maybe that's all it is."

BRIDGE OF SNOW

Marie Rutkoski

BY MARIE RUTKOSKI

The Shadow Society

~ The Kronos Chronicles ~

The Cabinet of Wonders

The Celestial Globe

The Jewel of the Kalderash

~ The Winner's Trilogy ~

The Winner's Curse

The Winner's Crime

The Winner's Kiss

Meet Marie Rutkoski

I used to be afraid of the moon. This was when I was little, and only in certain circumstances: in winter, just as we'd get out of the warm car after a long drive. I'd look up (sometimes I did it deliberately, to get that chill of fear), see the moon, and suddenly that brief minute between the driveway and the house seemed unbearable. What I felt: isolation, the alien, and some nameless peril close at hand.

As much as the night sky has fascinated humans with its beauty, it also represents the unknown. A couple of years ago, I read an article that told stories different cultures have invented to explain the Milky Way. I had known about the Greek version: that Hera, the queen of the gods, let Hercules nurse from her breast. The milk sprayed across the sky. But there were many tales I didn't know: the African one, invented by people in the Kalahari Desert, of a girl who threw embers into the sky. A Hungarian story said the stars were sparks thrown from the hooves of horses. An Asian one described the galaxy's curve as a bridge that could be crossed by two lovers. It occurred to me that it would be a great pleasure to invent my own explanation for the stars.

I also knew that I wanted to write a short story about Arin

as a child, from the perspective of his mother. "Bridge of Snow" is a prequel to my novel *The Winner's Curse*, which is set in a new world where an empire is conquering territories and enslaving the people who live there. Kestrel is the seventeen-year-old daughter of the highest-ranking general in the imperial army and has a luxurious life in Herran, a country conquered ten years ago. One day she finds herself at a slave market and buys a young man up for bid. This is Arin. He's full of secrets. He's even a bit secretive with the reader of *The Winner's Curse*. The book is Kestrel's tale, and although we're given glimpses from Arin's perspective, he really doesn't want to share. The thoughts and feelings he *does* give us are what he's accidentally let slip, rather than what he's chosen to show. So it was very satisfying for me to get a bit closer to Arin in "Bridge of Snow," and to portray someone intelligent, sensitive . . . and destined for loss. He's a child in "Bridge of Snow," sick in bed. There has been talk of war, and Arin has heard his family murmur worriedly about the empire's attacks on a nearby country. For now, though, Arin is safe. His mother is dressed for a party, but has made the carriage wait so that she can tell him the story of how the god of snow fell in love with a mortal, and the stars were made.

I made stories my life long before I wrote a novel. I majored in English at the University of Iowa and then went to Harvard University for my PhD in Renaissance studies with a focus on Shakespeare. Since 2007, I've been a professor of English at Brooklyn College, where I teach Renaissance literature, children's literature, and fiction writing. I'm married to an economist, which is how I know about the economic theory of the "winner's curse," the term that inspired my book. A winner's curse is, essentially, what happens when you win an auction by paying too high a price. I live in New York City with the afore-mentioned economist, our two small sons, and a cat. In addition to *The Winner's Curse* and its sequel, *The Winner's Crime* (the third book in the trilogy will be out in 2016), I'm the author of The Kronos Chronicles (including *The Cabinet of Wonders*) and *The Shadow Society*. My guilty pleasures are French fries and ice cream. But not at the same time.

BRIDGE OF SNOW

by Marie Rutkoski

The boy was sick.

It wasn't that, so much, that worried his mother. He was often sick, and she had grown used to that fever-dazzled quality to his eyes. Sometimes she secretly enjoyed his illness, once the fever had broken and the worry was past. She got to keep him all to herself. His tutors were sent away. His limbs, heavy with sleepiness, seemed ironically healthier than usual—solid, with a good weight. He was a spindly creature. Tall for his age. Large eyed, bony. She thought he would grow up handsome.

His father disagreed. The disagreement was matter-of-fact, even fond: an excuse for him to praise the boy's bookish ways. "Not *handsome*," her husband would say when they were alone in her rooms and the fire burned low. "Clever."

"Can he not be both?"

"Gods, I hope not. One of *those* is enough."

She sighed, now, remembering it. She sat by her son's bedside, careful not to crease her gown, and stretched an arm across a pillow. The boy, turning a page, nestled into her. He didn't look up from his book. His shoulders were rigid, his face tight. Whatever simmered in him wasn't fever.

She stroked his dark hair. "It's almost time. The carriage is waiting."

"A little longer."

Her arm ached from the awkward position and the boy's weight. She shifted.

"Don't go," he said.

"Arin. I must."

He jerked away. "Why? Just because Anireh wants you to? All *she* wants is to gobble up the prince. She's a spider."

"I'm not sure that spiders *gobble*."

He slammed his book shut. "A fox, then. A mean, sneaky fox."

"This ball is important to your sister. It's important that your father and I attend it with her. Nurse will take good care of you while we're gone." Yet she didn't like to leave Arin. It was his fury, grasped tight and trembling, that made her reluctant, not the sickness, which had almost run its course. "What did your sister do?"

He rolled over and buried his face in a pillow. "Nothing," came the muffled answer.

"If you tell me, I will tell *you* something."

He shifted so that one gray eye peered at her over the pillow's snowy slopes. "What kind of something?"

"A secret."

He looked at her fully now. "A secret . . . and a story?"

"Little trickster. You hope to make me forget the ball with tale-telling. What will the royal family think if I am not there? You don't need a story. You have your book." But then she looked more carefully at what he'd been reading and frowned. "Out with it," she said more sternly than she had intended. "What did Anireh do?"

"She said she was there when I was born."

"Yes." Her daughter was a full ten years older than him—a young woman now.

"She said," Arin whispered, "that I was born in the year of death. That you waited for months to name me so that my name day would be in a different god's year."

"Well." She fiddled with an emerald earring. "Yes. All parents did the same that year." Except perhaps, she supposed, for a few who thought that being born under death's sign would make their children fit for war one day. But who— she shuddered—would want that? "How silly to fret over this, Arin. It's the name that matters, not the birth." Yet he had gone nameless for two full seasons. He had been born in the peak of death's sign.

She looked away from the boy's pale face.

"Anireh said that I was born a skeleton."

Her gaze snapped back. "What?"

"She said I came out all bones. My knuckles looked like pearls."

Now it was she who had to hide her anger.

"Anireh said you prayed to the gods to give me flesh," he continued, "and they did—but not enough. That's why I'm so skinny."

"Sweet child, that's not true."

"I *know* it's not true!" But Arin's gray eyes were shiny with fear, and something in him saw that she had seen this. That lurking anger from before suddenly barreled through his fear, shoved it aside. "I hate her."

"You don't mean that."

"Yes," he said, "I do!"

"Shh. Your throat's raw already from the fever. Do you want to lose your voice?"

He gulped. He choked on the sucked-in air. Tears spilled down his cheeks. "I hate her," he said hoarsely.

She wasn't feeling kindly toward her firstborn either. To tell a child such frightening nonsense! "Let the carriage wait. You shall have your story as well as your secret."

Tears made his lashes spiky, his eyes luminous. "Both?"

"Both," she assured him. She picked up his book from where it lay on the bed. It was written in another language— one she didn't like. "I can certainly offer you something better than this."

He had stopped crying. "I like that."

"What could you possibly like about a Valorian book?"

"Valorians are interesting. They're different."

"Indeed they are." It stirred a dread in her, simply to see the printed language stamped on the pages. She had never been to Valoria, but everyone knew what people from that country were like: irreligious, brutish. Bloody-minded. Why, even the women took up arms. She could not imagine it. And there had been rumors . . .

She set the book aside. "A story, then."

Arin was calm now. He lifted a hand to touch the back of hers in thanks, then curled his fingers into hers. She cherished that little warmth. It nested in her palm like a bird. "Tell me how the stars were made," he said.

"You are too young for that tale."

He pulled her hand from hers. "I've had eight name days."

"Yes, exactly."

"I know the story already, Amma. I just want to hear it in your voice." When she hesitated, he said, "Did you know that Valorians say the stars are sparks shot from the hooves of galloping war-horses?"

The words made her heart race. Yet her country had no reason to fear Valoria. A mountain range stood between Herran and Valoria. The rest of Herran was surrounded by water, and the Herrani ruled the seas. We are safe, she thought.

"I hear that Valorians eat gold," the boy said.

"No, of course not." But *did* they? She wasn't sure to what lengths their barbarism went. Eating gold seemed perfectly benign compared with the massacre in the southern isles. The Valorians had waded in blood, she'd heard. Those they didn't kill, they enslaved.

She wondered how much Arin knew about the wars beyond Herran's borders.

"Now, you will be quiet," she said, "and you will listen. No interruptions."

He snuggled down, easy now. "All right."

"There was a young man, a goatherd, who lived in the mountains. His days were filled with bells and the scattering sound of goat hooves on loose rock. Nights were darker then than they are now—starless, lightless, save for the moon that hung like a jewel on the chilled black silk of the sky. He was alone. His heart was still. He remembered each god in his prayers.

"He hadn't always been alone. The days grew shorter, colder. Heavy gray clouds tore themselves into shreds on the mountaintops. Had he left behind the people he loved, or had they left him? No one knows. But he remembered them in the fading warmth of autumn. He heard voices ringing in the first frozen wind of winter. He told himself they were goats' bells. Maybe they were." She looked at her boy. He knew her weakness for storytelling. And it was, after all, only a story. Still, she wished he had chosen a happier one.

"Go on," he said.

"He was poor. His shoes were thin. But he was hardier than he looked, and he had a gift. In the icy pink mornings, he would select a charred stick from the dead fire. He would go outside where the light was best. Sometimes he used the wall of his hut; he had no paper. Sometimes he used a flat stretch of rock in the cliff, letting its texture give dimension to his charcoal images. He drew. Fingers black, he sketched his memories, he shaded the lost faces, he rubbed a line with his smallest finger to soften what he had known.

"The goats milled about him. There was no one to see what he drew.

"But the snow saw. Winter's first snow came. It lay a white palm on the charcoaled stone. It drifted over his hut. It eddied at the door as if curious, and wondering whether more drawings were hidden inside.

"The goatherd's skin prickled. Perhaps he should stay indoors.

"He didn't. He led the goats. He drew. And the snow came for him.

"In those days, the gods walked among us. The goatherd knew her for what she was. How could he not? She was silver haired. Clear ice eyes. Faintly blue lips. The air around her seemed to chime. It was the god of snow."

Arin said, "You forgot something."

She hadn't. Slowly, she said, "The god smiled, and showed her pointed, sharp, crystal teeth."

"I'm not scared," said Arin.

But how to tell her son the rest? The way the god silently followed the goatherd, so close that his shoulders grew frost? He drew for the snow god, whose frozen diamond tears fell at the sight of his images and rang against the rock. Every morning, he looked for her. He began to love the chattering of his teeth. When she appeared, the air sheered and sharpened. It became hard to breathe. Still, he longed for that painful purity.

When she was not there, he remembered the goats. He probably smelled like them. Was warm and stupid, like them.

Yet one day she touched him. It was a cold so cold it burned. It locked his jaw.

She drew back, and tried again. This time, it was all soft hushes, the sort of snow that changes the world by claiming it. A pillowing snow. It feathered down. She layered herself on him.

The burning cold came again. He begged for her bite.

She left him. It was that or murder him, so he was alone again with his goats and his fire-black sticks and the smudged walls of his mountainside hovel.

"They became friends," the mother said finally.

"Not *friends*." Arin was reproachful.

The boy read beyond his age, that much was clear. She frowned, but said only, "He didn't see the god again. He saw what most mortals saw: snowflakes, brilliant in their white geometry. He watched the snow by day, he watched it by night . . . when he could. The moon was waning. Then came a night when it vanished altogether. The night was as black as snow is white. He could see nothing. I wish I could tell you, Arin, that he said his prayers as always, remembering each one, but that night he neglected the god of the moon.

"He woke to the sound of footsteps crunching in the snow outside his hut. He knew it wasn't *his* god—she moved hissingly, or was silent—but any stranger on this mountain was strange indeed, so he stepped through his door to see.

"The newcomer was a man—or so it seemed. The goatherd wasn't sure, suddenly, what he beheld, unless it was *seeming* itself. The visitor had black eyes—no, silver, no, yellow, or was that a glowering orange? Was he shrunken, or enormous—and wasn't he, after all, a *she*?

"The goatherd blinked, and although he didn't recognize who stood before him, he at least understood what kind of visitor had come to call.

" 'You want to be with my sister,' said the god.

"The young man flushed.

" 'No, don't be shy,' said the god. 'She wants what you want. And I can make it happen.'

"The gods do not lie. But the goatherd shook his head. 'Impossible.'

" 'Mortal, what do *you* know? You're too far from the realm of the gods down here. You need a bridge to go up into the sky. The air's different there. *You* would be different up there. More like us. I can build that bridge for you. All you have to do is say yes.'

"Wary, the goatherd said, 'If I took that bridge, would it kill me? Would I live?'

"The god grinned. 'You'd live *forever.*'

"The young man said yes. He would have said yes anyway, he would have chosen death and snow together, but he had been raised to know that you do not enter into an agreement with the gods without asking the right questions.

"He should have asked more.

" 'We'll meet again tonight,' the god said, 'and build the bridge together.'

" 'Tonight?' It seemed terribly far away.

" 'I work best at night.'

"You must understand, it wasn't that the young man was a fool. He had a lively mind, sensitive to details, and if the conversation had been about any other matter than his lost god, he would have been suspicious. But we don't think too well when we want too much. He forgot that hole in the fabric of his prayers the night before. It didn't occur to him that such a hole might widen, and stretch, and become large enough for him to fall through.

"As agreed, he met the strange god that night. Although there was still no moon in the sky, he had no trouble seeing. The god glowed." In some versions of the tale, the god had the youth strip naked on the frozen mountain, coyly demanded one kiss, and was refused. "The god touched the young man's brow. In that last moment, he suddenly understood that he had been bargaining with the moon. He saw that he had wrought his own doom. But there was nothing he could do.

"He began to grow. His bones screamed. His joints popped. Muscle stretched and tore and disintegrated. He arched into the darkness. The mountains dwindled below. He left his flesh behind. It was as the moon god had promised: He was thrust up into the realm of the gods . . . but he *himself* was the bridge. He spanned the night sky.

"It is true, for gods as well as mortals, that it is impossible to love a bridge. The snow god came, walked the length of him, and wept. Her tears fell and froze. They scattered the sky, piercingly bright. They fell in patterns, in the images he had drawn for her. That is why we see constellations. The stars show his memories, which became hers. We still see them when we look up into the night at a black bridge covered with snow."

Arin was quiet. His expression was unreadable. She wondered why he had asked for this tale. His eyes seemed older than he was, but his hand younger as he reached to touch her satin sleeve. He played with the fabric, watching it dimple and shine. She realized that she had, after all, forgotten the ball and the waiting carriage.

It was time to leave. She kissed him.

"Will Anireh marry the prince?" Arin asked.

She thought that now she understood his interest in the story. "I don't know."

"She'd go away and live with him."

"Yes. Arin, the sibling gods can be cruel to each other. Is that why you asked for the story of snow and her brother-sister moon? Anireh teases you. She can be thoughtless. But she loves you. She held you so dearly when you were a baby. Sometimes she refused to give you back to me."

His troubled gaze fell. Softly, he said, "I don't want her to go."

She smoothed his hair off his brow and said gentle things, the right things, and would have left then to attend the royal ball with an easier heart, but he reached for her wrist. He held it, his hand a soft bracelet.

"Amma . . . the goatherd wasn't *bad*, was he?"

"No."

"But he was punished."

Lightly, she said, "Well, all boys must remember their prayers, mustn't they?"

"What if I do, but offend a god another way?"

"Children cannot offend the gods."

His eyes were so wide she could see the silvery rims of them clear round. He said, "I was born in death's year, but I wasn't given to him. What if he's offended?"

She suddenly realized the full scope of his fascination with the tale. "No, Arin. The rules are clear. I had the right to name you whenever I liked."

"What if I'm his no matter when you named me?"

"What if you are, and it means that he holds you in his hand and would let no one harm you?"

For a moment, he was silent. He muttered, "I'm afraid to die."

"You won't." She made her voice cheerful, brisk. Her son felt things too deeply, was tender to the core. It worried her. She shouldn't have told that story. "Arin, don't you want your secret?"

He smiled a little. "Yes."

She had meant to tell him that the cook's cat had had kittens. But something in his tentative smile caught at her heart, and she leaned to whisper in his ear. She said what no mother should say, yet it was the truth. Months later, when a Valorian dagger pressed into her throat, and there was a moment before the final push, she thought of it, and was glad she had spoken. "I love you best," she said.

She rested her hand on his warm forehead and said the blessing for dreams. She kissed him one more time, and went away.

DYNAMITE JUNIOR

Jennifer Mathieu

BY JENNIFER MATHIEU

The Truth About Alice

Devoted

Meet Jennifer Mathieu

When people ask me how long I've been a writer, I always answer, "Since before I could write." It's not a joke. I used to dictate stories to my mother before I could put words on paper, and after she transcribed them, I would illustrate them. One of my favorite stories was about a sad, lonely cat who finally finds a tribe of friendly yellow felines.

I majored in journalism because it seemed like a way I could write and still make a living—even though I did harbor fantasies of living in New York City and owning a claw-foot bathtub and writing fiction that was taken seriously by all the important critics. After I graduated, I worked as a reporter, but I didn't have the taste for blood that journalism requires. I always felt like I was bothering people when I asked if I could interview them. But working as a journalist gave me many opportunities to observe how humans behave in all sorts of situations—critical stuff for a writer of fiction. So in the end, I'm glad it worked out the way it did.

I became an English teacher in 2005, and it was one of the best decisions I ever made. In addition to falling in love with teaching, my students introduced me to a new generation of incredible writers of young adult literature, including

E. Lockhart and Laurie Halse Anderson. I decided I would try and write for teenagers, too, and many years later I published my first novel for young adults, *The Truth About Alice*. It was one of the best moments of my life.

The Truth About Alice tells the story of a girl named Alice Franklin who lives in a small Texas town called Healy. After rumors get started that she slept with two boys in one night at a party, she's labeled a slut, but things go from bad to worse when she's linked to the death of one of the boys she supposedly slept with—Healy's football quarterback and hero, Brandon Fitzsimmons. Ostracized by the town and almost all of her classmates, Alice endures, eventually finding a friend in the form of a boy she'd never paid attention to before.

The idea for this book came from my interest in small-town life and in telling a story with multiple, unreliable narrators, as well as from a *Seventeen* magazine article I read in high school. The article was about a teenage girl who'd been the victim of terrible, sexually explicit graffiti written about her in a bathroom stall at school. The school refused to clean it up and subtly suggested the girl was responsible for what happened. I was outraged. That piece became a seed for *The Truth About Alice* many years later. Just like the young woman in the article, Alice is also the victim of graffiti in a bathroom stall that the school chooses to ignore.

My short story for this collection is told from the point of view of a tenth grader named Carmen, a new student, who has moved to Healy from Houston because of something traumatic that happens in her family. In my very early drafts of *The Truth About Alice*, Carmen was actually a major character, but I decided there were too many voices and I ended up cutting her—something that really saddened me even though I still feel it was the right decision for the novel. I'm thrilled to get to visit with her again. While her backstory is mostly as I'd originally planned, I've changed a few key elements. For example, in this story she's new to Healy and no one knows about her past. While it's connected to *The Truth About Alice* in that it's set during the events of the novel, it makes sense as a stand-alone piece of fiction, too.

If you've enjoyed *The Truth About Alice*, I hope this story adds an interesting layer to the world of Healy High, and if you haven't read *Alice*, I hope it sparks an interest in checking out my first novel.

Oh, and by the way, you might want to know that I did end up with that claw-foot tub after all, even if I live in Texas instead of New York City. But honestly, I wouldn't have it any other way. Thanks for reading!

DYNAMITE JUNIOR

by Jennifer Mathieu

"Check it out," says Sadie Salazar, "there's new shit written in here."

I'm at the sink washing my hands, and Sadie's voice echoes from inside the bathroom stall. When I hear it, I roll my eyes a little. I've only known her for a few weeks, but this fake tough-girl Bronx-accent thing Sadie does is annoying. She was born in this tiny Texas town. She probably hasn't even been to New Orleans, much less New York.

"Let me see," says Claudia Sanchez, because whatever Sadie tells her to do, she does. This bugs me as much as Sadie's voice, but new friends who annoy me are better than no friends at all.

I follow Claudia inside the stall. The black Sharpie marks look fresh and the words are printed in neat block letters, like whoever wrote it practiced beforehand.

ALICE ALICE IS A WHORE
DID IT WITH THE BOY NEXT DOOR
DID IT WITH THE FOOTBALL TEAM
ALICE ALICE BLOW JOB QUEEN

"Jesus, those white girls are bitches," says Claudia, like she's bored more than surprised.

"White girls started it but everybody's writing in it," says Sadie with a shrug. "And that girl *is* a slut."

Claudia nods in agreement. Of course.

This Slut Stall was already a thing when I started tenth grade at Healy High in early October. The bathrooms at my old high school got tagged sometimes, but nothing like this. And the Slut Stall keeps getting worse, too. Back in Houston, they were super intense about cleaning up the graffiti because of gang members tagging everything, but here in Healy there are no gangs. No Galleria shopping mall or freeways either.

There's not much of anything, actually.

"Who sleeps with two dudes in one night?" Sadie asks us, but she doesn't expect an answer because we all know the answer. A slut. "We got, what, ten minutes till bio?" she continues. "I'm bored. I'm gonna add something."

"Me, too," says Claudia. Of course.

I stand there watching as Sadie fishes in her backpack for something to write with. The stale air around me smells like cheap cleanser and even cheaper perfume. I don't want to stay in here a second more than I have to, but Sadie and Claudia are the only two girls that I really know at this school, and I have too much time to kill before my next class.

So I watch as Sadie uncaps her marker and finds a clean spot in the stall.

∽

I'd found out I was moving to Healy just a few weeks before, when I was tucked under the covers in my family's apartment in Houston, trying to read *Animal Farm* for English class. My mother walked in and asked if we could talk. "We're sending you to live with Tía Lucy," she told me from her seat at the foot of my bed.

"You're sending me where?" I said, shutting my book, which was the only good part about having this conversation. I swear, if this dude wanted to write about the Russian Revolution, why not just write about it and skip the animal stuff?

"To live with your tía Lucy," my mother repeated, even though she knew I heard her the first time. "In Healy. We're driving you there Friday." She patted my leg and looked like she was trying not to cry.

I think she'd waited until I was in my pajamas to make this announcement, maybe because she thought I wouldn't throw a fit and run out of the house dressed in old boxer shorts and a black T-shirt with holes in the armpits. Which I didn't. But I definitely thought about it.

I stared at my mom, trying to take in her words. She's beautiful, my mother, with olive skin and hands as soft as a baby's even though she works as the manager at the Happy Washateria and does laundry all day long. But lately there are gray hairs popping up around her temples and she has a new, tiny double chin. She's gained about twenty pounds since everything that happened with my brother, Jorge. My dad's lost exactly the same amount.

"Mom, no," I answered, sitting up. "I don't want to go live with Tía Lucy in Healy. I want to stay here. With you and Dad." And with my friends, I thought to myself. Even if lately there had been a lot of awkward glances at the cafeteria table and too many texts that they responded to with just a K.

"Carmen, please don't fight me on this," my mother said, taking a deep sigh. "This is only for a little while. Maybe only until Christmas or just for this school year. I think it would be good for you."

I guessed my mom had seen what Luis and Nestor had scribbled on my red school binder. When she'd come home from work, it had been sitting on the kitchen counter with all my other school junk. But it was nothing. I knew it was just a joke because when Luis and Nestor laughed at it, I did, too.

"What did I do to deserve this?" I asked, and my throat tightened up. "Why are you kicking me out?"

My mother winced and I felt both glad and guilty.

"We're not kicking you out, *preciosa*," she said. Then she did start to cry—not sobbing hysterically or anything, but there were tears sliding down her round apple cheeks. "We all need a . . . little break. A fresh start. And your dad and me need . . . some time."

Before everything that happened with Jorge, my dad used to hurry home to our apartment from his job at Discount Tire and kiss my mom's neck and growl like a tiger in a way that made me roll my eyes even though I knew I was lucky to have parents who were still in love when almost everyone else I knew had parents who were divorced. But not long after the start of the school year, Dad had started coming home hours after his shift had ended and sat in the living room, flipping through the channels on the TV and picking at a plate of leftovers that I warmed up for him. Sometimes if I stayed up late enough I would hear him yelling at my mother through the wall that separates their room from mine.

My mother never yelled back. She just cried. Like she was doing now, here in my bedroom. I stared at my legs. They looked like two long, skinny mountain ranges under the quilt my abuelita made me. Everything felt off balance and strange, like we were rehearsing a scene from a play we might perform someday. A tragic play like Shakespeare would write if he wrote about Mexicans living in Houston in the early twenty-first century.

"Carmen, your dad and I love you so much," Mom said, leaning over to touch my face. I let her even though what I really wanted to do was shrink back and slide under my quilt and turn out the lights and imagine I lived in a parallel universe where everything in my life was like it was before.

"I love you, too," I said. Because I did, even though I was upset.

My mom smiled, still touching my face.

"Listen, you don't have to go to school for the rest of this week," she said, her voice dropping to a whisper. "Not if you don't want to."

I looked at my copy of *Animal Farm* and thought about what Nestor and Luis had written on my red binder. I remembered the tight smile Ana gave me in the lunch line when I asked her what was going on this weekend.

"Nothing really," she'd said.

I looked at my mom and nodded. "Okay," I answered. "I'll stay home and pack."

✀

On my first day at Healy High, I had to beg Tía Lucy not to go in with me. It was bad enough that she had to drive me when I could just as easily have walked.

"Honey, I know you're a big girl, but I just want to make sure you get inside all right," she said. When she called me a big girl I gave her a look. Tía Lucy is a nurse at a pediatrician's office, and sometimes she forgets I'm not five and she can't bribe me with lollipops. Besides, the walk from Tía Lucy's beat-up Toyota Corolla to the front doors of Healy High School was about twenty feet.

Still, I knew she was just trying to be nice to me. She had tiptoed around me the entire weekend, ordering pizza for dinner and letting me watch whatever I wanted on television.

And she never mentioned Jorge once.

That first day I finally persuaded her to let me go in by myself and I found the main office and got my schedule and, just like that, I was a tenth grader at Healy High School, Home of the Tigers.

At my school in Houston you had to wear a mandatory school shirt and jeans and everybody had to have a laminated student ID on a lanyard around their necks at all times. The words SAFETY EXCELLENCE RESPECT were printed on the lanyard. Or at least they were until kids starting blacking out some of the letters so they just read SEX. Then they started giving out lanyards without words.

But at Healy High you can wear whatever you want as long as it's not too short or too tight or too revealing. Also, there isn't a police officer patrolling the campus all the time, and the sport everyone cares about isn't soccer but football. There are more white kids at Healy High than at my old school, but just like at my old school all the white kids sit together in the cafeteria and all the black kids sit together and all the Mexican and Salvadoran kids sit together, which is how I ended up with Sadie and Claudia on my very first day, eating my lukewarm school cafeteria pizza while they asked me about Houston.

"What's it like living in the city?" Claudia asked, picking at her roast beef sandwich but not eating it.

"It's okay," I said. Obviously, they didn't know about Jorge. I mean, what happened was in the news, but they wouldn't have heard about it all the way out here in the middle of nowhere. "There's a lot more to do there," I continued.

"Like, do you go to clubs?" Sadie asked in her tough girl voice, and I could tell she was sizing me up.

"Sometimes, if we can get in," I said. This was a lie, but it impressed Sadie anyway, even though she nodded like she wasn't impressed at all.

"So why'd you move out here then?" Claudia asked. I wasn't prepared for this question, which was stupid on my part, but my first lie led to another. I thought about something a girl who goes to clubs would say.

"I got into some trouble," I answered. "I really don't want to talk about it." I liked how it sounded. Mysterious. Back in Houston during freshman year I'd had a pretty decent group of friends and we'd done our homework most of the time and sometimes we went to parties where a few people smoked pot but never me. I'd been one of those kids who belonged to the big mushy middle of high school. Not popular but not a total freak either. I was just a regular girl, living my ninth-grade life. Most of the upperclassmen hadn't known I'd existed until everything happened with Jorge. Then everyone knew who I was, but it wasn't because I was popular.

Claudia and Sadie seemed satisfied with my answer about getting into trouble. Sadie finished her Dr Pepper, and Claudia and I followed her when it was time to leave the cafeteria.

"Let's go chill on the benches outside the library," Sadie decided. "Sometimes Alex Villalobos is out there, and he is so fine. You'll see, Carmen." Sadie giggled and Claudia giggled and I giggled, too, but I felt a heavy weight on my chest as I understood that this was My Life now. This school where I only knew two girls. This town where I lived with my tía Lucy. This place without my parents. Without Jorge.

As we made our way down the hallway, I spotted a girl coming toward us from the opposite direction. She was wearing a big hooded sweatshirt even though it wasn't very cold and her hands were stuffed in its pockets. She had her head down and her short hair was tucked behind her ears. When she walked past us, Sadie whispered, "*Slut!*"

My mouth dropped open and my eyes got wide when the girl just kept walking. If Sadie had tried that at my old school, there would have been a fight right there in the hallway and Sadie would have gotten a beatdown until the police or some teachers broke it up. Honestly, Sadie deserved a beatdown for being so nasty. But the girl just kept going, her head bowed. Her hands still jammed in her pockets.

"That's Alice Franklin," Claudia explained as we headed

toward the library benches. "She slept with two guys at a party this summer. Like, in the same night. And then she killed one of them when she sent him these nasty texts while he was driving."

"The dude she killed was fine, too, and the quarterback of the football team," Sadie added. "Brandon Fitzsimmons. Of all the dudes to kill, she picked the wrong one. Now basically we all hate her."

"Oh," I said, nodding, the sound of Sadie's whispered *slut!* still stuck in my ears.

We made it to the benches outside the library, but Alex Villalobos wasn't there. Claudia had some Pixy Stix in her backpack and after she let Sadie choose what color she wanted, she let me pick one, too. I tossed the pink sugar down my throat and let it dissolve into nothing on the back of my tongue.

❧

When everything started with Jorge the summer before I had to move to Healy, he also wore a hoodie a lot even though it wasn't cold. And he started taking five showers a day and refused to eat food he didn't make himself. And even though it was summer, he didn't want to go skateboarding with his friends anymore like he used to. He just shut himself up in his room all the time and played the same three Ramones songs over and over again until I heard the lyrics in my dreams.

His phone would ring and I would find it buried in the couch or under the coffee table and I would answer it.

"Is Jorge there?"

I would knock on his bedroom door covered with Los Crudos and Massacre 68 stickers and one that said SKATEBOARDING

IS NOT A CRIME. I would yell, "Jorge! Phone!" but he always just ignored me. Pretty soon his friends stopped calling.

Jorge and I used to spend the summers together watching television and having competitions to see who could make the tallest sandwich. Mom would leave us a list of chores to do while she and Dad were at work, and when we had one hour left before they got home, Jorge would yell, "Let's do this thing!" at the top of his lungs, and we would race around doing everything on the list as fast as we could while Jorge's punk music played super loud.

But the summer before I had to leave home, none of that happened. And every day it got weirder and scarier. Like the night I went into the kitchen to get a glass of water and found him dressed in his black hoodie and sweatpants, staring at the refrigerator.

"I'm hearing them behind there," he whispered.

"Hearing who?" I asked.

"Them," he said. His dark eyes were frantic and he was covered in sweat. He kept staring at the refrigerator like he thought it would come alive.

"I'm going to get Mom and Dad," I told him, but Jorge shook his head and walked past me and back inside his bedroom without saying anything else.

On the first day of school Jorge said he wanted to get there early, so he took the first bus. My parents just went along with it. I think they were happy he was going to school at all. I knew they'd had to see how odd he'd been behaving, but I heard Mom tell Dad it was a phase and I noticed Dad coming home later and later from work so he wouldn't have to deal with it at all.

I took the second bus to school with Nestor and Ana and

some of my other friends. We were all excited because we weren't freshmen anymore. We sat toward the back of the bus and shared headphones and listened to music and talked about how none of us wanted to get Mr. Haymes for math.

Sometimes I try to remember that Monday morning bus ride and how normal I felt during it. I didn't know how nice normal felt until I didn't feel that way anymore.

∽

It had only taken me a few weeks at Healy High before I realized that independent study was a great place to take a nap. As long as the teachers didn't catch you.

"Carmen. Wake up, please."

I lifted my head off my desk and blinked a few times before looking at Healy's most ancient teacher, Mrs. Gallagher, who was sitting at her desk at the front of the room like a lump with a frown and two beady eyes.

"Sorry," I mumbled, but I bet Mrs. Gallagher could tell that I wasn't. I couldn't really help it if it was the last few minutes of independent study and I'd already finished my homework. Healy High is easier than my old school. Way easier. They don't assign as much and I get plenty of time in school every day to finish my assignments. And there's never any homework on the weekends during football season because they expect everyone to go to the game.

Sitting there in independent study, I wondered whether I was getting dumber just because I was living in Healy.

"Why don't you make yourself useful and take this down to the vice principal's office for me?" Mrs. Gallagher asked. She held up a sealed envelope.

"Sure," I answered, sliding out from my desk, happy to get out of there a little early.

I headed down the hall and, just past the big GO HEALY TIGERS! banner hanging outside the cafeteria, I saw Alice Franklin at her open locker. She wasn't wearing her hoodie like that first time I'd seen her with Claudia and Sadie. She just had on a black top and black jeans. She was reading some piece of paper and frowning at it, and she folded it and shoved it back into her locker.

"Hey," I said to her. I didn't know I was going to say it until I did.

She turned and looked at me with a scowl on her face. I guess if people constantly called me a slut in the hallway, I'd have a scowl on my face all the time, too. But even with a scowl Alice Franklin was one of the prettiest girls I've ever seen.

"What?" she said.

"Uh, do you know where the vice principal's office is? I'm new. I have to take this there." I held up the envelope Mrs. Gallagher gave me as proof I wasn't lying.

"Oh," said Alice, and the scowl softened. She shut her locker and pointed down the main hallway. "Head straight that way and make a left. His office is the first door on the right."

"Okay, cool," I said. "Thanks."

Alice's voice was very quiet in return, but I heard her say, "No problem."

I headed down the hall, and when I looked back over my shoulder I saw Alice walking in the opposite direction, her backpack slung low, her head down.

I knew where the vice principal's office was. Healy High School is smaller than my middle school. But I guess I thought it would be nice if for one minute someone was halfway nice to Alice Franklin, even if it was just to ask for directions.

∿

The first assembly of the year at my old school was always in the gym, and as me and Nestor and Ana and everyone crowded into the tenth-grade section, Luis yelled, "It smells like ass in here. Don't they clean it during the summer?"

"No," Ana responded, wrinkling up her nose. "The sweat smell just intensifies in the heat."

Lately, when I think back to that morning, I try to picture the senior section in my mind. I try to find Jorge's face in the crowd. But I never can. I don't know why I try. Maybe because I want to know what he looked like right before it happened. Did he look frantic like he did that night he heard "them" behind the refrigerator? Calm because he knew what he was about to do? Happy because he was going to do it? I hope he didn't look happy, but maybe he did.

"Fighting Hornets, welcome back to another great year at Jackson High!" Principal Carter yelled into the microphone, instantly sparking some squealing feedback. Everyone groaned, from the high-pitched sound and probably from Principal Carter's words, too.

"God, I'm already bored," said Ana. And that's the last thing I remember right before the loud boom that came from the senior section on the other side of the gym. Everyone jumped, including Principal Carter and all the other administrators who were seated on folding chairs in the middle of the floor. Suddenly there was a pocket of gray smoke billowing out from the senior section and kids were jumping from the top bleachers and racing out of the gym. Two girls ran right into each other and the smack caused them both to fall down.

"What the hell?" said Luis, and we were all standing up now, turning to look at one another, our mouths hanging open. My heart was pumping hard, and the boom was still ringing in my ears. There was a smell of something rotten in the air, like milk that's gone sour.

Somehow we were herded into the hallway and then teachers were screaming at us to exit to the football field. Some of the girls were crying and I heard one boy talking about how a bomb went off and I heard another one talking about Erica Garza and Darrell Curtis and that they were bleeding pretty bad.

And then I heard someone mention Jorge.

We were excused for the day and I got a ride home from Luis's older brother. I didn't know where Jorge was and no one in my family was answering their phones. By the time I got home there were news trucks around our apartment complex. I didn't know how the school got hold of my parents so fast but they did, and our apartment was full of police officers and some people from the school district and two ladies wearing name badges that read PSYCHOLOGICAL SERVICES and a woman I later found out was a social worker who smelled like cigarettes. My mother was curled up in the corner of the couch crying and my dad was sitting next to her staring at nothing and nodding as different people came up to talk to him, but he was barely saying anything back.

"What's going on?" I shouted, and all of a sudden I was sobbing. Hard. I was sobbing right there in the family room where I used to watch television with Jorge and he would set the timer for our speed hour of chores and we'd eat sandwiches that were six inches tall.

One of the Psychological Services women pulled me aside and in a voice like a kindergarten teacher's she explained that Jorge set off some sort of explosive device he said he built in his bedroom to keep awful voices away. It wasn't as bad as it could have been, she told me, but some people were hurt. Jorge wasn't. She asked me how Jorge had been acting recently, and I tried to explain. She told me Jorge was sick and what happened wasn't his fault and he was going to get the help he needed. Then she asked me how I was feeling, and I couldn't decide if I wanted to slap her for asking or hug her for at least saying what happened wasn't Jorge's fault.

Because in the weeks that followed, it seemed everyone thought it was Jorge's fault. Or my family's fault. The story was on the news more than once. Some reports were saying the parents of Erica Garza and Darrell Curtis wanted to sue my parents because they didn't get Jorge help when he was sick, and Erica had a broken leg and Darrell couldn't stop the ringing in his ears. Erica's friends gave me dirty looks in the locker room, like their friend being in a wheelchair was all my fault, too. Erica was very popular. Last year she was homecoming queen.

Teachers were either so nice to me it seemed fake or they watched me so carefully it was like they thought I might set off some bomb, too. Ana and Nestor and Luis and all of my friends still talked to me, but it was almost as if they were thinking about everything they said before they said it. Sometimes I sat down at the cafeteria table and the conversation stopped and Ana brought up something stupid, like what did we think was going to be on the math quiz tomorrow.

Jorge was sent to some state facility in Austin, and I never even got to say good-bye. My parents stopped talking about him. Once my mom drove up to visit him, but she didn't let me come with her and my dad didn't go. The door to Jorge's bedroom was kept shut. My mom peeled off the stickers and threw them away, but I found the SKATEBOARDING IS NOT A CRIME one in the garbage can and kept it in the drawer in my nightstand.

Then just before my mother told me she was going to send me to live with Tía Lucy in Healy, Nestor and Luis grabbed my red binder from me in English class and started doodling on it. I let them because we were always doing stuff like that—joking around with one another and drawing on each other's arms and everything. For a second it felt normal.

When the bell rang, I grabbed my binder back. Nestor and Luis were snickering a little.

DYNAMITE JUNIOR.

The words were written in big block letters in black marker. They even drew what looked like a cherry next to it but what I guessed was supposed to be a bomb because there were little sparks around the stem.

"You know we love you, Carmen," said Luis, grinning. "We're just messing with you." Nestor was laughing like he could hardly breathe.

I slid the binder into my backpack and rolled my eyes.

"Ha-ha," I said, doing the fakest laugh I could, like the two of them were boring me to tears.

I spent my lunch period in the library, curled up in the corner by the old encyclopedias that no one used anymore, staring out the window at the bright blue sky. I wondered if, wherever

Jorge was, he had a view of the sky. I wondered if he was feeling better and if he was missing me.

~

Sadie is done writing on the Slut Stall and now Claudia is having her turn. Sadie's written ALICE DOES IT WITH YOUR DAD which is stupid not to mention unoriginal. Claudia just writes ALICE=SLUT which is even stupider.

"Your turn," Sadie says. Claudia hands me the Sharpie. I hold it up to my nose and sniff it.

"Do you like to huff paint, too, or something?" Sadie asks, wrinkling her nose. Claudia laughs like it's the funniest thing ever.

I step back and move into the next stall, which is mostly blank except for a couple of hearts with people's initials written inside of them. I slide in past the toilet.

"What are you doing?" says Sadie. "That's not the Slut Stall."

"Yeah, I know," I answer.

Holding the marker tight, in big letters I write SKATEBOARD-ING IS NOT A CRIME.

"What the hell?" says Sadie. "You're high from sniffing that marker."

I hand the Sharpie back to Sadie and admire my work one more time before stepping out of the stall.

"I didn't know you liked to skateboard," says Claudia.

"I don't actually do it yet," I answer, picking up my back-pack and heading for the door. Claudia follows me and Sadie does, too. "But I'm thinking about maybe starting it up."

"Oh," says Claudia. "Do you know any other girls who skate?"

"That's a dumb question, Claudia," Sadie snaps.

"No, it isn't," I answer, and Claudia shoots Sadie a triumphant look. "And I don't know any other girls who skate, but it could still be kind of cool."

"Yeah," says Claudia. "It could be." Sadie keeps her mouth shut.

The bell rings, and I give the two girls a half wave and head to class. Shouts from other students fill the hallway, their shoes squeaking on the linoleum floor, their metal locker doors slamming shut. For the first time since Jorge did what he did, I feel pretty okay. Pretty good, actually. There's something about starting at a school where nobody knows me that's sort of freeing. Like every day I could be someone new.

MONSTER CRUSH

Anna Banks & Emmy Laybourne

Meet Anna Banks

Truth be told, I never considered myself a writer. It wasn't an aspiration of mine. Not to say that I wasn't *good* at it—I'd write papers for my classmates for money in high school. I'd cater to their voice and the expectations of their teacher and made the prose as realistic to each individual as I could. I just always thought my classmates were lazy. It never occurred to me that they might not have the ability to write, that it didn't come naturally to them like it came to me.

It wasn't until my late twenties that I decided to write a book. I had just read the Twilight series, and thought to myself, "If this girl can get published, I get can published." Yes, I know that sounds like a jerk-face thing to say (and, yes, she will probably punch me in the face one day) but actually it's a compliment to Stephenie Meyer. She made me believe that easy reading is easy writing. Oh, naive little me. Any good author will tell you, easy reading is freaking difficult writing. And trying to get published is a hard-knock life. But once I started writing, I couldn't stop. And I'm glad I did, because if not, Galen Forza (the hot guy from my Syrena Legacy series) would never have existed.

Fast-forward to today. As of writing this sentence, I've

published five books. My newest one is called *Joyride*. If I had to describe it, I'd say it's *Bonnie and Clyde* meets a Latina *Pretty in Pink*. You should check it out. For reals. It was fun (but not easy!) to write, and hopefully it will be fun to read.

Speaking of fun, have I ever told you about that one time when Emmy Laybourne and I wrote a Sasquatch romance? No? Here, sit back, relax, and have some popcorn while I regale you with the story:

One day, while I was minding my own business (←a lie), Emmy Laybourne calls and says, "Hey, Peaches, how are you doing?"

ME "Hey! Fine. You?" (←or something just as generic)

EMM "Well, I kind of entered us in this Twitter contest
  thingy to write a Sasquatch romance. And they
  kind of picked us. So here's how I thought we
  could do it—"

ME "&%#@!" (←use your imagination)

I was under deadline with a manuscript at the time and was insanely busy. But as with all things concerning Emmy, I couldn't refuse her. We decided that we would each take on bits of the story, and tweet it one after the other during our hour-slot time. Writing with another author, and especially Emmy, is the best kind of challenge, because you strive to be the best version of yourself so you don't let your partner down.

Writing "Monster Crush" was so satisfying, too, because my original idea for a YA novel was actually a Sasquatch romance—but I didn't think the market was ready for that quite yet. In the midst of searching for something else to write about, I was watching this documentary on the giant squid. Before 2005, scientists thought the giant squid was just a myth, fishermen's lore. We've all seen those drawings where an old ship is being hauled underwater by enormous tentacles, right? But in 2005, a dead one washed up on shore and everyone had to say, "Just joking! Giant squids are real!" I thought to myself *What else could be out there? Mermaids?*

And so I set out to prove mermaids could exist; *Of Poseidon* was born months later. People ask me all the time if I really think mermaids or bigfoot could really exist. My answer? Remember the giant squid, my friend. Remember the giant squid.

Meet Emmy Laybourne

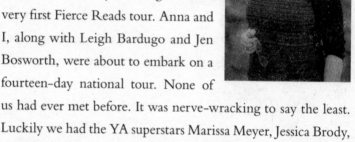

© Fernando Lopez

I love a good premise, don't you?

When I met Anna Banks in 2012, it was on the very first night of the very first Fierce Reads tour. Anna and I, along with Leigh Bardugo and Jen Bosworth, were about to embark on a fourteen-day national tour. None of us had ever met before. It was nerve-wracking to say the least. Luckily we had the YA superstars Marissa Meyer, Jessica Brody, and Lish McBride do some of the events with us along the way to teach us what the heck we were doing!

As the tour developed, I started hearing Anna joke about a premise. Anna would mention an outlandish idea she had for a paranormal romance featuring a Sasquatch. The audiences would always laugh. I would always laugh. It was a great, crazy idea.

I loved that Sasquatch premise.

And I loved touring with Anna. She's got a very dry wit and she would just sit there and then—*zing*—come in with a line so funny we'd all be knocked on our butts. Man, was it ever fun to set her up to tell a joke.

Every time she'd mention the Sasquatch idea, I'd mull it over—could it be pulled off? Could you get a reader to imagine a Sasquatch in a remotely sexy or romantic way? Would there be a way to write a scene where a girl kisses a guy who might turn into bigfoot without conjuring for the reader the sense-memory smell of wet dog? I really wanted to find out . . .

So when I heard they were looking for entries for the first Twitter Fiction Festival—and that collaboration was encouraged—I thought: Anna! And then: Sasquatch premise!

Fortunately, Anna Banks is up for anything.

We had so much fun writing this story. Going back and forth with Anna was tricky at times—but a very fun challenge. Can you tell I tried to set her up for some zingers along the way?

Another exciting thing about this collaboration was that it's a pretty big departure from the Monument 14 series. In *Monument 14*, a group of kids are stranded in a superstore while civilization collapses outside the gates. The kids don't want to go outside because there's been a leak of a vicious chemical weapon that divides the population by blood type, sending some people into a bloodthirsty rage, while others are made paranoid or infertile or just blister up and die. Okay, it's pretty intense. Dark in tone. The *New York Times* called it "frighteningly real" and that's good enough for me.

When it came time for Anna and me to write "Monster Crush," I was delighted by how light and breezy it was. I wasn't wrestling with life and death and chemical warfare—we were writing a love story. And a pretty dang good one. One hundred and forty characters at a time! It was very liberating to play so hard with my dear friend. Playing is good, people.

Once the Monument 14 series was complete, I moved on to a project with a bit more sass. Anna, you inspired me, baby! My next novel is called *Sweet*. It's about a luxury cruise to promote a new diet sweetener that makes you lose weight. Only, when the sweetener turns out to be highly addictive, the cruise goes comically, then tragically, then terrifyingly wrong.

Thanks, Anna, for sharing your awesome premise with me. A Sasquatch-human love story is possible . . . and here's proof:

MONSTER CRUSH

by Anna Banks and Emmy Laybourne

 (Emmy Laybourne): Jen was supposed to be on a plane. Amherst started in a week.

 (Anna Banks): But she was looking forward to going back to college for her junior year like you look forward to an appendectomy.

 And there was also the issue of the bartender, Ian. Sandy-blond hair, strapping physique, sparkling gray eyes.

 Why, oh why had they met on the last day of her Colorado vacation? It wasn't fair.

 She had watched him all night as he tended bar. Since she was only 19, she couldn't drink.

AB But he had made her a virgin Harvey Wallbanger that was pretty darn tasty and served it with that tasty smile of his.

EL When Jen had gotten up her nerve to approach him, they'd hit it off. As the regulars drifted out, they'd talked into the night . . .

AB A night that ended with her in his arms and him kissing her all over.

EL Kissing on the mouth is boring, he'd said. Instead Ian had kissed her on the shoulder, the neck, the palm of her hand.

AB And what his mouth didn't touch, his hands did.

EL Jen walked up and down the length of the bar now. She couldn't wait to see Ian again.

AB He would be so surprised, and so psyched that she had decided to stay in Colorado.

EL Who knows, Jen thought. Maybe I can even get a job here at the bar.

AB She knew her parents would flip out, but Amherst was their idea, not hers. In fact nothing was ever her idea—except this. Ian.

EL Finally, around 8:30, Ian walked in. Jen jumped up from her stool and rushed to his arms. He looked surprised, that's for sure.

AB She knew that look. It's the look someone makes when they're surprised by a hair or a bug or a razor in their strawberry cheesecake.

EL Yep. It's a kind of look you really don't want to see when the surprise is . . . you!

AB "What are you doing here?" he said. His gray eyes flashed angrily.

EL "I-I-I wanted to see you again," Jen stammered. Ian stalked behind the bar and hung his jacket on a hook.

AB He ran a hand through his hair and sighed. He leaned across the bar. "I thought you understood last night was just a onetime thing."

EL Jen slumped into a booth. She couldn't believe this. Sure, he'd said that. And, yes, she'd agreed. But how could he still feel that way?

AB The way they'd talked and laughed and shared—a onetime thing? He was wrong. It was more than that.

EL She decided to stay and talk to him later, once the crowd thinned out. She watched him, pouring drinks for the regulars.

AB He was so gorgeous, chatting and laughing. A pretty blonde woman spit out her drink at something Ian said.

EL Ian was funny, Jen thought. And everyone seemed to like him.

AB But not funny enough to laugh the way that blonde was laughing. She was braying like a donkey!

EL A scruffy man in coveralls noticed Jen noticing Ian. "He's an odd duck," the man said. "Been tending bar here a few years now."

AB "He lives up in the woods somewheres," the man said, picking his teeth with a matchstick.

EL The old man patted Jen's shoulder kindly. "If I were you," he said, "I'd set my sights on someone a little more . . . run of the mill."

AB Jen watched Ian go to get ice from a cooler out back. She followed him, proud of herself for being assertive for once in her life.

EL Why couldn't she have been this direct with her

parents when they sat her down and forced her to pick Amherst over Colorado College?

AB Ian makes me feel strong, Jen realized. Like a stronger version of myself.

EL Jen cleared her throat and Ian spun around. "Ian, it's just me," she said. "Why are you being like this? I don't understand."

AB "Of course you don't understand!" he snapped. "You don't know anything about me. You need to get on a plane and go back to your life, kid."

EL Kid? Jen shook her head. "Just because I'm under 21 doesn't mean I don't know what I want."

AB "Yeah? What do you want?" Ian asked.
"I want to be here with you, dummy!" Jen said. "I want the chance to get to know you better!"

EL There was just no way he didn't feel something for her.

AB Maybe he didn't feel the same way she did, but he had to feel *something*.

EL "Listen," she said softly, "if you say you feel nothing for me, then I'll have to accept it. But for me, last night was . . . pretty much . . . magic."

AB Ian looked at her with a sadness in his eyes she felt she could fall into forever. "I just can't," he said. "I'm sorry—it can never be."

EL He went back into the bar. She should have left. Of course she should have. Maybe before she'd met him, she would have. But she didn't.

AB She had grown this brand-new backbone because of him, so technically it was his fault, right? Right, she told herself.

EL She waited in a coffee shop across the street, drinking cup after cup of the brackish house roast.

AB When he closed the bar at 2 a.m., she followed him.

EL Ian walked up the side streets with the little, slumbering Victorian houses sitting in rows. Past the gas station and into the woods.

AB It seemed like he hiked for hours, up through the pines and aspens. The ground grew rocky underfoot.

EL Jen followed from a distance, a little scared by the woods, but determined to learn more. Once Ian stopped & turned, as if he'd heard her.

AB Even if he can't hear me, she thought to herself, then he can probably smell the sweaty stank I'm emitting all over this poor forest.

EL What did he mean, "It can never be." Why? Was it just because she was a college girl and he was a bartender? That was stupid.

AB Finally, she saw Ian approach a rock wall at the base of a cliff. And she saw a dark opening in the wall—a cave. No effin' way!

EL Ian lived in a cave?! Oh man, Jen thought, just my luck. The first guy I really feel something for is some kind of spelunking fanatic.

AB Then she had another thought: He could be homeless and ashamed of it. Hmm, a real homeless guy. Was there something kinda sexy about that?

EL No, there wasn't.

AB Yes, maybe there was . . .

EL He's homeless, Jen thought, getting her head back in the game. He's homeless and that's why he's pushing me away.

AB Too bad so sad for him, Jen smirked to herself. I'm not going anywhere. Except right into that thar mancave!

EL Just as Ian ducked into the cave, Jen heard a sound behind her.

AB She turned and caught a glimpse of something tall.

EL Something wild.

AB A bear? A gorilla? A huge-freaking-something coming at her.

EL The huge-freaking-something picked up a rock the size of her carry-on luggage.

AB *Bam,* carry-on luggage to the head. And everything went dark.

EL When Jen woke up, the constant rhythm of a headache thumped at her temples.

AB She found she couldn't move—she had been tied up with some kind of homespun twine that smelled like wet Chihuahua.

EL Jen looked around, taking in her surroundings with disbelief and spiraling dizziness. The walls and floor and ceiling were rock.

AB The air smelled damp and masculine. Musky, even.

EL Jen was lying on some kind of bed made out of piles of animal skins. "Hello?" she called. "Ian?"

What had happened to her last night? She remembered seeing the bear-gorilla-thing before she was hit. What the eff *was* that thing?

Jen shifted to get a better look at the cave. There were lots more animal skins and also some strange tufts of wool on the rocky floor.

The tufts had collected in the corners, sort of like snowdrifts. Stinky, hairy snowdrifts. Nice.

A few human objects were here and there—some folded clothes, tin mugs and plates, and a mirror and wash basin set on a small ledge.

Definitely a mancave, Jen thought to herself. The only things missing were a neon beer sign and a dart board.

There was even a poster tacked up onto one of the boulders—a street in Cairo at twilight. Huh.

This is where Ian lives? Jen thought. But why? She looked at the piles of skins. And did he kill these himself? Hadn't he seen *Bambi*?

Ian's living quarters seemed . . . less than ideal. The opposite of ideal.

No cable, no running water, and the nearest Starbucks was a sweaty 8 miles of hiking away.

EL Then again, so was civilization and with it her parents and the subtle but constant pressure to become a stockbroker like her dad.

AB As she glanced around, the cave and its possibilities began to flourish with appeal.

EL Then she remembered she was there more as a hostage than a guest. After all, people didn't usually tie up their overnight guests.

AB No, people usually didn't tie up their guests . . . unless they had been reading *Fifty Shades*.

EL "Hello? Ian? I'm awake," she called.

AB There was movement at the head of the cave but it was too dark to see anything.

EL A single candle offered the only light, and its glow only illuminated so much.

AB Maybe with more candles she'd see a toilet and a flatscreen. One could hope, right?

EL "Ian?" she called. "I'm sorry I followed you. I shouldn't have."

AB She tried not to panic. Please, she prayed, don't let Ian be some kind of serial killer. Let there be a good reason I'm tied up.

EL And then she saw it.

AB A towering form entered, hunched considerably by the cave ceiling. 8 feet tall, maybe more. Covered with long, shaggy fur.

EL The hands of an ape. The face of a monster.

AB Probably the teeth of a shark, but Jen didn't foresee him smiling anytime soon.

EL He was . . . he was . . . there was no use in denying it. He was a Sasquatch.

AB Jen felt like she was gonna go nuts, but he was real! Not legend, not myth. She was looking at a big living breathing freaking bigfoot.

EL One that knew how to knock humans unconscious and bind them with homespun ropes.

AB The beast shuffled forward, holding something in his giant, wooly mitt. He grunted and then lunged forward.

EL Jen struggled and kicked, trying to back away. "Get

away from me!" she screamed. The huge animal pulled back.

The daylight from the cave's entrance went dark as he backed out. And then the sunlight returned.

The small waft from his exit caused the lone candle flame to dance. He was gone.

Good, she thought to herself. Maybe he realized how close he was to getting his Squatchy balls kicked.

And then she saw that the Sasquatch had set something down—a tin cup full of blueberries. It lay close to Jen, right at her side.

Oh geez, she thought. The Sasquatch was gentle. He meant no harm. And apparently he had opposable thumbs, too.

Jen looked at that tin cup for a long time and then her headache-ridden, fully uncaffeinated mind pieced together what must be happening.

 Ian had somehow tamed a Sasquatch. He must take care of it and act, somehow, as his protector, she realized.

 It explained why the animal had attacked her the night

before. The Sasquatch must have thought she was a threat.

AB It didn't know that she loved Ian, too. Or maybe it did, and it was jealous of her. And maybe it should get over it.

EL "I'm sorry," Jen called. "I understand you won't hurt me. Come back, please, Mr. . . . Beast-thing-fellow."

AB The Sasquatch stuck his shaggy head into the cave. "Please," Jen said. "Can you untie me?"

EL The Sasquatch grunted in the affirmative.

AB Or at least, that was what it sounded like; her aunt Lucy always made that same sound when offered a second helping of fried chicken.

EL His giant fingers were clumsy with the twine. She tried not to shrink back from him. Animals smell fear, she reminded herself.

AB He began to grumble in frustration. "Easy now," Jen murmured. But the animal bared his teeth.

EL A scream rose and then died in Jen's throat as the Sasquatch leaned forward and bit through her bindings.

AB Not her wrists. Not her throat. Just the dumb rope.

EL "Thanks," she said, wondering when, when, when Ian would show up and explain his living situation and his unique, hirsute roommate.

AB He grunted in reply. And Jen officially decided he must be related to her aunt Lucy.

EL Jen got to her feet wearily. She saw a canteen filled with water and drank from it. She couldn't ever remember being so thirsty.

AB Luckily, she had a Nature Valley granola bar in her purse. So what if they were little-kid-ish—they were delicious!

EL She gobbled it down, then assaulted the tin cup of blueberries.

AB What she would have given for a double red eye with a foam cap. But still, it was breakfast.

EL The Sasquatch watched Jen eat and drink. When she was done, he raised a hairy paw and pointed toward the mouth of the cave.

AB "You want me to go?" Jen asked. He grunted.

EL "I want to wait for Ian," Jen said. "Please, I need to talk to him before I go." The beast pushed her toward the exit. And daylight.

AB "I don't want to hurt him!" she said. "I'll never tell his secret—that he's your protector. I just want . . . I want to tell him I love him."

EL It had slipped out of her mouth, but Jen realized it was true. She did love Ian.

AB The idea of insta-love had always repelled her. All those idiot Disney princesses falling for a guy after a ballroom dance and a kiss.

EL But here she'd gone and done the same thing. And they hadn't even had a real, *real* kiss yet, for goodness' sake!

AB The Sasquatch watched her, his eyes looking sad, somehow.

EL Maybe he's seen other lovesick girls up here, trailing after Ian. Maybe this happens all the time.

AB What a great reality show this would make, Jen thought as she polished off the last blueberries. *He, She & It!*

EL Then there came a sound—a horrible animal bellow from outside.

AB Next to Jen, the Sasquatch growled—more fiercely than Aunt Lucy ever had.

EL He rose and prowled out of the cave. Jen stumbled to her feet.

AB The sounds that came from outside were horrific: snarling, pounding, branches and skulls cracking.

EL Jen slowly approached the mouth of the cave, afraid of what she would see . . .

AB Outside, the Sasquatch fought another of its kind. Teeth gnashed. Fur flew.

EL Their howls and war cries filled the woods. The beasts attacked each other with a raw and deadly grace.

AB And somehow, to Jen's watchful eye, the fight seemed personal. The Sasquatches were pissed—at each other.

EL Ian's Sasquatch threw the other into a tree. *Snap* and *crash*—the pine toppled over and finally, the attack ended.

AB The other brute slunk away, giving Jen a dirty look over its shoulder. She wondered whether it would understand the middle finger.

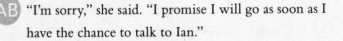 "Was that . . . was that about me?" Ian's Sasquatch grunted in the affirmative as it squatted on the ground to lick his wounds.

 "I'm sorry," she said. "I promise I will go as soon as I have the chance to talk to Ian."

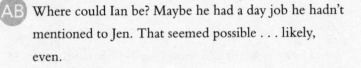 The beast shot her a look that said, You'd better. Together, they settled in to wait.

Where could Ian be? Maybe he had a day job he hadn't mentioned to Jen. That seemed possible . . . likely, even.

 She'd just have to wait.

 "Well," she said. "Might as well make myself useful!"

 She started to tidy up a bit. The cave certainly needed it.

 Jen took the animal skins outside and beat them against the rock wall of the cliff, holding her breath from the stank that wafted up.

She folded Ian's clothes and put them in a tidy pile.

She wanted to smell them, to take in Ian's yummy scent, but for some reason she would feel humiliated if the bigfoot saw her do it.

EL   The Sasquatch was keeping busy, too, running some secret Sasquatchy errands, Jen supposed. Every so often he came and checked on her.

AB   For the moment, he was just squatting by the entrance to the cave, watching her and picking his teeth with a twig.

EL   Jen's stomach growled. Loud. The Sasquatch gave a huff. A laugh, maybe? He beckoned to Jen.

AB   I hope he doesn't think I speak Sasquatch, Jen thought. His body beard will grow gray before that happens. He grunted again.

EL   "I'm coming, I'm coming." She followed the animal out of the cave and up a switchback path that lead to the top of the cliff.

AB   There she saw an abandoned campsite, with a fire blazing cheerfully in a pit. So the Sasquatch was a Boy Scout?

EL   Two skinned rabbits were roasting above the flames on a spit and a skillet filled with wild onions sat steaming off to the side.

AB   A Boy Scout and a chef? Jen was impressed! She couldn't remember the last time she cooked— burned—something without a microwave.

EL "You did all this?" Jen asked the Sasquatch. He shrugged in a demure way that nearly made Jen laugh out loud.

AB Who knew Sasquatches could be demure? And who knew Sasquatches could shrug?

EL The food was delicious. The Sasquatch squatted on his haunches and ate along with Jen, both of them tearing into the food with abandon.

AB She knew if Ian were here, she'd probably try to be a little feminine and maybe chew her food. But she ate as wildly as the bigfoot beside her.

EL Eating like a beast—with a beast—on the top of a mountain cliff. My parents should see me now, Jen thought. She felt fierce.

AB Ian makes me brave and this Sasquatch makes me feel wild. Okay—am I really assessing how a Sasquatch makes me feel?

EL "Yum," Jen said. She lay on the ground, watching dreamy clouds drift above.

AB It felt like watching a baby's mobile made by Mother Nature, with the wind in the scrub oak as her lullaby.

I could get used to this, Jen thought. And she drifted off to sleep as the Sasquatch sighed.

When she woke, it was the late afternoon. She sat up with a start. Was Ian back yet? Where was her 'Squatch?

From the shadows, the giant beast grunted to her. He had been keeping watch, she realized. It was kind of sweet.

Did he have a crush on her? Did Sasquatches even get crushes? Did sane people ask themselves if Sasquatches got crushes?

The fire burned, making a pretty glow as the sun, finally, began to set. The Sasquatch started crooning. His song was somehow . . . familiar.

"Is that 'What Makes You Beautiful' by One Direction?!" she asked in shock.

The Sasquatch grunted in the affirmative and kept on humming. He was . . . well . . . he was pretty good.

If his mouth could form words, he could be the sixth member of One Direction, Jen thought.

 That band could really use a basso profundo to

ground their sound. Then she shook herself out of her reverie.

AB "When will Ian be back?" Jen said. "Do you think . . . do you think he's staying away because I'm here?"

EL That was probably it. He didn't want to face her. Or he thought she was nuts.

AB Tears slipped from her eyes. What was she doing here, on a cliff top, with a Sasquatch, watching the sunset?

EL . . . while he serenaded her with a teen pop ballad?

AB Suddenly the Sasquatch patted her on the back. She looked up. There was a kindness in his gray eyes.

EL He pointed out to the sunset. "Yes," Jen said. "It's beautiful . . ." He pointed with more urgency. "It's really beautiful."

AB And then the Sasquatch began to shake. Violent spasms tore through his body.

EL "What is it?" she cried. "Are you okay? What's happening?"

AB He was shaking so hard some fur was flying off. Then

she realized *all* his fur was coming off. Like mange at the speed of light.

EL As the sun flared behind the horizon, a golden light burst from the body of the Sasquatch.

AB She gasped. It was . . . He was . . .

EL Ian. He stood there in all his naked glory.

AB And "glory" was the understatement of the millennium.

EL Jen backed away, looked away, but then took another good look. Yep, it was Ian all right.

AB She would know those, uh, shoulders anywhere.

EL "Jen," Ian said, "I never wanted you to see. To know about me."

AB "You-you-you're a Sasquatch," Jen stammered. A man by night and a bigfoot by day.

EL "Yes," Ian answered simply. "That's what I couldn't tell you. This is the reason we can never be together."

AB It was too much for Jen. The tears that had fallen before were nothing compared with the sobs that wracked her now.

Disappointment and confusion overwhelmed her. Ian knelt and held her in his arms.

 Which made it a million times worse.

 "I fall in love," Jen cried. "I fall in love and it's with a freaking bigfoot!"

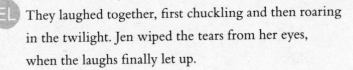 "We really prefer the term Sasquatch," Ian said. He cracked a smile and Jen laughed.

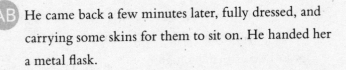 They laughed together, first chuckling and then roaring in the twilight. Jen wiped the tears from her eyes, when the laughs finally let up.

 "You do realize you're naked, right?" Jen asked.

"Yeah," Ian answered. His bashful grin made Jen blush. "You stay here," he said. "I'll be right back."

He came back a few minutes later, fully dressed, and carrying some skins for them to sit on. He handed her a metal flask.

"Is that whiskey?" Jen asked. "You know I'm underage."

"No, it's coffee."
"Coffee! Where was it?" she said. "I would have killed for some coffee before!"

"You have to know where to look," Ian said. "I have a lot of stuff hidden away in that cave."

"Do you have a hot shower hidden there?" Jen asked dryly.

"God, you're funny," Ian said. "And beautiful. It was all I could do to keep my hands off you all day."

"That would *not* have been cool!" Jen laughed. Being macked on by a Sasquatch? No thanks.

Ian handed her the coffee again and she drained the last drops.

"I should take you back down the mountain while there's still a little light," he said sadly.

"No," Jen said. "But I-I want to . . . I want to—"

"You want to what?" he said, desperation rising in his voice. "Stay with me? Live this insane life with me— beast by day, man by night?"

"It's absurd," he said, looking away from her. "You have to go."

"Maybe later," Jen said. "I waited all day to talk to you."

"All right." Ian sighed. "What do you want to talk about?"

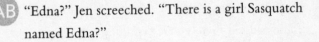 "Well, for one thing, who hit me on the head? It was a Sasquatch, but it wasn't you because you were, um, in your man form."

 "My 'man form,'" he said. "I like that. It was Edna. She, uh, she likes me."

 "Edna?" Jen screeched. "There is a girl Sasquatch named Edna?"

 "Yeah," Ian said. "Edna. She used to be human at night, too, but after a few years, your human hours dwindle away."

Ian looked into the fire. His future was grim, Jen realized. "Oh, Ian," she said. "I'm so sorry."

"There are upsides to being a Sasquatch," he said. "I have superhuman strength and I heal crazy, crazy fast."

"But I do miss my mom. And I'll never get to travel. I'll never get to see the pyramids at Giza, or the Taj Mahal."

"But, look"—Jen gestured to the mountaintops, the

sandstone vista painted purple and navy by the evening—"this is better than the Taj Mahal."

(AB) "I'm dreading going back east," Jen confided. "My parents want me to conquer the world of high finance and I'd rather fall off a cliff."

(EL) Ian shot her a glance. "Not this cliff here," she joked. "But you know what I mean."

(AB) Ian took her hands in his. "You're going to go back home and tell them you're changing your major," he instructed her.

(EL) "And then you're going to find a great career and marry some great guy and be happy," Ian said.

(AB) He looked so sad, Jen felt like her heart was collapsing inside her chest.

(EL) Instead of speaking, she leaned over and kissed him on the cheek. Then the back of his hand. Then the delicious area under his jaw.

(AB) An area that now smelled nothing like wet Chihuahua and everything like the Ian she knew and craved.

(EL) The skins they lay on were warm and the fire burned brightly against the blue-black sky.

She couldn't keep her hands off him and he couldn't keep his off her either.

 "I should get you down the mountain," he murmured. "We need to stop."

 "Don't tell me to stop," she pleaded. "Not when we just got started . . ."

 A few hours later, Jen awoke to the feeling of Ian's fingers brushing a few strands of her hair out of her face.

 What a great view to wake up to, Jen thought. In the embers of the firelight he looked like a blond Jensen Ackles. Supernatur-yummy!

 He was sitting up, gazing down at her with an expression so tender and full of regret that Jen's heart caught in her throat.

 It was the kind of look that had "never" written all over it. As in they could *never* be together.

 But Jen ignored his glum expression. There had to be a way to work it out.

 If he loved her . . . if he wanted to be with her as much as she wanted to be with him—they could find a way to make it work. They had to.

EL "It will be dawn soon," he said. "Let's get going. I'd like to get you as close to town as possible before I turn."

AB "But there's something you never told me—"

EL "I have to be really careful around town," Ian interrupted. "If anyone catches sight of me as a Sasquatch, I'll be hunted day and night."

AB "There's just one thing I want to know," she said, stalling.

EL She wanted to know if he loved her as much as she loved him. But somehow her nerve failed.

AB "How did you get this way?" she asked. If he says "I was born this way," I'm going to freaking pass out, she thought.

EL He rubbed his stubbly face. "I guess you deserve the story," he said.

AB "I had a fight with my dad and I left home in a stupid fit. I was determined I would make it by myself," he told her.

EL "I was only 16 and I got a job washing dishes down at the tavern. Then this woman came in. She was . . . she was gorgeous."

AB There was a faraway look in Ian's eye that Jen did not like. She snuggled nearer to remind him where he was—and where he wasn't.

EL "She was exotic. Sophisticated. Wild. At the end of the night she said . . . she said . . . Well, it doesn't matter what she said. She kissed me."

AB Jen *really* didn't like the way he looked now! He was clearly lost, remembering a kiss from the past.

EL Jen gasped. She realized that for all their making-out and romantic moments, they still hadn't kissed on the lips.

AB This mystery woman not only enjoyed a permanent space in Ian's memory, she'd also enjoyed his lips!

EL I'm going to kiss her right out of his memory, Jen decided.

AB She put one hand on the back of Ian's neck and drew close to him, closing her eyes as her lips moved toward his—

EL "No!" Ian shouted. He stood up. "Are you crazy?"

AB "Crazy to want to kiss you?" Jen cried. "You're foaming at the mouth about some old biddy from the past."

EL "And I'm right here in front of you. I feel like a chump!"

AB Ian strode away from Jen and faced the edge of the cliff.

EL "She turned me," Ian said softly. "Edna kissed me on the mouth and turned me into this half man/half beast."

AB "Edna?" Jen gasped.

EL "Edna." He spat her name out like a curse. "She wanted me for a mate. She still does. It's dangerous here for you."

AB "She's the one who hit me over the head," Jen said. "Shouldn't she have been in a human form then?"

EL "After a few years, Edna stopped turning human at night." He shrugged sadly.

AB "Do you think that's what will happen to you?" Jen asked. "That'll you stop turning into a human?"

EL The sky was beginning to glow.

AB The question hung in the air like a pestering mosquito.

EL "I don't know," Ian said bitterly. "I'll probably die a

monster. Hiding from hicks with iPhones. Eating rabbit and foraged weeds. Alone."

(AB) "But I'm not like Edna," he said. "I'd never turn someone to keep me company."

(EL) He looked down into the woods as if Edna were there, watching them. Listening.

(AB) Jen tossed a dirty glare toward the tree line, just in case she was. She wondered *again* whether Edna would still understand the middle finger.

(EL) Ian kicked at a rock and sent it tumbling down the hill.

(AB) It felt like all Jen's hopes and dreams were on that rock, now irretrievable.

(EL) "Why don't you just go already?" he shouted. "Go now, before I turn!"

(AB) "Okay . . . Okay," Jen said. The sun was cresting the mountain. But she didn't move. Couldn't.

(EL) Ian began to shake. He gritted his teeth, growling. "GO!"

(AB) "But you love me," Jen cried.

"No, I don't!" he snarled. "GO!"

 It was just too much. Jen tore down the cliff side, tears coursing down her face.

 She loved him, she loved him. She did. But it was impossible. Ian knew it already.

 And she'd better start getting used to it.

 Crashing down the mountain, roots seemed to grab at her ankles and branches snatched at her hair.

No detangler would win in a fight against her rat's nest of a hairdo now.

She ran and ran, getting nearer to civilization all the while when she tripped over one last rock.

Jen fell, sobbing, to the ground. Dirt in her mouth, hair, nostrils. She didn't care.

This was the end of something big. This was the end of something she wanted more than anything else. An end before it ever really began.

Sitting there, crying in the clearing, Jen realized she'd left her purse in Ian's cave. She snorted with a derisive laugh.

EL What was she going to do? Hike up the hill and face Sasquatch Ian again?

AB Or maybe she'd just leave it, cancel her credit cards, and start over. It wasn't like Ian was about to use them anytime soon!

EL Only then did she hear the snarl.

AB Jen looked up. There, on top of a boulder, was a mountain lion, poised. Ready to spring.

EL She reached out and grabbed a stout scrub oak stick.

AB In a flash of golden fur and jagged teeth, the beast was upon her.

EL Jen pushed against the snarling lion with the branch, shoving it away as it swiped with razor-sharp claws.

AB It turned out she did have fight left in her, even it was just pent-up frustration. She whacked the massive feline with the branch.

EL "Help!" Jen screamed. "Ian, if you can hear me—Help!"

AB The lion clawed her ear and neck with its claws. A scream rang out—a scream that mingled with Jen's. It was the lion. Her victory cry.

EL And then Ian, Sasquatch Ian, was there. He grabbed the cat by the back of the neck the way a housewife would handle a kitten.

AB Well, maybe not as gentle (depending on the housewife).

EL He threw the cat off to the side and squared off, ready to fight. Jen watched the lion—tail twitching in anger—size up the Sasquatch.

AB It was sizing up Ian. Her Ian.

EL Jen pressed her hand against her neck. There was blood. Lots of blood. And her ear. It was . . . it was torn and dangling.

AB She was glad she couldn't see it. As it was, she was trying to keep from passing out.

EL Maybe she was in shock. Maybe she'd lost too much blood. Maybe she was dying.

AB She fought to regain full consciousness. Her eyes struggled to focus. On Ian. On the lion.

EL Just as Ian the Sasquatch moved threateningly toward the giant cat, a third figure stepped into the clearing.

AB It was just a blurry shadow in Jen's vanishing sight. But she knew what—who—it was.

EL Edna! The She-squatch launched herself at Ian, grappling with him.

AB What was she doing? Why was she choosing this moment to show up?

EL Jen got her answer as the mountain lion turned its merciless golden eyes back onto her. Not the fighting Sasquatches. Edna was distracting Ian on purpose!

AB The lion licked its chops and let out its blood-congealing victory scream. Then it took a step toward her.

EL Jen shook her head, trying to clear it. Everything felt like a daydream.

AB Or, maybe a day-nightmare resulting from blood loss.

EL Edna wanted Jen dead. And all she had to do was keep Ian busy until the lion finished Jen off.

AB Which might be pretty freaking soon if she didn't do something!

EL Ian pulled free from Edna and tried to reach the

mountain cat but it jumped and sped ahead—bounding toward Jen with a wild cry.

 Jen reached for another branch—a rock—anything she could use as a weapon. There was nothing.

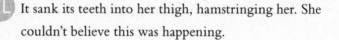 Jen pushed back, scrambling to get up, to run.

The effort was laughable—the massive feline was on her in a flash.

 It sank its teeth into her thigh, hamstringing her. She couldn't believe this was happening.

 Of all the things she accepted in the last 24 hours, she couldn't accept this. But, hey, who really can accept their own death?

 The mountain lion threw Jen to the ground and sank its deadly teeth into the back of her neck.

She was in so much pain her whole body felt like one giant scream.

But then the animal whimpered and released its hold.

She didn't care.

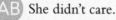 Jen fell face-first onto the ground.

AB She didn't care about that either.

EL She looked up to see Sasquatch Ian twisting the lion's head sharply, with a resounding *crack*. He threw the cat to the ground.

AB And still she didn't care. What was there to care about? She was dying and death has a way of keeping you from sweating the small stuff.

EL Jen saw Edna's motionless form lying beyond the cat. This she cared about. A little.

AB Edna was dead—good! It felt like a thorn had been removed from Jen's side—but the rest of her body was still ripped to confetti.

EL Sasquatch Ian squatted down and grunted at Jen. He touched her face gently with one thick-skinned finger pad.

AB "It's okay," Jen said. "I'm going to die. Just . . ."

EL She sputtered as blood bubbled up in her mouth.

AB Death, real death, was not like you see in a play or a movie. And whoever heard of a Sasquatch *Romeo and Juliet*, anyway? Nobody. That's who.

"Leave my body somewhere the cops will find it," she rasped. "So my folks won't worry . . ."

 Sasquatch Ian shook his head, No. She saw determination in his eyes.

 He picked her up, as if she were a small, frightened child, and cradled her to his chest.

 He does love me, Jen thought. She was weakening by the moment. But in that thought, a tiny hope sparked. It was faint, but it was hope.

 Jen felt her warm blood wetting Ian's thick pelt. I've got to hold on, she told herself. We must be nearing town now . . .

 All she could do was cling to Ian. And to her hope. Somehow consciousness came easier.

 Her head bobbed against the thick, muscled chest of the Sasquatch. She tried to hold on, but she was so weak . . .

 She'd heard of people fighting off death. How they weren't "ready" to go yet. She'd never put stock in that. Until now.

 The Sasquatch gave no sign of slowing. Oh no.

 There! Ahead, down through the trees she could see

the winding gray road—the town's only highway. And the gas station . . .

EL The beast—Ian—looked into her eyes.

AB "Wait," Jen cried. "No! You can't take me into town. They'll see you. They'll capture you."

EL "No!" she shouted. But only when she struggled to get free did Ian stop running.

AB She could read his expression. His face said he didn't care about being caught. That her life was worth his. That he'd already decided.

EL She lifted a weak hand and put it to Ian's ape-like face.

AB Pure love shone down from his gray eyes.

EL And then she did what she had wanted to do from the first moment she laid eyes on him . . .

AB With the last energy in her body, Jen reached up and kissed him on the lips.

EL An electric shock shot through her body.

AB A golden light poured from Ian's hairy body and filled up her own.

EL The light . . . it was healing her wounds. She looked at her body.

AB She was leaking light through all the slashes and punctures and wounds.

EL And before her eyes, they began to close up. She was healing so fast the wounds were gone before she could blink.

AB She no longer felt the fingers of death coaxing her away from the mountain.

EL Then the light was within her and Jen became aware that she was still kissing Ian.

AB Now she knew what all those Disney princesses were talking about. This kind of kiss could make a girl do crazy things.

EL The light pulsed between their two bodies then faded away. Leaving her . . . feeling *awesome!*

AB She felt strong. And she was. Stronger than death. She felt like a sharpened version of herself.

EL Ian dropped her to her feet and she stretched her arms. They were hairy and long.

AB Gillette didn't have nothin' on these pits now, she

thought. And she laughed—her laugh was something like a grunt crossed with a woof.

EL She was covered, head to foot, in downy, auburn fur. And she was beautiful.

AB Her parents might not think so . . .

EL But she would call them, and tell them she was staying in Colorado forever. They would accept it. They would just have to.

AB "My beloved," grunted Ian. Maybe "beloved" wasn't the exact word, but this kind of communication was different than human language.

EL She could understand his grunts perfectly now. They didn't form structured sentences, but emotion and meaning came through.

AB "A human observes us," he grunted, pointing.

EL Jen saw a gangly gas station attendant watching them. He had a doughnut crammed in his mouth and the keys to the station in his hand.

AB Well, "watching" wasn't the right word in English (or in Sasquatch).

EL It was more like "ogling in slack-jawed disbelief."

AB "Ogling in slack-jawed disbelief while choking on his frosted rainbow-sprinkled cruller."

EL "We must flee," Ian grunted. "Can you run?"

AB "You bet your furry hindquarters, I can," she told him.

EL They ran up into the hills. She could move so fast now! The trees blurred past her.

AB The kid at the pump dropped his keys as he fumbled for his camera.

EL Hands shaking, he took a shot of the two giant beasts disappearing up the hill.

AB He looked at the photo. Dang it, he thought. Not good enough to sell to the *The Sun*.

EL Just good enough to get me laughed out of Billy's Tavern. Still, he dialed his best friend's number.

AB "Hey snot-face, get up. It's me, Gary," he said into the phone. "Yeah, I know it's 6 o'clock in the a.m."

EL "Look, you and me's going bigfoot hunting this afternoon. I got a real good line on a couple of lovebirds."

Gary shut his phone and looked at the shot he'd gotten. It was blurry and questionable. But he knew what he'd seen.

 A couple of primo class-A Sasquatch lovebirds.

AB THE END

EL Yes, THE END!

Courtney Alameda

BY COURTNEY ALAMEDA

Shutter

Meet Courtney Alameda

My favorite biographies often have bibliographic leanings, as I believe books create watershed moments in the lives of their readers. For me, two books altered the course of my life so drastically, I often wonder what I might have become without them—Ray Bradbury's *Fahrenheit 451* and Garth Nix's *Sabriel*. The former taught me the language of symbolism and made me want to major in English. The latter made me realize I wanted to spend my life writing for young people.

Thanks in part to those books, my entire career has had a bookish bent: I spent seven years working for Barnes & Noble and had the good fortune to watch the young-adult section grow and flourish with the commercial success of titles like *Harry Potter* and *Twilight*. In 2009, I made a shift into library services, first as an events coordinator, and later as a young-adult librarian. Over the years, I've realized that my joy doesn't just come from working with books, but from connecting people with great literature of all shapes, sizes, and classifications.

I started writing in college. I dallied with all kinds of genres, forms, and markets; but it wasn't until I took a graduate-level writing seminar during my senior year that I found my voice. I met twice a week with a wizened old professor who owned a wicked red pen. He slashed through my fiction, rolled his eyes at my attempts at humor and romance, and declared me an outright failure at mystery. Science fiction and fantasy weren't entirely forbidden, but frowned upon.

About halfway through the term, the professor took off his glasses and said, "Stop trying to impress me, and write whatever exists in your head without you having to forcibly *put* it there."

So I wrote him a ghost story. He read the entire piece through without picking up his red pen, and afterward declared me an idiot. "You're a horror writer and you don't even know it, and there's talent here reminiscent of a young Stephen King. Mark my words, girl, in ten years, you're really going to be something."

I'm afraid my work doesn't live up to his pronouncement yet—but I still have a few years before I can celebrate the tenth anniversary of those words.

Shutter came about the way most of my novels do, through mind's-eye glimpses of a young person doing something incredible. In Micheline's case, I imagined a girl fighting an ultraviolet ghost with a Nikon camera. The more time I spent with her, the more her story and world expanded. A few weeks into our acquaintance, she spoke her first words to me: *"Call it reaper's insomnia, but the dead won't let me sleep at night."* Those words now comprise the novel's opening line.

"Fixer" is a prequel short story to *Shutter,* as told from Ryder's point of view. The story examines some of the emotional trauma dealt to Micheline and Ryder on the night

Micheline's mother and brothers die, which presented me with several unique challenges. I spent several weeks trying to write this story from Micheline's perspective, but her memories of what happened in the panic room were too raw and painful for young-adult fiction. So I switched to Ryder's head, which meant I had to invest time in fleshing out his voice and unique worldviews. He's significantly less observant than Micheline, especially in terms of texture, color, and shape; which makes sense, he's not a photographer like Micheline. Also, his voice is rougher around the edges, less lyrical, and so very Aussie.

If I can claim any literary godparents, I would name Michael Crichton for his monsters; J. R. R. Tolkien for magic and myth; and Stephen King for the macabre. Also, Robin McKinley bestowed the blueprints for the strong, dynamic heroines in novels like *The Blue Sword* and *The Hero and the Crown*. I see their influences—among many others, including Bram Stoker's—in *Shutter*'s pages.

FIXER

by Courtney Alameda

NOW

It's a rare night I can't fix broken with a bullet—any reaper knows how to stop the dead. But when the monster you're aiming for wears a familiar face, the trigger kills on both sides of your barrel. It's not the kind of broken I can fix: The nightmares in my head can't be shot down and nothing will erase what happened to Micheline and me that night, or what I did to save her.

"Hey, slacker," Jude says as I climb into the Humvee. It's been ten nights since Micheline's mother and brothers died and the bastard's finally shown up at the Helsings' safe house. But he's not here for Micheline, no. He's here for me.

When Jude arrived, honking in the driveway like the bloody redcoats were coming, Micheline's old man handed me his Colt .45 and kicked me out of the house, promising me he'd keep an eye on her. But I know old man Helsing won't look after her right—he's suffering almost as bad as she is, but he's old enough and stubborn enough to tough it out . . . least on the outside.

As for Micheline? Damned if I couldn't fix her kind of broken, either. It wakes her up screaming, has her breaking glass to cut her wrists or dyeing her hair black with ink milked out of Sharpies. I might've saved her life with a bullet, but I can't mend my girl's heart. I stop, wondering when Micheline became *my* girl. Rather than face the thought, I settle into my seat and say, "Last time I checked, *slacking* was your prerogative, mate."

"*I'm* the slacker?

You've been holed up here for more than a week. If we don't post numbers tonight, those asshats in Chicago are going to catch up to us on the killboards," Jude says, backing out of the driveway. "How's Micheline?"

"Go in and see her yourself." I don't give a rat's arse about the killboards tonight. Jude hasn't visited Micheline at all, not even with Ollie, and it pisses me off to the point of wanting to adjust that cocky jaw of his with my fist.

"*Somebody's* cranky," Jude says. "You forget *I* held her hand during the funeral—"

"And you're a goddamn saint for it, you're right."

He scowls at me. "Hey, *mate*, it gave me a real good look at what happened back at the big house that night." Jude's a perceptive bastard, and he picks up on memories and possible futures just by touching someone. "She doesn't need me in her headspace, adding to the noise. I'm doing her a favor, okay? Just tell me how she's doing."

Now it's my turn to scowl, because we both know he's doing *himself* the favor. I thump my boot up on his dash and he groans about the detailing, but doesn't force me to ease off, either.

Honestly, I'm not sure how to answer his question. Over the last week, Micheline's hollowed out, speaking no more than a handful of words at a time. Her gorgeous peacock blues look as vacant and eventual as open graves—she cries little, never complains, and says nothing about what happened in the panic room that night. I wish she'd scream, throw a punch at me, do *something* to tell me the girl I knew still exists inside her, somewhere, and wants something more than to write her own life off.

I settle for saying, "She's holding up best anyone could, I reckon."

Jude lifts a brow. I'm a shitbox liar and it shows to anyone with a pulse, but he doesn't press the issue. Typical of him. "Did you get the new brag tag already, or what?"

He means the Harker cross tattoo I got for saving Micheline's life. The three-day-old ink on my biceps aches like a new bruise, but I shrug. Thanks to my bloody waffling that night, Mrs. Helsing's teeth missed Micheline's jugular by inches. I don't deserve the Harker cross for saving her; I'd been one bite away from losing her for good.

The Harker cross is a medal that can't be taken off; like they say, once a reaper, always a reaper, and nobody walks away from Helsing alive.

"You want to stop acting like a douche and actually answer me?" Jude asks.

"The tat's a beauty, hey?"

He groans. "Let's hope a good hunt loosens you up so you can pull the stick out of your ass." He waves to the guards as we drive through the safe-house gates.

I *tch* and look out the window, watching the upscale Palo Alto neighborhood blur by. Guess I couldn't expect him to understand what it was like to pull the trigger on something . . . no, some*one* you loved. We're killers, Jude and me, but we're used to cutting down faceless things: Point, shoot, and don't think twice about the trigger. If I told him what happened that night, 'specially the parts nobody else knew, he'd bluff his way through his shock, shrug it off, and tell me to man up. And I swear, that's all I've been doing since I shot Micheline's mum dead.

"The boys are meeting up at Potrero Point," Jude says. "Travis found a big pod of Glasgow girls in the generating station. You game?"

Like I've got much choice. I chuckle darkly and say, "Hells yeah."

Jude hits the gas as we merge on the freeway toward San Francisco. "That's all I wanted to hear."

☙

THAT NIGHT

I started up the road to the Helsings' big house after finishing my homework at the shooting range. Fog twisted through the compound's big eucalyptus trees and softened the sounds of traffic on Highway 101— the big road cut through the Helsing compound at the Presidio on its way to the Golden Gate Bridge.

The wind whistled and shrieked, cold from skipping over the bay. I grit my teeth, ignoring how human it sounded. But a heartbeat later, there was no ignoring the shriek that cut through the night. The sound was faint, maybe tires squealing on the highway. The night raged too late for civvies to be messing around, 'specially on a weeknight. Maybe it'd been an animal, or even a few cadets playing pranks somewhere in the trees.

The noise cut through the fog again—a scream ripped straight out of the big house.

Micheline.

I dropped my backpack and sprinted up the road. Dead run, full tilt. The copse of trees cleared out, and all the lights in the Helsings' house blazed bright. The house looked homey, cheery even; but the screaming sliced through the pounding in my ears. I leapt up the steps and found the front door locked.

"Micheline!" I shouted, beating the door with my fist. Another scream slammed into the wood and cut off mid-pitch. I kicked the door, once, twice. When it held, I shot out the lock and shouldered the door open. Everything looked normal save for the bloody handprint stamped onto the stairwell wall.

"Micheline!" I shouted again. Screams raced down from the second floor to answer me.

Bracing myself for the worst, I leapt up the stairs.

∽

NOW

Jude parks the Humvee outside the generating station's gates, his lights flashing over a rusted red sign that reads POTRERO POWER PLANT, 1201-A ILLINOIS STREET. Two other Helsing Humvees sit on the road, their boxy forms outlined in the street lamps. There's no light beyond the gates and no moon, so I barely make out the shapes of power poles, sagging cables, and smokestacks. Jude whistles. "Old and abandoned, just the way the necros like 'em."

"Who else's here?" I ask.

"Travis and Elena scouted the pod," Jude says, nodding to the other trucks. Guys are jumping out, arming up, and pounding fists. "Looks like Garrett and Rory are with them. Did

Trav have to bring the ginger Wonder Twins? Rory likes to spray-and-pray with an M-sixteen, so watch your back out there. His aim's some scary shit."

We need six top-tier cadets? "How big's this pod?"

Jude waggles his eyebrows and jumps out. "Big enough to remind the Chicago kids that the top academy killboard spots belong to us."

I grin and grab an M16 rifle from the munitions locker in the back of the truck. Maybe Jude's right—a hunt will do me good. Micheline will survive a night in her old man's care.

Maybe.

When the other guys see me walking up with Jude, their faces fall. I know it's nothing personal, and it's got everything to do with respecting the girl back at the safe house. The blokes nod; Elena steps forward to give me a loose hug.

"We've missed you in class, Ryder," she says, and her voice is all Spanish lilt and honey. Deceptive, because I've seen the girl take out reanimates at thirty yards with throwing knives. "How are you?"

It's the first time in days anyone's asked me how I'm doing, and the answer sure isn't *bloody gorgeous.* So I shrug, 'specially with the guys around—I don't want them to think I'm going to puss out. "We're all taking things a day at time." *An hour at a time, sometimes.*

Elena steps back, her lips pressed together, doe's eyes soft and sad. "And Miss Helsing? I'd hoped she'd be . . . Is she . . . ?"

"Okay?" I shake my head and wipe my jaw with my hand. If it was just Elena and me, I'd tell her how I broke Micheline's bathroom door down two nights ago and pried a butterfly knife from her bleeding hands, or how I spent half the day today holding her when a night terror shook her awake. Maybe I'd tell her that the half-moon-shaped cuts on my arms are from Micheline's nails, or that I hadn't slept in a proper bed since that night.

Or maybe . . . *maybe* I'd tell Elena what happened *after* I carried Micheline out of her home or hell or whatever the big house was to us now. But how does a bloke say something like that out loud?

I shot . . .

No. *I had to shoot . . .*

He was . . .

He was just a kid.

No. *He was already dead.*

None of those words would make someone understand what I had to do or how the memory would stalk me till I died.

"Damn, I feel like I should salute you, man," Travis says. We clap hands, and he pulls me in for a half embrace. He's not my crew; but if I didn't hunt with Micheline, Jude, and Ollie, I'm dead sure I'd be reaping with Travis and Elena. Their skills are heaps better than everyone else's, and I trust them with my life.

After everyone makes nice, Elena pulls out the business: "The pod's holed up in the basement of the generating station." She motions to a building about two hundred meters up the road. "We'll move through the switchyard together and split into three teams once we hit the tank farm. Hang right and head for the smokestack near the shore, taking out any bogeys as you go. We'll regroup at the plant. Everyone clear?"

Nods. We sync our headset comms and move out. The

night's clear and fogless, so the switchyard's towers cast shadowy skeletons over the road. Elena takes point, followed by Travis and the twins. Jude and I bring up the rear. I brace my rifle's stock against my shoulder and flick the mounted flashlight on, downshifting into the rhythm of the hunt. Adrenaline drips into my system, sharpening my senses. For the first time in days, I remember how I live for this.

After fifty meters, we reach three massive tanks. Travis motions the twins forward, then points Jude and me left, toward the tanks. He and Elena move right, headed for a redbrick building.

The tanks used to house fuel oil for the plant and stretch some twenty meters in diameter apiece. Jude and I skirt the edge of the first one, our rifles pointed at the ground to decrease our chances of our flashlights being spotted. The place is silent except for the city's whispery, AM-radio-like chatter and the soft hiss of the bay surf. Nothing moves in the switchyard. No cars pass on the street. My adrenaline hikes, but I'm grinning like a fool. After being cooped up so long, it feels good to be out in the night air, hunting deadly things.

We round the tank at a jog and halt. There's a necro standing in our path by the second tank, his back to us, hidden in the deep shadows. Long, tangled hair spills over his shoulders. He's dressed in a ratty white shirt and torn jeans, and he shivers and jerks in the breeze.

"It's gotta be a bait-and-switch," Jude whispers. Glasgow girls hunt in packs, luring prey to the bait while the others sneak up behind and slash the victim's mouth from ear to ear with their claws. Victims die a day or so later and join the pack—females become hunters, males are scapegoats and reaper bait. Clever as hell, Glasgow girls. Just not clever enough. "Where's his partner?"

"Dunno." I glance back at the switchyard, but the darkness lies still.

Gunshots break up the silence. The guy's head snaps up, and he shrieks when our flashlights hit him in the face. Blood still weeps down his gashed cheeks, and his teeth glow like bloody pearls.

An answering cry echoes overhead. Footsteps pound the top of the empty tank.

"Heads up," I shout. A black form leaps off the edge, landing like she's boneless and darting toward us fast. The necro lunges for Jude—and before I can react, stabs her claws into his mouth.

I squeeze the trigger and freeze—

'Cause I swear it's Mrs. Helsing standing there.

⟨∾⟩

THAT NIGHT

Nothing could've prepared me for what I found.

I ran up the stairs and hit the second-floor landing. The lights in the Helsings' panic room blazed, throwing the scene at the end of the hall into high definition: Micheline, scrambling backward as her mum lunged. Gore gloved the woman's hands and arms, aimed at Micheline's throat for the kill.

I tore my handgun from its holster. My sights wavered, because in no world I knew could Mrs. Helsing turn necro and attack her own kids.

Micheline screamed, and the sound drove nails into my heart and

ripped it in two. I punched the trigger. The gunshot cracked the air open,
leaving me alone with the shock of silence. Mrs. Helsing crumpled.
Christ, I heard my own pulse pounding in my ears. Gunsmoke burned
my throat. Nothing moved in the panic room, except for the cherry ooze
dripping out the back of Mrs. Helsing's skull.

Bloody,
Bloody,
Bloody,
Hell.

⌒

NOW

Jude drops his gun and grabs the Glasgow girl's wrists, keeping her from tearing into his face.

The male rushes me, his claws spread wide. His shriek
snaps me back, and I realize the girl Jude's fighting looks *noth-*
ing like Mrs. Helsing—she's a brunette and too tall. I shoot her
off him, then pivot to face the male charging at me. My rifle
shouts and bucks into my shoulder. The male tumbles to the
ground, loose-limbed. He rolls to a stop just a few feet away
from me, his vacant eyes staring at the sky. Blood seeps out
from the hole I punched in his corpse, his dead blood black as
crude oil.

Jude hunches over, hands on his knees, coughing and spit-
ting. He uses his index finger to check the corners of his mouth
for cuts. Glaring at me, he grabs his gun off the ground, straight-
ens, and kicks the Glasgow's corpse as he walks away.

Jude can walk away; Micheline almost didn't. My bloody
hesitation's almost killed two of my best mates now.

That night broke me, too, the way it broke Micheline and

her old man. I never guessed my cracks would spread so easy—
if I want to help Micheline, I've got to start by keeping my own
shit together.

Setting my rifle's stock against my shoulder, I follow Jude
to the rendezvous point.

I won't hesitate again.

∽

THAT NIGHT

*"Micheline?" I pointed my gun's muzzle at the floor, surprised by how
hoarse my voice sounded. By the way it echoed, as if I were the last
thing living in the world. "Micheline?" I asked again, louder this time.
She didn't answer.* Dammit, don't die on me, girl, *I thought, sprint-
ing for the panic room.*

*I shut out the gore on the walls and the small, tattered corpses on
the floor. I grabbed Mrs. Helsing by the shoulder and yanked her away,
and damned if the body wasn't still warm. A freshie, even, her mouth
a smear of red and her eyes all fogged up. My .45 caliber bullet smashed
her forehead open. White-blond hair fanned out around her, soaking
up the blood on the floor. Her fingers still twitched.*

*Micheline sobbed and scrambled away from her mum's body, spattered
in blood and bone, bruised, and bleeding from a bite in her trapezius
muscle. She pressed two shaking fingers against the wound, her chin trembling when she pulled her hand back and saw her bloodied fingertips.*

*She lifted her gaze from her fingers to my face. "Ryder . . ." She
hiccuped, her breaths fluttering in and out of her parted lips. "Y-you
shot her."*

Yeah, but not fast enough. *I knelt in front of her to block her
view of the little boys' bodies. Wet warmth seeped into the knee of my
jeans. I holstered my gun and put two fingers on her throat, her skin*

clammy, her pulse weak and rapid. The bloodstain on her T-shirt spread fast.

I'd seen enough shock in the field to recognize it on Micheline: the vacant gaze, the light breathing, and the damp skin. The confusion. No Helsing reaper in her right mind would be surprised to have a necro shot off her; but how could anyone be in her right mind when she watched her mum go all Night of the Living Dead and kill her little brothers?

I rolled my jacket off my shoulders. Micheline and I had given death the finger more times than I could count. I wouldn't let her die from a bite wound I hadn't been fast enough to prevent.

"She's dead," Micheline said. "My mom's dead."

"I know, love. Stay with me, I'm going to fix you right up," I said, using my hunting knife to slice my jacket into strips. If she didn't get the H3 antinecrotics in the next twenty minutes or so, her chances of surviving the infection from the bite dropped to fifty percent. I can fix this, I told myself. I can save her.

Micheline grabbed me by the arm as I laid a strip of canvas on her wound. "The boys first," she said, those blue eyes of hers glittering with dammed-up tears. "Help my brothers first."

I looked away, unable to tell her there wasn't enough of those boys left to help. I could deal with people dying; it was the crying that turned me chicken. 'Specially her. My girl could be stubborn as stone, but she wasn't unbreakable.

"Ryder," Micheline insisted, gripping my wrist tighter.

All I could do was shake my head. She'd know what it meant; she read my wordless gestures better than anyone. Her face crumpled. I wiped some of the gore off her cheek with my thumb, and then laid three more strips of fabric over her wound. I'd save her life first, and fix her heart later.

"Ethan?" Micheline asked in a small voice, calling for her brother. "Fletcher? Guys"—she hiccuped again—"it's not funny, answer me."

I tied two large strips around her chest and one under her arm to create some pressure, then took her left hand and clamped it over the makeshift bandage.

"Ethan?" she cried, louder this time. "Fletch?"

"Hold tight," I said, scooping her off the floor. I edged out of the panic room, shielding her from the horror show. No need to stab a stake into the shreds of her heart.

"Oh God," Micheline said as I carried her down the hall. She tried to look over my shoulder, but winced and gasped. "Oh God, she killed them, it's my fault she killed them, I couldn't stop her . . ."

"Shh, it's not your fault," I said.

"She killed them, she killed them . . ." Micheline repeated the words over and over again, down the stairs and through the foyer, her voice dying to a whisper. I clung to her, the last bit of home I had now. Her family took me in, gave me a place in a world that'd kicked me into the gutter and left me for dead.

Now Mrs. Helsing had a bullet from my gun in her skull. And as for the littlies . . . I'd never forget the sight of them limp and lost to us, not so long as I lived.

I kicked the front door open. Old man Helsing's truck sat in the driveway, doors unlocked. I helped Micheline into the passenger seat. She stared straight ahead as I buckled her in, shaking, eyes unblinking. The sight of her could've broken my heart if I looked too long, so I didn't spare her more than a glance.

I dashed around the truck's hood and jumped in, but the keys weren't in the visor. Or the center console. Or in the glove box, goddammit.

"Micheline, where are the keys?" I asked. If she heard me, she *didn't respond. Cursing, I sprinted back into the house. I searched through the foyer table drawers, knocking family pictures to the floor. The keys weren't in the bloody kitchen, or in old man Helsing's study. I hustled up the stairs double-time, thinking maybe he'd stashed them on his bedside table, and froze.*

A small figure stood in the hall, outlined by the panic room's light. Ethan wavered on unsteady legs, his right ankle bent at an angle. His head lolled on his tattered neck, blood gelling down the front of his shirt. He looked at me with the foggy eyes of the dead. It wasn't right, freshies were supposed to take at least twenty minutes to turn. The kid hadn't been dead more than three minutes, tops.

"Oh shit," I said softly. "No, kiddo, not you, too."

He snarled at me, his voice raspy, the vocal cords shredded. My hand shook as I took aim at his forehead. This trigger would fuck me up for real, fuck me up forever, but there was only one way to fix dead and mobile.

We both crumpled under the pressure of the trigger.

⌘

NOW

Jude and I don't talk for the rest of the hunt, both of us bloody ruthless, both of us angry. My kills cool me off quick, but Jude throttles the steering wheel all the way back to the safe house, popping a couple of stitches in his shooting gloves.

When he finally parks in the drive, all his frustration explodes.

"Where was your head tonight, McCoy?" he snaps. "That necro was inches"—he pinches the air between his thumb and index finger—"away from ripping my face open."

I scrub my face with my palms—I can't do this anymore,

can't bottle it in, can't pretend like I'm stone cold when all I can think about is that kid and his mum. "I know, mate, I'm sorry."

"*'Sorry'*?" Jude asks. "Were you planning on telling me *sorry* while they stitched my face back together? For God's sake, you looked like you were about to piss yourself out there."

I tune out his bellowing, realizing I'd only disarm him with the truth. But it doesn't matter what he thinks of me anymore, because all I want is for him to shut up, pull his head out of his arse, and realize I walked out of the big house alive but not unscathed.

The words slide out of me so easy, they take me by surprise: "I shot Ethan."

Jude stops. Some of the red rage drains out of his face. He blinks. Breathes. "What?" he asks, his eyes narrowing to slits.

"That night . . . the kid turned, and fast," I said, swallowing hard and looking straight ahead, out the window, anything to avoid Jude's gaze. "Micheline, she . . . I'd already taken her outside. When I went back in for the car keys, I found the kid on his feet, his whole bloody throat ripped out and *shit*—" I shove my hands into my hair. I'd loved that kid, taught him to do proper cannonballs into the pool and to trap small game in the woods around the big house. "His head sounded like a melon when it hit the ground—hollow, y'know? *How* can I forget that? How can I *ever* get that out of my head?"

Jude's silent for a long moment. When I look at him, he sniffs hard and swipes his upper lip with the back of his hand. The tendons in his jaw contract, relax, and contract again, as if he's trying to stop himself from saying something thoughtless.

"Goddamn," he finally says. His seat creaks as he leans back, and he presses the heels of his hands into his eyes. "This shit-show gets worse by the minute, doesn't it?"

"Just wait till you see Micheline," I said. "She dyed her hair black the other day."

Jude scrunches his face up. "You didn't tell her about Ethan, did you?"

"Hell no," I say. "Do I look like a dumbarse?"

"I'd say you're a *jackass*, but *dumbass* is an acceptable substitute." He grins when I cuff him on the shoulder. "Get out of here, and tell Micheline I'll see her later today."

"You'd better damn well make good on that promise," I say.

He rolls his eyes. "Get out, McCoy, before I decide to be pissed at you again."

I kick my door open and jump out of the Humvee. Dawn's graying the sky up a bit, and I jounce my shoulders to shake the night off. I feel . . . lighter, but not better. Everyone knows I shot Micheline's mum to save her life; but hardly anyone knows I shot her little brother, too—just the coroners, investigators, old man Helsing, and now Jude. That's it.

I find Micheline sitting on the marble floor in the foyer, resting her head on her knees. When she looks up at me, I do my best to keep my poker face. Dead easy for a reaper, even when her vibrant, peacock-feather blue eyes make me feel like the floor will fall out from under me. I might've saved her that night—the new tat on my arm and the ragged space in my chest's proof enough of it—but how do you save a girl from her heartache?

Micheline pushes off the floor and runs to me, throwing her arms around my waist. She sniffles and shakes, but she's still too proud or too stubborn to cry. This girl's my Micheline and yet she's not; this girl's the one I've grown up with, the one I'd learned to shoot with, the one I'd sworn to protect with my life. She's mine, and yet she isn't; she's alive, and yet something about her died back there with her mother and brothers, some part of her I couldn't save. The thought makes me want to hit something. Hard. I want to make something bleed for it, even if that thing's me.

"What's wrong?" I ask, kicking the door closed behind me.

"Nothing," she whispers. "Everything. Do you know what a fixer is, Ry?"

She's talked a lot of nonsense over the past few days. I let her go, chucking her under the chin so she'll look up at me. "A fixer? What are you talking about?"

"It's the chemical I use to stabilize photographs after I expose them. A fixer removes the silver particles from—" But her eyes well up, and she presses the back of her hand against her mouth and nose, stopping up her tears. "At least I don't look like her anymore. I don't have to look in the mirror and see her dead face staring back at me."

"Aw, Micheline." I put my arms around her again. "Is that why you dyed your hair?"

She nods against my chest. "Does it look awful?"

"No, you've always looked badass in black." I put my chin on the crown of her head, soaking up the fact that she's said more than twenty coherent words in a row. "Everything's a fixer now," she says. "The dye. The black. You."

Fixer.

Fix. Her.

Problem is, I don't think I can. The best I can do is be here for her when she needs me, and hope that, someday, she picks up her exorcism cameras and Colts and rejoins our crew in the field. I have to believe she's not so far gone.

"You stabilize me, Ry," she whispers.

I hold her so tight, I hope I squeeze all her broken pieces back together.

UNSTOLEN

Jessica Brody

BY JESSICA BRODY

52 Reasons to Hate My Father

My Life Undecided

Karma Club

~ *The Unremembered Trilogy* ~

Unremembered

Unforgotten

Unchanged

~ *The Unremembered Novellas* ~

Undiscovered

Unleashed

Meet Jessica Brody

Writers like to say that inspiration is everywhere. You just have to let it hit you over the head like a coconut falling from a tree. I never actually believed this overly whimsical theory of creativity until it happened to me.

It wasn't a literal coconut, but it was close enough.

I got the idea for the Unremembered trilogy while reading a newspaper a few years back. (For you younger readers, in case you don't know, a newspaper is this thing that used to come to your door every morning before the invention of Twitter.) I wasn't looking for a book idea—I wasn't really looking for anything in particular—but a book idea is exactly what I found.

I read a headline that said, TEEN GIRL IS LONE SURVIVOR OF COMMERCIAL AIRLINE CRASH.

And the world stopped.

A teen girl survived a plane crash when no one else did?

How?

I proceeded to read the article, hoping to answer this very question. It provided no explanation beyond the all-encompassing, overly simplified rationale of "miracle."

That wasn't good enough for me.

I started asking myself questions. What-if kinds of questions. And anyone who knows me knows that when I start asking

what-if questions, an outline of a new book idea is soon to follow. "What if she has total amnesia and doesn't remember *anything* before the moment of the crash?" "What if she wasn't on
the passenger manifest?" (This question made me shiver.)
"What if no one shows up to claim her, and her DNA and fingerprints aren't in any databases?"

And then came the question that changed everything.

"What if the real reason she survived the plane crash is . . ."

Well, I can't tell you that because that's the ending of the
first book.

Within thirty minutes of reading this article, I had a rough
outline of an entire trilogy. A trilogy that all begins with a girl
floating in the ocean, surrounded by plane wreckage, who can't
remember a thing.

It's a sci-fi thriller with a little romance, a little mystery, and
a *lot* of twists that I hope you won't see coming.

The Unremembered trilogy (*Unremembered, Unforgotten,* and
Unchanged) was my first foray into the world of science fiction.
As an author of five previous contemporary young adult titles
including *The Karma Club, My Life Undecided,* and *52 Reasons
to Hate My Father,* writing science fiction was a challenge I'd
always wanted to take on. Can I build my own world? Can I
invent my own technology? Can I create an entire story around
a speculative reality that may or may not ever happen?

The books are all written from the main character Seraphina's point of view. I did this on purpose. I wanted you, the
reader, to be just as lost and disoriented as she was. I didn't want
you to have any information that she didn't have. I wanted you
to *discover* her secrets and her past right along with her.

But after writing the first book, I was left with a feeling of longing. I wanted to know what happened when Seraphina wasn't around. I wanted to explore this world without her in it, from someone else's point of view. Someone who, maybe, is a bit more reliable of a narrator.

There's a scene in the first book in which Zen, the mysterious boy who seems to follow Seraphina wherever she goes, shows her a tiny hard drive and explains that *this* is where he's stored some of her lost memories.

"I stole them," he tells her, "from the people who took them from *you*."

Every time I read this scene as I was revising and proofing the book, this one line stood out to me. I pictured an *Alias*-esque spy-thriller-type scene in which Zen has to break into the top-secret research compound where Seraphina used to live and retrieve the stolen treasure, aka her memories.

I desperately wanted to write this scene. And I wanted to write it from Zen's point of view. But what I found, as I dove into it, was that the heart of scene wasn't really a spy thriller. Or some kind of great action-packed heist. It was more of an internal story. A small piece of chilling truth that Zen discovers about Seraphina's past and how that one discovery shapes the rest of their journey together.

I hope you enjoy "Unstolen."

You can read more about me and my books on my Web site, JessicaBrody.com. Or follow me on Twitter (@JessicaBrody), Instagram (@JessicaBrody) or Facebook (@JessicaBrodyFans), where I post an overwhelming amount of pictures of my four children who are very furry and often slobbery. (Spoiler alert: They're actually dogs.)

UNSTOLEN

by Jessica Brody

The files were marked by numbers.

For some reason I felt disappointed by this convention. As though it should have been more ceremonious than that. More elegant. These were pieces of her life. Bytes of her experiences. And they'd been reduced to a sequence of digits.

Then again, I guess I shouldn't be surprised. They'd failed to humanize her in every way possible. Why should cataloging her memories as though they were payment transactions in a register be any different?

I'll never forget the day I found them. Or rather, the day I *saw* them. Finding them is one thing; experiencing them as though I were in her head, as though I were watching it all through her eyes, is something else entirely. Something that stays with you. That mars you.

I knew they had done things to her. Unspeakable things. Before erasing them from her memory. But no knowledge of the horror could prepare me for the horror itself. Of seeing it played back in supreme definition on the Revisualization monitor.

Although I suppose the monitor provides somewhat of a buffer from the experience itself. A playback is still far from the real thing. Still far from what *she* had to go through.

How could they think it wouldn't scar her permanently? How could they think that simply erasing the recollection of the acts themselves would ever erase them from who she is? It's this kind of infuriating arrogance on the part of the scientists here that makes me want to live a life of piety in a Far East temple somewhere. Just to spite them.

I located the first encrypted pod shortly after hacking into the system's mainframe. I knew I would never have time to find all her memories. For one, there was no way they'd be stored in the same pods. Or even in adjacent pods. The monsters who ran this place may have been arrogant, but they weren't stupid. And if there was anything they were especially careful about, it was security.

But hacking had always been my specialty. And having a mother with a high clearance level who was too absorbed in her work to notice that her son had been stealing her fingerprints off coffee mugs and wall panels for years didn't hurt either.

I had to be fast. I had to get out before anyone realized the protocol had been breached. The last thing I needed was for them to wipe *my* memories as well. Then we'd both be lost forever. Apart. And she'd never come to know the truth.

They'd find her where I left her. They'd bring her back here. They'd rewire everything. They'd fix the loopholes they left behind last time. The very loopholes that allowed her to fall in love with me.

And where would I be?

Shipped off to a boarding school in Europe somewhere. Made to study useless things like Latin and physics and quantum theory. Imprisoned by haunting, incomprehensible dreams of a strangely familiar girl with purple eyes. And then maybe one day I would meet someone. I would get married. I would live out my life with a woman I thought I loved. But it would be an empty arrangement. There would always be a chasm I would never be able to fill nor understand.

I knew it was risky to come back here, but it was my only choice. After our meeting at the supermarket, it had become clear that Sera wasn't going to trust me. Not until I could show her proof. And this time, we didn't have the luxury of being able to wait for her to come around. It was only a matter of days, minutes, seconds before they would be able to track her.

I just needed to collect enough memories to convince her.

But I never expected to find what I found.

I never expected to be so permanently changed by something with a name as harmless as #989970.

989970.

Six numbers that will stalk me forever. Like a ghost with rattling chains.

I had been sifting through files for the past thirty minutes, the microspeakers lodged comfortably in my ears, my finger resting on the scrub wheel. I fast-forwarded through hours of countless footage. Tedious memories of meals and pointless conversations and walks down dimly lit restricted hallways that I'd never seen before.

I had already had the good luck of stumbling across several useful files—the last of which was the memory of the day I first met her. I felt considerably fortunate to have found that one. Like a gold nugget magically appearing in a cast-iron pan full of dirty water and dull rocks. Not only was it magnificent to be able to relive that day from her perspective, but it served as an excellent motivator for me to keep searching.

A reminder of everything they stole from her.

A reminder of how many times they tried to erase me.

It fueled my resolve.

With each new valuable memory file that I found, I transferred it to the cube drive and kept going. Kept fast-forwarding through all the forgotten moments of her life.

It was the scream that halted me. That caused my finger to slip from the scrub wheel like tires skidding off a road.

That scream.

Sera's scream.

It shrieked through the microspeakers in my ears, echoing off the chambers of my brain, reverberating against my skull. It sent tiny shivers pulsing through my body. It turned everything cold. Colder. Coldest.

I should have kept going. I should have advanced right through it, on to the next. No good can come from watching the Revisualization of a memory that begins with a scream like that. No good. But the cold had reached my fingers. The frost had congealed everything, including my common sense. My finger hovered above the scrub wheel like a bird afraid to touch down upon volcanic ash.

The scream was still going. It felt unnaturally long. Surely, sooner or later she would run out of breath. But it was as though she'd had an infinite supply. As though the agony bursting from her was fueling the heart-wrenching wail all on its own.

The only consolation was that I couldn't *feel* what she was feeling.

The sound of it was bad enough. The way tears coated her eyes and blurred the interior of the room was sufficient to mutilate my heart.

It was a white, sterile room with no windows. Lots of machines.

Having lived here for so long, I recognized it as *any* room within these walls. After a while, the labs start to blend together. But from the angle of her perspective—ceiling and heat ducts and light fixtures—it was clear she was lying down. Probably on some sort of table or gurney. I couldn't see any of her appendages. Which meant they were probably restrained.

A male voice came from somewhere behind her head. Somewhere unseen.

"Left tibia," it said stiffly. Emotionless.

I felt my toes curl inside my shoes.

A robotic metal arm protruded from the ceiling, flashing in and out of her view as it descended toward the bottom half of her body. The sight of it was followed quickly by a sharp cracking sound. Another scream erupted from her, blasting my eardrums.

Her eyes closed, turning the monitor to black. When they opened again, she had managed to rotate her head slightly to the side, revealing a screen with a live feed from the inside of her body. The atom-sized nanocam maneuvered effortlessly beneath her flesh, traveling to her lower leg. The handiwork of the metal arm was revealed a moment later.

I shuddered as I saw that her long, perfect white tibia bone on the inside of her calf had been snapped in two, causing the muscle and skin to bulge unnaturally around it.

"Fracture complete. Starting clock," another voice said. This one female. Also unseen. They were probably both hiding behind a wall of glass like the cowards they are. While they let their machines do the dirty work.

The screaming had stopped. Replaced by a low whimper. My view was clouded by more tears and excessive blinking, but Sera continued to stare straight at the monitor. At the inner workings of her own anatomy. Almost as though she were just as curious as the spineless scientists hiding behind their wall.

I loved her infinitely more for that.

With mouth open and eyes wide, I watched the two halves of the bone start to progress toward each other. Like a magnet pulling at metal. They interlocked as seamlessly as puzzle pieces sliding into place. And then in complete disbelief, I watched the fissure between them . . . cease to exist.

It was as though someone had recorded a video clip of the fracture and simply played it in reverse. Erasing any evidence of a break. Any evidence of heartless violence.

"Two minutes, fifteen seconds," the female voice reported.

"Impressive," came the response.

Sera turned her head, providing me a view of the ceiling again. I could tell the pain had vanished because she was no longer whimpering and her breathing had evened out.

I leaned over the side of my chair and vomited the contents of my stomach.

I retched and retched until there was nothing left. And then I retched air for good measure. It wasn't the lack of bile that finally stopped my heaving. It was the sound of the man's voice from the memory, yanking me back in.

"Moving on. Right wrist and left ankle simultaneously."

Sera's eyes closed tightly, filling my monitor with swift darkness again. Panicked, I lunged for the controls, slamming my hand down on all of them at once. The Revisualization screeched to a halt just as the tip of her scream penetrated the air.

With numb, fumbling fingers, I logged out of the pod and shut down the system. I grabbed my cube drive and jammed it into my pocket. I couldn't stay there any longer. The files I had found so far would have to do. I couldn't risk accidentally running into anything else like that.

I swore right then that I would never repeat to Seraphina what I had witnessed. I would take it to my grave.

I never thought I could ever be thankful for what they did to her. But removing this moment from her memory, banishing it forever . . . I'm thankful for that.

No one should have to remember #989970.

I often find myself wishing it could be erased from *my* mind, just as it had been erased from hers. But, at the same time, I don't. It's a burden I need to bear.

To this day, I use it as a reminder of why we ran. I call on it for renewed strength when I feel weary or hopeless. I let it keep me from ever giving up. From ever failing to protect her. This will never be her fate again.

With the cube safely in my pocket, I stood up and stepped over the pool of my regurgitated stomach matter. I knew, once the breach was detected, that they would easily match the DNA to me.

Fine, I thought to myself. *Let them work themselves into a frenzy knowing their precious security protocols have been violated. Let them deploy mass numbers of agents to the far corners of the earth. Let them try to find me.*

And let them fail.

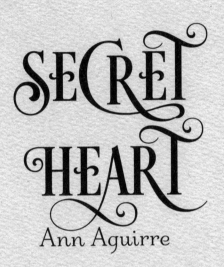

Ann Aguirre

BY ANN AGUIRRE

The Queen of Bright and Shiny Things

~ The Razorland Trilogy ~

Enclave

Outpost

Horde

~ The Immortal Game ~

Mortal Danger

Public Enemies

Meet Ann Aguirre

My road to becoming a published author was long. Ever so long. It started well enough. When I was eight, I wrote a story for a school writing competition called "The Mystery of the Gold Doubloon." This seminal, self-illustrated work was about two best friends who went to Florida on vacation and busted an illegal treasure-hunting ring. I won the contest. I went to the state finals and met Shel Silverstein, who read to a bunch of us from *Where the Sidewalk Ends*. In that moment, sitting on my square of carpet, I thought, *They pay him for his words. This is what I want to do.* Later that same year, my teacher told me writing wasn't a real job and I should pick something else. As it turns out, I am stubborn beyond the point of common sense, as I never did choose another career.

I wrote my first novel at fifteen. I sent it to New York. At sixteen I got my first rejection. This pattern continued at nineteen, and again at twenty-one, although I did interest an agent at that early stage. Unfortunately, the historical romance I had written was too dark for the market, though the editors all agreed I could write and that I had talent. I wrote more. In the meantime, I got married and had some babies. I kept writing. More rejections. I hit my thirties, signed with an agent, and got more rejections. By this point, I had, oh, eight books that had been rejected. In utter despair, I wrote a sci-fi novel. I decided, *You know, if I'm never going to sell, then I am going to write the novel I want to read. I'm going to write for myself, for fun, for pleasure, and without regard for market.* The result was *Grimspace*. Unfortunately, my agent at the time thought it sounded unsellable. I had to choose between my book and my agent. It was a terrible decision, but I believed so strongly in that project that I gave notice. I went back to cold querying. I was thirty-six by this point. An agent pulled me out of the slush pile—and that was the start of a really magical career with my current agent, Laura Bradford.

Laura Bradford is a romance specialist. (I thought I'd written a romance with futuristic elements. Turns out, no.) But she loved *Grimspace* so much, she learned the market, just for me. She said, "I've never sold sci-fi but I want the challenge, so if you're okay with that, I'm offering you representation at this time." I chose passion and enthusiasm over experience. I signed with her on March 31, 2007. We pitched *Grimspace* on April 11, my husband's birthday. Within a couple of weeks, we had a nibble. An editor loved it and was taking it to acquisitions. She updated the rest of the editors, who were then motivated to read faster. Before we heard from the first editor, we had an offer from Anne Sowards. That day, I cried in excitement and disbelief. This sale was over twenty years in the making, closer to thirty if you count the story I wrote when I was eight. We accepted the offer at once, and since then, we've sold thirty-three books together in the last seven years. It's been a long time since I've had a day job, and it's my plan to write for the rest of my life.

So that's my story. I currently live in Mexico with my family, I was raised in the Midwest, and I graduated from Ball State University in the early nineties. I write steampunk fantasy, romantic science fiction, new adult romance, and several genres of YA. As of now, I'm a *New York Times* and *USA Today* best-selling author with books in print in many countries. And I'm so glad to be living my dream.

The short story you are about to read takes place in the world of my YA post-apocalyptic Razorland trilogy (*Enclave*, *Outpost*, and *Horde*). And here is how the trilogy was conceived. First, I was a child in the eighties, when we lived with constant fear from nuclear stockpiling and the Cold War. In grade school, they actually showed us films on what we should do if a bomb dropped. As a result, I've always had some issues from that constant anxiety. When I'm afraid of something, I tend to work it into my books, so it was natural that I would, someday, write about the end of the world as we know it.

Furthermore, I've always been a fan of apocalypse movies. The first one I saw on my own was *Night of the Comet*. (Don't laugh!) As a kid, I was alone at the mall with a friend for the first time, and we decided a zombie movie would rock. The flick was awesome, campy, and it imprinted me for life. Later, I took a film class as part of my English degree, and I wrote a paper analyzing the themes in George Romero's *Night of the Living Dead*.

Since then, I can't get enough of the genre. Most of the apocalypse movies I've loved over the years haven't been as silly as *Night of the Comet*. Some of my favorites include *Terminator* (the future is bleak indeed), any Resident Evil film, *28 Days Later*, *Undead* (a wicked awesome indie Aussie film), *Daybreakers* (by the same directors who did *Undead*), *Zombieland*, *12 Monkeys*, *Children of Men*, *The Road Warrior*, *Shaun of the Dead*, *Logan's Run*, *Blade Runner* (some might argue its inclusion), *Equilibrium*, *Tank Girl*, *The Postman*, *Escape from New York*, *The Blood of Heroes*, *Reign of Fire* . . . hmmm. I should stop now.

The final piece of the puzzle came when I read *The Mole People* by Jennifer Toth about the folks who live in the tunnels below New York. I started to wonder, *What if they were the ones who survived when the worst happens?* Before I wrote the Razorland trilogy, I hadn't read extensively in the genre, mostly because I intended to take a crack at it, so I wanted to be able to say, honestly, that any similarity came from a collective zeitgeist. Before I finished the series, I had only read *A Canticle for Leibowitz*, which is post-apocalyptic but not YA, and *Lord of the Flies*, which is more about the savagery that lurks close to the skin. Since completing the Razorland trilogy, I've discovered a long list of dystopian authors I cheerfully recommend, including but not limited to, Paolo Bacigalupi, Veronica Rossi, Patrick Ness, Courtney Summers, Meg Rosoff, and more.

For me, every book starts in the same place—with the characters. They tell me their names and then I listen as they share their stories. I write them down. So far, it's working really well. "Secret Heart" first came about when I asked readers what they wanted and they said something that would give them a hint about how Fade felt, long before Deuce had any clue what was going on. "Secret Heart" is a scene from *Enclave*, rewritten from Fade's perspective, giving the reader a glimpse into his hidden longings. While readers may suspect that he had feelings for Deuce long before she figured it out, they can't be sure until they see for themselves. And being in the hero's head is pretty delicious. The result is both sweet and tender, romantic and protective. It should make Fade fans swoon. The best thing about him is that while he adores Deuce, he doesn't want to change her. He loves the fact that she's fierce, every bit as much as he fears the possibility of losing her before she realizes how he feels.

SECRET HEART

by Ann Aguirre

You lost her.

I turned slowly, keeping my movements quiet. Calling out would draw the monsters. Yet the tunnel didn't lend a clue to what might've become of Deuce. I froze, listening to distant movements. Once, caution had kept me safe against overwhelming odds. Good ears and quick feet saved me more than once. Maybe I could save her, too. Impossible to think about losing somebody I didn't want to care about; she *shouldn't* matter. I was only biding time here anyway until I was big enough, strong enough, to return to the surface. It had been years, though. No telling how dangerous it was now. Before, the gangs were bad enough, but we hadn't been harassed topside by the Freaks when my dad was alive.

Be brave, Semyon. I heard his voice in the dark, like he was right next to me. People would think I was crazy, if I ever told

them I felt him with me sometimes, usually at the worst moments, like this one, with panic clawing at my neck like bloody
talons.

Sickness rose in my gut, the blade edge of failure. I was a
knife to the elders who ran the enclave, and they wouldn't hesitate to discard me if I failed them . . . but I'd just started to
think maybe I could trust this girl. Like all who had been born
and bred in darkness, she was obstinate and blind, but unlike
most, she seemed willing to learn. She didn't flinch from me
or act like I was a dirty savage.

Before I could decide where to start looking, a faint whisper reached my ears.

"Fade?"

I liked hearing her call for me. *Me.* Though I fought the
reaction, it came anyway, a slow curl of warmth that meant she
hadn't left me when we got separated. *She came back.* Determined now, I moved toward her, using my ears more than my
eyes. She resolved in the darkness into a girl-shape, her eyes
wide, face a pale blur in the dark. But I didn't need to see her
features to remember them.

Sometimes I even saw them when I closed my eyes.

Reaching for her was instinctive, though I wasn't supposed
to touch. Her muscles were smooth and sleek, her skin warm
beneath my palms. "Are you all right? Where were you?"

"Come on. No time to explain."

I followed her; she was quick and graceful. Since before her
naming, I had been watching as she trained, admiring her in-
tensity and dedication. For just as long, I had wondered what
it would be like to have her focus on me. Which was why I'd

asked Silk to partner us. She had been reluctant at first, as Deuce was one of her best, but I convinced her I could be trusted—that I deserved one more chance.

Between the blind brat and the Nassau run, it hadn't worked out all so well for Deuce. But at least I hadn't lost her, as I'd feared. That was something.

This time, I saw the hand come out to grab her. I lunged, but then I noticed she wasn't fighting.

Her other hand came out, tangled with mine, and that distracted me to the point that I didn't fight when she tugged me into a narrow channel between the stones. My shoulders scraped as I slid in behind, unbearably conscious of her fingers on mine. There was a creature in the shaft with us, and it started replacing the rocks to hide evidence of passage.

Soon I smelled the reason why. Freaks weren't far behind. I narrowed my eyes, taking in the odd settlement. "What is this place?"

"Home," one creature said.

They were odd looking, but not dangerous, too small and weak to pose a threat, unless they attacked us in our sleep. Deuce seemed to trust them, and as I respected her judgment, I kept my hands away from my weapons. There were times to fight, but this wasn't one of them. I hardly dared to breathe, actually, because at any moment, she would realize we were still holding hands.

"We need a place to rest before the last leg of our journey. They've volunteered. In return, we'll try to set up some trade." Deuce paused, lowering her voice. "Freaks are following us."

"Instead of attacking, they're looking for the bigger prize." That behavior tracked with what we'd seen on the journey.

Increased intelligence would make life a lot harder down here, not that I intended to stay. But after seeing what it was like to fight beside someone I trusted, I didn't want to go alone.

"They want to see where we live," she guessed.

I nodded. "We have to lose them before heading back to enclave."

"Yeah."

I leaned in to whisper. "You're sure we're safe here?"

Deuce scanned the creatures head to toe and then shrugged. "Relatively. We're bigger and stronger, and I *do* think they want to trade. They wanted me for breeding at first, but I convinced them it wasn't an option."

Though I had no claim on her, I hated the idea of anyone touching her but me. There was no reason to feel that way; she had given no hint she had any softer feelings.

So I covered with a smile. "And no bodies? Impressive."

When Deuce slid to the floor in exhaustion, I sat beside her. She still hadn't noticed we were holding hands, and I didn't intend to change our status. Which meant I had to sit close. Eventually, our rescuers delivered dinner in the form of mushroom porridge. I ate it one-handed, tipping the stuff straight down my gullet. It was disgusting, borderline rancid, but if she could stomach it, I could. After we finished, I entertained myself drawing little lines on her palm, wondering when she would realize this behavior was unbecoming to a Huntress and shove me away.

Before that happened, a short, bug-eyed man bowed before Deuce. "Am Jengu."

"Deuce." She pointed at me and said, "Fade. You want to tell us what you have to trade?"

"Why doan I show you?"

She let go of me in clambering to her feet. I fought the urge to help her, but she wouldn't thank me for it. As with everything, she was fierce in her desire to be self-sufficient. But I did stay close to her; there was no way I was letting her out of my sight again. The tunnel twisted, cut a sharp right, and the air was close, stinking of charred meat and unwashed bodies.

We came to a platform littered with rock. I scanned, determining there was no outlet on the other side. Despite the blockage, there was more light than in the tunnel, better air, too. Deuce wasn't taking in the environment, however; she was staring, wide-eyed, at all the topside junk these odd creatures had collected. I had seen such things repeatedly and used some of them, so they didn't impress me like they did her. She seemed to think this was a vast treasure instead of an unholy junk heap.

"Worth a few fish?" Jengu asked.

"And then some," she answered.

Mostly, I was tired. I wanted to stretch out and get some sleep if we were safe. Failing that, I'd like to hold her hand again. But I didn't ask. It was too hard to put that stuff into words when the person you felt it for had no idea what you were talking about. There were other girls in the enclave, easier girls—and some were willing to sneak kisses in the dark—but I didn't want them. I wanted Deuce, so much it hurt. And I didn't think she'd ever desire anything more than her two blades.

"Do you mind if we sleep here?" I asked. "You can search our bags now to see what we have, and then again before we go. We won't take anything."

"You wan sleep in storage?" Jengu seemed puzzled.

"If you don't mind." Deuce held out her pack so he could riffle through it—and I was gratified that she understood why I'd asked to bunk on the platform. The inner tunnels really did reek.

"Got dis where?" he asked, pulling out one of the slim books.

"On the way back from Nassau. There was a room up some stairs—"

"Ah," he said. "Up near Topside?"

She nodded. "I guess."

"Anything else?"

"Sure," I answered. "We didn't take it all. Couldn't carry it."

Jengu seemed pleased, which I didn't care too much about. Deuce seemed to have some idea about brokering a trade agreement between these creatures and the College enclave, but based on what I'd seen of the elders, I didn't see that ending well. Maybe I just pictured death everywhere because of the way life had gone. It didn't change my secret heart.

Everyone dies. Everybody leaves. Just once, I thought, *I'd like someone to stay. Let it be* this *girl.*

"You're all right?" I asked, once Jengu left. "They didn't hurt you?"

She shook her head. "They're harmless. It would do the enclave good to make friends of them, I think. Look at this place."

"It's amazing," I answered, mostly because she wanted me to be impressed. "They must've been scrounging for generations."

Her eyes went serious, lashes spiky and dark against her pale skin. I could stare at her all day; her eyes were like the sky before a heavy rain—stormy but so worth the wreckage. Looking at Deuce made me feel like I was about to be knocked off my feet.

"Thanks for waiting for me. But it was a big risk. Anything could've happened to you."

I touched her cheek tenderly, hardly daring to believe she'd let me. The words I could muster weren't the ones I wanted, but they had to do. "I have your back. I didn't mean only when it's easy. *All* the time."

Her face softened. In any other girl, I would take those parted lips as an invitation to a kiss. Certainly I'd gotten such subtle signs before, but I didn't think she knew enough to offer them. I imagined how her mouth would taste, the soft slide of her hair through my fingers, but I didn't bend down. Not then. *Someday,* I promised myself. *Soon.* The ache curled through me, sharp and sweet, fierce as hunger, but not as easily quelled.

"This should be our last stop. Tomorrow, we make it home." She got out her blanket and wrapped up in it.

We will, I vowed silently. *I'll never let you down. And I'll always be there for you. Always.*

I fell asleep listening to her breathe.

DEATH & WAFFLES

Lish McBride

BY LISH MCBRIDE

~ The Necromancer Series ~

Hold Me Closer, Necromancer

Necromancing the Stone

~ The Firebug Series ~

Firebug

Pyromantic

Meet Lish McBride

"Death & Waffles" started out like a lot of my writing does, with a sudden image. This one was of a girl in a Catholic school uniform and saddle shoes walking into a diner. Along with the image came a line about her being Death in saddle shoes. I thought the image was funny. At the time I was in graduate school in New Orleans. I was in my last bit of school and working on my thesis novel to graduate. (That thesis would later become my first book *Hold Me Closer, Necromancer*.) While working on my novel, though, I was still taking classes, which meant I had to produce a few short stories and a screenplay at the same time. As I wrote about Ashley, I liked her so much that she made her way from the short story and into the novel. She continues to be one of my favorite characters. There's just something about her—snarky, dry humor in a tiny package, and yet for all her tough talk, there's a core of loyalty and kindness in Ashley. I suspect that's what makes her so good at what is a very tough job.

Ashley has made it into three novels now—*Hold Me Closer, Necromancer*, *Necromancing the Stone*, and (hopefully) my third book, *Firebug*. Though "Death & Waffles" doesn't connect to *Firebug* per se, it's all one big world just waiting to collide.

I've always wanted to be a writer, but it's one of those jobs no one thinks you'll actually get. Even now when I tell people what I do they're surprised when I tell them I'm published and that you can buy my books almost anywhere. It just seems like such a long shot to many people, and it is. Which makes me feel so grateful that I get to do what I do. I get to be silly for a living.

I got my BA degree in writing at Seattle University and my MFA from the University of New Orleans. That's not a sure-fire degree. I went in knowing that the probability of me getting a job in my field was low, and to be honest, sometimes that would make me panic. Then my mom would call and talk me down and tell me that "no, I shouldn't become a plumber and that everything would be okay." That "no education is ever a waste, no matter what comes of it." Ultimately, I went not because of job security or anything like that, but because I wanted to be a better writer. I wanted to tell stories more than anything. I needed to try at my dream because the fear of not getting it wasn't nearly as powerful as the fear of not trying.

So I went to school and survived Hurricane Katrina and then moved back to Seattle where the weather is a little less deadly. I sold my first two books right after graduating from my MFA program and now I work at a local indie bookshop as well—and it's great. My entire life revolves around books. It's a lot to juggle, but at least I love it. The only downside is it takes me a little longer to tell my stories than I'd like. I've had Ava, the character from *Firebug*, in my head even before I began telling Sam's story (from *Hold Me Closer, Necromancer*). Sam started as a combo of concepts, the biggest of them being what would someone like Sam (vegetarian and all-around nice guy) do if he found out he had a power that forced him to hurt others or kill things . . . and what if not using that power wasn't an option? What would that situation do to someone like that? Ava was a similar idea—what would happen to someone who could start fires with their mind . . . especially if they had to exist in a world with powerful vampires? (In most mythologies, vampires don't do well with fire and in fact tend to be quite flammable.) Ruthless people in power often stay in power by removing anything that might be a threat to them. Ava, as a firebug, is a huge threat, and because of that she's been hunted her whole life. She has lost everything, and now that she's rebuilt her life, what if that were threatened? That's how a lot of my books start—with a character and a what-if scenario.

Once I have that base, I get to have fun. I add in biker were-hares, pygmy chupacabras, and zombie pandas. I get to be scary and silly and let me tell you, it's a blast. I can only hope that people enjoy reading the books as much as I enjoy making them up.

DEATH & WAFFLES

by Lish McBride

The sharp rapping of knuckles on my windowpane woke me up. I'd like to say the noise surprised me, but Ashley had been showing up a lot lately. I rolled out of bed and walked over to the window.

"Matt," she hissed, teeth flashing in a fierce and happy way, "open up."

I stopped in front of the window, arms crossed. "Does it matter if I do?"

"It shows you've got some manners, jerk-wad."

I sighed and flipped the latch so she could open the window and crawl in. She seized me in a hug the instant her feet hit my floor. Ash had always been affectionate to the point of exuberance. At least, she'd always been that way toward me. She said my family didn't hug enough.

"C'mon, get your coat on," she said after she'd let go of me and collapsed onto my bed. "And ditch the pj's."

I pulled some jeans on over my boxers and searched around in my drawer for a clean sweatshirt. The weather hadn't turned to snow this week, but that didn't keep the cold from hanging around. I finally grabbed my gray sweatshirt off the floor, deciding it was more clean than filthy.

"Hurry up, blondie," she said. Ash swung her feet back and forth, saddle shoes flashing as they caught the moonlight.

"Do I even want to know where we're going?"

"Probably not. But I want waffles and fries, and you're my ticket to a night free of harassment. For some reason, a little girl alone in a diner at night is questioned."

"Good to know I'm useful."

Ash shrugged, an easy roll of shoulders. Her shrugs had always been graceful. Mine looked more like shoulder spasms.

I pulled on my hiking boots and grabbed my keys off my nightstand.

"Finally," she said.

"Aren't you forgetting something?" I jerked my chin toward her getup. Tonight, Ashley wore the tartan skirt, white button-up, and sweater of some Catholic school. I knew for a fact that she'd never once set foot in any private school, Catholic or otherwise.

She cocked her head to the side and raised one sable brow. "Like what?"

"Jacket," I said.

"Oh, come on, Matt. It's not like I get cold."

"You wanna blend, right?"

She huffed out a dramatic sigh and snapped her fingers. Ash became instantly wrapped in a large parka. She was nothing if not practical.

I looked at her dark pigtails, each one tied with shiny red ribbon. "What, no hat?"

"Don't push it."

"Fine," I said, walking softly through the hallway even though I knew my parents wouldn't wake up. They'd have to be home for that. Ash didn't bother trying to be quiet. In fact, she skipped down the hall.

"Mom at a conference?"

"Yeah," I said, "New York, I think. I forget exactly."

"Where's Daddy Dearest?"

"Your guess is as good as mine."

My dad had stopped taking interest in me as soon as he figured out I wouldn't be following in his footsteps in pretty much any way. Not in his love for baseball, not in his vocation as an architect, and certainly not in his frequent skirt-chasing. I guess my ability to see women as people and not disposable objects sort of killed any last chance we had. Pity.

By the time he realized my savings fund was for a new camera and not a sweet-sixteen hot rod of some sort, I knew we'd never really understand each other. I cared more about taking pictures than cruising. To me, cars were a method to get from point A to point B, period. Dad just shook his head and muttered, a little disgusted. Mom bought me the Toyota so I could get to school when she was away and ignored the rest.

I unlocked the front door and waved Ash through. "And what's with the snapping thing? Don't you think that's just a little cheesy in a sort of *I Dream of Jeannie* way?"

"She nodded her head."

"Fine, *Bewitched* then."

"She twitched her nose. Besides, I'm not a witch."

"I know," I said, "but don't you sometimes wish you were?"

Ash laughed but didn't answer.

I'd always been able to make Ash laugh. That seems like a simple thing to take joy from, but for me it was rare. Other kids made it look so easy. Not just laughing, but talking, playing, hanging out. I wasn't good at it when I was five, and I'm even worse at it now at seventeen. The only time I ever got it right was with Ash. For some reason, she didn't make me anxious. Didn't make me feel like any second I was going to trip over my own shoe and embarrass myself forever. Maybe it was because, even then, she had the uncanny ability to not just accept, but glory in her own shortcomings.

When I first met Ash she'd moved into a place a few houses down, and even though she'd only been there two weeks, she always had someone to play with. I'd lived in that neighborhood for most my life, yet I usually had to be both Batman and the Joker. There never seemed to be anyone around to fill the other parts. I didn't mind—I was used to it, really—but it was always kind of hard to capture myself and beat myself up all while I was doing the Joker's evil monologues.

One day I looked up from my new Batmobile toy, and there she was. The sun was behind her, so all I could see were inky pigtails and freckles.

"What do you got?" she asked.

"Batmobile," I said.

"Well, duh. I meant what one? That one looks different from mine."

"Oh." Even at six I was old enough to know that "different" was bad. "I don't know," I said. "One of the old ones, I guess. My mom found it at a yard sale."

"Cool," she said. "We should build a Batcave."

After that, I always had someone to play the Joker. At least, until she died from cancer four years later. I put all my Batman toys in a box after that and shoved the box under my bed, and that's where they stayed until she started showing up again a few years ago. Then I began to find Batman under my pillow, Batman in my underwear drawer, and—my own personal favorite—Batman and Joker in compromising positions in the Batmobile. I found that one a little disturbing. Mostly because the last time I'd seen my Batmobile it had been in Ash's coffin.

I let my car warm up for a few minutes. I sat huddled in my sweatshirt, hunched over the steering wheel, doing my best to collapse in on myself for warmth. Ash breathed on the windows and drew little stars in the fog. I wished I could ignore the elements like she could, but then I suppose she'd paid the price for her little benefits.

"Can we go now?" she asked.

"You're not working tonight, are you?"

She raised an eyebrow. "Would it matter if I was?"

I released the brake and backed out of the driveway.

Ash, or Death as some probably called her, pushed open the door to the diner, her saddle shoes making clacking noises on the floor, her pigtails bobbing with her excited movements. Okay, Ash wasn't Death-death, but she was as close to it as I had come. Still, I've always wondered whether people are surprised when they see her instead of the traditional Death with the scythe. Are they disappointed? Relieved? I looked around at the people in the diner: some travelers, a random trucker, a couple groups of kids in all black, a rowdy group who'd obviously come from a bar, and a handful of couples out for a late meal. Did they know, on some level, that my Catholic-schoolgirl-looking companion was a harbinger of death? Nobody screamed and pointed, so I guess not.

We pressed ourselves into a booth, the vinyl making a slick sliding noise as we moved to the end. I wasn't that hungry, so I just got coffee and a piece of lemon meringue pie, even though I felt that, given the circumstances, a meringue was just too cheery. There is something almost optimistic about a slice of lemon meringue pie. I'm not sure why. Is it the bright yellow or the fluffy white topping? But I didn't trust the cherry pie, and bread pudding just freaks me out because I can't imagine bread as a part of a dessert, so I had to go with the lemon. Ash ordered waffles with whipped cream and strawberries, with a side of chili cheese fries. I'd blame the odd mix on her being dead, but she'd eaten like this when she was alive.

"Hey, Ash?"

"Yes?" She didn't look up from the creamers she was building into a pyramid.

"I know you can't really tell me, you know, about your job, but are people ever let down by you? I mean, because they don't get actual Death killing them?"

Ash looked up from her creamer stack. "I don't kill anyone, Matt. Heart attacks, old age, an unchewed hot dog—those things kill people. I'm just their guide."

"Sorry."

"Sometimes. I mean, most people are relieved to see me. Death is scary, and I'm not very intimidating. On the other hand, sometimes it takes people longer to believe that they're dead because of it. Some people don't care. Others have such a fixed idea—they expect the bright light and the tunnel, or pearly gates and a cloud, and I don't look like either of those things."

The waitress dropped off my coffee, and I stole the top of Ash's pyramid for my cup. I stirred slowly, watching the white of the creamer take the edge off the darkness.

"So, no pearly gates, huh?"

She smiled and put her chin in her hands. "I didn't say that. I just said they weren't expecting to see me first."

"You don't find it depressing? Being Death?"

"I already told you, I'm not Death."

"Fine, a psychopomp then."

"Actually, we're generally called Harbingers now. Most people don't even know what a psychopomp is, so management called a meeting and changed our titles."

"Wow, even when you're dead they have boring meetings. Good to know."

The waitress brought out our orders, but they were out of the strawberries so Ash had to eat her waffle plain. The frazzled-looking waitress seemed apologetic, so Ash accepted her food with a "that's all right" and a "thanks."

We talked for a few minutes about nothing really: movies, books, whatever. It didn't matter what we chatted about, it felt good to have someone to talk to. Ash had only gotten about a fourth of the way through her fries and one bite of her waffle when she jumped a little in her seat. I hadn't even started my pie. I'd been too busy talking. Chances for me to have conversations were rare.

Ash pulled out a BlackBerry and started typing away on it. She sighed.

"You have to go, don't you?"

"I'm sorry, Matt." She looked down regretfully at her food. "She's early." She gave another heavy sigh. "I didn't even get to finish my waffles."

"Where do you have to go?" I asked.

She didn't look up.

"It's here?" Leave it to Ash to be pragmatic, even in choosing her waffle joints.

She nodded. "I'm sorry. I really didn't think—"

"Can I come with you?"

She blinked at me, surprised, I think.

I knew, theoretically, what she did, but I had never seen it. I wasn't sure I was allowed, and I'd never had interest in accompanying her before. In fact, I'd always been slightly repulsed by the idea. No, not repulsed, scared. I'd like to say I was trying to face my fear, but in reality I think I just wanted to stay with her a little longer. Or maybe I couldn't handle that Ash had a separate life I'd never seen. I felt a little guilty when I realized that, if our places had been switched, she would have asked much sooner than I had.

"Yes," she answered slowly. "You can come." She rubbed her mouth and chin with her hand, an adult gesture that sat weird on her. "For the collection anyway. I can't take you where I'm going."

"Okay."

We both slid out of the booth. I waited for a second while Ash finished typing something on her BlackBerry. Then she flipped it shut and I followed her back to the bathroom. She walked right into the ladies' room, the yellow door swinging behind her. I paused for a second, a built-in hesitation about entering the girls' bathroom. Then I went in.

The room continued the overly cheery yellow of the door. The walls were yellow, the counters were made of a yellow tile, and the stalls were yellow. Only the sinks, floor, and ceiling were white. I once heard that yellow was a color of aggression and that restaurants only used it so that people wouldn't linger. I guess the diner didn't want people to hang out in their bathroom.

Ash was at the back by the third stall, waiting for me. Once I caught up, she knocked on the door.

"Marjorie?" she asked.

"Yes?" came a muffled reply.

"Marjorie Anne Clausen, wife of Harold, mother of Todd and Judy?"

"Yes, but how did you know that?"

Ash didn't answer but continued. "Marjorie Clausen of Thirteen Forty-Two West Highland?"

"Why, yes. Do I know you?"

"No, ma'am," Ash said, "you don't."

She gently pushed the door open and revealed Marjorie sitting on the floor. It was the same frazzled waitress who'd served us a few minutes ago. She had slouched to the floor but looked exactly the same as earlier except for a few smudges and wrinkles on her uniform. She brightened when she saw Ash.

"Oh, it's you, dear. The waffles." She smiled, revealing a few off-white teeth.

Ash nodded. "It's time to go, Marjorie."

"Call me Marge, please. And go where? I'm right in the middle of a double shift."

"Not anymore you're not," Ash said. She pinched the bridge of her nose. "I hate it when they don't know." She squatted down so she could look into Marge's eyes. "You know that heart arrhythmia the doctor told you not to worry about?"

Marge nodded, a confused look on her face.

"Well, you should have worried."

"But he said it was just stress," she said.

Ash shrugged. "Not to be insensitive, Marge, but you should have gotten a second opinion." She held out her hand. "You need to come with me."

Marge squinted at her hand but didn't take it. "I don't think I like you. I've changed my mind; you don't get to call me Marge."

Ash didn't answer. She just continued to hold out her hand, like a mother waiting patiently for a child to stop throwing a tantrum. Which seemed weird, since Ash looked like she was ten and Marjorie had to be in her upper forties.

Marjorie still wasn't taking her hand. "You're too rude to be an angel." She folded her arms and looked away. "I'm not dead. I feel fine, great even. This is just a stupid prank." She looked back at Ash suspiciously. "Did the cook put you up to this?"

Ash took back her hand and stood up. "I'm not an angel, Mrs. Clausen, nor am I a devil. I'm just a Harbinger. I simply take your soul on to the next step. That's all. And of course you feel fine. You don't carry aching joints and sore muscles into the afterlife."

"That's what a devil would say to trick me."

I had been feeling bad for Marjorie, but I didn't like anyone giving Ash a hard time. I started to get ticked off.

Ash put her hands on her hips. Through gritted teeth she said, "I'm just one of Death's assistants. I promise you that I'm a neutral party, Mrs. Clausen."

"Death. Right." Mrs. Clausen looked over at me. "And who's he, the Muffin Man? Santa?"

I cleared my throat. "I'm Batman."

Ash threw me a dirty look, and I just shrugged at her. It was all I could think of.

"He's an intern," Ash said.

That seemed like a much better answer. Book smart I'd always been, but Ash was quicker on her feet.

"I refuse to go with an intern," Marjorie said with a sniff. "I've been a good Christian woman my whole life. I want an angel, or I'm not going."

"Fine," Ash said, "kicking and screaming it is, then."

I edged along the wall to the left. I'd heard Ash's angry tone before, and that was it. I didn't know what was going to happen, but I knew that a small buffer zone would be a good idea.

Darkness swirled around them, blocking out most of the cheery yellow of the bathroom. A vortex opened in the ceiling and a flock of swallows flew out. They perched on the stall doors and looked down on Marjorie Clausen.

Marjorie slapped the stall with the flat of her hand. "Shoo!" she said. She glared at Ash. "That's a health code violation, missy."

Ash stamped her foot and another portal opened, this time behind Mrs. Clausen where the back of the stall had been. Out of the darkness, a few shapes materialized. Three cats came out of the shadows: a Siamese, a white Persian, and a fat orange tabby. The Persian circled around and pounced on Mrs. Clausen, knocking her back so she lay half in and half out of the portal. The orange tabby sauntered forward and sat on Mrs. Clausen's chest.

"Oh. Hi, kitty," she said, scratching the orange tabby tentatively behind the ears. The other two leaned down and grabbed Mrs. Clausen's uniform at each shoulder with their teeth and began to slowly drag her away. Or part of her anyway. Marjorie's body stayed put on the floor while the cats pulled her soul into the portal. I think it was her soul. I'd have to ask Ash if management had another term for it. Mrs. Clausen looked back at both of the cats, startled. She began to yell. The cats, being cats, ignored her in that complete way only cats seem to be able to manage, and continued to drag her soul into the darkness. After Mrs. Clausen's ghostly white shoes vanished, the portal shut.

Ash's tense stance relaxed. "I hate it when they do that." She turned to me. "I have to go after her. See you later?"

I looked at the birds. The swallows returned a glassy black stare. I hate birds. "You're going to take them with you, right?"

For some reason Ash threw herself at me and grabbed me in a big hug. I slipped my arms out of her grasp, since it was awkward being pinned by a little girl, and wrapped them around her shoulders. She went up on her tiptoes and kissed me on the cheek.

"What was that for?"

Ash leaned out of the hug and smiled at me, even though her eyes looked like she was about to cry.

"For never making me feel like a freak," she said. She turned and held out her arms. The swallows flew down, grabbed bits of her clothing in their beaks, and pulled her off the ground. The birds flapped madly one second and then an instant later, they were gone, taking Ash with them.

I was left alone in the suddenly empty girls' bathroom. A girl entered, one of the goth kids I'd seen earlier. All the black eyeliner she used didn't darken her bright blond looks.

"Sorry," she said, and she looked back at the door. She frowned at the woman symbol.

"Me too," I said, and I walked past her.

I slid back into our booth. My pie was still there. For some reason, it seemed like that shouldn't be. Hadn't I been gone a long time? I felt like a death should resonate, like the whole diner should have felt it. The pie should have crumbled into dust by now. People should be somber. But the goth kids still laughed over their coffee, the drunks were still drunk, and my pie refused to mourn.

The goth girl came out of the bathroom a few minutes later. She looked the same, so I assumed she hadn't looked in the last stall. If she had, she was handling it very well.

I grabbed my fork and slowly finished my pie. I don't like to waste things, and it seemed to make just as much sense to sit there and eat in silence as it did to go home and sit in silence. If you're going to think and be depressed, you might as well do it with pie, right?

I paid at the register, leaving a tip on the table. Would it end up with Marjorie's family, or would the staff split it, deciding they'd earned it in her stead? On my way out I overheard one of the other servers asking where Marjorie had gotten off to. I quickened my step, hoping to get to my car before they started looking.

∽

The next day I drove my battered Toyota to Highland and stopped in front of a white house with blue trim and a hand-painted sign that read THE CLAUSEN FAMILY next to the mailbox. I parked across the street and watched for a while. I'm not sure why.

A green SUV pulled into the Clausens' driveway. A young woman, tall and slender, got out carrying a foil-covered dish. Her brown hair was loose and a little messy from the drive, but she didn't bother to straighten it. Instead she knocked immediately on the Clausens' door. If a knock could sound worried and heartfelt, then that's what the woman's knock would have been. I wished briefly for someone to arrive on my doorstep that way, but felt instantly guilty for it. I wasn't the one on the block with the fresh hurt. Mr. Clausen deserved this visitor, not me.

A man answered. I assumed the man was Harold Clausen. He hugged the woman and took the dish. Harold was balding and fat but in a robust way. The hug looked stiff, like he wasn't used to public displays of affection, but he did it anyway. They went inside.

Through the window I could see Harold sitting at a table and talking to the young woman. A china hutch stood behind them, covered in floral arrangements and framed photographs. An altar to the Clausen family.

Two kids came out of one of the doorways. The girl looked

like she might be at the age where My Little Pony toys were still cool, but the boy looked preteen, spiky haired and a little angst ridden, but still shiny under the bitter layer. He wasn't old enough yet to have lost the hope and innocence of youth. Since they both looked like Harold and Marjorie squashed together, I guessed these were Todd and Judy. They seemed sad, their faces pinched and drawn, but they mustered up a hug and smile for the young lady. Even their mother's death couldn't dampen their obvious joy in seeing her.

Harold got them all sodas and a plate of cookies that were probably brought over by another visitor. They sat and talked, the lady smiling and touching cheeks, shoulders, hands, like she was trying to let her joy rub off on them. Judy even laughed a few times.

Todd never got further than a smile, but it appeared less forced after a while. When Harold started to cry, the kids and the woman immediately closed in around him, making a tight knot of affection. I felt more instant guilt when I realized I was jealous of a widower and his family.

I started my car and drove back to my house. There was nothing for me to see there. I'd seen the process before, anyway. So I drove home and wondered why people always bring food to mourners. When Ash died, the last thing I wanted was a chicken casserole.

Ashley didn't die fast like Mrs. Clausen, but she didn't take months either. She got sick and withered away. You could measure the time from the first symptom to the grave in weeks. At the time, it felt like forever to me, and also too fast. I sat by her bedside whenever they let me. My mom wasn't the type to worry about me catching things, and lymphoma isn't contagious anyway.

Sometimes we talked, if she felt up to it. Sometimes we watched movies. Sometimes I sat in the chair by her bedside and watched her sleep, glad that she was still with me, even if she was only sleeping.

Her funeral was open casket. Most of the other kids wouldn't go up to her, but I don't remember being afraid. Death hadn't turned my friend into a bogeyman. I still couldn't catch what she had by being near her. I remember thinking that, even though she looked the same, she wasn't Ash anymore. Something had fundamentally changed. That a vital part of her was gone and wouldn't be stuck in the ground to rot. That made me feel better, but only a little. I put my Batmobile in beside her, tucking it down by her hand, touched her cheek, and went home. I didn't need to stay to hear more words from people who didn't really know her. Not like I did.

∞

This time, when Ash rapped on my window, I wasn't asleep. I wasn't even in my pajamas, but sprawled out on my bed in my jeans and a Pac-Man T-shirt. My feet made soft sounds on the carpet as I walked over to let her in. Then I sat down on the edge of the bed.

"Thanks," she said. She crawled in and closed the window behind her. She sat next to me.

"You just do that to make me feel better, don't you? The knocking, I mean. You could just pop into my room anytime you felt like it, right?"

Ash nodded. "I suppose, but it's rude. I have to force people to do what I want all the time. It's nice to give someone a choice."

"And this"—I waved my hand at her image, this time in jeans and a KISS T-shirt—"is this also for my benefit? I mean, if you can wear whatever you want, can't you also look like whatever you want?"

"I guess," she said, "but this is how I'm most comfortable, and, again, it helps people not be afraid of me. I died at ten. I'm content with ten. I could look twenty-five, change my hair, whatever. Some of the other Harbingers do but most of us stay the same." She shrugged. "I guess it's one of the few things we have left of our earthly selves."

"Do you visit anyone else?" I asked.

She shook her head. "No. I check in on my parents, but I can't talk to them. Generally, it's frowned upon. Most people don't see me unless they're dead, anyway." She picked at a loose piece of thread on my comforter. "Except you."

"Why me?"

She shrugged. "Some people are just more sensitive to other things." She kicked my foot lightly. "And maybe it's because you're not really alive."

I blinked at her. "What does that mean? I'm not dead."

"No, but you're not really living, either. You aren't connected to anyone. You go to school, come home, and go to your room. You're like a phantom."

"It's not that easy. People aren't that easy."

Ash shook her head. "What's hard? You walk up, you shake hands, and you talk. Easy."

"It doesn't seem that simple," I said. "Not for me."

"I know, but you can't expect other people to do all the work for you all the time. If I hadn't approached you, would we have been friends?"

I looked down. "I'd like to think so. That us being friends was inevitable."

Ash leaned into my shoulder.

"Can I come with you?"

"No," she said.

"Why not? You said it yourself, I'm not really living."

"But you're not dead, either."

I opened my mouth but she cut me off. "Don't go getting any ideas in your head about killing yourself, either. Not a good idea, Matt."

My mouth snapped shut. I hadn't actually been considering it. Not really.

"You shouldn't be in such a hurry to come over."

"I know," I said. I didn't want to die; I just didn't want to lose her again. It seemed a cheesy thing to say, though, so I kept my mouth shut. Ash guessed my thoughts.

"Matt, you ever wonder why I took this job?"

I shook my head. "I just assumed you were assigned it, or it was a punishment or a reward or something." I'd never been able to figure out whether Ash's job was a good or a bad one. Some days it looked good, some days I wasn't sure.

"No, I chose it." She went back to picking at the thread on my bedspread. "This way, I could wait for you." She smiled at me wanly. "I guess you're not the only one having trouble moving on."

"Great," I said, "Death is waiting for me."

She pinched me. "Harbinger," she said.

We sat in silence for a minute. I was always happy to be around Ash. I felt half empty whenever she was gone. And as weird as it was, it felt good to know that she'd been hanging around for me. That I could move on with my life without leaving her behind.

"Grab your parka," I said. "I owe you some waffles." I hesitated as I reached for my keys. "Let's go to a different diner, okay?"

She grinned and, just for me I think, did the *Bewitched* nose wiggle to get her parka.

I thrust my keys into my pocket and slipped my sweatshirt over my head. "And, Ash?"

"What?"

"Thanks for never making me feel like a freak, either."

"You're welcome, freak," she said. "Meet you in the car." She winked at me and was gone. I heard my Toyota shudder to life outside. I guess now that I'd seen her work, the magical gloves were off.

I went out to join her, gently closing my bedroom door, safe in the knowledge that Death's Harbinger would wait for me no matter what. As long as I could bribe her with waffles, anyway. It's amazing what makes some people happy.

KRISIS

Lindsay Smith

BY LINDSAY SMITH

Dreamstrider

~ The Sekret Series ~

Sekret

Skandal

Meet Lindsay Smith

Hi, Fierce Readers! I'm Lindsay Smith, author of the paranormal Cold War thrillers *Sekret* and *Skandal*. My books follow the struggles of a Russian teenager in 1963 named Yulia who's learned to read thoughts and memories by touching people and objects. She's captured by the KGB, the premier spy agency and secret police in the Soviet Union, and is forced to join a team of psychic teens who use their powers to hunt traitors and spies. "Krisis" takes place about a year before *Sekret*, during the Cuban Missile Crisis, when the United States and Soviet Russia came incredibly close to launching a nuclear war with each other. The main character in "Krisis," Larissa, has been with the KGB for a while, and she's gotten accustomed to her ability of foresight being exploited by the KGB, but when she meets a new teammate, she finds herself wanting to enjoy the present as well as the future.

I studied Russian language and history in school, and I've always wanted to write a story set in the Soviet Union—I think it's a woefully underexplored time period, but also an important one. The idea for the Sekret universe came to me when I was contemplating daily life in Soviet Russia and the intense amount of scrutiny people felt as they tried to go about their business. They couldn't trust their friends and neighbors with their most private thoughts—the only safe space for dissent was inside their own head. So I thought, what if I took even that away from them? That's how the "psychic spies" twist came to me, and the book really just wrote itself after that!

Sekret is my first published novel, though it's not the first book I wrote. I'm a firm believer in National Novel Writing Month, or NaNoWriMo (nanowrimo.org), which taught me the value of perseverance and finishing the writing projects I'd begun, no matter how awful I felt they were by the time I got deep into the middle of them. Every book is its own learning process, but I think there's great value to be gleaned from getting a feel for the rhythm of working on something as massive as a novel, and it makes the next one just a little bit easier to write.

The Fierce Reads program is so fantastic—I've gotten to meet some incredible authors, as well as wonderful readers, whose enthusiasm for books and reading are truly an inspiration! I have a few more books on the way from Macmillan as well, and I can't wait to share them with you. The next one, *Dreamstrider*, is a young-adult high-fantasy novel about a girl whose ability to manipulate people through their dreams causes problems when nightmares start to escape into the waking world.

 KRISIS

by Lindsay Smith

MOSCOW. OCTOBER, 1962.

Sometimes I pretend that, instead of being lost in these visions, I'm drifting underwater. That the scenarios I see, the strange what-ifs and could-bes, are just vague shapes darting through the depths, content to leave me be if I'll give them the same courtesy. That down here, where it's cool and dark, I'm a world away from whatever's playing out above me, and all I need is to surface for a quick inhale of breath and then I can plunge back down, away, into the echoing silence and solitude.

But sometimes my masters hold me under.

"Boats or planes?" The KGB officer's voice rumbles through the darkness. "Which will they use?"

Boats or planes, bombs or blockades, the visions spark and sputter into existence, then extinguish just as quickly, before I can examine them. My gift to see the future has its limits, and

I'm slamming up against those walls. The officer's questions help me focus on the future, spreading the options before me like the pages of tomorrow's news. But I can only foresee like-lies and possibilities and maybes, and the KGB demands certainty from me.

I can see the American president, so young, so lost, as he hunches over the photographs. His brother's finger traces the strange objects in the jungles of Cuba, slender as pencils, but far more deadly. Missiles—our missiles—each one with a tip that can turn a city into a smudge. Two plans spread out before them. Boats to block our ships as they carry in more missiles, or planes to obliterate the ones already in place?

"Which is it, girl? Can you answer or not?"

As if they're giving me a choice. The voice plows through my concentration with the force of an icebreaker ship. I know all about choices that dangle from a single branch like ripe fruit. Which one looks the freshest? Which one looks most likely? I pluck the brightest possibility and offer it up for inspection: This, here, is the future that you seek.

"Boats." Snarling, now. "Or planes."

Each option is a blur, equally likely and unlikely; until the scale starts to tip, they will remain ghosts, and only certainty can give them flesh. "I can't see it clearly yet."

This is not an answer they care to hear.

I try to explain. "There are too many possible futures, none looking more likely than the rest—even the Americans can't decide."

But still the men hover over me. I can't breathe. This room, the chair I'm sitting in, I can see only in flashes. I lurch forward, light and noise and pale pink walls swimming around me. "I need air—"

A hand shoves me back down into the chair. "Answer us! We must know now!"

"Comrade Rostov." Another voice wafts through the murk, though this voice, too, wields an edge. "If the future hasn't yet been determined, then she cannot help us. Perhaps we should take a break."

The hand on my shoulder digs harder, nails piercing the thin fibers of my sweater, then slowly relents. "One hour, Larissa. Then report back to me."

I don't need foresight to know I won't enjoy it.

⸎

Winter has settled into the ramshackle mansion where the KGB keeps all the psychic children like me—every surface bites with chill, every chair promises numbness. At dinner, I stir the sour cream into my soup, watching the drops of oil spin and separate, though my teammates' eyes are all on me like winter-starved wolves. They want answers—same as the KGB does—they want to know if we are moments from a blinding flash and then nothingness. If we are leaning into the wind at the edge of the cliff.

No one has slept much since we learned the Americans found our missiles in their backyard. But I have nothing to offer them. I am elsewhere, walking a thousand paths, bracing for blows yet to come.

"Such a pity," Masha says, looking right at me, "that we have to be burdened by dead weight who can't even use their gifts."

Masha, a remote viewer, and her mind-reading twin brother, Misha, are the easiest of my fellow teammates for me to read. Their choices are always the most obvious, and always follow the same course. I could say something cutting, I could defend myself, I could leave the room. But none of those futures look satisfying, so I just stir my soup.

"Are we really ready to go to war?" Sergei asks. Like Masha, he's a remote viewer, but his choices are less certain than hers; I'll think he's barreling toward a future full-speed when at the last moment, he jukes to another one. It must serve him well in his hockey games.

Masha peers down her nose at him—he's so tall she's really looking up, but she makes it seem like she's peering down all the same. "We should. It would serve those imperialists right for putting their missiles in Turkey."

"They ought to be wiped from the face of the planet," Misha agrees. "Stalin had it right—we must bring about change in the world order, instead of waiting for the world to revolt."

"No one deserves such a death."

Everyone turns to the far end of the table, where Valentin, dark-faced and solemn, pushes a crumbled pirozhki around his plate. His futures are harder for me to grasp, turning to smoke as soon as I think I've captured them. Lately, though, there's a sting to them, as if they'd grown thorns. I do not like dealing with Valentin much, with his caustic power to change thoughts and his piercing stare; even Misha and Masha tend to leave him be. Only Anastasia ever hovers around him like a shadow, but tonight it appears she, too, is staying away.

"Of course they deserve it," Masha says, but she speaks softer now, gaze hurrying back to our end of the table as she reaches for the plate of pickled herring. Valentin watches her for a moment longer, eyes narrowing, before looking back at his food.

The new boy, Ivan, is fidgeting beside me. Like Sergei, he eats his meals in about two gulps, but unlike Sergei, he makes no effort to redirect the twins' insults or, really, to take part in our conversations at all. I don't know where he came from; I've never had much use for the past. All I know is his future is wide-open, undetermined, as blessedly empty of grim certainties as a cloudless summer sky.

I wonder whether that'll change once Lieutenant Colonel Rostov, our KGB commander, finishes training him.

Something rumbles outside, far beyond our mansion walls. Everyone looks up with their breath held in their throats. Possibilities spark and dance before me—enemy planes soaring overhead and bombs clattering to the cobblestones. But it's only the Red Army across the river, rehearsing in Red Square for the October Revolution anniversary parade. A million future Moscows spread before me—all tenuous as a spider's web— bombs raining down instead of fireworks, bodies strewn instead of confetti throughout the streets.

"This is your big opportunity, Larissa. A real chance to serve the motherland. You should be honored." Masha jabs her fork in my direction. "Sergei and I are doing our part, watching their air bases. Don't let us down."

It doesn't feel like an honor. Lieutenant Kruzenko steps into the dining room, slumped forward, eyelids heavy. Hers was the kinder voice in the interrogation room, but I know how quickly it can sharpen. I can see the possible futures the night holds for her—shouting matches with Lieutenant Colonel Rostov, or else biting her tongue. A quick and mostly painless session trying to divine the future from me, or another sleepless night.

"Come, Larissa." Kruzenko flexes one hand, then tightens it into a fist. "We must continue our work."

The twins watch me as I drop my spoon into my barely touched soup and stand from the table. "Try not to get us all killed," Misha says. The others' stares around the table don't look too optimistic on those chances.

Then the new boy, Ivan, looks up at me. "Not flesh, nor feathers," he says, with the slightest twist to his lips. A superstitious old way of wishing luck. When our eyes meet, a thousand moments spawn from that point, though I don't want to consider them yet.

Some futures are better left unexamined.

I smile as I give him the traditional response. "Go to hell."

Turns out, it's boats.

Finally the possible futures narrow and coalesce to show me an impending naval blockade around Cuba—not that it'll help the Americans much, since we already have more than enough missiles in place to melt their entire continent away, a possibility that hangs so tantalizingly close to my grasp. I see it lurking behind every future I consider, a thin scrim with the scenes projected onto it like a film as the Secretariat considers it. Mushroom clouds. Buildings worn down into broken little teeth that poke from land rendered as foreign, as barren, as the surface of the moon. A foot, a skull, a flash burn on a brick wall where once there was a man.

But in my visions, it's not only American cities that suffer this fate. Soviet cities burn and crumble in retaliation. Retaliation feels like breaking your hand against someone's face. This is what our world has become—dead man's triggers crisscrossing the world to ensure no cruelty goes unpunished.

The next few days are a haze. I am trapped in a room with a single question looming from the fog—*Will they bomb our missiles and our soldiers already in place on Cuba's shores?* Sometimes I can hear the engines roaring in my ears and feel the thick jungle air, so full of chirping and buzzing, as the American bombs begin to fall. But other times, the only sound is a voice, crackling out of a badly tuned radio set. *My fellow Americans.*

The wooden chair is like glass shards under my skin. Three hours, five, eight. Closed away in a classroom, guards at the door, KGB officers crowding around me like each word I utter is a prophecy. They spread maps before me; the pen cuts through the paper as I trace, retrace, scratch out, and draw anew the troop positions and flight plans that crowd inside my head. I'm their oracle, sifting through the future, barely able to hold on to right now.

Nine hours, ten. The smell of sweat and exhaustion, thickening in the room like a snowdrift. "You're pushing her too hard—"

"We have to know. How else can Comrade Secretary make the right choice? We must know what they will do if we attack!"

Apologies and excuses fill the future, transmitted across red phones. Warnings. Accusations, negotiations, begging, threatening, screaming—

No, the screaming is from me. I am screaming because it

feels like my skin is on fire, my hair is falling out, my insides are thickening into a cancerous soup. Someone tries to touch me, but their fingers sting like lemon on a wound.

"First strike," I scream. "They'll hit us first if we don't stop!"

Everything pauses—and then everyone speaks at once, pointing and barking out commands.

I blink, and fling myself back into the future, a world where the KGB officers' faces run like wax. Our mansion slides down its embankment into the Moskva River, now thickened like stew with debris and blood as the bombs rain down. Get me out of this future. No—I can't escape. This is real, this is happening, they wouldn't listen to me.

"Sedative," a voice calls, sparking a thousand futures. Do I fight—claw my nails into that face, push at this chest, kick those knees. Or do I succumb? I try to weigh the possibilities but it's all so useless. We're all going to die. Isn't that the possibility that no one wants to hear but everyone knows is true? Every branch has an end, a point where it will split no more. But does it have to end like this? With fire in my veins and poison on my skin?

The futures retreat as a soft white nothing settles around me, quiet as snowfall, soft as fresh-spun wool.

$$\backsim$$

I awaken twisted in my bed sheets, blankets cast off, bare toes jutting out into the sharp cold of nighttime. My mouth bears the distinctive aftertaste of standard-issue sedatives, cottony and tinged with a hungry ache. How long have I been out? I glance at Masha in her cot to my left, issuing soft sighs with each exhale, and Anastasia to my right, her whole body curled tight as a fist under the covers. I like my teammates best when they're asleep. It's the only time Masha's mouth stops moving. The only time I don't see the flash of possibilities running through Anastasia's head, glinting as if against the edge of a knife. No matter what future I see, Anastasia craves the only certain escape from our prison—the kind where they carry you out in a bag.

As prisons go, ours isn't so bad. I have a bed to myself and warm clothes up to the task of the winter already frosting across our windowpanes. I rummage around in the chest at the foot of my bed and pull on two pairs of socks, add another sweater, and twist my hair into a bun at the back of my head. I glide down the second floor hallway, kept company only by the roaches and rats as they skitter out of my way. All but the night-shift guards and the vermin are asleep now, and I can come up for breath—stop worrying about what might come and pretend that anything could happen. I might even feel real surprise, genuine anticipation—that dual-edged blade of excitement tempered with nerves. It never turns out that way, but I like to pretend.

I reach the linen closet and push open the side panel that leads into the secret vault—a gift from the imperialists who built the mansion. Futures spin and coalesce in my mind as they become more tangible—glimpses of smiles and winking blue eyes and things yet to come, awaiting me at the tunnel's end—but I ignore them as I walk down the dark passageway. An amber glow up ahead fills the vault. The future presses in on me, but I try to push it away. Let me cling to this moment of candy-sweet ignorance before whatever future awaits me becomes right now—

"Oh. Hi. Sorry, I didn't think anyone was awake . . . ," he says. It's the new boy, Ivan, stomach down on the cold stone floor, a book spread open before him. An illustrated collection of folktales—not the sort of thing boys like to be seen reading. But he's looking at me, not trying to hide it away. The possibility doesn't even register in his mind. I smile.

"Sorry to intrude." I perch on the edge of a sheet-covered sofa and draw my knees up under my chin. I wonder whether he's going to ask me about my screaming episode—surely the whole house heard—but he doesn't look too interested in anything besides his book. "I suppose Sergei showed you this place?"

"Valentin, actually. I was—I was having trouble shutting off all the voices, you know? My head was full of everyone's thoughts, and I couldn't stop hearing it and I couldn't hear anything else, so I just had to get away—" His cheeks flush red to match the red-and-gold illustration in front of him. They're good Russian cheeks, angled, but not so sharp you could cut yourself on them. The red brings out the icy sparkle to his eyes. "But I suppose you know what that's like."

Planes and boats, bombs and tanks, threats and pleas . . . "You aren't going to ask me what will happen?" I raise one eyebrow at him. "It's always the first thing people want to know when they learn about my power. Whether or not they're about to die."

He lifts his shoulders. "If you know, then you'll tell us. No point in pushing you, right?"

Softer than Sergei, happier than Valentin, kinder than Misha. But carefree boys, incurious boys, don't belong on this team. We're in the cruelty business, breaking into heads and futures and lives. I like that he doesn't belong, but I don't like to think about what futures it might bring.

"What are you reading?" I ask.

He blushes again, and a grin spreads on his face. "Well, I couldn't find any copies of *Midnight at the Moscow Nursing School,* so I had to settle for Maksim Gorky stories instead."

A laugh bursts out of me before I can suppress it. I remember finding a racy photo book like *Midnight at the Moscow Nursing School* buried under my brothers' side of the mattress. All right, so Ivan's not *that* good-hearted. I hide my smile behind my knees. "Sure. I've heard what they teach at that kind of nursing school."

His face is deep crimson now, the color of Rostov's patriotic medals, but I think he senses that I'm not letting him out of his joke so easily. "Anatomy, mostly." He waves one hand in the air. "It's a very serious text. Lots of illustrations, to teach you proper technique."

"Well, Gorky must pale in comparison." I slip down from the sofa and sit across from him on the floor. The future is lighting up, quick-fire, flashing like an aerial bombing in the night, but I shove it aside. I like this moment as it is, isolated, untouched by what's happened or what's yet to come.

Ivan gestures to the illustration. "Why, my dear comrade, nothing can compare to the proper socialist teachings of the legend of Danko. Danko tried to lead his village out of the dark forest when it threatened to consume them, and here he is, selflessly dismembering himself to illuminate the night. Ripping out his heart to light their way. Because, as every good worker knows, your body parts can be used as torches to fend off evil spirits."

I lean over the illustration. Sure enough, Danko has wrenched his heart from his chest, and the light from his heart is guiding the rest of his village out of the forest to safety. "What a brave and resourceful comrade he is, to sacrifice himself in such a way," I say. "I never even would have thought to do such a thing."

Ivan nods sagely. "We should drop leaflets with the story of Danko over America. Then I'm sure they will understand the rightness of our cause."

Our heads are looming side by side over the gruesome illustrations, made all the more grim for how genuinely happy Danko looks to sacrifice himself. Maybe he secretly was thrilled to find a way out of his village. Maybe after twenty years of cabbage soup and kasha every day, he couldn't take it anymore. I glance at Ivan from the corner of my eye, wondering whether he's thinking the same thing. Wondering how long he can live in this mansion, with this team, with the KGB ordering us around, making us into weapons because of an irrational gift we possess.

I rock back from the book and clutch my knees once more under my chin.

"How bad is it out there?" I ask, voice muffled by my knees. "What have they said on the news?"

He shrugs again. Russians shrug for the same reason a baker rolls her dough—to flatten everything out, hide the imperfections. "The Americans declared DEFCON-2. Kruzenko explained this is their second-highest level of military alert."

"But no one's attacking anyone yet."

"Not yet," he says.

I lean back against the sofa, Ivan watching me, our gazes locked. There's no aggression in his stare like from Masha's; no pity or contempt like Sergei's and Valentin's. He simply looks at me, and for once I think about the past, about whatever sequence of choices has brought this calm, quick-smiling boy into our midst.

I'm glad for it.

⌒

Sometimes, the question is more important than the answer. Ask me, *Lara, what's going to happen with the Americans?* and don't expect anything brilliant in reply. They'll eat hamburgers, probably, or listen to their rock and roll. Someone will say something funny on a TV show and the Yankees will win it again. I've told Rostov before—ask with the answer in mind. But he never sees what he's not looking for.

Someday, though I don't yet know how, this will be useful to me.

"How do we stop the Americans from invading Cuba?" Rostov's boss asks, a thick-skulled man, KGB something or other, colonel, major general, I forget. Sometimes when I look at him, I see a glimpse—just a glimpse—of him hunched over a desk, worry deepening the folds of his face, a shadow in the doorway catching his eye. But no one ever asks me about that.

How do we stop the Americans? How isn't relevant to me. I'm no military planner; I'm a girl with a pinhole peek into the future. Point me in the right direction. "It doesn't work that way." I rub at my eyes. "Give me a scenario, a possibility— something to explore."

He peels off his hat and dabs away the thick smear of sweat across his forehead. Consults a well-loved notepad in his breast pocket. "What if we agreed to remove the missiles?"

Rostov steps forward, lip twitching into a sneer. "Comrade, that is not a feasible option—"

"Comrade First Secretary Nikita Khrushchev wants to know," the other man says, the words pointed like a gun. "If we remove our missiles from Cuba, will it keep the Americans from invading? Will it keep us safe? Will it keep Comrade Castro's Cuban people safe?"

"Castro himself asked for us to strike the Americans first," Rostov says.

But they are fading, fading away as I sink into the depths, letting the new future that's arisen drag me in.

The tang of frying Chinese food floods my nose as the scene coalesces around me. Only a few hours ahead of right now—this one's a near certainty. Two men, emissaries both of their respective countries, hunch over the crusty diner table deep in Washington, gesturing at the dark silhouettes that freckle the maps in front of them. Soviet missiles in Cuba, just beyond the American shoreline. American missiles in Turkey, butting up against the Soviet Union. Each pressing like a knife into the other's back.

The diners around them chatter away in English, oblivious to the nuclear weapons being plucked off the table one by one, like pawns eliminated in an aggressive game of chess.

"Offer to remove the missiles from Cuba," I say.

Rostov stares at me, slack-jawed, darkness smoldering in his eyes.

"If you offer it, then the Americans will take their missiles from Turkey. They will agree to the trade."

Rostov and his commander face each other, neither breathing. Slowly, Rostov's shoulders shrink back until he stands at military posture. Deferent. But his clenched fists show how it pains him to submit.

"Thank you, comrade, for your service," the commander says to me with a quick nod. Then, to Rostov: "Fetch my car. I must head straight to the Kremlin."

Rostov's dark eyes burn through me as he holds the door open for his boss.

❧

Everyone's gathered in the old ballroom. Misha and Masha press up against the monolithic radio, Valentin practices his scales at the baby grand, Anastasia clings to the piano like a piece of driftwood saving her from a shipwreck, and Ivan and Sergei speak in hushed tones on the sofa. When I enter, however, all heads swivel toward me, as if I were magnetic north, the only way out of this mess. I tug my cardigan tight around me and lower my head.

"Well?" Misha asks, as he and his sister rise to their feet. "Have you managed not to kill us all?"

I shuffle toward the couch, but they step into my path. I glance up, quick, then duck around them. "It'll be fine. Everything's fine now."

Somehow this does nothing to ease the thick pressure in the hall.

"How do you mean, it's fine? Last time you were screaming

that we were all about to be nuked into oblivion." Masha trails me to the sofa. "How can you be sure? You've missed things before."

I bite my lower lip. No, I've chosen not to see things before. But the difference would be lost on her. "Well, it's fine now."

"This is a matter of life and death! I know you don't give a damn about the rest of us, but if you could think of someone besides yourself for once, you selfish capitalist swine—"

Ivan hops up from the sofa. He's a few inches shorter than the twins, and wirier than Sergei, but the future spreads out from him, containing several possible endings in which he puts his fist through Misha's nose. "And what have the rest of you done to help? I may be new here, but I'm pretty sure moping around listening to radio dramas isn't helping us dodge the capitalists' bombs."

Masha's mouth flaps open and shut. "Why, I've been trying to remotely view the White House, see what Jack and Bobby Kennedy are plotting—"

"Trying," Ivan echoes. "And how successful have you been?"

Sergei saunters toward us, hands in his pockets. "Hey, now, remote viewing's tough work. I wouldn't expect a meager mind reader like you to understand."

"We all have a role to play. Isn't that what Marx, Engels, Lenin were all about? Doing our part?" Ivan's eyes flick toward mine. "Maybe you should worry about what you're doing—or not doing. Let Larissa worry about herself."

A high-pitched flurry of beeps cuts through the droning

voices on the radio set, indicating breaking news. Then the cheery, waddling brass chords of "The Internationale" fill the ballroom. As one, we crowd around the wooden radio, wordless, transfixed. The future looms large before me, but I push it away; I drop to the floor beside Ivan, shoulder pressing against his.

"Comrades. Workers of the world. We interrupt this Radio Moscow broadcast to read you a letter from the First Secretary of the Communist Party of the Soviet Union, Comrade Nikita Sergeyevich Khrushchev." The announcer clears his throat. " 'The Soviet government has given a new order to dismantle the weapons in Cuba that the Americans have described as offensive, and to crate and return them to the Soviet Union.' "

Anastasia and Sergei cheer, and briefly embrace; Valentin slumps forward with a relieved sigh. "What?" Masha screeches. "We're pulling our missiles back?" She and Misha turn their rage on me, chattering back and forth with each other about my incompetence.

My heart is hammering in my throat; my nails dig into my palms. I stare forward, beyond this moment, feeling the cold water of another future flood around me. I have to be sure. I find the image—the pillar of smoke, the radioactive rain, the corpses that crumble to ash. It's still there, but faded now, as if washed over with bleach. Maybe it will never be gone entirely. But the details are gone, the pain, the smell.

For now, we are safe.

I surface again to find Ivan watching me with a tentative smile. "Well done," he tells me. His arm is now pressed against the length of mine, and it feels like a million new possibilities blooming on the horizon.

I curl my fingers around his. "And I didn't even have to tear out my heart."

✑

Of course, it's weeks before anything is official, but after the requisite rounds of bluster and speeches and hollowed-out threats, the missiles are removed. Rostov gets promoted, to colonel—for what, I'm not sure. Proper handling and employment of his weapon, I suppose, and I'm the weapon of choice. For my service, I'm given a color television with which to watch black-and-white Russian broadcasts, with the occasional burst of color from films like *Five Days, Five Nights*.

I'm of little use in fieldwork, but I knew it would be only a matter of time before Rostov and Kruzenko deemed Ivan ready. For a time, we could curl up on the couch and watch the Soviet variety shows on TV while the others trained in the field, but after lunch one day, he sits down beside me, boots in hand, and begins to lace them up. "I'm afraid I'll have to miss the new episode." His face is soft as he looks into my eyes, but the frost in his gaze has returned. "My first big mission. I suppose I should feel honored."

Honored. I shrug, and try not to see the ache that an afternoon without him holds, but that future is right here in front of me, unavoidable. I like this boy who smiles, who believes in things like honor and loyalty but never believes in them too much. I reach out and grab his hand before I have a chance to see what consequences such a future would hold. Don't think, Lara, just savor this moment. No future, no past. The present is his warm skin against mine and his dark blond hair on his forehead just begging for me to brush it back.

"Lara," he murmurs, and it sounds well rehearsed. Like this moment is a future he's dreamed about.

I press my lips to his, and everything else retreats. We are now: soft flesh, warming against the dead of winter. Hot breath to melt away fear. Two hearts that beat, defiant of the future that could have been. Fingers tangled in honey-gold hair.

He gasps for air and plants one last kiss on my forehead. "Maybe we can revisit this when I get back, huh?" he asks.

I smile; it's my turn to flush deep red. "I'd like that." The future flashes, white-hot and urgent, a fresh possibility needling its way in. No. Not now. I cling to the simplicity and innocence of the moment and refuse to foresee what is about to happen to us. Instead I ask him: "What is your mission?"

He finishes tying off his snow boots. "We're hunting a scientist who tried to defect."

Then the future plows into me, now, too leaden to ignore. It's gone as fast as it came, but the threat is unmistakable—a white as vast as the tundra, as biting, as scouring and cold. I lean back with a gasp. No, no, no, the word clings to my lips, but I can't speak it, I can't let on. This future can't be true.

Ivan's forehead wrinkles up. "Lara? What's the matter?"

I search for the possibility again, but it's evaded my grasp and slipped off into forever. Maybe it was only a remote chance; so far away, there's plenty of time to change it. I tighten my grip around Ivan's knee and force myself to focus, to ask the right question. *Will Ivan return from his mission tonight?*

The answer is as vivid as his kiss. Yes. He'll walk through that door, perhaps with some minor success, perhaps not, but he'll return.

"It was nothing." I pat his cheek. "Not flesh, nor feathers."

He smiles and stands. "Go to hell."

Nothing is set in stone. Futures dart like fish in the depths of time, and some can escape us forever. The future is malleable. Even atomic winters can thaw, with the right choices.

As I watch Ivan leave, I promise myself I'll cherish the present, the firm sofa beneath me and the scratch of cheap wool. The scent of boy that lingers on my hands. We could have lost it all, just a few short weeks ago. Maybe, just maybe, I can keep us from losing again.

BROKEN HEARTS, FENCES, AND OTHER THINGS TO MEND

DELETED SCENES

Katie Finn

BY KATIE FINN

~ *The Broken Hearts & Revenge Series* ~

Broken Hearts, Fences, and Other Things to Mend

Revenge, Ice Cream, and Other Things Best Served Cold

Hearts, Fingers, and Other Things to Cross

Meet Katie Finn

© Gina Stock

*Volunteering for Things You're
Unqualified For!
Or, How I Became a Writer*

Back in the long-ago days of 2007 (like
a lifetime ago, right? We had electricity,
but that was about it. Tumblr didn't exist. Nobody used emojis
or said "yolo." It was the dark ages, truly), I was working in
YA publishing as an assistant. It was my first real job, like, one
with a salary and a desk and nobody asking me to put their
dressing on the side. Since this was 2007, MySpace was still a
thing (see how long ago this was?) and my boss wanted to
know what the "MySpace book" would look like. I had been
working on some mostly terrible book ideas—like one about
the lives and loves of teenage ambulance drivers called *Sirens*
(egad)—but none had gone anywhere. (In retrospect, this was
not at all surprising.) So when my boss mentioned this book
idea, I immediately volunteered to write it, despite having no
idea what a MySpace book would look like, and having never
actually finished writing a book before. My last effort had
been a *terrible* five-hundred-page attempt with no plot.

But as I sat down to work, I found that I was greatly helped by
a deadline. My publishing house had given me an advance, half
of what I would get paid, and I had used it for my astronomical

Brooklyn rent. If I didn't finish the book, they would take it back—and I'd already spent it! It also helped that while I had a germ of an idea, the rest of it was mine to play with. I had no guidelines beyond "something about the Internet," which might explain how I turned the book into an Agatha Christie–style whodunit about a hacked account that was later called *Top 8*. It became a series, I went on to write two sequels, and I had a blast doing it.

I think if there's any advice from this I could pass on, it's that you should always volunteer for something, even if you don't know you can do it. You can figure it out once you're doing it.

Oh, and never write a book about teenage ambulance drivers.

Revenge Inspiration. Revengespiration? Inspirevenge!

I had a great time writing my Internet trilogy, but after I finished I was ready for a change—and a challenge. Those books were a lot of fun, but even though I put my heroine through the ringer, I never really doubted that everything would work out for her in the end. I was really interested in the idea of a book where a happy ending wasn't nearly so assured.

But the absolute worst way to try and think of an idea is to tell yourself, "Hey! It's idea-thinking time now. Go." But I didn't know that then, so I was trying really, really hard—always a mistake—to come up with new ideas. I knew it was time to give up when I started thinking about those teenage ambulance drivers, and wondering whether that idea—now five years old—had really been so terrible after all. (Short answer: yes.) So finally I decided to give up for a while, and was watching a lot of TV while feeling guilty for being a not-writing, no-idea-having writer. At one point, I was scrolling through shows, looking for something to watch . . . and ended up devouring the entire first season of the show *Revenge* in a day and a half. Suddenly, it was like all the idea circuits in my brain started lighting up again. Now I wanted nothing more than to write a revenge book. I pitched my idea to my agent, who was . . . lukewarm about it. When I described it to her, it was a straightforward revenge story—a girl tries to get revenge on the girl who ruined her life when she was eleven. But my agent felt like she'd seen this story before. So I thought about it, and while I was thinking about it, came up with the title *Revenge, Ice Cream, and Other Things Best Served Cold.* I liked the construction of that so much, I started playing around with other titles, and hit upon *Broken Hearts, Fences, and Other Things to Mend.* I didn't even know what it meant, really, but I liked it. Someone had a broken heart . . . someone had a fence to mend . . . and like that, I had my idea. It would be a *reverse* revenge story. The girl who'd wrecked someone else's life would try to make things right, years later. And just like that—after despair and soul searching and lots of TV watching—a series was born.

The Series

The Broken Hearts & Revenge series is three books: *Broken Hearts, Fences, and Other Things to Mend* (book 1); *Revenge, Ice Cream, and Other Things Best Served Cold* (book 2); and *Hearts, Fingers, and Other Things to Cross* (book 3). The heroine of these books is Gemma Tucker. Gemma's been dating her totally perfect, do-gooder class-president boyfriend, Teddy, for the last two years. But then he dumps her unexpectedly in a Target (while she's wearing what in hindsight was a terrible outfit choice of red shirt and khakis), turning her world upside down. Since she and Teddy had planned to go on a volunteer trip over the summer, Gemma finds herself at a loose end. She ends up going to the Hamptons to spend the summer with her screenwriter father, but she's dreading it. Not only is she nursing her broken heart, but the last time she was in the Hamptons—five years earlier—she wrecked the life of her then–best friend, Hallie. When she bumps into Hallie—and her incredibly cute brother Josh—a small case of mistaken identity ensues. Hallie thinks that Gemma is actually Gemma's best friend, Sophie, and Gemma realizes this could be her chance to make things right with Hallie. But as mishaps and hijinks—and a growing crush on Josh—start to take over the summer, Gemma wonders whether she can make things right before her secret comes out . . . or whether it's already too late. The first book ends with a twist, and the second book in the series picks up twelve hours after the first one ends. It's impossible to go into details of books 2 and 3 without spoiling book 1, but trust me when I tell you that in book 2, things in the Hamptons are more dramatic—not to mention funny and heartbreaking—than ever.

~~Very Necessary and Important~~ Deleted Scenes

So I wrote the first draft of *Broken Hearts, Fences, and Other Things to Mend*, turned it in to my editor with a song in my heart (if memory serves, it was by Taylor Swift) and went about my day. It happens to me every time I write a book, but I was dismayed to find, a few weeks later, that not only did she have (brilliant and sensible) ideas about how to make the book better . . . she claimed it was too long (it was). I agreed that it was *maybe* too long, but her solution for fixing this was to delete scenes. Some of which were my favorites! Some of which I loved! But of course, she was right. We went back and forth, talking about which scenes absolutely needed to be in to keep the story moving forward, and how to make everything as clear as possible. There's also an element of mystery to the book, so we were also very aware of making sure we didn't reveal too much. Because my editor is smart and wise and I had waaaay more scenes than necessary in which not much happened except people ate pizza (these scenes were usually written just before dinner), a lot of scenes ended up being deleted. But I still like them (obviously more than my editor, at any rate) and I thought it would be fun to provide a look-behind-the-curtain and show you scenes from *Broken Hearts, Fences, and Other Things to Mend* that *almost* were . . . but didn't quite make the cut. A small description will precede each one, along with a little bit of info about how it fits into the story. Enjoy these previously unseen (except by my editor) scenes from *Broken Hearts, Fences, and Other Things to Mend*.

Broken Hearts, Fences, and Other Things to Mend

DELETED SCENES

by Katie Finn

#1—The Carnival

There had originally been a subplot where a charity carnival is set up in Quonset. Gemma, Hallie, and Josh attend, and things start going wrong for Gemma right away—she can't win at any of the games, she somehow ends up in the dunk tank, and she gets caught on the Ferris wheel with Josh when it stops working. The chapter was funny, but it was just too long, hitting too many beats we would see in later chapters, and it didn't feel beachy enough. So the whole carnival thing had *to go. But this is one of my favorite scenes from it, when Gemma and Hallie wander into the fortune-teller's tent.*

☙

I blinked as my eyes adjusted to the dim, incense-filled air. It was late afternoon outside, and still really sunny, so the contrast in here was jarring. It was a small room, the floor covered with threadbare woven carpets and the walls with hanging scarves. There was a woman sitting behind a table, and I took a step forward to make her out better.

I'd expected something like the fortune-tellers I'd seen in movies—flowing clothes, turban, hands covered in rings. But the woman was petite, wearing jeans and flats, and a white shirt. She looked about my mom's age, and could have easily been any of the women I saw fighting for parking spots outside the South Fork. She was sitting with her hands folded, a deck of cards to her right. "Come in," she said in a quiet voice that nonetheless carried across the tent. "Don't be afraid."

Hallie nudged me and gave me a smile, and I tried to smile back, like this was just a silly goof. But I could feel that my palms were starting to get clammy. What if, on the off chance, this fortune-teller was actually real? What if she was a psychic who would be able to tell that I was currently pretending to be Sophie? What if she told *Hallie*?

"I'm not sure," I said, hanging back at the entrance. "Want to just get a funnel cake instead?"

Hallie shook her head and took a step forward. "It'll be fun," she said as she walked right up to the table. I bit my lip, but then followed behind her, trying to talk myself out of this nervousness. After all, most of the people working these booths were volunteers. Probably this was just somebody's mom. There was most likely a *Tarot for Dummies* book under her chair that she'd stashed out of sight when we came in.

"What would you like?" the woman asked, still in her same quiet but commanding voice. She gestured to the tarot deck next to her. "I can only read one person at a time if we use the cards. Otherwise, I can try and do a general reading for you both."

I was about to tell Hallie that she should get her tarot cards read, and I'd go out and finally try to make the ring-toss thing happen, but Hallie was already nodding and sitting down at the table. "Why don't you do us both?" she asked, as she reached into her purse for her wallet. She grinned at me, and placed a twenty on the table before I could protest. She nodded at the seat next to her, and I sat down, trying to tell myself that this was just a random mom. She'd probably tell us both that we were destined to meet tall, dark strangers and come into money and take a long journey soon, and then we'd both laugh about it and get some funnel cake.

The woman nodded and gave us a brief smile. Then she closed her eyes and let out a long breath, fluttering her fingertips by her eyebrows. Hallie looked over at me, and I could see she was fighting not to crack up. I pressed my lips together, hard, because otherwise I knew I'd burst out laughing. It was just so stereotypical and theatrical, I could feel myself start to relax. I had nothing to worry about here.

"I sense . . ." The fortune-teller's fingers stopped moving, and she raised her head and looked up. She looked at Hallie, then me, long enough that I started to feel uncomfortable, and pretended to be interested in the scarves draped above me, just to have an excuse to break eye contact. "There is so much *anger* in this room," she finally said, looking a little bit surprised, as she looked from me to Hallie.

I could feel my eyebrows rise. I wasn't sure, but it seemed like, next to me, Hallie's posture stiffened. Of course this woman was just casting around in the dark. But who goes to a carnival if they're angry? Maybe she was betting on the fact that everyone else had failed at the ring toss, too. "Really?" I asked, but she was back to closing her eyes. This time, though, neither Hallie nor I laughed, and I felt myself leaning forward.

"There is also . . . ," she went on, her eyes still closed, "deception. There is dishonesty and false fronts. False *friends* might be more accurate. And . . ." The fortune-teller's fingers started fluttering again.

I drew in a sharp breath. This woman was talking about me. She had to be, right? How did she *know* that I was currently pretending to be Sophie? How could she? Nobody here knew. Nobody knew at all except the actual Sophie, and she was hundreds of miles away in Connecticut and wouldn't have gone around telling random fortune-tellers my secret. Panicked, I looked over at Hallie, expecting her to be staring at me with suspicion, maybe even finally putting together who I really was. But Hallie had turned pale, and it looked like she was as discomfited by what this woman said as I was. I tried to meet her eye, but she seemed to be deliberately looking away from me.

The fortune-teller looked up and blinked at us. "Just . . . be careful," she said, and I couldn't tell who she was talking to—but I had a feeling she was talking to me. "Things could go wrong here. Very wrong, very quickly." I felt a shiver go down my spine, despite the fact that the temperature outside had been hovering near ninety all day, and it was especially warm inside the tent. "There are many obstacles ahead."

Hallie took a breath, like she was about to say something— maybe ask this woman for more details—but before she could, the fortune-teller swept the twenty off the table and folded her hands as she had in the beginning. "Would you like another reading? Tarot, maybe?" Her fluttering fingers and quavering voice had disappeared, and she was back to being all business again.

I just blinked, startled by this transformation. I tried to use it as evidence that she'd been making the whole thing up. But . . . what a *weird* thing to make up. Was she going around telling everyone that they had false friends and their lives were filled with deception? It didn't seem to me to be a good way to get more business.

"No," Hallie said, as she pushed herself back from the table. She glanced at me briefly, and I shook my head. "We're done." She walked straight to the tent entrance, not once looking behind her, and I pushed my chair back and hurried after her. I turned and glanced back as I approached the exit, and saw the fortune-teller shuffling her cards, slowly, her eyes on mine. She gave a small shake of her head—so quick a moment later I wasn't sure if I'd imagined it—before looking back down at her cards again.

I stumbled out into the sunlight, and it took a moment for me to adjust—to the sunlight and noise and sounds of other people. It was like we'd been underwater and were just now coming up to the surface. I looked over at Hallie, nervous.

What if she put it together? What if she wanted to talk about what this woman meant? Would this be the moment she'd realize I wasn't Sophie Curtis—the moment this would all come crashing down?

But Hallie just gave me a quick smile that didn't quite meet her eyes. "So that was weird, huh?" Her voice was just a little higher than usual, and it didn't seem like she was going to want to discuss this at length. I could already hear the changing-the-subject tone in her voice.

"Totally," I agreed, falling into step next to her as we started to cross to the other side of the carnival. I could hear the occasional high-up yell from people on the Ferris wheel. "Do you think she says that kind of stuff to everyone?" I held my breath, hoping that Hallie would go along with this.

"Probably," Hallie said, giving me another smile. "I bet she has like four things she says. And maybe if you come in with a friend, that's what she says to you. Probably if we'd stayed, she would have offered up a charm to dispel disharmony, or whatever."

I felt myself relax as I smiled for real. *Of course* that's what it was. She had just been setting us up to sell us another reading. There was no reason to assume anything else. And Hallie's strange reaction had just been because she was confused. "Sorry you had to spend your money on that," I said as we sidestepped a guy staggering under the weight of a huge stuffed teddy bear. "Can I buy you a funnel cake to make up for it?"

Hallie raised an eyebrow at me, and the tension I thought I'd seen when we were inside was now totally gone. She linked her arm through mine and started to steer me toward the snack booths. "Totally," she said with a grin. "Let's go."

#2—TALKING TO FORD

Ford Davidson is a character who appears mostly "offscreen" in book 1. He's the son of Gemma's family friend Bruce Davidson—whose house Gemma and her dad are staying in for the summer. Gemma's always had a little bit of a crush on him—but nothing's ever happened with this, mostly because he lives across the country from her, and she'd been dating Teddy (until he dumped her). But Gemma and Ford have a few scenes together, either through video chatting or talking on the phone.

This deleted scene was another Gemma-Ford video call, in which Ford starts to put together that maybe the things that keep happening with Gemma aren't actually accidental at all. We decided to take it out, because my editor was worried that it made Gemma too suspicious too early, when that wasn't part of her character arc yet. I loved it because Ford became one of my favorite characters in this book—even though we don't see him a ton, he's a much bigger presence in book 2—and I always wanted more Ford scenes. But I was overruled, so here's the Ford-and-Gemma scene that didn't quite make it in.

∽

"Hey!" I said, as I propped up Bruce's iPad against the stack of diet books he had decided he no longer needed, now that he was focused on the caveman diet. I straightened the top one—*Do I Dare to Eat a Peach? Overcoming Your Fear of Carbs*—and smiled at the familiar figure onscreen.

Ford was yawning, and his eyes still looked a little bleary, like maybe he'd just woken up. I tried to do the math to figure out what time it was in Hawaii, then gave up when I realized I wasn't entirely sure if they were ahead or behind the

Hamptons. Ford sleeping at strange hours also wasn't that unusual, because when he was really on a coding streak, he'd work for hours at a time, then crash, and it never seemed to matter what time it actually was. Even though he'd clearly just woken up, Ford was, as usual, almost unfairly cute. I knew that I certainly didn't look that good when I was just rolling out of bed. His black-black hair was sticking up in little spikes and there was a pillow crease across one side of his face. He looked even more tan and golden than he had when I'd last video chatted with him. It was also funny to see Ford without his glasses, which over the years had just become part of his identity. He looked younger without them, and it felt a little bit like I was seeing him with his defenses down.

"Hey there," he said around a yawn, giving me a sleepy smile. "How's it going?"

"Bruce is out of town," I said, by way of answering that question. I wasn't sure I wanted to go into how it was *actually* going here. My stomach still wasn't entirely settled from the spoiled-lobster food-poisoning incident of the night before. "Want me to tell him you called?"

"And what if I was calling to talk to you?" Ford asked. "Did you ever think about that?" He shot me a faux-offended look and I couldn't help but laugh.

"Then I take it back," I said. "How's Hawaii?"

"Hawaii's fine," he said. "Working on a new project that's taking up most of my time. But the waves are killer, so I'm not complaining." I nodded, so used to Ford that none of this was surprising—he somehow managed to be both a tech geek and a surf champion. It made sense when you were around him, especially when he started talking about the mathematical properties of wave curves. "But seriously, what's going on?" he asked, leaning forward a little more. "Are you okay? You look kinda pale. Don't they have sun in the Hamptons? I know they don't have surfable waves . . ."

"I'm fine," I said, maybe a little too quickly. I didn't want to take the bait to get into an argument about East Coast surfing, which Ford was a huge snob about. "And I had food poisoning last night, so . . ."

"What happened?" Ford asked, his brow furrowed.

I decided he didn't want to know the gross details of the night—and I didn't really want to go into them, especially now with food actually starting to sound appetizing again. I decided to keep it vague—not only because I felt weird telling Ford that I'd been on a kind-of date when it happened. And though nothing had happened between me and Josh, the fact we'd fallen asleep together on the couch was information I wasn't sure I necessarily wanted to share with Ford. "I was at this seafood place, and the lobster must have gone bad. It was a lobster roll, so maybe the mayo had been sitting out? Anyway, the worst of it seems to be over now." I smiled at him, even though just saying the word *lobster* had been enough to make my stomach clench.

Ford's frown deepened. "Seriously?" he asked, and I could hear the skepticism in his voice.

"Yeah," I said, trying not to be offended—and failing—as I settled into one of the bar stools and crossed my arms over my chest. "Why would I make that up?"

"No, I believe *you*," Ford said as he ran his fingers through his hair. He leaned out of frame for a moment, and when he popped back onscreen again, he was wearing his glasses, hipster-cool black square frames that were miles away from the deeply dorky thick lenses he'd worn when he was a kid. "I'm just surprised it happened, that's all."

"We were, too," I assured him.

One of Ford's eyebrows quirked up. "We?"

"Me," I said immediately. "I meant it in the general sense." Ford continued to look skeptical, and I added quickly, "What do you mean by surprised?"

Ford looked away, and let out a long breath. "Okay, I might be going all math geek on you for a minute here."

"I can't wait," I assured him and was rewarded when he shot me one of his rare, wide smiles.

"So," he said, and from the way I could see his hands reaching out for nothing, I could tell just how much he wanted to either be figuring this out with a pencil or typing on his laptop. "It's a numbers game. It's a seafood place, right?" I nodded. "So seafood is what they do. And the law of averages states that the more you do something, the more the possibility for error *reduces* as long as none of the elements change."

"Okay," I said, nodding, pleasantly surprised I was able to follow this.

"If you'd ordered a lobster roll at a diner and you got sick, not surprising," he said, and I could tell he was warming to his theme. "Or if you got a bad hamburger at a seafood place. Not weird, right?"

"Right," I agreed. "Because . . ."

"Because it's not what they *do*," Ford said, leaning forward. "It's not what they're making a hundred of, every day. So the margin for error is vastly increased. But a place where they only do fish? To randomly get sick?" Ford shook his head. "It's unlikely. Mathematically, at any rate."

I straightened Bruce's pile of cookbooks while I let this sink in. I'd been so focused on getting home without throwing up all over Josh—and then so focused on just doing things like walking upright and trying to keep down liquids—that the *how* of the food poisoning had never occurred to me. But now that Ford was pointing it out, with his unassailable logic, I was beginning to question the whole situation. How *had* it happened, exactly? "So what are you saying?"

"I'm not saying anything," Ford said. "I don't have enough data to make any conjectures. But unless all the diners around you were getting sick simultaneously, there's something fishy—so to speak—going on."

"Fishy?" I echoed, rolling my eyes, smiling despite myself. "So what does that mean? That someone . . . sabotaged my food?" Even saying it out loud sounded ridiculous. Who would want to do that?

"Maybe," Ford said, completely serious. "Is there anyone out there who would want to cause you pain?"

I just blinked. There was one person, of course . . . but she didn't know I was actually me. It couldn't be . . .

Could it?

#3—Pizza with Josh
(KF = Katie Finn. ED = her editor.)

KF *So this was one of my favorite sections of the book. It was just a little scene, but I really liked it.*

This was understood by the fact you kept inserting it back into every draft.

 I just love these little scenes that really don't have to move the plot forward much—

 (or at all)

—and are just about the characters getting to know one another better.

Did you really think I wouldn't NOTICE that you kept putting this scene back in? Did you think I wasn't reading these drafts or something?

 This scene is Gemma and Josh, sharing a pizza in the back of the SUV.

As I pointed out, there is another scene where Gemma and Hallie share a pizza in the back of the SUV. I also encouraged you to work on this after eating dinner, not before.

 The Gemma-Josh relationship is so fun to write and I loved this scene. I also liked Gemma getting so caught up in Josh that she forgets about the double life she's living.

 Me too. But still—we didn't need another pizza/SUV scene.

 I still think this scene is great—

ED *(sigh)*

KF *—but can maybe see my editor's point of view here.*

ED *Thank you.*

KF *So here is the Gemma-Josh pizza scene that I loved—*

ED *(we know)*

KF *—but ultimately had to go.*

❧

"Cheese?" I leaned over to look at Josh's slices in the pizza box. I had ordered, without thinking, my usual—pineapple-sausage-pepperoni. I was now just crossing my fingers that Hallie hadn't told him about the pizza preference that would reveal me to be Gemma Tucker. But he hadn't said anything, just looked a little surprised—like most people did. I'd been so worried about my order, and berating myself for slipping up on something so basic, that I hadn't paid attention to what he'd gotten until now.

"What's wrong with cheese?" Josh asked as he picked up a slice and leaned back against the car windows. We were in the back of the SUV, parked in Josh's driveway. The rear door was up, and we were sitting on opposite sides, our legs stretched out in front of us. I could hear the ocean waves crashing, and the moon was bright enough that the back of the car was flooded with light.

"Nothing," I said, as I reached for one of my own slices, then leaned back before taking a bite. "I guess I was just expecting some toppings or something." It seemed like everyone

I knew had complicated pizza orders, from Sophie, who liked so much extra cheese that the crust sometimes sagged under it, to Walter, who wanted every kind of fish topping available (which almost always meant I was striving to keep his anchovies from migrating onto my slice).

Josh gave me a smile and set down his slice. "It's habit, I guess," he said. "When I was growing up, we used to go to this pizza place in Brooklyn. It wasn't even really a restaurant—there was only one table, it was more like a stand."

"Brooklyn?" I asked, trying to sound surprised, like this was new information to me, like I wasn't well aware of where Hallie and Josh used to live.

"Yeah," he said, nodding, a tiny, nostalgic smile creeping over his face. "We lived there until I was like thirteen. Then . . . we moved to Manhattan." He said this with a note of finality, like I wasn't supposed to ask why he'd moved to Manhattan, even though I was really curious, and had been all summer. "But anyway," he said, the natural warmth in his voice returning, "this pizza place was my favorite. Hallie didn't like it as much as me, but I loved it. And the owner was this crazy old guy who'd been there forever. And he didn't believe in toppings."

"He didn't *believe* in them?" I echoed, speaking around a bite of pizza. I hadn't realized toppings were something, like Santa Claus, you could choose to buy into.

"Nope," Josh said with a smile. "He was a pizza purist. He claimed if you needed anything else, it was because your pizza wasn't good enough. I guess his influence stuck."

"I guess so," I said, smiling at him. Josh took a bite, and ended up with a glob of sauce just under his bottom lip. "You've got—" I said as I reached over with my napkin and swiped it off. It wasn't until I had done this—still leaning across the car toward him—that I'd realized what I'd done. It was such an intimate gesture that I could feel my cheeks getting hot.

"Thanks," Josh said. He didn't look embarrassed, and when he looked back into my eyes, I realized just how close we were. My heart started to beat hard, and I realized that despite the fact there were two slices of pizza between us, we were close enough to kiss. This realization was enough to make me lean back, fast, returning to my side of the car. "You could try it, you know," Josh said after a moment of silent pizza eating in which I tried to persuade my face to cool down.

"What?" I asked, finishing my slice and setting my crust back in the pizza box.

"The pizza that needs no toppings," he said. "We could . . . go there together. When we're back after the summer. You're not that far from the city, right?"

I shook my head. That was the one answer to all of this that I did know—Putnam was a quick train ride from New York. But the rest of it . . . Josh was essentially asking me out on a date *three months* from now. I could feel myself start to smile, the kind of smile that takes over your face before you can stop it. "That sounds great," I said, trying to get myself to stop smiling like an idiot. But I couldn't believe this—we hadn't even kissed yet and Josh was talking to me about going on a date in the fall.

"Well, I'll put it down on the calendar, Sophie," Josh said with a smile.

Just like that, I felt my smile fall off my face as reality brought me back down to earth. Josh didn't know that he was talking to Gemma Tucker. In fact, Josh probably hated Gemma Tucker.

He thought he was talking to Sophie Curtis, the nice girl with no baggage he'd met on the train. I blinked, and the vision of me and Josh, walking around Brooklyn with topping-free slices of pizza, suddenly disappeared.

"You okay?" Josh asked, his brow furrowed.

"Fine," I said quickly. "Just . . . hungry." I picked up another slice, my thoughts spinning. If I was able to pull this off—if I was able to show Hallie that I was a good person and get her to forgive me—maybe Josh and I could have our September pizza date after all. I could practically *see* it, and I suddenly wanted it to happen more than I could say, because if Josh and I were eating pizza together in Brooklyn, it would mean that Hallie had forgiven me. That everything was okay. I looked up and smiled at him. "September," I said with a nod. "It's a plan."

Caragh M. O'Brien

BY CARAGH M. O'BRIEN

~ The Birthmarked Trilogy ~

Birthmarked

Prized

Promised

~ The Vault of Dreamers Trilogy ~

The Vault of Dreamers

The Rule of Mirrors

Meet Caragh M. O'Brien

If I'm to elucidate the truth about my background and my writing career, I might as well start with the story I gave my Nona for Christmas back when I was in junior high. It was the tragedy of a wispy girl who took walks on the beach and didn't realize she was dying of cancer. The story was bleak in every conceivable way, and when Nona loved it, I beamed.

From seventh grade on, I kept a journal, and later I took creative writing in college, so by the time I graduated from Williams with a BA in physics, I was ready to move into my parents' attic and write a romance novel. *Mirage*, set in romantic Death Valley, California, was picked up by Silhouette, and I was ecstatic to be a published writer.

Off I went to Johns Hopkins University to earn my MA in the Writing Seminars, and then I spent a couple decades writing, raising my family, and teaching, until one day, on a leave of absence, I started writing *Birthmarked*.

I had the first ideas for Gaia's story after driving through a drought in the southern US. The miles of dry landscape made me consider what sort of people would survive climate change, and how they might adapt. The social and political repercussions seemed huge, and I had the inklings of an isolated, walled city in a wasteland north of Unlake Superior. I wrote the first chapter, in which Gaia, a young midwife, has to bring a newborn baby to authorities inside the wall, and then I wrote the rest of the book to see what would happen.

Birthmarked was my first YA novel, and to my amazement, Roaring Brook Press/Macmillan offered me a three-book contract. That's when I realized I was writing a trilogy, and two years later, I resigned from teaching high school English so I could meet my deadlines. I've been writing YA ever since.

These days, I'm deep into a new series. *The Vault of Dreamers* is a novel about a girl attending an arts school/reality TV show that hides a nefarious secret about dreams. It involves some psychological twists and a narrator who is not 100 percent reliable. I love it. I'm revising *The Rule of Mirrors* (book 2) at the moment, and I can say truthfully, it's my biggest challenge yet. Nona would be proud.

What you'll find here next is my short story entitled "Tortured." It's intense. I'll say that much. It features a young captain on the night he leaves the Enclave, and as one might infer from the title, it's a dark little tale of pain and determination.

This bridge story takes place chronologically between books 1 and 2 of the Birthmarked trilogy, which means it's a spoiler for the first novel. In fairness, I should warn you not to read it if you want to be completely surprised by the ending of *Birthmarked*, but read it if you're okay with knowing some pertinent facts or if you're the sort of person who mentally ignores previously acquired info by the time you read through a whole book. I fall quite easily into the latter category, so I would read it, but it's really up to you.

If, on the other hand, you've already read the Birthmarked trilogy, we have no spoiler problems whatsoever. Go ahead and read "Tortured" pronto.

As for quirky facts about writing "Tortured," I have three.

First up, to be honest, the Birthmarked 1.5 story was an experiment that originated in marketing. Writing it was not my idea, but I was, as always, game to try something new, and I liked the idea of a free e-story for loyal readers to tide them over until *Prized* (book 2) was released. That, at least, was the plan, but tie-in stories were not common for Roaring Brook at the time, and we were inventing a wheel. As it happened, legalities slowed us up, and we had snags with the e-publishing lead times, so the story didn't go live until several weeks *after* book 2 came out. It was a 1.5 that came out of order.

Second, the story went through five or six drafts in a very short time, and the deadlines hit while I was supposedly on vacation. My editor, Nancy Mercado, was relentless about fine-tuning it, so I ended up working on my laptop in the car while my husband drove. I distinctly recall revising in a traffic jam south of DC.

And last of all, the title was proposed by my publisher, Simon Boughton. When I heard we were calling it "Tortured," I winced. Part of me couldn't believe that I, sunny little me, had written a story that deserved such a title. But, of course, the title made perfect sense for the story, and I instantly knew it. After all, I'd been writing bleak stories since junior high.

Enjoy!

TORTURED

by Caragh M. O'Brien

(SPOILER WARNING: The following story spoils the ending of *Birthmarked*.)

"I'm not going to fix him up if the Protectorat is just going to have him worked over again," Myrna said from the doorway of V cell. "I won't be part of that."

Leon heard her dimly through a haze of pain, and stirred in his chains.

"If we can get him out of here before Miles changes his mind, it'll be over," Genevieve said. "Please, Myrna. You have to help me. Give him something, please."

Kneeling, Leon lifted his head to see Genevieve, his step-mother, working the catch on the metal cuff that held his left wrist, and then she caught his arm when it fell. She retrieved his white shirt from the corner of the cell and wrapped his hand in the makeshift bandage. He tried to straighten, not to sag his torso's weight by his other chained wrist, and the doctor, Myrna Silk, came forward to help support him. A second later, he felt a sting in his shoulder, and Myrna withdrew a syringe.

He swallowed thickly, working his dry throat. "Did they find Gaia?" he asked.

"Your father's searched all of Wharfton and can't find her," Genevieve said. "They've tracked down her old neighbors and her friends but she isn't with any of them."

"So she got away?" Leon asked. If so, it would be the first good news he'd had in four days.

"Yes. So far, at least," Genevieve said. "Guards are looking for her in the wasteland. Why? Did you think we'd found her?"

"Iris told me at one point that they did. I didn't know what to believe," Leon said.

"She'll have to come back," Myrna said. "She can't keep that baby alive in the wasteland."

His other wrist came loose, and with the lowering of his arm, tiny explosions of new pain stretched across his back. Shirtless, he surveyed his bare arms and torso, finding the raw streaks in his skin where the whiplashes on his back trailed around his sides.

The two women helped him to his feet, supporting his arms over their shoulders.

"Watch his back," Genevieve said.

"I know," Myrna replied.

Leon struggled to coordinate his feet, clenching his body as each step triggered pain upward through his muscles.

"Buck up," Myrna said. "No fainting, now. Hear me?"

He focused all his concentration on the cement floor before him, and then the steps as the women guided him down.

Disoriented, he began to fear it was only a nightmare, that they were leading him deeper into the prison or a stone tomb where he'd awaken to another round of torture. His instinct was to struggle.

"Leon, please," Genevieve insisted. "You'll be all right, but you have to let us help you."

"You let them do this to me," he said.

"I made them stop," Genevieve said, plainly stricken. "I've been pleading with your father ever since I learned he turned you over to Mabrother Iris."

They reached a tunnel next, and lights that were thinly spaced down the rugged corridor came on one by one as they approached. Though the air was cool, Leon was sweating from effort, and by the time they reached another staircase leading upward, he couldn't go farther. He sank to the steps, breathing hard, grasping his wounded hand with the other to apply pressure. The fabric was saturated with blood.

"Get Mabrother Cho for me, Myrna," Genevieve said, urging the doctor onward past Leon. "He's in the kitchen. Quickly."

Myrna's footsteps vanished up the stairs.

"I'm sorry, Leon," Genevieve said.

Her apologies didn't interest him. "Tell me what I've missed."

"They've focused in on a Wharfton girl named Emily who was a friend of Gaia's, and she verified that Gaia went into the wasteland."

"Emily wouldn't volunteer that information."

"She was interrogated last night." Genevieve's lips tightened. "Miles gave her baby to Masister Khol. They intend to recover the ledgers you stole, unless Gaia took them with her. If she did, they won't rest until they find her. Does she have them?"

He looked bleakly at the floor between his boots. "I don't know where the ledgers are." He'd said it a hundred times in the last few days.

"You must see it's a matter of the utmost importance," Genevieve said. "Those records could guide birth parents outside the wall to the families inside who are raising their advanced children. It would cause widespread panic if parents in the Enclave believed that their children could be identified. They'd be afraid their kids could be stolen."

"Like you'd have cared if my birth parents came for me?" he asked.

"Leon," Genevieve said. "Of course. You're my son no matter what's happened."

Wincing, he tightened the fabric around his injured hand, even though it was doing little to stanch the blood. The tip of his ring finger had been severed from the knuckle up, and his efforts to arrest the blood flow when he'd been chained had not succeeded. Only the combination of his hand being raised high and his wrist shackle restricting his circulation had prevented him from losing more blood.

"I wish you'd just cooperated with him from the start," Genevieve said. "Do you know where Gaia is now?"

"No."

"Or where she's gone? Didn't she tell you anything?"

He glanced up grimly. "You think I'd tell you if she did? Now that they've found Emily, my resistance didn't make much of a difference anyway," he said. "That's why the Protectorat is letting me go now, isn't it? He's done with me. Why doesn't he just kill me?"

She put a hand on his arm, and he went still at her touch.

"Don't, Mom," he said.

"Your father's never known how to handle you," she said quietly, releasing him. "But this is the worst of all."

He didn't want to hear it. The man had ceased being any decent kind of father long before he'd ordered Leon's torture. What Leon didn't understand was why Genevieve was still with the Protectorat. How could any woman stay with a man who hurt his own son? She must not love him as a son, either. That's what it felt like to Leon, no matter what she said about protecting him. Her lies only added to the betrayal.

He didn't need this. He had to get out of here. He took a deep breath as the noise of footsteps came down the staircase and he shifted. A compact, strong man in a white chef's apron preceded Myrna past Leon.

"What's this?" Mabrother Cho said with false levity. "In trouble again?"

Leon looked up to see the cook scowling at his back.

"You don't seem surprised," Leon said. "Give me a hand?"

Mabrother Cho stooped instead and hauled Leon over his shoulder, careful not to touch his ripped back. He carried him up the rest of the stairs into the kitchen, where he gently deposited him on the long wooden table. Leon shifted heavily over the edge to sit on one of the stools instead.

"If I lie down, I'll pass out," Leon said, and glanced up at the doctor. "See what you can do, Masister."

He held out his hand first. The doctor took it tenderly

between her hands, turning it carefully, and unwrapped the torn, blood-soaked fabric. "A bowl of water," Myrna said. "And more so I can wash his back. And towels. This is ridiculous working like this. At least get me better light."

"I'll get the lamp," Genevieve said.

Myrna opened her black satchel and began laying out medical supplies, including a metal scalpel that she propped over a candle flame. She readied another syringe.

"What's that?" Leon asked.

"Another dose of morphine. It's going to hurt, what I'm about to do for you."

He shook his head. "I can't have it. I have to be able to think."

Myrna regarded him soberly for a second, then set the syringe and the little bottle of morphine aside. "I'll send it with you. When you reach the point you need it, you can take it."

Mabrother Cho returned with a metal bowl of clean water. Genevieve had an extra lamp, which she arranged near Myrna's shoulder.

"Put the bowl there, and stay out of my way," Myrna said, directing Mabrother Cho. "You, too, Masister. No hovering."

Leon was slouched forward, elbows on the table, and when Myrna immersed his hand in the bowl, blood immediately began to seep into the warm water, turning it red.

"You're reported to have a great bedside manner, Masister," Leon said. "Where's that tonight?"

"That's only for patients I don't care about," Myrna said.

Yet when she began cleaning the wound, her touch was gentle and sure. He winced when she snipped away a dangling bit of torn skin and blotted at the blood with a cloth. Then she hitched the lamp nearer. "It's a clean amputation at least," she said.

"Glad you think so," Leon said. He refused to turn his mind back to how it had happened.

Myrna peered at it closely again, tilting her face as she inspected it from every angle, and then she folded Leon's undamaged fingers down into a fist, keeping his wounded one extended over a clean towel.

"Mabrother Cho," Myrna said. "I need you to hold his arm. Here."

Startled, Leon tensed as the chef pinned his forearm securely against the table.

"You don't want to watch this," Myrna said, tightening her grip around his finger.

Before Leon could argue, she took her hot scalpel from over the flame and pressed the flat side of it firmly against his raw fingertip, cauterizing the flesh with a sharp, sizzling noise. The sensation knocked Leon backward and he would have fallen except that Mabrother Cho kept his arm pinned to the table. A pungent, burning scent soured the air.

"Thank you," Myrna said curtly to Mabrother Cho. "You can let him go."

She set her scalpel aside.

"Are you done?" Leon asked, breathless with pain.

The doctor was frowning in concentration, examining his finger again. "Yes," she said. "With this at least. Let's see your back."

She released his hand. He curled his fingers slowly toward himself, scrutinizing the seared end of his finger. The burned tissue was damaged in a controlled, scarlet burn, the bleeding had stopped, and the skin at the edges had singed to a tender brown. His pulse was still hammering in his veins but the pain, oddly, was deadening a little, as if the nerves to his fingertip, which before had been ragged and shrill, now were short-circuited. The significance struck him for the first time: His wedding-ring finger had been deliberately stunted, as if he'd never make a fit husband.

"Ouch," he said softly.

"Change your mind yet about the morphine?" Myrna asked. "I could put you out for a couple hours." She put a light dressing on his finger to keep it clean.

"No." He glanced over at Genevieve, who had gone very pale. "You said he could change his mind?"

She hesitated, then nodded.

"Would he come down here?" Leon asked.

"I don't think so," Genevieve said.

Leon heard the uncertainty in her voice. "Can you get together some supplies for me?"

She nodded and slipped quietly out.

He'd been barely aware of his surroundings, but now he glanced around the great kitchen of the Bastion, with its rafters high above and a row of ovens near the open fireplace. A bowl of brown eggs was in a familiar place on the counter, and he remembered a blue ceramic teapot on a shelf by the window. How long it had been since he used to sneak down as a kid to visit the cook, he couldn't recall, but little of it had changed. Though most of the cooking equipment was tidily put away, four pie dishes on the counter were filled with unbaked crusts that draped gracefully over the edges, and he could

see a big bowl of apples had been sliced and sprinkled with cin-
namon. In fact, now that he looked more closely, he saw traces
of flour across the top of the wooden table, and Leon guessed
that Mabrother Cho had hastily moved things out of the way
to clear room for his unexpected guest.

"Pies?" Leon asked.

The cook gave a shrug. "I couldn't sleep."

"I'll need some food to take with me," Leon said.

"Where are you going?"

"Into the wasteland. Mycoprotein mainly would be good,
and some powdered baby formula," Leon added. "And whatever you have for canteens."

"You're going after the midwife? Do you know where she
was headed?" the cook asked.

Leon knew only that Gaia was heading north, and that she
had at least a four-day lead on him. Anxiety made him rest-
less.

"Here, hold still," Myrna said. "What's this?" She touched
the back of his head.

"I was hit there when they arrested me." He lowered his
head to rest on his folded arms, and she cleaned the tender lump
on the back of his skull.

"Have any headaches?" she asked.

"Not so bad now."

As the doctor turned to work on his back, he could feel her
cleaning the scabby wounds from his floggings and couldn't
help flinching. He tilted his face, staring blindly at the piecrusts,
and gritted his teeth. He searched mentally through his body
for one place of him that didn't hurt and settled on the big toe of

his right foot. Deep inside his black boot, under the table, that one part of him was okay and he concentrated on that.

Then, after the cleaning was finished, he felt the careful tugs at his back as she sewed the worst of his shredded skin.

"Is that necessary? I won't be able to reach to take the stitches out," Leon said.

"They'll dissolve by the time you heal," Myrna said.

The little snipping noises continued as she tied off the knots, and finally she set aside the curved needle and scissors on the towel in his line of vision. Mabrother Cho brought him a bowl of barley soup to drink. Leon couldn't relax, couldn't let down his guard against pain, but he swallowed the salty, steamy liquid and dipped a crust of the bread in the dregs to swab them up.

"More?" Mabrother Cho asked.

Leon nodded.

"Hold still," Myrna said again.

Next he could feel the doctor dabbing something on his back, a light, cool substance that pulled some of the pain away.

"That's good," he muttered.

She kept at it, working her way from the top, and in the path of her touch, he felt the merciful easing of pain across the back of his shoulders, toward the middle of his spine, and then outward.

"What is that you're putting on?" he asked.

"The sort of thing your girl would appreciate. It's mostly an antibiotic, but I added some tansy she told me about. That's what's soothing. I'll give you some of this to take with you, too."

"You called her 'my girl,'" he said, surprised.

"Isn't that why you're going after her?"

He shifted slightly. "Did she ever talk about me?" he asked.

"Not much," Myrna said. "She liked the orange. That was from you, wasn't it?"

"Yes," he said.

"I guessed as much."

He would have appreciated a little more to go on, but then, Gaia herself had never been particularly forthcoming. She was the most direct, fearless person he'd ever known, except where admitting her own feelings was concerned. At least, he hoped she had feelings for him. When she'd said that thing about respecting him, as if that was all she did, he'd been startled by how much it hurt, like a clean gouge right through him. Still, she'd gone on to let him kiss her, and that counted for something.

He wanted Gaia to trust him or, more exactly, he wanted to be a person that Gaia would trust, even if no one else ever trusted him. He wondered whether she realized he'd risked his life for her. Not that it mattered. He'd have done it anyway. But still, he wondered.

Why did he want so badly to be with her?

"Look at me," Myrna said, sitting down beside him on another stool. Her fingers were still smeared with the frothy, white salve.

He looked up doubtfully to meet her gaze. Myrna's shrewd eyes were devoid of sympathy, but he could see that didn't make her heartless.

"Don't ever blame Gaia for this," Myrna said.

"I don't."

"No. I mean later. Whether you ever find her or not. None of this was her fault."

"I know," he said. "It was my decision. I knew what could happen to me. I know what could happen to me in the wasteland, too."

Myrna rose to rinse her hands at the sink, leaving Leon to rest another minute. His one comfort was that he'd succeeded in helping Gaia escape. He could only believe she was surviving somewhere, somehow. A girl who could come out of prison stronger than she went in, who let hardships deepen her rather than rigidify her thinking, had to be able to handle the wasteland, and as long as she was alive, there was a chance he could find her.

Genevieve returned with an assortment of supplies and a rucksack. "You can't carry anything on your back, obviously," she said, "but is your neck all right? You could hang something around your neck, in front of you."

He lifted a hand to gingerly touch the nape of his neck, which was unscathed. "That'll work," he said.

"I think this will keep the sun and flies off your back without clinging," Genevieve added. She'd brought a loose, lightweight shirt and a bowed, oblong framework that he recognized from a kite kit his brother Rafael had owned once. She clipped the framework to the inside of the shirt collar so the material would drape loosely behind him, not touching his skin. The resulting contraption had a flimsiness he doubted, but she tested its spring with a tug, and it rebounded in a way that was flexible and durable enough to last, at least for a while.

"Feeling any better? That first dose of morphine should have kicked in," Myrna asked, taking the stool again.

He was.

The food was helping, too. Mabrother Cho handed him another bowl of soup and more bread. Then he set before Leon a saucer with a few of the cinnamon-and-sugar-coated apple slices. "You always liked these," he said.

Leon looked up, noting the cook's kindly expression.

"You know each other," Genevieve said, as if she were just figuring that out.

"More or less," Mabrother Cho said, smiling. "He used to sneak down here nights when he was little, now and again. Your boy here's made lots of friends I suspect you've never known about."

Leon reached for an apple slice and bit into the sweetness. "Not so many," Leon said.

"Enough that you'll be missed," Mabrother Cho said. "Don't be gone forever, Mabrother."

Leon didn't know what to say. He had no idea what he might find in the wasteland or if anything lay beyond it. It seemed unlikely he'd ever come back. He watched while his mother and Mabrother Cho packed food and supplies in the pack: mycoprotein, dried fruit, cheese, a little tea, flatbread, and a canister of baby formula. They added matches, a candle, flint and steel, a small pot, and a knife. Mabrother Cho filled four lightweight, metal canteens, capped them, and looped them to a sturdy belt.

How many supplies had Gaia taken? Leon wondered. How long could she last on what she could carry? And she had the baby, too. The thought made him impatient to leave.

"You want a blanket?" Genevieve asked. "It'll get cold at night when the sun goes down. I can pack it small."

"All right," he said.

"A hat," Myrna said.

"I have one here," Genevieve said, offering a beige one with a wide brim.

Myrna showed him where she was putting medical supplies in the outer pouch of his pack. "Your back will start to itch when it's healing," she said. "You won't win any prizes for enduring the pain. Use the morphine, and keep up with the antibiotics." She shook a small container. "Two pills a day until they're all gone. Promise me."

He lifted the bottle to eye the contents. "If I outlast them."

"Don't say that," Genevieve said.

He glanced across the table to her. His mother stood with her shoulders proudly straight, but he could see the fear and stress in her troubled gaze. He accepted her help with putting on the shirt, which billowed slightly behind him. Then he dipped his head into the strap of his pack, straightening to lift its weight and shift it to the most comfortable place along his chest.

Genevieve reached for the water belt and slung it over her shoulder. "I can take this as far as the wall for you."

He didn't argue with her. Donning his hat, he took a last glance down at the table with its bowl of reddish water, the dirty towel, and Myrna's tools. Myrna was regarding him gravely, but she held out a hand to shake his.

"Good luck," she said simply.

Mabrother Cho lifted a hand in silent farewell.

Strangely moved, Leon reached past the cook to snag a last slice of apple from the bowl. "Thanks," he said.

The cook gave a twisted smile. "Get going, then."

Leon followed Genevieve out the back door of the kitchen, past the rubbish barrels and the empty crates left from deliveries. The night was edging toward dawn, and Genevieve's white sweater was visible as muted gray over her slender form, sliced by the black of the belt and canteens over her shoulder. As they headed uphill, side by side through the dim, cobblestone streets, he watched warily for guards, still not trusting that he was safe with his mother. The open space of Summit Park was quiet except for a lone cricket, and from that elevation, the high point of the Enclave, he had a view out toward the wasteland, where the horizon was visible as a line of gray meeting with faint pink above. Vast seemed the wasteland, and trackless. Finding Gaia was going to be nearly impossible.

The alternative was staying in the Enclave and waiting for the moment his adoptive father decided to put an end to him once and for all.

They left the park and headed down the last curving streets. The occasional streetlights flickered on as they approached, triggered by sensors. At one corner, a mute camera was aimed at the intersection.

"He's watching us go, isn't he?" Leon asked.

"Yes," Genevieve said. "He'll paint you as a coward and a traitor, but you'll be safe. You'll be gone."

He glanced at her profile. "He can't be very happy with you," he said.

"I'm not very pleased with him, either," she said, and smiled. "Don't worry about me."

He considered that. "I will, though."

She laughed briefly. "Just so you know, Emily turned in the ledgers tonight. I just heard, when I was gathering your things."

"Did they give back her baby?"

"No. Miles advanced the baby. He thinks she had a copy of the birth records made. She had enough time."

Leon stared ahead to where the wall that surrounded the Enclave was coming into view. Gaia's friend Emily must be frantic about her advanced son, and she'd be helpless against the injustice of the Enclave. He was glad Gaia didn't know, for he was certain she would blame herself if she did.

"See what you can do about that," Leon said.

"I will. I'll try. But we also need to be sure our children are secure."

"It proves Gaia didn't take the ledgers with her," Leon said.

"I know."

"So will he call off the search for her?"

"That I don't know. She's still a criminal for stealing them in the first place," Genevieve said.

"Advancing the babies in the first place, though," he said dryly. "That doesn't count as theft?"

"You know it doesn't," Genevieve said. "That's completely different."

"Tell that to Emily."

"No, you think it over yourself," she said, "and imagine what your life would have been like if we hadn't raised you."

He laughed bitterly. "You can still say that, when my father has just had me tortured for four days?"

She paused, and he was compelled to turn beside her. "I'm not going to try to excuse him," she said. "But can we not argue about him? Just for now?"

He could make out her eyes enough to see how troubled she was. His feelings for her were confused by the bitterness he felt toward the Protectorat and her own complicity in his cruelty. On the other hand, she was likely the only one in the Enclave who had the power to save him from his father, at what personal cost to her own well-being, he couldn't guess. He couldn't stay hardened against his mother, not when they only had a few more minutes together.

"All right," he said.

"Thank you."

The North Gate, seldom used, was smaller than South Gate but it, too, was patrolled by the requisite guards. They nodded at Genevieve as if expecting her, and when they opened the tall wooden gate, Leon passed under the arch to the outside. He glanced behind him for the last time, at the quiet, treelined street and the lightless towers of the Bastion, just visible over the rise of the hill.

Before him, the hill sloped down toward an arid, windswept, shadowed landscape of boulders and stunted brush. His future. The cold uncertainty of it chilled him, and yet he did not look back again. The likelihood of finding Gaia's tracks was essentially nil. He could scan for movement by day, and at night it was possible a campfire would show to guide him to her, but probably his best chance was to head north, looking for civilization, and hope Gaia found the same place.

He briefly considered circling back to ask Emily what she knew of Gaia's departure, but it would be risky, and set him back several hours, and he already knew Gaia intended to head north for the Dead Forest. If it existed. Gaia believed it did.

I've done smarter things than this, he thought.

Wordlessly, he took the belt from Genevieve, settling it

around his waist so that the canteens rode to the sides where they wouldn't impede his stride.

"Here. One last thing," she said, and passed him an extra roll of socks. "For your feet," she added, as if he didn't know. "It's important to take care of your feet when you're going so far."

The ball was soft in his hand. "Mom," Leon said, strangely moved.

"I'm just so sorry about this. If there were any other way—"

He shook his head, and pulled her near to wrap his arms around her. She couldn't hug him back properly because of his wounded back, but she held tight to his collar and kissed his cheek.

"Please be safe," Genevieve said.

"I will. Give my love to Evelyn and Rafael," Leon said.

"Come back to us," she whispered.

There was no answer to that. For a last, long moment he held her, filling with sad tenderness, a kind of forgiveness and loss that normally would have made him feel weak. Instead, he felt human, honest. "I'll miss you," he said, and knew it was true, despite everything.

When he left his mother and started down the hill, he trod carefully in the shadowed space between boulders. He hitched once at the belt around his hips, tucked the socks in his pocket, and began his vigilant search for motion along the horizon. Somewhere ahead of him, Gaia was traveling with her baby sister. Whether what he was doing was stupidly reckless or nobly brave didn't much matter, because the only thing left to do was try to find her.

BLUE MOON

Nikki Kelly

BY NIKKI KELLY

~ The Styclar Saga ~

Lailah

Gabriel

Meet Nikki Kelly

I was born and raised only minutes away from the chocolaty scent of Cadbury World in Birmingham, England. So it will probably come as no surprise that, when I'm not dreaming in vampires and angels, I dream in chocolate. At age seventeen, I packed my bags and moved to London, and for ten years enjoyed a career as a personal assistant. I now write YA fantasy fiction full-time, and I live with my husband and my two gorgeous and equally naughty pups—Alfie (the pug) and Goose (the Chihuahua).

As a tween and a teen I spent hours and hours reading books and, when I wasn't doing that, I was busy writing my own short stories—usually involving animals and, of course, cute boys. I had a short story published at age twelve, and my dream was to one day write a novel and see it on a bookshelf. Initially, there was the first spark for what became *Lailah*, which emerged in the form of a dream I had one night. Now, to be fair, I had slightly overdosed on vampire-themed TV that week, so perhaps that's why I dreamt what I did. In my dream, there was a girl who was helping what was very obviously a vampire in a derelict shell of a building.

I remember the scene so vividly, even now: The girl never

came into focus; all I could see was her long blond hair streaming down her back while she aided the vampire, who was injured. But then, from nowhere, and somewhat like a horror film, she snapped her head over her shoulder and all I remember seeing were striking sapphire-blue eyes. As she blinked, they changed into a fierce red, and it startled me so violently that I woke up.

The nights that followed I continually found myself thinking about the girl and asking myself, *What is she?* It was shortly after that that I realized I was asking the wrong question. While the *what* was important, the far more imperative question was the *who. Who was this girl?* I decided to find out by telling her story. And so, I began to write . . .

One thing I was really set on doing was creating something original, and I wanted to give a rich and deep history behind the supernaturals of the story. While the journey is centered on Lailah, and she is the pivotal point, there is always something greater going on beyond her (as in our own lives), and so came the world-building. I wanted to ensure that all my supernaturals were as unique—and as different—as possible. For me, that stemmed from asking various questions: Where did they come from in the first place? When, and how, did they come to be here? And then the two most important questions (you might notice a theme here!): What are they and who are they? The final questions that needed answering were, of course, what motivates them all? What do they want?

In answering all of the above, and borrowing a little here and there from my own belief system, I was able to create new worlds and beings, but utilize existing belief or myth on which to base them. For example, the two worlds the beings emerged from were based on the concept of Heaven and Hell. I then spun that into something else entirely. I took the myths about vampires and angels, etc., and tried to demonstrate how, through storytelling and the game of telephone, the idea of what they are has become quite different from the truth—the truth of course being the reality of things in my books!

The setting of *Lailah* features some fantastic locations, including Ireland, Wales, England, and France. I like to write about places that I know well and, for those that I don't but want to include, I will visit them to get a sense of the place and the people firsthand.

About half of the book is based around the Carcassonne area in the south of France, ranging from a small village called Neylis, where Lailah resides for some time, and branching out to various other locations, such as Mirepoix and Limoux. I am very lucky that my auntie Gill and uncle Ken retired to Neylis a few years ago, because they hosted me for various weekly visits so that I could both conduct research and write in their beautiful garden. My uncle is fantastic, and he loves the history of the towns, villages, architecture, and art. He took me on countless day trips and excursions, and when we weren't doing that, he was keeping me well fed and watered.

Towards the end of the novel, the Pyrenees Mountains—which sit behind the barn conversion that Lailah stays in—become a setting. Having spouted all my talk of making sure I saw everything with my own two eyes, my auntie and uncle insisted that we go to the exact spot, high within the mountains, where I wanted to set the final scenes. Great, I thought, until they explained to me that you could only travel so far by car and then it was a further two-and-a-half-hour hike up the steep mountain through the forested tree line! Yeah, not so great. Used to spending most of my time behind my writing desk, with a teapot and an endless supply of cookies, and as someone who denies that exercise is important, you can imagine my horror at the thought of such a climb. But I conceded. I'm not the type of writer to put my characters through something that I wouldn't myself be prepared to do or face (I say this with reasonable limits, as it is a fantasy after all!), and so I agreed—albeit with much fear. The trip was planned for the final day of my visit, but due to freak weather conditions on the day, it wasn't safe enough to do the climb up Monts d'Olmes. (Phew! Dodged a bullet there.) In the end, I drew from photographs my auntie and uncle had taken on their last climb, which was probably for the best—I really did think that I might not return.

My journey to becoming a fully fledged published author, I think, is a good representation of the modern and connected world we now live in. After writing *Lailah,* I soon discovered Wattpad—a community for readers and writers. I serialized the novel, and within six months, *Lailah* had garnered over one million reads and thousands of comments and votes. There was some press around the success of the story, which happened to be seen by just the right person, at just the right time. I was approached by the assistant editor at Feiwel and Friends and was asked to send over my manuscript. Three weeks later, I received an e-mail from the editor-in-chief, offering all three books in the saga a traditional publishing deal. In just one e-mail, the dream I had worked so hard to realize had become a reality.

What you'll read here is a story called *Blue Moon,* a mini-prequel to book 1 of The Styclar Saga, *Lailah.* The story unfolds a few nights before the opening of *Lailah*. The story is told from Lailah's perspective, and I think the most exciting element is the introduction of Darwin, a young gentleman from Chelsea, who is not featured in *Lailah*; instead, we meet him in the second book, *Gabriel*. He's a super-important character who will play a pivotal role in the final book of the trilogy, so I was delighted to be able to show Lailah and Darwin's first encounter by writing this short story.

BLUE MOON

by Nikki Kelly

The moon is so beautiful. It's a big silver dollar, flipped by God.
And it landed scarred side up, see? So He made the world.

—Two-Face
Arkham Asylum: A Serious House on Serious Earth

THE WATER RIPPLED AROUND HIM AS HE SANK
TO THE CENTER OF THE PLACID LAKE. The shining
blue moon acted as a button, bringing together the night's navy
sky and the undulating water.

As the blond-haired boy released the buckle that held together his shirt, his movements pulled the seam that stitched
the two worlds together.

He hesitated before tugging away his shirt, peering up at
the fair-haired girl who watched him at the shore. A wondrous
smile crept up his cheeks, causing his dimples to deepen and
his iridescent eyes to beam.

The girl rested her palm flat against an aging yew tree, as she carefully slid off her shoes. Then she tiptoed barefoot over the yew's curling roots. She swept her long braid over her shoulder and nervously placed her fingers on the Juliet sleeves of her white muslin dress. She paused, and the boy slid his arms from the soaked shirt, letting it drift behind him. He nodded encouragingly, treading water while he waited.

The girl blushed at the sight of his exposed shoulders. She took a deep breath and then pulled her full-length gown up and over her head. She giggled nervously as she discarded it on the grass. Her tight cotton corset overlapped her petticoat and she shifted uncomfortably within her undergarments as she dipped her toe into the icy water.

The boy tucked his loose blond curls behind his ears and then extended his hand to her.

She hesitated; the water was cold. He swam to her, grasped her hips, and drew her close.

Bobbing backward, he carried her to the middle of the lake. She tilted her head back and peered up at the dusting of gold sequins in the sky. When she finally met the boy's shining eyes, she blinked hard, unable to distinguish the difference between them and the stars.

He was a miracle.

He pressed his hand to the back of the girl's neck, bringing the tip of his nose to her cheek, where he lingered. He affectionately ran his hand down her nape, and she flinched when his arm brushed her bare shoulder blade. She bowed her head and held her breath as the boy drifted behind her and unlaced her corset.

She exhaled when he tugged the last of the ribbon free and

pulled the corset from around her body. Two welts branched out from between her shoulder blades, dry blood clotted down the marks. The boy's pupils dilated in surprise, and his lips strained in a tight angry line, but then his expression fleeted to one of concern.

Careful not to touch her skin, he found her braid and unfurled the plait. Her hair dropped to the surface of the crystal water, before she gathered it to cover herself. The boy spread his palm wide across her belly, easing her backward, and she began to float.

As the girl's lash marks became submerged in the chill, she jolted . . .

✑

I SAT BOLT UPRIGHT, the cocoon of my sleeping bag falling down to my waist. I automatically reached for the top of my back, squeezing the skin painfully between the tips of my fingers. I panted, trying to catch myself, as I returned from the depths of a dream.

Tears pricked my eyes, and I realized I must have cried as the wounds had stung in the water that night. Now the tears gushed out of frustration, not pain.

Dreams were supposed to be the mind's way of busying itself. But, like everything else in my troubled existence, I didn't believe that was true for me. My dreams, my visions felt real. He felt real.

I allowed my eyes to flutter closed once more, hoping to see his face again. I didn't entirely understand the dream, but I preferred to linger there rather than face my present reality.

The alarm I'd set on my cell buzzed, and I smacked it in an

attempt to stop the piercing siren. I quickly checked the time; it was almost five o'clock and I had a shift at the pub in an hour.

I glanced around the living room, but it was hard to see; the fire had gone out while I slept. I had no electricity. So despite my lack of inclination to get up, I did.

I used my cell phone as a flashlight and freshened up as best as I could, using the last of the water that I had collected in a bucket from the stream that ran through the back of the property. I rooted around in my backpack, pulling out a plain T-shirt and jeans. I made a feeble attempt to brush out my long, matted hair, realizing it desperately needed washing, but I was out of shampoo. I searched the bag and found the small bottle of talcum powder. Shaking the last of it out, I massaged it into my scalp. When you have next to nothing, you learn to get by.

I was sliding my old, beaten Nokia into my back pocket when I heard the creak of a floorboard. I twisted to face the doorframe, panic hitting me quickly. Despite it being a decrepit, derelict building that no sane person would want to reside in, it had provided me with shelter and I was most grateful for it. But I was squatting, and that was illegal. What worried me most about being discovered was having nowhere else to go in the middle of a bitter British winter.

"Hello?" I ventured in a mousy voice.

The noise stopped abruptly.

"Hello?" I tried again. When no reply came, I strode cautiously to the doorframe, and squinted into the diminishing daylight, trying to see who was there.

The hallway was empty.

I wiggled my nose as I considered that the property was very old, and it did have a tendency to make old-house sounds;

on windy nights it practically howled as the air thundered through it.

I decided to pack up the few bits and pieces I possessed, tidying them away into the broken storage cupboard underneath the stairs before I left, just in case.

ℰℴ

I MEANDERED DOWN THE UNLIT, winding road to the pub, hurrying as the last of the daylight dwindled. I stayed as near to the forest line as possible, though cars seldom passed by.

The tall trees swayed overhead as gusts of wind bobbed and weaved through bare branches, almost sounding like whistling panpipes. As I rounded the corner, I stopped briefly to rub away the chill that nipped at my ears. The wind dropped suddenly as though time had stopped; the forest around me became still.

Just like the trees, I paused.

I glanced to the woods, a tingling sensation running up my spine as though I were being watched. But if there was someone, something, following me, then it was staying well hidden.

I was about to look over my shoulder, but my attention shifted as my crystal ring, which was threaded through the chain around my neck, grew warmer against my skin. I placed my palm under my jacket and it felt cool; I thought for a moment that I might have imagined it.

I glanced to the woods as if they might provide me with some sort of answer, but they only ever kept secrets. We were alike, the trees and I: many years older than we appeared.

The girl in shadow came to my mind quickly—she was a mystery. A girl who appeared when I was faced with terrible trouble, but then simply disappeared. She blended into the night; I had never seen her face. I had no idea why she would be spying on me, but she was the only person that I could think of who conceivably might.

I hurried on to the pub, relieved to finally see it ahead. Inside, I scanned the tables and bar stools, but as usual, it was pretty quiet. Only a few of the locals sat clutching their pint glasses and looking up at the flatscreen, where a roundup of the day's rugby match had captured their interest.

"Francesca, good, you're early. You can restock the crisps," Dwyn shouted at me from over the bar.

I took my arms from my jacket, hanging it on a hook behind the bar, and rubbed my arms, trying to warm up. Haydon appeared from the back and, seeing me, pulled a tight smile and said, "Pour yourself a whiskey, you're bright red." He walked over to his wife and kissed her on the neck, ogling her cleavage in the process. Dwyn batted him away playfully, but I didn't miss the revulsion that showed with the roll of her top lip as she repositioned her expensive necklaces and jiggled her gold bangles lower on her wrists. I did as I was told, and sipped the spirit.

"Be sure to put it on your tab, I'll take it out of your pay," Haydon added, turning to me and giving me the once-over with a raised eyebrow. "You know, you'd get better tips if you dressed more like Dwyn. Something to think about?" He slapped his wife's bottom hard as he strode back to his office.

Dwyn lifted up a box of crisps and thrust it into my arms. "He's a pig, of course, but he's not wrong. You could make a little more effort when you're behind the bar; you never know who might walk through those doors. And believe me, the

Haydons of this world expect a little more." She puckered her lips together, evening out her bright pink lip gloss as she fingered her permed hair that, to my mind, resembled more of a crow's nest.

"I'm not searching for a Haydon," I said coldly, placing the box at my feet and pulling back the packing tape.

Dwyn bent down to face me, her eyes narrowing. "Perhaps you're better suited to sweeping the floors than being swept off your feet. And if that starts to feel too much like hard work, don't you forget that Haydon belongs to me, missy."

I waited for her to turn before I rolled my eyes. If I wanted to eat, I needed to keep this job.

⸎

I'D BEEN PULLING PINTS FOR SEVERAL HOURS, making idle chitchat with Mr. Broderick, one of the regulars, when the doors swung open and a group of young men loudly entered the pub. I glanced at them as I ran a tea towel over the countertop. There were four of them in total, and one was wearing a bright red rugby shirt with the letters CYMRU stamped in white across the front. They didn't resemble the average rugby supporters, though, with their expensive-looking blazers and designer jeans. Two of the guys sank into the fading cushions of the sofa along the back wall, while another pulled out a chair on the opposite side of the table, and they began talking amongst themselves. The fourth guy made his way over to me at the bar.

"Evening," he said, smiling. He perched on one of the tall stools and removed his unusual retro orange eyeglasses, placing them down in front of him.

"What can I get you?" I asked, throwing the damp rag over my shoulder and kicking the empty crisp box out of the way of my feet.

The guy's eyes slanted to his left, assessing a pint I had just pulled in the hands of another customer. Seeing that it was all mostly froth, he looked over my shoulder to the fridges behind me. "Bottled beer, three, if you would be so kind. And a water for me, I'm driving," he said.

"Any particular brand?" I asked, stepping backward and opening the fridge door, acting on autopilot.

"Buds will do fine," he replied politely. I couldn't help but notice that he was extremely well spoken, with an upmarket London accent, and I wondered for the briefest moment what he and his friends were doing in Creigiau—a tiny Welsh village in the back of beyond. But it was a fleeting thought; it neither mattered nor made any difference to me.

An uncomfortable silence drifted between us. I thought then that perhaps he was expecting me to make polite conversation with him, so I obliged. "What brings you here?" I popped the bottle caps off one by one.

"I have some business to see to near Dublin. A few of my old Eton buddies thought we could make a weekend of it, and stop in on the rugby game en route. Will, over there—" He stopped, turned round, and nudged his chin up. His friend raised his eyebrows in reply. "He was born in Cardiff. He seems to think that makes him Welsh, even though he's lived in Chelsea all his life." The guy smirked, straightening his dark green tweed jacket, the color of which complemented his jade-green eyes.

"Right . . . so what, this is a pit stop on route to Holyhead?"

I asked, throwing the caps into the bin, not bothering to make any eye contact.

"In a manner of speaking. The Range broke down. I've called for assistance, but it's freezing out, so we thought we'd have a tipple instead of waiting in the car. Can't say how long they will be."

I couldn't help raising my eyebrows; I doubted he really knew what freezing, real cold, felt like. I scooped a tray from underneath the till and proceeded to place the bottles on top.

"Would you like glasses?" I asked.

He nodded, and then reached into his back pocket, producing a wallet, and offered me a black credit card. "Run a tab for me, if you wouldn't mind, and charge it at the end."

I reached for it, my face still bowed down. But he didn't release the card immediately, which forced me to look up and meet his eye. "My name's Darwin. It's a pleasure to meet you . . . ?"

"Francesca."

"Pretty name. Do your friends call you Fran?" he inquired, loosening his grip around the plastic.

My shoulders slumped as I tucked his credit card away and I said, "No, not exactly. I've been called . . . Cessie." I struggled to take a breath as I said it, my mind immediately fleeting to Frederic; he was the last friend I'd had who'd called me by my nickname. The very same friend who had tried to kill me.

I chewed my lip and furrowed my brow. Darwin offered me a reassuring smile, as though he somehow knew that I had suffered, that I was suffering still.

I was aware that I appeared detached; I preferred it that way.

If I let people in, they couldn't or wouldn't be able to stay. My existence was between reality and dream; I drifted through life, a silent observer. I let the noise of the living echo around me, but never allowed it to touch my skin.

I gathered myself quickly and stepped unsteadily from behind the bar.

"Let me help you with that?" Darwin called as I scuttled ahead of him, but his offer was a little too late. As I tried to balance the tray against my waist, I realized that I hadn't evenly distributed the weight, and the glasses began to clatter together. Darwin's bottled water went over first, soaking me through as it spilled down my chest. I jerked backward, and then two of the glasses tumbled, hitting the floor and shattering.

Darwin hurried to my side, took the tray from my hands, and placed it on the table in front of his friends as they howled with laughter. "Ah well, never mind . . . she looks in need of a bath anyhow," the dark-haired guy jeered, and I cringed in embarrassment.

"I told you, Welsh girls—filthy little devils, in every way. Maybe you should slum it with her for a night, then you'll know what I mean," Will joined in as though I weren't there, and my cheeks grew hot.

"Will!" Darwin barked.

"I'm sorry," I said, turning to Darwin. "I'll fetch you another water, and new glasses." I stumbled away, pinching my wet top from my skin.

"Cessie—"

I ignored Darwin, as I bumped into Dwyn, who had reappeared at the commotion. She saw the mess I was in, but then that was nothing new—I had barely made any money the first week I had worked here, with all the deductions from the glasses I'd smashed.

"Really!" she wailed at me. Then she noticed the group of guys staring after me from across the room and she broke into a wide smile. "Francesca, go to my room. There's some fresh laundry at the end of the bed, help yourself to a shirt. I'll take care of these gentlemen." Her pitch leveled out, as she made her way over to Darwin and his friends.

I made my way through the hall and up the stairs to Dwyn's bedroom. Opening the door, Haydon was sitting half naked, perched on the side of the double bed. I realized then why I hadn't seen either of them for a little while.

"Sorry, I just came to borrow a top . . ." I trailed off, averting my eyes and grabbing the first garment my fingers could find.

"Spilled a drink again?" he asked smoothly.

I glanced up as he proceeded to pull a cigarette out of a packet using his lips, while he reached for his lighter resting on the bedside table. "Yes, sorry," I said, shuffling back toward the door.

The end of his cigarette glowed orange and he puffed, blowing the smoke from his nose and out the corner of his mouth. "You can change in here, you know. I don't mind."

I bit my tongue; I needed this job too much to be sacked from it. Haydon paid me in cash, and I was pretty sure he knew I was lying about my age.

"I need to dry off first," I replied, trying not to let the disdain show through my voice.

Haydon merely shrugged, flipping his feet up onto the bed,

he propped himself up against the pillows. Holding his cigarette in his lips, he scraped his fingers through his thinning hair, and reached for a newspaper.

I ducked into the bathroom and changed quickly, frowning as I slid Dwyn's tight-fitting V-neck shirt over my curves. Not only was the top cut a little too low for my liking, but it also had an open back, which would show my scar. But I didn't have much choice; I had no desire to go back into the bedroom to search for something else to wear.

I tucked my ring under the delicate material and I made my way to the bar.

When I returned it was a little busier, and a frosty wind was traveling in through the side door, which the smokers had left ajar while they sat in the gardens. I immediately began serving another customer, who seemed disgruntled that he'd had to wait; he pawed at his wiry beard as I pulled his pint, grumbling underneath his breath. My eye wandered over to Dwyn, who was busy flirting at the guys' table. Darwin looked over his shoulder, locking eyes with me. He smoothed his dark blond hair, tying the top into a small elastic, above the short back and sides, and scraped his chair as he stood up. I opened the till, plinking in the coins, before sliding it closed.

"I should apologize on behalf of Will, and what he said before—that's no way to speak to a lady. And you are a lady." Darwin's calming voice traveled over to me.

I hesitated before replying. "Did you want another drink?" I asked, staring at the floor and pretending to shuffle something under the counter.

"I'm quite fine for now, thank you."

He didn't move, and I wondered what he wanted. "Did you come over just to apologize on behalf of your overprivileged, obnoxious friend?" I asked a little too sharply.

"Well, yes, and I left my glasses." He put the bright orange specs over the bridge of his nose. Still he didn't leave. I turned to another customer, who was leaning up against the bar next to Darwin, and took his order.

I finished serving and began tidying the glasses behind me, once again trying to avoid any eye contact with Darwin, who was still hovering. He cursed lightly under his breath, and I realized that he could see the bare skin of my back. I swiveled around too quickly, and I almost lost my footing.

"Cessie, are you okay?" he asked as if he'd known me all my life.

"Yes. Thank you." I kneaded my lower back with my fingertips, thinking that maybe, if I rubbed hard enough, I could erase the terrible mark Frederic had left on me.

"So, what business do you have in Ireland?" I asked, trying to change the subject. He was clearly in no hurry to leave, and I didn't want to talk to a stranger about my scar.

"There's some unusual activity in a town not far from Dublin. I'm heading over to analyze what I can."

"Unusual activity? What do you do exactly? For a living, I mean?" I ventured.

"I'm a scientist and a fully fledged geek. I just graduated from MIT. Right now, my focus of study is all related to dark matter, particles . . . I spend my life dreaming about the stuff that makes up the universe." He stopped and then, quoting Shakespeare, added, " 'Such stuff as dreams are made on.' " He pushed his glasses farther up the bridge of his nose.

"You don't look, or sound, much like a geek," I said.

"Oh, really?" He grinned. "And what do you think defines a geek?"

"I guess I'm not sure, really. Here." I reached into the fridge and offered him a bottle of water, which he took. Now I was feeling slightly bad about how quickly I had made assumptions of him, based purely on his clothing and his accent. It made me no better than his friends.

"In science, you only need to scratch the surface of something, to reveal the elements that make up what's beneath it. The same can be said for people." Darwin proceeded to unbutton his tweed coat, and then unzipped the lining beneath it. He yanked the two lapels apart dramatically and said, "See!" He was wearing a Comic Con T-shirt.

"Ah," I said. "See, I would never have guessed." I offered him a small smile.

"Well, I wear two faces. A gentleman in constant conflict, you might say. Maybe I feel like I want to reveal my hidden identity to you, so you'll offer me yours."

I scratched my cheek, unsure of the reason he was showing an interest in me. And while I was in no position to share any details about my past, for it was one I didn't understand, I also wasn't about to reveal what I did know of my peculiar present, either.

"Conflict?" I backtracked, again diverting the conversation away from me.

"Nature versus nurture. Nurture being all the influences from the environments I have been privileged enough to be placed in. And of course, nature being my moral fiber, what's bred into me," he explained.

"Yes, I do understand the concept." I drummed my nails on the bar top.

"Well, my nature is the product of an affluent man, driven by money, status, and family." He paused. "But I am also a free-minded geek who devotes himself to uncovering the mysteries of the universe."

"So what—preppy and posh on the surface, mad scientist who perhaps dreams of becoming a superhero underneath?"

"Not quite. Theoretical physicist, emphasis on theoretical. I let others do the practical implementation, I just set the wheels in motion and then stand back and watch. Sadly, I am but a mere mortal, capable of the very best and the very worst of my own humanity. And there's not a lot I can do about the preppy-and-posh part, as you put it. So, tell me, what's going on below your hard exterior?" He unscrewed the cap of his bottle and took a swig of water.

I fidgeted uncomfortably. Darwin had asked the very question that I myself was searching for the answers to. "I didn't realize I came off as hard," I said.

I caught sight of Mr. Broderick loitering at the other end of the bar, and so I seized the opportunity. Excusing myself from Darwin I made my way over to our best customer. I poured Mr. Broderick a pint and as I mopped up the spilled fizz from the countertop, I peered at Darwin, who had followed me down the length of the bar. He placed his water down and, once again, eyed me as though he were trying to strip away my layers to see what my insides were really made of.

"I don't mean to keep you from your friends." This was my way of asking politely why he was still here.

"You're not. Besides, I far prefer your company to Betty Boop's over there. She's quite scary."

Unable to stifle a laugh, I let a small snort escape. As wisps of blond hair fell into my eyes, and I reached to push them away, Darwin's fingers met mine. He reached over the bar and twirled the hair around his fingers, tucking the messy strands behind my ears. "Your smile is very lovely, you know. You should let yourself laugh more often," he said. His hand grazed my cheekbone. "You're avoiding all my questions. Despite my best efforts, all I know is your first name. Your eyes give nothing away, they are . . . absent." His words sounded almost caring when he said, "What did you lose?"

A lump began forming in my throat.

Darwin's hand moved under my chin, where he tipped it up. "Maybe I'm asking the wrong question." He paused, stroking his thumb against my skin. "Who did you lose?"

I blinked rapidly. My body stiffened. I placed my hand over his arm, but instead of batting him away as I had intended, I found myself gripping it tightly. Finally, I whispered, "I don't know anymore."

He sat back and nodded thoughtfully, as though I had answered in some profound manner, gifting him with a surprise add-on to the puzzle he was trying to solve.

A chill spread over my arms, and the rattle of the side door sounded as it met the exposed brick wall. I felt a pinprick of heat on my chest—my gem sparked. I reached for it, sliding my hand below Dwyn's top, pressing my palm to its edges.

"Did your necklace just . . . glow?" Darwin asked, startled.

I ignored him, my gaze fleeting down the corridor, where

I caught a glimpse of long hair whipping behind a woman's back as she left. I sprinted toward the door, and it swung closed as I reached it, slowing me down. I yanked it open and propelled myself onto the grass, scanning the area. For the second time this evening, a strange sensation crept over my skin. I turned suddenly—I thought I saw something, but it disappeared into a shadow, melting into the darkness of the night.

My thoughts instantly turned to the girl in shadow, but as quickly as I thought it, I tried to unthink it. Maybe the sounds in the hallway had just been house sounds, maybe no one was spying on me in the woods, and perhaps whoever just left the pub had nothing to do with me whatsoever. I hoped that was the case. Given the nature of my existence—knowing that I was able to die, but that I would wake up again, that I was some weird, immortal freak of nature was one thing—I didn't want to add schizophrenia to my long list of crazy.

I ground my teeth together, perplexed, and marched back to the bar, where Darwin was waiting for me. "Everything quite all right?"

"Uh-um," I replied.

Darwin leaned back over the countertop, eyeing the gem around my neck with a look of avid curiosity. To my relief the crystal had reverted back to cool against my skin, and oddly it made me feel more assured that I hadn't imagined it before.

"May I ask how you came into possession of that crystal?" Darwin's gaze remained steadfast.

Protectively, I tucked it back into my top, another question I was not going to answer—yet something else I didn't even have an answer for.

Darwin's cell phone started to ring loudly, breaking his

concentration—a well-timed distraction. He slid off the tall stool and answered the call.

"Two more hours," he said as he hung up. "They're busy tonight, it seems, rugby fans on route home from Millennium Stadium. I don't think we'll make the last ferry, after all," he informed me.

"What's wrong with your car?" I inquired.

"Can't say I know. It just stopped." He shrugged. "I'm a physicist, not a mechanic."

"Why don't I take a look?" I offered, walking around the bar.

"You know your way around an engine?"

"I worked in a garage, once—picked up a few things." I was about to call over to Dwyn, but Haydon stumbled through from the back shouting to her first, clearly annoyed at seeing his missus being overly tactile with one of Darwin's group.

"Oi! Dwyn! Get yer arse back over to the bar!" He turned his attention to me and said, "Where are you going?"

"I hope you don't mind, sir. I just need a moment of your bar staff's time." Darwin placed his hand on my lower back and extended his hand in front of him, guiding me forward. "You can charge me appropriately for her time—my Amex is behind the bar."

Dwyn's brow dipped as I walked past her toward the door, but she didn't watch me for long. Haydon was hollering for her again and she scuttled off, tutting as she went.

Darwin's truck had broken down directly in front of the pub.

"A spot of luck that it conked right outside where there happens to be a girl who knows a little something about cars serving this evening," I said.

Darwin placed his hand inside his jacket pocket, checking for his keys, I assumed, but he didn't produce them. "No such thing as luck. Men make their own—or rather they take advantage when they see an opportunity," he replied.

"Well, you didn't see an opportunity with me—I had to reveal. But I guess I did offer you something to take advantage of."

Darwin observed me shivering and said, "Yes, and rather to your own detriment—look where it got you. You're now standing in the dark, dead cold." He quickly unfastened his checked coat and placed it around my shoulders. I grasped the wool together, snuggling my nose deep into the collar. An exotic, musky scent met me, and I flinched. It reminded me of the way Frederic had smelled.

As we approached, the locks automatically released, and Darwin opened the door. He bent over, pressing a button underneath the steering wheel to pop the hood.

"Turn the key in the ignition, get her started," I said, eyeing the expensive wooden dash, and the cream leather seats.

"That's the problem, it won't start up again." Darwin slid a square card from his pocket and placed it into a slot. Nothing happened.

"Hmmm." I walked over to the hood and gently lifted it, where it hovered without the need for the use of a stick to hold it in place. "Might just be your battery. Did you try pumping the gas pedal before trying to start it? Could it just be the cold?" I said.

"Yes, I tried that. No joy," he said, making his way around to my side.

I crossed my arms, thinking, as I looked over the inner

workings of the engine. "Did you hear a sort of clicking sound when you tried to start it before?"

"Yes, actually. And the headlights came on and the radio played, so all signs point to the starter, correct?" He actually sounded quite proud that he knew what a starter was.

I leaned over to have a quick peek at the battery. "Not necessarily. That sound you heard is probably the solenoid within your starter, which means it's likely just a case of your battery not transmitting enough voltage, that's all," I said, jiggling some of the cables.

Darwin's phone beeped, and he excused himself, turning around to check the message. I didn't need to ask in order to know that it was likely one of his friends back in the bar, asking what on earth he was doing outside with the likes of me.

I placed my fingers to the negative and positive terminals of the battery, checking for any sign of corrosion. I wiggled the two round caps; it probably just needed a jump start. Suddenly, a weird feeling—a pulse almost—exerted from my palms. The headlights flipped on, producing a blinding full beam, and I stumbled back from the truck as the engine kicked in, growling angrily.

Darwin spun around, his hand falling down to his side, as he looked at me with a curious expression. He shook his head. "What did you do?"

I honestly didn't know. I quickly convinced myself that I'd done nothing; The engine had kicked in all by itself, perhaps a delayed response to Darwin's key card. "I didn't do anything. It must have warmed up on its own." I smeared the grease from my hands, down the top of my jeans.

Darwin looked from me to his truck, and then hesitantly lowered the hood.

"I guess you can leave now." I shrugged off his jacket and passed it to him. I cupped my hands together and blew into the center.

Darwin hesitated for a moment, then placed his hands over mine, and rubbed them gently, creating additional friction. He looked to the night sky and then finally to me. "Your eyes are like the moon, you know."

I gazed up at the sky. A bright half-moon shone down. I squeezed a sad smile, remembering the dream, and knowing that the moon would never appear full again. It would always be cast in a shadow of secret, until I found the blond-haired boy. I wondered whether Darwin saw a half-moon, or whether he was able to see what the sun tried to hide in the dark—could he see the moon's true fullness, even if it didn't reveal itself?

"I knew someone like you, once," he said quietly. "She had the same look in her eyes that I saw in yours tonight."

I listened, hearing the slight warble in his voice, and I knew it was not born from the cold breeze. "Who you lost?" I whispered.

"Yes. The words she wouldn't speak, the things she found herself unable to say. I should have heard them through her eyes. I wasn't listening." He moved his hands to the tops of my arms, and squeezed, as though he were comforting me the way he wished he had comforted her.

I felt a stab of pain on Darwin's behalf, but it didn't seem right to satisfy my own curiosity by asking him questions, when I was unprepared to answer any of his.

"Life goes on, and I understand, memories fade. Whomever it is that you are struggling to remember, I am not offering to replace them. I'm looking in your eyes and I'm listening, Cessie. I think you need a friend."

I half wondered if Will had bet Darwin to hit on me or something. I think, somehow, I would have preferred that to be the case. The word *friendship* was now something that filled me with a sense of dread.

Frederic had been my friend, but in the end I had fallen victim to the hate he had hidden from my view. I distanced myself from others, favoring dreams of the blond-haired boy as my company, even if they reminded me how alone I was now.

"I will drive back through here on Sunday night. Will you be working?" Darwin asked, breaking my train of thought.

"Yes," I answered. "But you should take the M40 from Holyhead straight back to London. You'd be coming out of your way to stop here."

"It's not out of my way if I am picking you up. I'd like you to come to Chelsea with me," he said.

I took a step back from him. "Why?"

"We'll figure that bit out. I didn't help her, but I can try to help you, Cessie."

I wasn't sure what to say. I didn't trust easily, I barely knew Darwin, and I had no clue as to what his idea of help meant.

No.

I shook my head. "Thank you, but I'm fine, really." Holding my elbows with my hands, I offered him a sincere and grateful smile. I stepped up onto the pavement, and began to stroll back up the slope.

Darwin shouted after me. "Please, just consider it."

"I'll tell your friends that you're ready to leave. I'll give them your credit card," I called behind me.

As I neared the doors, Dwyn's shrill voice invaded my thoughts. She was arguing loudly with Haydon, and in front of the customers no less. My chest fell, knowing that whatever Darwin was offering, it had to be better than this. I hesitated for the briefest moment.

It didn't go unnoticed.

"Think it over, Cessie, and I'll see you on Sunday," he shouted. "You'll definitely be here?"

I stopped.

Slowly, I turned back to him and with a frayed tone I replied, "Yes, Darwin, I'll be here." I bowed my head as my shoulders sank, but then as I thought of his name—*Gabriel*—I found my gaze sweeping up toward the moon instead. "Unless of course, a miracle occurs . . ." I paused, and smiled. "'Such stuff as dreams are made on.' But the kind that only happens once in a blue moon."

The Cypress Project

Gennifer Albin

BY GENNIFER ALBIN

~ The Crewel World Trilogy ~

Crewel

Altered

Unraveled

Meet Gennifer Albin

My debut novel, *Crewel*, the first in a trilogy, focuses on a group of talented girls who can manipulate the fabric of reality. The idea for the novel was inspired by a painting called *Embroidering the Earth's Mantle* by Remedios Varo. In the painting, girls sit in a tower embroidering fabric that flows out the tower windows and becomes the world. If you look closely at it, one of the girls is watching the audience as she embroiders herself into the fabric—and by doing so, into the world. It's a pretty awe-inspiring piece. One day I was thinking about it and I sat down and wrote the prologue to *Crewel*. From there I had to figure out a lot of about how this world came to be. It would have been easy to make it magical, but I like to do things the hard way, so I chose to give it a science-fiction backdrop. The novel came together for me when I realized that our own history could be twisted to create the world of Arras. Inspired by Albert Einstein's regret regarding his role in creating the atomic bomb, I asked myself what if the scientists had chosen a different option. That's when I realized the history of the Looms.

Set in World War II America, "The Cypress Project" offers an insight into exactly where our reality and the Crewel World diverged. It was also an excellent chance to write science fiction with a historical backdrop. Sprinkled throughout the story you'll find references to people, places, and events from the 1940s. And, yes, Marlene Dietrich really was the first woman to wear pants into the exclusive Beverly Hills Hotel.

Of course, look closely and you'll also find plenty of subtle references to the people and places of Arras. If you've read all the Crewel World books, you might discover a few familiar characters as well.

Before I wrote *Crewel*, I earned my master's in eighteenth-century literature and women's studies from the University of Missouri. As it turned out there's not much of a job market for people who can tell you all about the history of the novel. So, as a recovering academic stuck at home with a new baby, I turned to writing my own books. It turns out that it's a lot more fun to make up stories than to write long research papers dissecting them.

I always considered being a writer, but usually found myself lured by other possibilities. For a long time I wanted to be an actress. In college an English degree seemed, inexplicably, like a more solid option than a theater degree. Now I understand that at my core I just love stories. I love to watch them, read them, and write them. I'm very fortunate to have the opportunity to spend my day in other worlds with strange characters caught in remarkable circumstances. Now that is a job anybody would love to have, and it's mine.

In my free time I sit on the National Novel Writing Month Advisory Board and watch too much *Doctor Who* (if that's possible). I'm currently at work on a new young-adult series that bridges my love of adventure with my obsession with conspiracy. It's completely different, apart from also having a feisty heroine, and lots of fun.

THE CYPRESS PROJECT

by Gennifer Albin

Marion, Illinois

The air was heavy and thick, drawing beads of sweat from Lucy's forehead and neck as she fought against her victory garden. Weeds choked the turnips and she tore at them, determined not to lose a single precious plant. She and Mother were terrible gardeners, but if there was going to be enough food on the table for the two of them, they would have to make it work.

Lucy's heart sped up as a figure came into focus. She didn't dare look past the crisp ironed slacks and recently shined boots, both standard military issue, even as the messenger knocked on her front door.

She hesitated, remaining hidden among the tomato vines. Whatever news the man had brought couldn't be undone by ignoring him. There was nothing for it but to be bold. Lucy pushed to her feet, wiping her dirty palms against the jeans she'd stolen from Nicholas's room and brushing loose hair back under the handkerchief wrapped around her head.

"Hello," she called out.

"Mrs. Price?" the messenger asked.

She nodded. He wanted her mother, but she wouldn't be home from her shift at the munitions factory for hours. He would probably give her the message anyway, but if he wouldn't she'd never sleep tonight, waiting for him to return. Not with both her father and brother at the front.

"I have a telegram for you." It took the messenger an eternity to cross the yard and hand her the small yellow telegram. A wisp of paper that could shatter the fragile normality she clung to. She shoved it into her pocket. It would be better to open it inside.

"I'm very sorry," the man said, the words as clipped and precise as his sharp turn toward the sidewalk.

Lucy had never counted the steps from the lawn to the front door before, but she counted them now, willing herself to breathe with each one.

One.

Two.

Three.

Twenty-five steps until her fingers found the doorknob and she crumpled against the foyer wall, away from the eyes of her neighbors.

❦

New Haven, Connecticut

Two gold initials were embossed on the leather suitcase: J. O. The letters mocked him, reminding him how impractical and flashy his father's gift was, as he made his way through the crowds of soldiers at Union Station. New Haven was a waypoint for most—some heading off to the front, others to training, but no one was headed home. This was the only similarity between the men in uniform and Joshua O'Donnell. They were all strangers headed off to what had been sold to them as an adventure.

Joshua didn't believe Yale University would be an adventure, though.

He gripped the handle of his case tightly, focusing his attention on the doors to the station and trying hard not to look at the men surrounding him. Men who were going to glory or death while he was forced to go to college. Joshua wasn't sure how his father had secured a 4-F for his file, but he was sure he'd paid handsomely for it. There was absolutely nothing wrong with Joshua and being handed a 4-F slip had stung. The army doctor hadn't been able to meet his eyes.

Joshua felt the shame as though it had been embossed in gold letters on his forehead.

A soldier knocked into him. "Watch it, daisy."

"My apologies," Joshua said, his jaw clenched.

"We're going off to fight for our country here," the soldier continued. His eyes traveled up and down, taking in Joshua's tweed jacket and shined shoes, and a sneer twisted across his lips.

"I'll pray for your safe return," Joshua said as he backed away. It took every ounce of self-control he possessed not to deck the soldier. In fact, the only thing holding him back was that the soldier was right. That man deserved Joshua's respect, but Joshua didn't deserve his.

Outside the station, Joshua leaned against the brick facade and inhaled the fresh air. Setting down his suitcase, he pulled a folded letter from his pocket. The paper was thin and worn from the number of times he'd read it over the last two months. Opening it, he read it again and noted the address. Joshua O'Donnell would go to Yale as his father demanded, but he would serve his country as well.

꒰ꔠ꒱

Los Angeles, California

A hostess beckoned for Harold Patton to follow her through the crowded restaurant. The Polo Lounge remained one of the few places that felt normal in spite of the war. Harold nodded at Spencer Tracy, who was dining with a collection of his fellow polo players. The number of starlets in the room would have turned most men's heads, but Harold was preoccupied. The only thing he noticed, to his dissatisfaction, was how many women had dared to wear slacks. First the Lounge had given in to Marlene Dietrich and now the entire Beverly Hills Hotel had given in to the modern sensibility. It was an unpleasant reminder that with so many men at war, there were fewer people around to keep women in their place.

"Mr. Patton." The hostess motioned toward his table. Two men wearing cheap suits were waiting in the green high-backed booth.

"I'll have an old-fashioned," Harold said to the girl as she turned to leave.

Harold settled into the booth, taking each man's hand as it was proffered.

"Dick Morton, and this is my colleague Walt Fitch."

"It's a pleasure to meet you," Harold said, although he wasn't entirely sure this was the case.

"You're probably wondering why the War Department asked you to lunch—" Dick began, but Harold cut him off with a wave of the hand.

"I assume you want something from me," Harold said.

"Well, yes." Dick shifted uncomfortably in his seat and tugged at his dime-store tie.

Walt jumped in. "But it's probably not what you think." He was younger than Dick, which meant his suit was even cheaper, but there was no hesitation in his words. He believed in his ability to land Harold's support.

"I'm a railroad man," Harold said, "so either you're after that or you're after my collection of Baroque paintings. I doubt the War Department has a need for Rembrandt."

"Actually, it's neither of those things," Walt said. He leaned in, dropping his voice as a waitress placed Harold's old-fashioned in front of him. "We want you to invest in a project."

"So you're after my money? How refreshingly honest of you." Harold took a long swig of his drink, studying his companions. Dick's tie had been loosened to hang around his neck like a noose and his eyes darted around the room. If Dick had been an ambitious man, he might have enjoyed lunch at the Polo Lounge, but it was clear being here unnerved him. Walt's eyes glowed, on the other hand. He didn't merely seem at ease, he appeared to feed off the energy in the room. Either he was very invested in what he was selling or he was too young to know that lunch at the Beverly Hills Hotel was likely to be a singular event in his life.

"I think you'll like what we have to offer," Walt said.

"Which is?" Harold asked.

"An end to the war."

"I know this is an unpopular opinion, Mr. Fitch, but I'm not eager to see the war come to an end. It's been very good for the Patton Railroad Company." Harold understood this would end the conversation and he would end up paying for the drinks the men abandoned when they took their leave of the unpatriotic fellow, as they'd be sure to call him.

Dick stood up, bowing slightly. "Mr. Patton, thank you for—"

"Sit down, Dick," Walt ordered. "We haven't explained to Mr. Patton what's in it for him yet."

Harold cocked an eyebrow as he raised his old-fashioned to his lips.

"You have money, Mr. Patton, but what about power?" Walt asked.

"Money is power, son."

"It won't be for much longer." Walt leaned back against the booth to let this settle in.

Harold's black eyes narrowed, looking for a tell in Walt's demeanor. He was sure the kid was bluffing him, but Harold couldn't help but respect him a little. "So you're going to win the war? How?"

Walt's mouth twitched into a smile. "The Cypress Project."

⁓

They buried an empty coffin in the Marion cemetery. The military sent them a medal and some unposted letters Nicholas had had on him when he died in a muddy field in France. It was all they had left of Lucy's older brother, and it was more than most of the other families in town had received. For many there had been only the telegram and the awkward apology of the army messenger.

Two months had passed, school had started, but like many of the other girls, Lucy didn't return. Learning about literature and geometry seemed increasingly pointless, and Mrs. Price hadn't raised a fuss when Lucy announced she had better ways to spend her time. Her mother's only requirement was that she didn't spend that time driving up to the Mattoon canteen to send off the young soldiers. More than one of Lucy's friends had found herself in a precarious situation following the deployment of a lover. A few had even come home married to boys they barely knew. But her mother didn't have to worry; those girls had been caught up in the romance of war, falling for the propaganda posters plastered throughout town. Those girls didn't dream of their brother's blood mixing with wet dirt and ash in a muddy field in France.

The weather would change soon, and Lucy canned the vegetables from the miserable victory garden. *Victory garden*— even the name now cut like a well-timed insult. The war would end as all wars must, she realized, as she stewed tomatoes over the stove top, but there would be no victory for the Price family. Her father would almost certainly come home soon. He'd telegrammed that his commanding officer had learned of Nicholas's death. The family would be complete then, as complete as it ever would be again. But like so many who returned from the war with legs and arms amputated, the ghost of what they'd lost would linger over the Prices forever.

A knock at the door startled her from her black mood, but she frowned as she answered it to find a salesman on the porch.

"No, thank you," she said.

The man caught the door, barring her from closing it. "Miss Lucy Price?"

Lucy took a step back, uncertain what to do.

"My name is Mr. Watson. I'm from the War Department—"

"Do you have news about my father?" Lucy asked.

"I'm sorry to disappoint you, but I do not. I'd like to speak with you, though."

Lucy's hand fluttered to her chest, the motion asking the question that had stalled on her tongue. *Me?*

"May I come in?" he asked.

She couldn't think of a reason to say no to the War Department, and besides, a strange sensation was creeping through the haze of grief engulfing her. Lucy had felt nothing but darkness since the day of the telegram, but now something else flickered into her chest.

Curiosity.

Lucy showed the man to the sitting room, whipping off her homemade apron when Mr. Watson's back was to her.

"Can I get you some tea?" she asked. It was all they had in the house except stewed tomatoes. Neither Lucy nor her mother had much of an appetite these days.

"I'm fine," Mr. Watson assured her. "I won't take too much of your time."

She nodded as she sank into a chair across from him. For some reason, she was relieved her mother wasn't there.

"The War Department is looking for young girls like yourself to help with the war effort," he said.

This time the question leaped from her lips. "Me?"

"Is it really that shocking? Our mothers and young women

are running our factories. Our fathers and brothers are fighting," he said.

Girls in Europe worked as nurses on the front. Lucy was too young to enlist as a nurse yet, but she planned to in a year and a half when she was of age. She hoped the war would be over by then, but now she knew it would never end. It would stretch on until there was no one left, until it wiped out the entire world. The realization colored her thoughts black with hopelessness, making her feel even more useless than when most of her victory garden had died after Nicholas's death.

It was time girls did something more than blow kisses to passing soldiers or dance with them at the USO or show them one last good time in the backseat of their daddy's Ford. Lucy knew that, but it didn't make her any less afraid of the strange man. "What would I be doing?"

"You'd be ending the war," Mr. Watson said.

"No one can end this war," Lucy said before she thought better of it. "This is a war between good and evil, Mr. Watson. It never ends."

Mr. Watson opened his mouth, but then paused, his eyes trained on her. Finally he reached into the inner pocket of his suit jacket and withdrew a business card, which he handed to her. "If you change your mind about that, you can reach me here. I'm on my way to Chicago this evening."

Lucy nodded, unable to speak, her mouth full of cotton and doubt. She showed Mr. Watson to the door. Then she made her way into the kitchen where she dropped the card into the garbage, but as it fluttered onto a discarded eggshell, Lucy spied: THE DRAKE HOTEL.

Lucy's mother didn't speak at dinner. Lucy hadn't been counting but she was fairly certain less than fifty words had passed between the two of them this week. It had been that way since Nicholas died. Nothing had happened between them. Rather, neither felt like talking. They'd tried at first, forcing empty conversations about rations and small-town gossip, and then they'd given up, lapsing into a perpetual silence. The house was quiet as death, which felt appropriate, and the words they shared were utilitarian. There was always a point to them.

Everywhere Lucy went in town there were signs urging citizens to do this and that to help the war effort. At the picture show they talked about war bonds and beating Hitler, and then played films about young men going off to become heroes. At church they prayed for an end to the war and read the names of the boys going to the front, asking for the heavens to watch over them, but God didn't seem to be listening. It was all hollow. Death had become routine. Sending boys to be slaughtered was simply a regular sacrifice. And the words on the posters and the film reels and in the mouth of her minister were hollow. They did nothing to calm the ragged anger that burned in her chest. They didn't fill the void carved from her belly by sadness.

So she stopped listening and then she stopped talking. They both did.

But words never left her mind, especially since Mr. Watson's visit, and now they were lining up to become questions that marched through her thoughts so swiftly she couldn't latch on to one long enough to find the answer. It left her temples throbbing and now, at dinner, she speared a turnip, holding it up for examination but not eating it, while the deluge of questions continued. Lucy set the fork back down and slumped against the table.

Mrs. Price watched her, but didn't say a word. Instead she rose and took her plate to the sink to be washed. It was then that Lucy realized how lonely it was to be stuck in one's own head. More questions joined the long marching line: Who had stopped talking first? Was it her or her mother? Followed by a perhaps more important one: When would they start talking again?

It wasn't until Lucy's head dropped to her pillow that night that she asked herself the question that would change her life: Why had a man from Chicago come five hours to speak to *her*?

∽

Two days later, Lucy dropped a note for her mother on the kitchen table and then boarded a train to Chicago. She hadn't called ahead and when she pushed through the revolving doors to the Drake Hotel and stepped into the opulent lobby she wondered whether she'd made a mistake. She stood there on the marble floor, lost in the *click-clack* of dress shoes, and marveled at the number of people. Chicago felt alive in a way that Marion, Illinois, hadn't since the U.S. had joined the war. Perhaps she could lose herself here, become a new person, and forget all the pain she'd left behind when she got on that train. It wasn't too late. She could walk back out to the busy Chicago sidewalk and disappear, but then she'd never get her answers.

Watson hadn't told her what they wanted her to do or why, but she couldn't stand the nagging questions circling in her brain any longer. She needed to know why he'd come for her. She needed to know why he thought they could end the war.

And why they hadn't done so months ago, before Nicholas was killed.

But most of all she needed to believe that good could still triumph over evil. Lucy supposed that was like wishing for a fairy tale; but she knew there would be no happy ending.

◇

Harold skimmed the file in front of him, paying no attention to the girl in the chair across from him. He didn't notice how she clutched the locket at her neck or how her eyes darted bird-like around the room. If he had, he might have discovered the girl was nervous, but he probably wouldn't have cared. Harold Patton wasn't in the business of sixteen-year-old girls. At least, he wasn't until recently. Somehow that bastard Walt Fitch had talked him into this little program the War Department needed to have financed, and because of the exorbitant amount of money the leeches had gotten out of him, Harold had insisted on being present for the process. Personally Harold thought these scientists were insane, but they had the backing of the US government, which meant that they had more than a theory. There was no way the War Department would have sanctioned such a ridiculous program, especially during wartime, without evidence that it could succeed.

He wanted to see that evidence for himself. If they could pull off what they'd proposed to him, Harold wanted in on the ground floor. But he also wanted to know how it would work. When Harold was fifteen his father had sent him out to help lay new track for the railroad. Harold had hated him for it at the time, but because of that experience he understood what business he was in, which meant nobody could pull one over on him. It had also provided him with near-limitless power within his own company. Power that could only grow—if he understood the implications of this little project Fitch had pitched him.

But that didn't make him interested in the girl.

She cleared her throat and he looked up, dropping the file on the table.

"Mr. Watson thinks I would be a good candidate," she told him.

He had to hand it to Watson. At least all the girls the man had recruited for the trials were lookers. This girl—Lucy, according to her file—could have been in pictures in a few more years with her wavy blond hair and fair skin. Right now she looked too young, too innocent, for Hollywood. That was the other thing Watson had a knack for—picking the gullible ones who believed it was their duty to help the poor boys overseas. Of course, Watson was working from a list of the survivors of those recently killed in action, so maybe he wasn't all that brilliant, but at least he brought back pretty girls.

Faces like hers would sell this program to every Tom, Dick, and Harry in the country. People wouldn't bat an eye at putting their fate in the hands of a sweet young girl from—he glanced at the file again—Illinois. It would make the transition simpler—for everyone.

"I think Mr. Watson is right," Harold said. He flashed her a brilliant smile as a young man entered the room. Harold's eyes flicked from Joshua to Lucy, waiting for a reaction from either of them. This was the variable no one wanted to talk about, but it was the one Harold felt would become more important than most. They needed these girls to be chaste. No man was going to allow his wife to work full-time once this war was over, so it was imperative that these candidates not be involved in romantic entanglements. It would make things easier for everyone.

Joshua was a good-looking kid, broad shouldered and dark haired, and nothing about his outward appearance gave away the 4-F Harold had discovered in his file. Then again Joshua came from money and Harold knew how easy it was to purchase a rejection from service. But Lucy barely gave the boy a second glance, although when Harold looked closer he saw her hands were balled into fists in her lap.

"Sir," Joshua said, handing him a new file. "Dr. Lucas sent this your way. He's ready to open up the next study."

"Thank you," he said, nodding to the door to indicate Joshua was dismissed. As the boy passed Lucy, he smiled but she looked away, a frown sagging over her fair features, and Joshua left the room with heat burning on his cheeks.

"May I speak frankly?" Lucy asked.

Harold leaned back in his leather desk chair and pressed his fingertips together. "Of course."

"I don't know why I'm here, but I do know that men are dying every second you waste reading my file."

Sass, Harold thought. Not a good sign at all. Lucas had said they needed a particular kind of girl, obedient girls who would do as they were told, but Harold Patton had to disagree. What they needed were girls like Lucy Price. They needed fighters.

"There's a trial beginning this afternoon," he said. "My secretary will show you to the laboratory."

⟡

A pretty nurse led Lucy to the laboratory. Half of the room had been converted to a makeshift exam area complete with a cold steel table; a tray of frightening instruments gleamed beside it. The rest looked like the lair of a mad scientist in a picture show. Beakers and microscopes next to a panel, covered with blinking buttons that stretched the length of the room. It was cold inside the sterile facility, and Lucy shivered in the thin cotton gown she'd been given for the procedure.

This place felt removed from reality, not quite of the world Lucy had lived in for the past sixteen years, and as she realized this, she wondered again whether she'd made a mistake in agreeing to be part of the project. Dr. Lucas appeared beside her before she could let this thought get too far.

"Miss Price." He flourished an arm toward the exam table and Lucy stepped toward it. Her body rebelled against her, slowing her down, until each step was smaller than the last.

"She's nervous," the nurse said in a tone usually reserved for small children. She looped an arm through Lucy's and guided her to the table.

The steel was as cold as it looked, numbing her skin as she lay back against it.

"B-b-blanket?" she asked through chattering teeth.

"I'm sorry, dear." The nurse patted her hand, shaking her head. "We'll need you uncovered for the procedure."

"Will I be asleep?" Lucy shut her eyes, remembering having her tonsils removed. They'd given her a shot and she'd woken later with a sore throat and fuzzy memories of strange and vivid dreams.

"It will be like sleep," Dr. Lucas said, coming into view above her.

A leather strap buckled over her wrist and Lucy's eyes flew open in surprise.

"Nothing to worry about. Just a safety precaution," the doctor assured her.

But Lucy couldn't help but worry. She wasn't sedated yet and a fourth strap was being fastened over her left ankle. She flexed her arms, testing the strength of the leather and found she could do little more than move her fingers.

"Nurse," the doctor said in a firm tone, and a moment later Lucy felt the prick of a needle in her arm. The effect was instantaneous. Her head lolled to the side and she couldn't pick it back up to see what they were doing now. It was too heavy, and besides she didn't want to. Not really. Their hands were on her body, but it felt nice. Fingernails grazed over her bare skin. She was colder than she had been a moment before, but she didn't mind.

"What was that?" she asked in a dreamy voice. She wanted more of it.

"A new drug, approved for use in this project," the doctor said. "Nurse, take note of the dosage we used and that the candidate seems exceptionally euphoric."

The nurse giggled at this, and Lucy heard the buttons on her gown unsnap. A cool breeze tickled over her. Her eyes wandered overhead, her vision blurring and refocusing, until they landed on a clear pane of glass. A group of men were huddled in an observation deck, watching the procedure from above. Lucy smiled at them.

"You're going to feel a few pricks now," the doctor said, and a second later there was a brief pinch on her chest, followed by one on her stomach and one on her hip.

A tremor rippled through her muscles and she convulsed on the table, held in place by the restraints. The doctor pressed a hand to her bare stomach so that she couldn't arch into the air.

She tried to breathe, gasping for air, but not catching any. Her lungs were frozen, turned to stone in her chest, weighing her down and suffocating her.

The doctor watched her with interest. "Note the violence of the muscle spasms in this case. I'd say that's very promising . . . if she survives the procedure."

His words jumbled in Lucy's head, refusing to make sense even as they cracked the glossy coat of calm the drugs had encased her in. What was happening to her muscles? And what did he mean by *survive*? But her own lips had stopped working, held captive by the pain searing through her muscles. The drugs weren't working to keep it away, but she couldn't bring herself to mind. She couldn't bring herself to *want* to fight the restraints holding her to the table even as her body bucked against them. Lucy's eyes rolled back and up to the crowd of men watching from overhead. Some had begun to take notes. One shifted on his heels and looked away as her eyes brushed past his. But then her gaze met with a young man's, surely not much older than herself, and locked. She'd seen him before on the compound. He had stood out then because a young man his age not wearing a uniform always stood out to her. That day the sight of him had turned her stomach. How dare he not enlist? How dare he walk by her when her brother never would?

But today his eyes were soft, concerned, as they met hers. The others had looked past her or away from her. He looked *at* her. And even through the haze she realized he was the only person here who had ever truly seen her.

⁐

Joshua couldn't turn away from the force of the girl's gaze. He wanted to look at his chart and find her name, but he didn't dare turn away from her. Whatever was happening to her body clearly scared her, despite Lucas's assurance to Joshua that the new drug Valpron would make the subjects oblivious to the physical effects of the trial. Like many of the others Joshua would have given his own mother's life to end this war. He could no longer count on both hands how many friends he'd lost in the war.

But something about the girl's eyes made him want to sweep her away from this place. It made him question every reason he'd come to believe in the Cypress Project.

Joshua had thought Dr. Lucas was joking when he told him to pack up his things two weeks into the school year. The professor barely knew him, although he'd been instrumental in bringing Joshua into Yale early. Something about his entrance exams had caught the man's eye, and from the moment Joshua arrived on campus Lucas had been watching him, quizzing him on some of the recent theoretical developments in physics. The whole thing had been unnerving for the freshman, but once Lucas had revealed his ideas and some background about the project he'd written Joshua of earlier in the summer, Joshua was entranced. There had been little hesitation on his part when he'd realized Lucas's offer was genuine. Yale could wait for Joshua to help end the war.

More than once it occurred to him that his father might have been right. Joshua could have been off lying in the mud in France, bleeding to death. Instead he was in Los Angeles using his brains to end the war. And what would his father say then?

And then he'd seen the girl on that table. She'd been cold to him in Patton's office, unwilling to give him so much as a smile, and Joshua knew why. He knew what he must look like—a strapping boy of eighteen in khakis and a button-down. She'd noticed the absence of a uniform, and he'd felt shame over it. Shame he thought he'd left behind him in New Haven. And just like that he'd gone from being a man doing important work to being a rejected boy holding a 4-F file. Joshua had hated her almost as much as he hated himself in that moment.

But all that changed as he watched Lucas inject her. A few of the men—all business types who were financing the project— had elbowed Joshua when the nurse undressed the girl, but he'd kept his eyes on her face until she began to fight the serum coursing through her. Then he'd seen her breasts heave into the air as her back arched. He'd noticed how long her legs were as they spasmed and kicked against the cuffs that bound her. But even then he'd watched objectively. He had remained a scientist, taking notes about the effect of each injection, for Lucas to use later in his reports.

Until he looked into her eyes.

Fear flashed through them, counteracted easily by the Valpron Lucas had administered before the procedure began, but in that split second something else had reflected from them: curiosity. She didn't know what was happening to her and if she had been able to ask Joshua in that moment, he wouldn't have been able to tell her, either.

He could give her the canned pitch they used for the investors or the suits from the bureaucratic side of the War Department: that the serums isolated particular genetic abilities and enhanced them. As Lucas had explained it to him, it was like giving someone better-than-perfect vision and reflexes. Not only would candidates be able to see the most essential components of the universe around them, best described as threads that made up all of matter, they would be able to manipulate these threads as well. The entire Cypress Project depended on it.

But Joshua knew that wouldn't answer the girl's questions, because it was about so much more than that. For the first time Joshua himself wondered what was really happening. There was a difference between theory and application. Watching her endure the serums showed him that, which led him to the same inevitable question: What would happen? If they were successful at harvesting and manipulating the material that comprised time and matter, how would that be used to end the war?

Those answers were classified, well beyond his level of security clearance.

But there was one thing that wasn't: the name of the girl.

❦

She was being watched. They hadn't bothered to hide it from her. There was a window in her quarters where scientists observed her sleep and dress. Nurses escorted her to every meal and meeting. Lucy's memory of the procedure was hazy at best, and now she wasn't sure what to expect. They certainly expected something from her, but she didn't feel any different. The mirror still reflected the blond waves and a freckled nose that she'd had every day of her life. On the outside there was no change.

At first she didn't think there was a change on the inside either. She was accustomed to questioning things, but since the procedure she'd been plagued by strange lapses in her memory. Every once in a while the light in the room seemed to catch like fabric on a nail, drawing her attention to the spot only to discover nothing amiss.

A nurse left her in a small waiting room, not unlike her doctor's back home, but there were no charts or posters about health on the wall. Everything was bare-bones, the room stripped down to an exam table and two chairs. She tried not to think about the cinder-block walls and lack of windows.

There was a knock at the door and she called out that she was ready. In truth, she hadn't known whether or not to get undressed. She had no idea why she was here and she wasn't going to hesitate now. Lucy wanted answers to all the questions tumbling around her head.

But when the door opened it was a young man. Lucy noted his strong, smooth jawline. He was handsome, but young. The kind of man who would only get better looking with time. There was something familiar about him, but she couldn't quite place where she had seen him until she realized that was an answer in and of itself. A memory of his eyes watching over her blurred through her mind.

Lucy's hands twisted in her lap. They were slick with sweat and she hoped the man wouldn't try to offer his hand in introduction.

"Miss Price, I hope you haven't been waiting for long," he said, dropping into the other chair.

"I haven't," Lucy assured him. "I wasn't sure if I was to be examined again. I should have asked. Do you need me to get undressed? Has the procedure worked? When will they stop watching me?"

Gennifer Albin

The man blinked at the onslaught of questions, then smiled. "I was about to ask if you had any questions, but I see that's unnecessary."

"I'm sorry. I tend to bottle them all up until they spill out . . . Doctor." She tacked on the title as an afterthought, although she stole a shy glance at him when she did.

"I'm not a doctor," he said in a rush. "I'm Doctor Lucas's research assistant. Joshua."

"I thought you looked too young to be a doctor," Lucy said, her blush deepening.

"Perhaps I'm a prodigy," Joshua said.

"You are involved with this project, so you must be smart."

"As are you."

"I'm a lab rat," Lucy said. They both knew that, but it was nice of him to act as if she were a vital piece of the program rather than the subject of an experiment.

Joshua shook his head. "No, you aren't. You have no idea how important you are."

"Because they gave me a few shots?" The prick of the needles was one of the only clear memories she had of the procedure.

"To start with." Joshua stood and drew a stethoscope out of his pocket. "May I?"

"I thought you weren't a doctor," she said even as she nodded her assent.

"This I'm capable of, but you probably shouldn't allow me to cut you open or deliver a baby."

"Thankfully, I've no need of either service."

Joshua stood over her and paused. She noticed the hesitation and realized he needed her to unbutton her blouse. She

331

tried to look confident and casual as though the thought of the handsome young man, who was definitely not a doctor, touching her bare skin didn't bother her in the least. But her fingers fumbled on the buttons and she had to try three times before she managed to open the top one.

"I'm afraid this is rather cold. Hold on." Joshua rubbed the stethoscope with his fingers. "A little better."

"It's fine," Lucy said, but her voice was high-pitched and unconvincing.

But when his fingers brought the stethoscope to her chest, they brushed along her skin, trailing fire in their path. Her breath hitched in her throat.

"Take a few deep breaths for me," he said in a low voice.

She did as he asked, and he listened. Lucy was certain that he was noting the rapid beating of her heart. He probably thought something was wrong with her, or even worse, perhaps he guessed that her body was responding to his touch. She wasn't sure which was more distressing.

Joshua moved behind her and gently slid the metal diaphragm of the stethoscope down her back. As he did, he swept her loose hair over her shoulder and for just a moment Lucy imagined his lips on the back of her neck. She pushed the thought aside. She was being silly and girlish, two traits she'd loathed in her girlfriends at school. And of all the places to lose her head! She had been recruited for a special mission. She was here at the request of the War Department. Now was no time to get goofy over a boy.

"You didn't enlist?" she asked him.

Joshua's hand slipped and the stethoscope slithered down the back of her blouse. He drew it up in a hasty motion.

That was when she recalled where she had first seen him: at her briefing with Patton. She'd been haughty to him, but somehow between then and now her impression of him had changed. She could only guess that it had to do with the barely recalled memory she had of him during the procedure.

"I was listed as four-F," he admitted to her.

"Oh." Lucy felt very stupid, and she had to bite back the question every girl thought of upon hearing a young man was deemed 4-F.

But Joshua seemed to know what she was thinking. "There's nothing wrong with me. I'm in working order. My father paid someone to get me rejected. He knew it was the only way to keep me from going."

"It's not really my business," she said.

"They'd like to run a few more tests," Joshua said, his tone becoming businesslike.

"Of course." Lucy buttoned her blouse and followed him out of the room.

The machine was unlike anything she'd ever seen. It took up half the wall with its gleaming gears and tubes. She wasn't certain she knew what to do, but she perched on the stool, which looked almost comical next to the great mechanical beast it sat before, and waited for instructions.

A few men with horn-rimmed glasses, including the one who had interviewed her when she arrived, waited nearby, but no one spoke.

Joshua flipped a switch and the gears whirred to life, revealing a panel of light and color that shimmered in front of her.

"What do I do?" she asked him in a quiet voice so the others wouldn't hear.

"Do you see it?" he asked.

"The web?"

Joshua's jaw tensed, but he bobbed his head.

"Yes. It's beautiful." And it was. There were colors Lucy had only seen in dreams, displayed with a sparkling vibrance that sent a chill up her back. What did they expect her to do with it? What *was* it?

But when Lucy looked up there was a gleam in Joshua's eyes and the men had come closer.

Whatever this web was, it was important.

❦

"Can you touch it?" This was the real test. Several other girls had been able to view the matter on the loom, but none had been able to capture it in their hands. A few had come close, but day by day the project team had grown more disappointed. Even now the War Department was considering disbanding the program. That was why they'd had to bring in the private financiers. Men like Patton, who watched everything too closely for Joshua's comfort.

Lucy reached out and brushed the large, airy panel in front of her. Whatever she could see, Joshua could not. Lucas had tried the serum himself, so he could be certain it worked, but he hadn't allowed any of the other men working on the project to do so. That meant that when he wasn't present, Joshua had to rely on the honesty of the girls. But he never doubted that any of them saw the weave. It showed in their eyes—the awe of it. He'd be lying if he said he wasn't jealous that he couldn't see the elements of the universe laid out before him, especially given that these girls didn't even know what they were looking at.

None of them had a clue that they had been given the ability to see the very threads of life.

But Lucy was different. Her awe was measured and removed. She seemed almost hesitant to go further, but as she did, Joshua's attention turned to the glass holding cell that sat in the middle of the room. To the average person it looked like a small greenhouse, full of leaves and vines, but the scientists had isolated the space inside for this very purpose.

"What should I do?" she asked him.

"Grab it," he ordered.

His eyes never left the holding cell. He couldn't bring himself to look at Lucy as she made her attempt; too much was riding on this girl, and it made Joshua uncomfortable. But not because of what it might mean to the project if she failed. Joshua wasn't certain he wanted her to succeed, which was what scared him. Nothing happened inside the cell and he dared a glance back at her.

Lucy's hands dipped through the space as though they were tangled up in the air in front of her. There was a gasp from one of the men in the room, and Joshua whirled around to discover that a large fern in the holding cell had begun to wilt before his eyes. It withered, its tips turning brown, and it shriveled, dying, until finally it disintegrated entirely.

Applause startled Lucy from her work and she turned to stare at the businessmen who were laughing and patting one another's backs. She looked to Joshua, but he couldn't think of a thing to say. His mind was too heavy with her success.

༄

Patton lingered as the other investors shook hands and patted one another on the back. All they could see was the small success the girl had managed, but he could see more than that. Much more than that. The girl had killed the plant, but not in the way he had been expecting. He'd been warned that there were implications to the loom technology, but where the scientists involved on the project saw only the risk, Patton saw possibility.

His eyes narrowed as he watched the young man guiding the girl out of the lab. That was a situation that needed to be controlled. Impressionable girls couldn't be trusted around young men, who could rarely be trusted at all.

Someone cleared his throat and Patton was startled out of his thoughts. He adjusted his bow tie and turned toward the other party without hurry. It was important that the scientists remember who was funding their little project after all.

"May I help you?" The man's white lab coat brushed the knees of his wrinkled slacks. Patton's nose wrinkled at the sight, and the man caught the look. "I'm certainly a mess, but I've been sleeping at my desk. Someone has ordered tests be conducted twenty-four hours a day."

Patton already knew that. As the project's largest financial backer, he had insisted the trials run continuously. He was certain this man knew exactly with whom he was speaking, which meant the man knew he was the reason for the exhaustive schedule. But Patton admired the arrogance of the casual remark enough to step forward and feign oblivion. He thrust a hand out. "Harold Patton."

"Dr. Lucas." The man shook his hand firmly but quickly, stepping around Patton to fiddle with a large panel of buttons.

"And you're the head scientist on this project?"

"I am one of them," Dr. Lucas corrected him.

"And the others?"

"What can I help you with, Mr. Patton?" he asked, skirting Patton's question none too subtly, and continuing to check down the row of panels.

"I have a question about the experiment I just witnessed," Patton said. He placed his body in front of the next instrument panel, so that Lucas was forced to look up at him.

The doctor raised an eyebrow as he crossed his arms, a clear signal of defeat.

"The girl didn't merely remove the plant from the weave. She mutilated it," Patton said.

"The important thing is that she was able to touch it," Lucas said. His eyes flickered past his visitor to the panel.

"This will only take a few seconds of your time." And if Patton was right, it could buy both of them enough time to waste. "The plant wasn't just mutilated, though. It seemed almost as though it was undone. How is that possible?"

Lucas scratched his head, surprised by the thought-provoking question. "These are the very building blocks of our world. It's not unthinkable that if she could touch the strands, she could destroy them. A child knows how to knock down a tower of blocks, after all."

"You noticed nothing strange then about what happened to the plant?" Patton pressed.

"I suppose I didn't," Lucas said, wondering when the other

man would leave so he could stop playing wet nurse to investors. "Did you?"

"She didn't destroy the plant, Doctor. Any child can knock down a tower or rip up a plant." Patton stopped, counting on the doctor's curiosity to show itself. Lucas finally stopped fidgeting with his equipment and gave him his full attention.

"I'm not sure I follow your meaning."

Patton's lip curled like a cat's. "The girl killed the plant, all right, but not by ripping it up. She pulled something out of it."

"And what do you think that was, Mr. Patton?"

"Life itself," he answered without a second thought.

✑

Chills shivered through Lucy's body, settling into her stomach, which rolled and clenched. She did her best to hide it from Joshua, not wanting to appear weak. There had been a breakthrough. She wasn't clear about what had happened exactly, but the investors had cheered and congratulated themselves. No one had spoken to her—it was as though she were just part of the machine—but her feelings hardly mattered. All she cared about was ending the war.

Joshua walked beside her, keeping pace with her slow steps without complaint. Lucy dared a glance at him and felt a flutter in her chest that wasn't an aftereffect of her time at the loom.

"I'll have the nurses bring you some food." Joshua's eyes swept over her. They crinkled in concern so she plastered on a wide smile.

"I could use something to eat," she admitted.

"Anything in the world," he said.

"Do you have any chocolate? I know it's being rationed—"

"You're working for the War Department," he reminded her.

"So I get a soldier's ration then?" she asked. A giggle bubbled past her lips, and she turned away, cheeks blazing, shocked at the girlish side Joshua brought out in her.

"Of course," he said. "You're defending our country now."

Lucy thought of Nicholas, alone and cold on a field in France, ripping open the K rations that served as his meals. She wondered how often he had received chocolate as part of his rations on those bloodied fields. She shook her head. "I don't need any," she said to Joshua in a strangled voice. "It wouldn't be right."

"Why not?" He grabbed her arm and forced her to stop in the hallway.

"Because soldiers are out there dying to save people they've never met and I caught a chill?"

A shadow passed over Joshua's face so quickly Lucy wondered whether she had imagined it. His lips pressed into a thin line that he managed to curve into a smile, but Lucy was certain she had upset him. She didn't quite understand why, though.

"Oh," she said as realization dawned on her. "I didn't mean that I . . . or that you—"

He held up a hand to stop her. "I'm overly sensitive and you're too selfless. It will never do."

Lucy cocked an eyebrow at him.

"We've had a major breakthrough today. Both of us. We should be celebrating," he said.

"I'm sure the cafeteria will have something delightful for us to eat," Lucy said, but Joshua was grinning at her now in earnest. "What is it?"

"I have an idea," he said. "What would you say to getting out of here tonight?"

She hesitated. No one had told her she couldn't leave the compound, but it had been implied by the tight security she saw throughout the halls. "Are we allowed to?"

"You're allowed to with me," he reassured her as they passed a group of silent guards. "What do you say?"

Lucy sucked in a breath and nodded. "Okay, I'll go, but it's on you if we get in trouble."

Joshua caught her hand and kissed it swiftly. "Leave everything to me."

∽

Lucy hadn't packed much when she boarded the train to Chicago. She'd thought she would return home. It was a rather foolish notion in hindsight, but Mr. Watson had insisted she leave straightaway for Los Angeles. His speech was impassioned enough to persuade her to board another train with the small case she'd brought with her. He'd promised to ring her mother for her, explaining that the secrecy of the project mandated all communication with her family go through the War Department. This hadn't seemed an odd request then, given that they'd received all correspondence from Nicholas through the army. His letters had been read by censors. He wasn't allowed to phone. Even the notice of his death had been filtered through the proper bureaucratic channels, delivered by a stranger in a stiff uniform.

She hadn't considered that she'd have occasion for more than a few pieces, so there was really only one thing to wear for an evening out with Joshua: a soft cotton sundress that had faded a bit with washing, leaving the dots pale, like they'd been left too long in the sun. It would have to do, though, and despite its weary appearance it clung to her body, accentuating the curves that grew softer and more womanly with each passing year. She had no makeup, but she twisted her hair into elaborate pin curls.

"You look lovely, miss," the night-shift nurse said as she made her rounds.

Lucy bit her lip and gathered her courage. "I'm meeting one of the scientists for dinner."

If this shocked the nurse, she didn't show it.

"All you need is this, then." The nurse drew a gold tube out of her pocket and whipped off the lid. "Summer cherry."

Lucy took the lipstick awkwardly. She'd worn lipstick before, but nothing quite this dramatic. One wrong swipe and she'd look like a traveling-circus clown. But she managed to apply it in smooth, precise strokes.

"You've got good, steady hands, miss," the nurse said as Lucy returned the lipstick to her.

"Thank you," Lucy murmured, but her eyes were frozen on her reflection, marveling at how different she appeared. One simple cosmetic and she looked years older. More sophisticated. A wave of confidence overcame her and she smiled to the girl in the glass.

"Have a nice night."

As soon as the nurse was gone, Lucy slipped into the hall. She had arranged to meet Joshua near the cafeteria. Neither had spoken much more about whether they would get in trouble if they left, but Joshua seemed eager to avoid any security entanglements. There was a back door near the cafeteria that led out to the parking lot and Dr. Lucas's car, which Joshua had arranged to borrow for the evening.

Joshua turned and caught sight of her heading toward him, and his mouth fell open. He had a single daisy in his hand, but when she reached him, he didn't speak.

"Are you ready?" she asked.

He nodded. "Yes," he said, recovering himself. "Lucas's car is out back."

"Is that—" She pointed to the flower that Joshua was suffocating in his hand.

"Yes," he said, thrusting it toward her. The stem was broken and the petals had been crushed. "A lovely gesture."

She followed him out the back door and to a Cadillac. Whatever Lucas did in that lab must have been important given his expensive car.

"It looks like a car fit for a movie star," Lucy said, but she immediately clamped her mouth shut. It was embarrassing to think that Joshua now probably suspected she read the Hollywood rags that reported on the most minuscule information available. She didn't really need to know what Judy Garland ate for breakfast or who was secretly in love with whom, but she read them anyway. They were an easier escape for her than the movies, which showed so much of the war in the shorts they ran between features.

"You follow the silver screen then?" Joshua's smile widened.

"Doesn't everyone?" Lucy couldn't really understand people who turned up their noses at actors and actresses.

"Then you'll like where we're headed tonight." He opened the door and helped her into the passenger seat.

They spoke throughout the ride, learning that they both

enjoyed reading more than going to movies. Joshua shared that he was an only child, and Lucy told him about Nicholas. He sensed a weight lift from her shoulders as she spoke her brother's name, and Joshua didn't interrupt her even when her tone grew distant and reverent. She was running from something. Maybe it was only memories, but it was something they had in common.

Joshua stole a glance at her and tried to think of something witty or funny to say. He wanted to make her laugh, to give her a moment's reprieve from the grief that hung over her like a heavy winter coat. But he wasn't the type. He read books and studied physics. Joshua was dependable. He wasn't the guy who swept a girl off her feet.

"Did you have a boyfriend back home?" he asked. It wasn't going to make her laugh, but his rational mind wanted to know all the variables he might encounter even as he was quite convinced there was no sense in trying to be rational around Lucy Price. She was too intoxicating for him to think straight, but if she was off-limits, he might as well know now.

His question tripped a bemused smile from his companion. "No. I was never one for fooling around with boys."

"But there must have been someone. A . . . ." Joshua trailed off before he could add *a pretty girl like you*. It was the kind of cliéd mumbo jumbo stars said to girls in motion pictures. But still, he reasoned, it was true enough. Lucy was too beautiful not to have attracted anyone's interest.

"A few tried," she said. "But I only recently shed my ugly-duckling feathers. The war was nearly on before I did, and girls can't compete with the call of fame and glory. What about you? Did you leave a girl back home?"

"My hometown is only a few hours from here, but I can assure you that no one misses me there."

"You don't know that," she said.

"I do actually," Joshua said, his eyes boring into the road ahead. "My father hasn't spoken to me since I informed him that I'd left Yale to work for the government."

"He must have been very angry," Lucy said.

"Yes. I suppose when you spend a small fortune trying to keep your son in a cage, you expect it to work," Joshua said dryly.

"I think he wanted to protect you," Lucy said in a soft voice. "My mother pretended to support Nicholas when he enlisted, but she cried every night for a month after he left. She told me that she didn't want him to go. That she'd never see him again. I tried to calm her down, but she insisted that he would never come home again. She said she could feel it."

Joshua heard the ache of tears in her voice and he slowed the car.

"Maybe parents just know," Lucy continued, her voice cracking. "Maybe your father knew and couldn't bear it."

"But your mother let you come here," Joshua said. "She respected your decision and your brother's."

"She doesn't know I'm here," Lucy confessed.

Joshua stopped the car entirely, the tires crunching gravel as they came to a halt. "You didn't tell her?"

"The man who recruited me told me that I couldn't," Lucy said. Her eyebrows knit together as she stared at him.

"Why would he say that?"

"For security reasons." Her answer felt rehearsed somehow as though she'd not only been fed the line but also believed it.

"You should tell your mother," he said.

"Weren't you the one just telling me how horrible your father was?" she asked, crossing her thin arms over her chest.

"Even still, I phoned him to let him know where I was," Joshua said. "I'll put in a request for you. She must be terribly worried."

"She's so sad about Nicholas that she probably hasn't even noticed I'm gone," Lucy said.

"Remember what you said about parents knowing a few moments ago? Right now she doesn't know and that's bound to be driving her more crazy," he said.

Lucy didn't say anything and they sat in silence under a blanket of stars. He started the car back up and continued down the road.

"Where are you taking me anyway?" she asked. "We appear to be in the middle of nowhere. Should I call my mother now?"

His lip twisted up. "You're safe with me, and it's a surprise."

"As long as you aren't taking me off to be murdered." She tried to keep her face straight but the twitch of her lips gave her away.

"I said it was a surprise," Joshua said. "I suppose you'll have to wait and see."

But she didn't have to wait long, and as soon as the sign loomed up over the horizon, he dared another glance at her.

"The Hollywood Canteen?" Lucy's eyes were as round as silver dollars and the stars overhead seemed to dance in them.

"Absolutely," he said. It wasn't that he wanted to impress her exactly, but he guessed that a girl from small-town Illinois might think it was swell to see movie stars. Joshua had seen them his whole life. He hadn't bothered to tell her that he'd spent a good portion of his formative years on back lots. It wasn't something he liked to talk about if he could help it.

A polished and obviously physically fit man greeted them at the door. "Tickets?"

"I'll be on the list," Joshua said.

The man gave him a disbelieving look but retrieved a small card. "Your name?"

"Joshua O'Donnell."

"Yes, sir," the man said, stepping aside immediately. "This way, please."

"Were you a movie star before you decided to take over the world?" Lucy whispered as they entered the swinging canteen.

It had been a country bar before a group of Hollywood elites had hatched their plan to open a canteen for soldiers. No one had bothered to update it to something more posh, so the walls were still painted with cartoonish Western scenes. Long, rustic beams lined the ceilings, in stark contrast to the ten-piece band playing on the stage and the celebrities sprinkled throughout the joint. It wasn't the kind of place starlets would normally flock to, but it wasn't for them—it was for enlisted men, and it was the best way showbiz could find to help, even if it was only giving them a good time before they left to die on foreign soil.

"No," Joshua said with a laugh, checking his fedora. The girl at the counter had ringlets of spun gold that hung perfectly to her shoulders and waved over her forehead. She was really much too pretty to be a coat-check girl. Joshua caught Lucy staring at her.

"Is she an actress?" Lucy asked.

"She'd like to be," Joshua said. "She's clearly been groomed for it, but the American people have less patience for new faces these days. They want their favorites, to keep their minds off the war."

"Are you sure you aren't an actor?" Lucy asked, her eyes narrowing. "You seem to know a lot about show business."

"I'm not an actor," Joshua said as a hostess took them to one of the best tables in the house. "But my father is."

"Wait!" Lucy shrieked. "Is your father Mickey O'Donnell?"

"The one and only," Joshua said. Now that she'd found out, he wished she hadn't. Any girl would want a piece of the fortune now that his father had begun producing films as well. There was even talk of making him head of MGM, but Joshua thought it was unlikely given his father's volatile temper.

"I saw one of his movies," she said. "And I've seen him in the gossip rags."

"Whatever you read isn't true. He'd want me to tell you that."

"Is any of it true?" she asked Joshua.

"Almost all of it, but actors are liars and they expect their children to be as well," he told her. "Lying is a family business in Hollywood."

"It's really too bad you don't get along," Lucy said. Her eyes darted around the room and she gasped, pointing out celebrities serving tables and dancing with soldiers. There was no more mention of Joshua's father, which Joshua found refreshing. She'd only seen one of his movies, after all, and, of course, she'd read about him. But she didn't seem interested past that.

"Do you want to dance?" he asked her.

"I don't really. I haven't ever . . . I don't dance." She stumbled over the words. "You should ask someone else."

Joshua felt a sharp snap in his heart as though it had broken and mended itself in a split second. He couldn't explain it. He simply knew he wanted to hold her, so he sidestepped her excuse and extended his hand. Their eyes met and she took the proffered hand without further protest, allowing him to sweep her onto the floor. They waltzed next to Bob Hope and later Joshua taught her how to jitterbug.

"You told me that you didn't dance," he admonished her as they stepped outside for air.

"I don't. I think I only could because you were here."

Joshua caught her in his arms and pulled her roughly to him. Lucy's face glowed in the moonlight. There was a pretty color in her cheeks, rose washed to silver in the dim night.

"Has anyone kissed you before, Lucy Price?" Joshua asked.

She shook her head, causing a single curl to loosen and fall across her brow. He brushed it away, trailing his fingers down her face and cupping her chin in his hand.

"May I kiss you?" he whispered. An eternity stretched between them before she said the word he needed to hear.

"Yes." She barely managed to push the word past her lips before his mouth was on hers. The kiss consumed her so fully that her body relaxed, nearly going limp in his arms, and she swayed just a little as he held her steady.

Lucy had never kissed a boy before. The war had broken out around the time they started to interest her, and while her friends listened with dreamy eyes to schoolboy plans for guts and glory, Lucy didn't have the stomach for it. But now with

Joshua's lips pressed hot to hers she crumpled against him, thoughts of the dead and the dying slipping as far away as the stars twinkling overhead. His arm wrapped more tightly around her waist, and she fell further into the moment until there was only the roar of her pulse urging the kiss on. When he broke away, he dropped his forehead against hers and they stared into each other's eyes, both knowing a line had been crossed.

But neither caring.

"We should get back to the base," he said. He stepped away from her and looked toward Lucas's car.

She knew he was right, although she wanted to stay here forever. The only thing that waited back on base were tests and scientists, needles and examinations. But Lucy looped her arm through his, allowing him to lead her to the car. It would be over soon. The war would be over and they would be free, but that all seemed too far away tonight when her life felt like it was finally beginning.

_____

Patton lounged in his chair as Dr. Lucas poured two bourbons and handed one to him. The man's office was small and spare, nothing like the places where Patton did business. It was a scientist's lair, stuffed with so many books and papers that there was no room for decorations or furniture beyond the two chairs and table Lucas used to do his research.

"Then you've found exactly what I thought?" Patton asked, wishing to clarify the good news Lucas had just given him.

"I believe so." The doctor's forehead creased as he sipped his drink. He clearly wasn't as thrilled at the unexpected development. "The implications of the findings are quite disturbing."

"I would think a man who had discovered the key to immortality might feel some pride." Patton chuckled at the dumbfounded expression on Lucas's face.

"But at what cost? We must consider the ethical issues at stake."

Patton set his glass on the table and chose his words carefully. It was important that he not sound threatening. "The Cypress Project needs more money. I have that money, and so do many of my associates. We've all done our bit for our country at this point, and more than a few of us are wondering how far you plan to drain our piggy banks to get this off the ground."

"I'm certain the investors understand that what they are doing—"

"The investors are quite simply that: investors. Businessmen don't get into business to help people out. We expect remuneration."

"And the War Department has already informed you that your places in Arras are secure."

"We don't just want *places* in Arras," Patton said. "This new world of yours is going to need leaders, and I can only speak for myself, but I'll be happy to step up in return for some special considerations."

Lucas pulled his glasses from his nose and ran a hand over his tired eyes. "Even without the ethical considerations, it could be years before technology enables us to accomplish what you're asking."

"And we will have years, Dr. Lucas," Patton reminded him. "Thanks to your machines, we'll be able to control time."

Patton sensed this line of argument was getting him nowhere. He needed to make the man see the possibility before him. "Think of what you can do with that time. How much you can accomplish. All it will take is a few words from you and some contracts with my lawyers. I can promise you that I won't be the only one who reaps the benefits of your discovery."

"My unintentional discovery," Lucas said. "And how can you promise me anything?"

"This administration is desperate to see the war end, as is most of the world. They'd promise a man anything if he could put a stop to it, and with my money I'm the man who can pay for that solution."

"I'm not certain you're wealthy enough for that."

"I've spoken with others. Hearst. Kincaid. They're all in as long as you continue the research privately. There's no need to involve the War Department."

"Money won't do you much good once the exodus is over. The administration plans to initiate a socialist structure while Arras is established. Everyone will have to work together—"

"And they will." Patton stopped him. "But until then, money can buy me power. You won't be left out in the cold, Lucas. We'll take care of you as long as you take care of us."

His companion opened his mouth to speak, but hesitated and clamped it shut again. Patton almost had him.

"We'll live forever," Patton promised. "Think of that."

"All of us?"

"The fortunate few," Patton said in a measured voice.

"And you expect people to go along with that? A good portion of Arras's population is going to be American, Mr. Patton. I can't imagine they'll take too kindly to a few men running the show in perpetuity."

"You're thinking of this too clinically," Patton said. "It's simple with a bit of creativity. Our names, the names of these 'few men,' will die and we'll be reborn as new men. The people won't know their leaders haven't changed. Given your experiments with alterations, I hardly think it will be difficult to smooth this over. And we'll have plenty of time to handle the arrangements."

"It strikes me that might be more a curse than a blessing."

"As my friend Kincaid would say, 'To be or not to be.' Are you ready to watch the world destroy itself? Because this war will spread. My sources expect it won't be long until it crosses the Atlantic, and then where will we find the solution when we're hunkered down in bomb shelters?" It was a carefully chosen lie. His sources thought nothing of the sort. Hitler seemed intent on Western Europe at the moment, but it *could* happen, which Patton knew, and which gave him the ability to sell it to Lucas. "In Arras you'll have time to eradicate disease and hunger. We will lift humanity up to the next stage of evolution. These boys you've been testing could be more important than doctors someday. Imagine being able to alter the foundational blocks of biology."

A gleam was growing in Lucas's eyes as Patton continued his speech, and soon the doctor began to nod in agreement with the promises.

"Perhaps I should send a telegram to Albert," Lucas suggested. "If anyone could foresee—"

"You've said yourself that the most important thing is to end this war. Let's focus on that for now," Patton said. He rose from his chair and retrieved his fedora. "I'll be in touch. I only ask you to keep this between us for now, and I'll see that you get what you need for the first stage."

He exited the room, but not before he saw Lucas begin to scribble furiously in the file. He would have to return for it later. For now he had more important things to do. One phone call and he'd be in charge of this alterations department. Then he would see what they could really do. Lucas's initial notes had been very *promising*.

And after that was final, he'd handle Lucas. He'd bought him off for the moment, but he couldn't be certain that would last long. The doctor was burdened with a conscience unsuited to ambition or science. He'd have to find someone else more flexible with his so-called ethics. Patton knew that wouldn't be hard. He'd never had difficulty finding people willing to sell their soul before.

∽

Lucas wrote with such speed that his hand cramped, but he ignored it. He had to reach Albert immediately, but it was difficult to get a line into Nevada at the moment.

Men like Patton were used to getting what they wanted and Lucas hadn't given it to him. Patton had some fair points. Things Lucas might have considered if he'd been given the time, but this world wasn't Arras. There was a war on, men were dying, and it would be all too easy for Patton to buy someone off. A senator, or a general, or even one of Lucas's own men.

Patton displays a near-psychopathic disregard for the general population, imagining the alteration technology will be the proverbial fountain of youth. His clear case of megalomania suggests he will try to buy this technology to further his own agenda. It's recommended that we sever our business relationships

*with Mr. Patton. We cannot wait for a moment of kairos for
this, we must seek resolution as swiftly as possible before it is
too late.*

Lucas sank against his chair and stared at the letter, remembering for a split second the wayward message sent by Friar Lawrence to Romeo, but this was not a love story and more than two lives hung in the balance. He'd take it there himself in the morning.

∽

The base was quiet when they returned, but Joshua knew the night guards would make a note of what time they'd come in and pass it up the chain. He hadn't actually told Lucas he was taking Lucy with him and he was pretty sure his mentor wouldn't have approved of him absconding with their prize candidate for the Cypress Project. But the real reason he wished he could avoid word of their date spreading was because he wanted to keep it himself. It was their secret sealed with a kiss.

Thinking of the kiss distracted him and he glanced over at her. She shifted her long, stockinged legs and smiled at him. He wanted to kiss her again, but he kept his hands on the wheel and parked the car. They were back on base and he needed to think with his head instead of with the other parts of his anatomy vying to run the show.

"Joshua," Lucy said in a quiet voice when he shut off the engine.

He turned toward her, leaning in to kiss her again before he could stop himself. She giggled and pulled back.

"I have a question for you."

"Shoot," he said, a little disappointed that she'd fended him off.

"What are they testing me for? What do they plan to do?"

He could lie and tell her he didn't know, that he didn't have the clearance, which would technically be true. But Joshua did know because he was a Hollywood kid and he'd learned a long time ago that nobody in business talked straight. To get the real story, you had to listen to the unspoken lines between sentences and to the conversations not meant for your ears, and Joshua hadn't been able to help himself. Some of it he'd guessed from the equations and models he'd helped Lucas with, but scientists also loved to talk to themselves as they worked through complex problems. And no one had a temper like a pissed-off researcher. One good rant could spill all the beans.

So he knew exactly what she wanted to know, but it wasn't going to be easy to explain. It all sounded so crazy, even after everything he'd seen. Lucy had managed to touch the quantum threads they'd given her. She'd even affected them, but he doubted that would be enough to make her believe him.

"It's better if I show you," he said.

Because of the success earlier in the day, the labs were dead now. The breakthrough had been enough to warrant Lucas giving everyone the night off. Joshua thought Lucas might have stuck around himself; he'd seemed preoccupied, but then the man was never relaxed. To Joshua's relief, though, even Lucas's office lights were off.

Every man and woman on Lucas's team had signed a contract stating that they wouldn't leave so much as a handkerchief lying around, but Lucas himself kept files in his office. Files that

Joshua had access to. He led Lucy through the dark, stopping at the office door to dig around for the key. It would have felt like a breach of trust if it had been anyone but Lucy he was showing the information to. She was directly involved with this project and she had the right to know what they were going to ask of her. The lock clicked open, and he went in first, fumbling for the lamp. But when he flipped the switch and light flooded the room, he wished he hadn't come.

Lucy's scream barely registered. He couldn't tear his eyes from the body of his mentor collapsed across his desk. The back of his head was missing, leaving behind a thick ooze of blood that swirled black and red. Hideous gray clumps were splattered on the chair behind him.

"Did he . . ." Lucy's voice trailed away, and Joshua was grateful. He couldn't believe Lucas would do this. He did not want to believe it. Not when he was so close.

"We should call someone," Lucy said, tugging his arm gently and trying to lead him away.

But Joshua ignored her. Once the guards came, there would be investigators and questions. They would ask him about what had happened. They would ask Lucy. And neither of them would have any real answers to give. Joshua had questions of his own, and right now they seemed more important. In particular, *why?*

"He wouldn't," Joshua said. It was more a wish than a fact.

"Maybe there's a note," Lucy suggested.

Despite the grisly state of the desk, Joshua stepped forward and carefully sorted through the papers around Lucas's body. There was nothing. No note. No report that might explain why Lucas had taken such a drastic measure. He went around to the back of the desk and opened the single drawer, only to find a few pens and a picture of Lucas's wife and son.

Perhaps it was that he didn't want to believe his mentor would take his own life or perhaps it was that photograph or maybe it was the different angle, but when he looked back up at the desk, it struck him that the desk was too neat. Too organized. Matthew Lucas was a genius at everything but organizing.

"Someone straightened his papers," he said in a hoarse whisper. Lucy moved next to him and took his hand.

"Maybe a secretary before . . ."

"No." Joshua shook his head. "No one was allowed to touch his desk but me. He said I was too young to know any better."

"Than to mess with his stuff?"

"Than to steal it," Joshua said. A chill began at the base of his skull in the exact spot that was now missing from his mentor's head. He had been murdered, Joshua was sure, but there was no proof. "Someone's killed him."

Lucy sucked in a breath, but didn't speak.

"There's no way to prove that. I'm sure I sound crazy, but I know it, Lucy."

Her girlish face was pale, maybe even a little green from their discovery, but she gave him a small, supportive smile. "I believe you. But if he was, maybe we should leave. Whoever did this—"

"Could come after us," he finished for her. She was right. The longer he stayed there searching for clues, the more danger he was placing her in. "Let's get out of here."

"Wait." Lucy grabbed his arm. "What's that?"

She pointed to the chair and Joshua saw a piece of paper

sticking out of Lucas's pants pocket. It had been shoved in hastily and Joshua was able to pull it free easily. He ignored the cling of iron on his tongue from the heavy scent of blood around the desk and smoothed the paper out. It was a note addressed to Albert. Joshua didn't know any Alberts on the base, but it was clear from the content of the note that this man was working on the Cypress Project.

"What does it mean?" Lucy asked. Her voice was high, but other than that and a slight tremble in her hands, Joshua thought she was holding up remarkably well.

"They're building a new world, Lucy," he told her, the truth spilling out. There was no time to wait for proof. Lucas had surely died because of what he'd discovered. "They're going to create a world with those machines they've been testing you on, and girls like you are going to create it."

"That's not possible," she said. "What is he talking about, though? 'Fountain of youth'?"

"I'm not sure. There are other experiments going on. Soldiers have been brought in. I haven't seen any of them myself, but I heard Lucas talking about the things they could do. They can manipulate people. Change them. There's an entire department devoted to studying this alteration ability."

"Change them how?" Her voice was hollow, and he worried she might faint.

"Change their memories. Maybe even their faces. Lucas said the experiments were a bust. Unethical. He was going to stop them," Joshua said. But he hadn't been able to. Someone had stopped him first. Up until this moment Joshua had believed he was working for the greater good. Now he wasn't so sure that the Cypress Project wasn't going to destroy the entire world. It was supposed to end violence, but now Joshua was staring at proof that it was going to do the opposite.

"We need to find out who Albert is," Lucy said. "Anyone here could have killed the doctor."

"But Lucas trusted Albert, and he kept this message safe. He didn't want his killer to discover it."

"No, he didn't." It wasn't Lucy's voice. It was a man's, and the couple looked up, startled.

"How long have you been there?" Lucy asked Patton in a whisper.

"Long enough." Patton snapped a finger and two guards rushed into the room. Joshua struggled against them and Lucy came to his aid, kicking at the guard. The man struck her hard across the face and the blow knocked her to the ground.

"Lucy!" Joshua cried, losing focus only to find his hands pinned behind his back as a pair of handcuffs snapped shut over his wrists. The guard pushed him out the door past Patton, but Joshua pulled away, cornering Patton against the door. "You did this!"

"I wouldn't say anything more," Patton said. "Your fingerprints are all over that room, and then you attacked that poor girl."

"What are you going to do to her?" Joshua snarled.

"She'll be fine, I can promise you. The Cypress Project needs her. You, however, are expendable."

And at a flick of Patton's wrist, Joshua was dragged away.

⟨∽⟩

She awoke under a light so bright that for a moment she thought she was blind, but as Lucy blinked, shapes swam around her.

As the seconds passed, the room stayed fuzzy and out of focus. If it weren't for the outlines of the light and the crease where the walls met in the corner, she might have thought she was dead. Then there was the matter of the cuffs that strapped her down to the bed.

Her throat felt stuffed with cotton, and she couldn't force a swallow to wet it. Although she was mostly blind, all her other senses were as sharp as the tip of a knife. Lucy felt the pulse of blood in her dry throat. She thought she might be able to count each hair on her body as they stood up, alert to the danger she'd found herself in.

Because despite having very little memory of how she'd got here, she knew she was in trouble.

Something had gone horribly wrong and it didn't take perfect vision or a clear memory to tell her that.

The door clicked open and Lucy heard the *tap-tap-tap* of shoes on tile, growing closer with each step, and then the stranger spoke, or rather barked, "Turn that light down."

She froze when she heard the voice, and a rush of memories came back to her in a tangle. She sorted through them until she found the face the voice belonged to: Patton.

"What have you done with Joshua?" The question scratched across her parched tongue.

"You're awake," Patton said.

Lucy fought against the panic tumbling through her body, but she stayed calm. Patton wasn't the type to take kindly to a hysterical girl, and thankfully Lucy had never qualified as one. The door behind her had begun to open and close to a stream of traffic, but Patton was the only one interested in speaking to her. The others didn't look at her, even as they came to check the monitor by her bed. A pretty young nurse with a freckled nose gave her a sip of water and then disappeared without a word. With others nearby, she was safe for now.

"Why am I in cuffs? And where is Joshua?" she asked again.

"Your young friend couldn't join us," Patton replied as he tapped a finger against her bindings. "He's been . . . reassigned to avoid further issues."

"We didn't do anything wrong," Lucy said. Her voice rose an octave, not from fear, but from the injustice of her situation.

"Of course you didn't, my dear. Young girls need to be protected from predators like Mr. O'Donnell. It was a mistake I won't allow to happen again." He hovered over her like a cat closing in on a mouse, and Lucy realized he'd only removed his competition. She shrank back against the exam table, but there was nowhere to go. She couldn't run. She couldn't call for help. No one nearby seemed concerned for her safety and without Joshua she was friendless here. She strained against her cuffs to distract herself from crying.

"I'm afraid that you're much too important to our plans," Patton said. "We can't afford for you to run off again."

"I'll cooperate," she promised, but she couldn't quite keep the hint of a lie out of her words.

"You *will* cooperate. I've already seen to that."

The night's events grew clearer with each passing moment, and bile rose in her mouth as she recalled Lucas's body collapsed on his desk with the back of his skull blown out. She was in danger, which meant she had to play the one card she had. Lucy dropped her voice to a whisper. "I know what you're planning."

Patton's jaw tightened, and Lucy thought he might strike her, but instead he straightened up. "Out!"

The others in the room exited swiftly and Patton locked the door of the lab behind them.

"I suppose you want to bargain then." He drew up a stool and sat across from her bed. "What's your *price* then, Miss Price?"

She narrowed her eyes at him.

"A little joke," he said, "to lighten the mood."

"I suspect most things about you are little."

The smug grin dropped from his face. "Let's talk business. Before one of us does something we'll regret."

"You're creating a new world," Lucy said. "And keeping it from this one."

"That's hardly a secret. We can't announce our intentions until we're certain we will succeed."

"And when you make the announcement, who gets to go and who will be left to die?" It wasn't so much a question as an accusation.

Patton didn't blink. "We can't save everyone. This war has taught us that."

"And who will you save? The rich? The powerful?"

"Yes, but we will also save the intelligent and the healthy and the strong. This new world—Arras—will be a fresh start for humanity. Imagine it, Miss Price. No wars. No famine. Soon not even disease. We can control it all."

Lucy had heard crackpots talking before, trying to sell their visions to eager buyers. A friend had dragged her to a Pentecostal church once and she'd watched people speak in tongues and men heal the sick of heart. It had been revolting, save for one thing: the fervent belief that had pervaded that tent. It had been palpable, hanging in the air like sticky, humid heat. How her heart had pounded, her cheeks growing red in the crush of the crowd. She'd almost believed it all herself.

She thought Patton could use a lesson or two in selling lies, especially to himself.

"And what about the alterations department?" she asked when he'd finished the last of his sales pitch. "What will you use it for?"

"Arras needs strong leaders to establish order—" he began.

Lucy laughed at him. "The same leaders in perpetuity? That's what those plans said. You called these alterations 'the proverbial fountain of youth.' You want to live forever. You don't care about saving anyone but yourself."

"It's fortunate for you that the alterations department exists." Patton stood and moved toward the door.

"And why is that? Are you going to kill me like you killed Dr. Lucas?" She spit the question at him, anger boiling over inside her. It was impossible to hide it.

"Alterations have another use, Miss Price. They can alter memories. Our tests so far have had varying success rates, but I'm sure our boys only need more practice." Patton's lips curved into a thin smile that didn't reach his near-black eyes.

"Is that a threat?"

"It's a promise. Prepare yourself, Miss Price. You've been chosen to help us build the new world," he said.

"And if I won't?"

"You will, because after my boys are done with you, you

won't remember this conversation. You won't even be Lucy Price anymore. Enjoy tonight. Tomorrow will be a whole new world."

And with that he flipped a switch, washing away the room in a torrent of light and screams.

THE
TOO-CLEVER
FOX

Leigh Bardugo

BY LEIGH BARDUGO

Six of Crows

~The Grisha Trilogy ~

Shadow and Bone

Siege and Storm

Ruin and Rising

Meet Leigh Bardugo

The idea for "The Too-Clever Fox" began with a moment in *Siege and Storm*, the second book in the Grisha Trilogy, when my protagonist, Alina, meets a privateer named Sturmhond. Sturmhond is a trickster—brilliant, glib, and cocky to a fault. As soon as you encounter him, you know that some of his schemes are bound to backfire. "He reminds me of the too-clever fox, another of Ana Kuya's stories," Alina says, "smart enough to get out of one trap, but too foolish to realize he won't escape a second."

At the time, that line was really all I knew about the story of Koja, the too-clever fox. I didn't know who he would meet, who he'd best, or who he'd fail to best. With my novels, I always create an outline. I don't feel safe writing without one. But with my shorter work I just let the story unfold. Sometimes, I begin by literally telling the story, speaking it out loud as if I were sitting by the fire on a stormy night. ("You want to hear a story? All right then, be very quiet and I will tell you the tale of an ugly little fox. What was his name? Well, he didn't have one to begin with . . .")

I've written three Ravkan folk tales now, and each is a (very loose) retelling of a well-known fairy tale. They're meant to be stories that the characters of the Grisha Trilogy would have been told when they were younger. "The Too-Clever Fox" is a retelling of "Little Red Riding Hood," but you'll find it heavily steeped in the magical-animal tales of Russian folklore. "The Witch of Duva" and "Little Knife" are based on two fairy tales that always bothered me as a kid, "Hansel and Gretel" and "Rumpelstiltskin," respectively. (If your dad lets your evil stepmother send you into the woods to die, why would you even want to go back? And who would want to marry a king who threatens to kill you if you don't spin a room full of straw into gold? Not a great way to start a relationship.)

For me, these stories are a chance to mess with some of the iffy ideas in fairy tales—the conflation of beauty and goodness, all those wicked witches and stepmothers. "The Too-Clever Fox" is a morality tale ("pride comes before the fall, kids!"), but I hope it's also a look into the loneliness we all experience. And the stories give me a way to shed light on how religion, superstition, and myth might blur in a world where magic really does exist. In the trilogy, the country of Ravka is protected by a magical military elite known as the Grisha. But though the Grisha train in a palace and live lives of privilege and luxury, ordinary Ravkans view them with fear and suspicion. There are also magical creatures that can increase a Grisha's power and that are often hunted by them—none of the animals talk in the trilogy, but in "The Too-Clever Fox," they get to weigh in on how they might feel about this state of affairs.

Okay, but how did Ravka and the Grisha Trilogy come to be? It really all began with a question—what if darkness was a place? In fantasy, darkness usually works as a metaphor (a dark age is coming, darkness falls across the land), but what if darkness had physical form? And what if the creatures you imagined lurking in the dark were real? What if you had to fight them on their own territory? Those ideas became the basis for the Shadow Fold, the swath of nearly impenetrable darkness that has torn the country of Ravka in two. Because the truth is, no matter how old we get, our fear of the dark never completely goes away. It's the monster under the bed, the creature in the closet waiting for you to turn out the light. As a child, I was convinced that there were a pair of two-headed red dragons living in my closet. Why two? No idea. You'd think one two-headed dragon would be enough to scare a kid. Of course they could only get out if someone accidentally left the closet door open. That's the thing about dragons and doorknobs—no thumbs.

I've been making up stories since I was lying in my bed trying to work up the courage to slam that closet door shut. In middle school, I discovered science fiction and fantasy and began writing down my stories as a way of dealing with a pretty rough reality. I always dreamed of becoming a writer and through the Grisha trilogy I've gotten to introduce readers to some of my favorite monsters, to a country of ice and snow and dark magic, and to a girl named Alina who discovers an extraordinary power that makes her the most valuable Grisha in the kingdom. In my new book, *Six of Crows*, I'll be taking readers to a different corner of the Grisha world, a city ruled by thugs and thieves, and a gang of young criminals who must pull off an impossible heist. And then who knows? There are always new worlds to explore and more monsters waiting in the dark.

The Too-Clever Fox

by Leigh Bardugo

The first trap the fox escaped was his mother's jaws.

When she had recovered from the trial of birthing her litter, the mother fox looked around at her kits and sighed. It would be hard to feed so many children, and truth be told, she was hungry after her ordeal. So she snatched up two of her smallest young and made a quick meal of them. But beneath those pups, she found a tiny, squirming runt of a fox with a patchy coat and yellow eyes.

"I should have eaten you first," she said. "You are doomed to a miserable life."

To her surprise, the runt answered, "Do not eat me, Mother. Better to be hungry now than to be sorry later."

"Better to swallow you than to have to look upon you. What will everyone say when they see such a face?"

A lesser creature might have despaired at such cruelty, but

the fox saw vanity in his mother's carefully tended coat and snowy paws.

"I will tell you," he replied. "When we walk in the wood, the animals will say, 'Look at that ugly kit with his handsome mother.' And even when you are old and gray, they will not talk of how you've aged, but of how such a beautiful mother gave birth to such an ugly, scrawny son."

She thought on this and discovered she was not so hungry after all.

∽

Because the fox's mother believed the runt would die before the year was out, she didn't bother to name him. But when her little son survived one winter and then the next, the animals needed something to call him. They dubbed him *Koja*—"handsome"— as a kind of joke, and soon he gained a reputation.

When he was barely grown, a group of hounds cornered him in a blind of branches outside his den. Crouching in the damp earth, listening to their terrible snarls, a lesser creature might have panicked, chased himself in circles, and simply waited for the hounds' master to come take his hide.

Instead Koja cried, "I am a magic fox!"

The biggest of the hounds barked his laughter. "We may sleep by the master's fire and feed on his scraps, but we have not gone so soft as that. You think that we will let you live on foolish promises?"

"No," said Koja in his meekest, most downtrodden voice. "You have bested me. That much is clear. But I am cursed to grant one wish before I die. You only need name it."

"Wealth!" yapped one.

"Health!" barked another.

"Meat from the table!" said the third.

"I have only one wish to grant," said the ugly little fox, "and you must make your choice quickly, or when your master arrives, I will be obliged to bestow the wish on him instead."

The hounds took to arguing, growling, and snapping at one another, and as they bared their fangs and leapt and wrestled, Koja slipped away.

That night, in the safety of the wood, Koja and the other animals drank and toasted the fox's quick thinking. In the distance, they heard the hounds howling at their master's door, cold and disgraced, bellies empty of supper.

❧

Though Koja was clever, he was not always lucky. One day, as he raced back from Tupolev's farm with a hen's plump body in his mouth, he stepped into a trap.

When those metal teeth slammed shut, a lesser creature might have let his fear get the best of him. He might have yelped and whined, drawing the smug farmer to him, or he might have tried gnawing off his own leg.

Instead Koja lay there, panting, until he heard the black bear, Ivan Gostov, rumbling through the woods. Now, Gostov was a bloodthirsty animal, loud and rude, unwelcome at feasts. His fur was always matted and filthy, and he was just as likely to eat his hosts as the food they served. But a killer might be reasoned with—not so a metal trap.

Koja called out to him. "Brother, will you not free me?"

When Ivan Gostov saw Koja bleeding, he boomed his

laughter. "Gladly!" he roared. "I will liberate you from that trap and tonight I'll dine on free fox stew."

The bear snapped the chain and threw Koja over his back. Dangling from the trap's steel teeth by his wounded leg, a lesser creature might have closed his eyes and prayed for nothing more than a quick death. But if Koja had words, then he had hope.

He whispered to the fleas that milled about in the bear's filthy pelt. "If you bite Ivan Gostov, I will let you come live in my coat for one year's time. You may dine on me all you like and I promise not to bathe or scratch or douse myself in kerosene. You will have a fine time of it, I tell you."

The fleas whispered amongst themselves. Ivan Gostov was a foul-tasting bear, and he was constantly tromping through streams or rolling on his back to try to be rid of them.

"We will help you," they chorused at last.

At Koja's signal, they attacked poor Ivan Gostov, biting him in just the spot between his shoulders where his big claws couldn't reach.

The bear scratched and flailed and bellowed his misery. He threw down the chain attached to Koja's trap and wriggled and writhed on the ground.

"Now, little brothers!" shouted Koja. The fleas leapt onto the fox's coat, and despite the pain in his leg, Koja ran all the way back to his den, trailing the bloody chain behind him.

It was an unpleasant year for the fox, but he kept his promise. Though the itching drove him mad, he did not scratch and even bandaged his paws to better avoid temptation. Because he smelled so terrible, no one wanted to be near him, yet still he did not bathe. Whenever Koja got the urge to run to the river, he would look at the chain he kept coiled in the corner of his den. With Red Badger's help, he'd pried himself free of the trap, but he kept the chain as a reminder that he owed his freedom to the fleas and his wits.

Only Lula the nightingale came to see him. Perched in the branches of the birch tree, she twittered her laughter. "Not so clever, are you, Koja? No one will have you to visit and you are covered in scabs. You are even uglier than before."

Koja was untroubled. "I can bear ugliness," he said. "I find the one thing I cannot live with is death."

♋

When the year was up, Koja picked his way carefully through the woods near Tupolev's farm, making sure to avoid the teeth of any traps that might be lurking beneath the brush. He snuck through the hen yard, and when one of the servants opened the kitchen door to take out the slops, he slipped right into Tupolev's house. He used his teeth to pull back the covers on the farmer's bed and let the fleas slip in.

"Have a fine time of it, friends," he said. "I hope you will forgive me if I do not ask you to visit again."

The fleas called their good-byes and dove beneath the blankets, looking forward to a meal of the farmer and his wife.

On his way out, Koja snatched a bottle of *kvas* from the pantry and a chicken from the yard, and he left them at the entrance to Ivan Gostov's cave. When the bear appeared, he sniffed at Koja's offerings.

"Show yourself, fox," he roared. "Do you seek to make a fool of me again?"

"You freed me, Ivan Gostov. If you like, you may have me as

supper. I warn you, though, I am stringy and tough. Only my tongue holds savor. I make a bitter meal, but excellent company."

The bear laughed so loudly that he shook the nightingale from her branch in the valley below. He and Koja shared the chicken and the *kvas*, and spent the night exchanging stories. From then on, they were friends, and it was known that to cross the fox was to risk Ivan Gostov's wrath.

⌀

Then winter came and the black bear went missing. The animals had noticed their numbers thinning for some time. Deer were scarcer, and the small creatures, too—rabbits and squirrels, grouse and voles. It was nothing to remark upon. Hard times came and went. But Ivan Gostov was no timid deer or skittering vole. When Koja realized it had been weeks since he had seen the bear or heard his bellow, he grew concerned.

"Lula," he said, "fly into town and see what you can learn."

The nightingale put her little beak in the air. "You will ask me, Koja, and do it nicely, or I will fly someplace warm and leave you to your worrying."

Koja bowed and made his compliments to Lula's shiny feathers, the purity of her song, the pleasing way she kept her nest, and on and on, until finally the nightingale stopped him with a shrill chirp.

"Next time, you may stop at 'please.' If you will only cease your talking, I will gladly go."

Lula flapped her wings and disappeared into the blue sky, but when she returned an hour later, her tiny jet eyes were bright with fear. She hopped and fluttered, and it took her long minutes to settle on a branch.

"Death has arrived," she said. "Lev Jurek has come to Polvost."

The animals fell silent. Lev Jurek was no ordinary hunter. It was said he left no tracks and his rifle made no sound. He traveled from village to village throughout Ravka, and where he went, he bled the woods dry.

"He has just come from Balakirev." The nightingale's pretty voice trembled. "He left the town's stores bloated with deer meat and overflowing with furs. The sparrows say he stripped the forest bare."

"Did you see the man himself?" asked Red Badger.

Lula nodded. "He is the tallest man I've ever seen, broad in the shoulders, handsome as a prince."

"And what of the girl?"

Jurek was said to travel with his half sister, Sofiya. The hides he did not sell, Jurek forced her to sew into a gruesome cloak, which trailed behind her on the ground.

"I saw her," said the nightingale, "and I saw the cloak, too. Koja . . . its collar is made of seven white fox tails."

Koja frowned. His sister lived near Balakirev. She'd had seven kits, all of them with white tails.

"I will investigate," he decided, and the animals breathed a bit easier, for Koja was the cleverest of them all.

Koja waited for the sun to set, then snuck into Polvost with Lula at his shoulder. They kept to the shadows, slinking down alleys and making their way to the center of town.

Jurek and his sister had rented a grand house close to the taverns that lined the Barshai Prospekt. Koja went up on his hind legs and pressed his nose to the window glass.

The hunter sat with his friends at a table heaped with rich foods—wine-soaked cabbage and calf stuffed with quail eggs, greasy sausages and pickled sage. All the lamps burned bright with oil. The hunter had grown wealthy indeed.

Jurek was a big man, younger than expected, but just as handsome as Lula had said. He wore a fine linen shirt and a fur-lined vest with a gold watch tucked into his pocket. His inky blue eyes darted frequently to his sister, who sat reading by the fire. Koja could not make out her face, but Sofiya had a pretty enough profile, and her dainty, slippered feet rested on the skin of a large black bear.

Koja's blood chilled at the sight of his fallen friend's hide, spread so casually over the polished slats of the floor. Ivan Gostov's fur shone clean and glossy as it never had in life, and for some reason, this struck Koja as a very sad thing. A lesser creature might have let his grief get the best of him. He might have taken to the hills and high places, thinking it wise to out-run death rather than try to outsmart it. But Koja sensed a question here, one his clever mind could not resist: For all his loud ways, Ivan Gostov had been the closest thing the forest had to a king, a deadly match for any man or beast. So how had Jurek bested him with no one the wiser?

For the next three nights, Koja watched the hunter, but he learned nothing.

Every evening, Jurek ate a big dinner. He went out to one of the taverns and did not return until the early hours. He liked to drink and brag, and frequently spilled wine on his clothes. He slept late each morning, then rose and headed out to the tanning shed or into the forest. Jurek set traps, swam in the

river, oiled his gun, but Koja never saw him catch or kill anything.

And yet, on the fourth day, Jurek emerged from the tanning shed with something massive in his muscled arms. He
walked to the wooden frames, and there he stretched the hide
of the great gray wolf. No one knew the gray wolf's name and
no one had ever dared ask it. He lived on a steep rock ridge
and kept to himself, and it was said he'd been cast out of his
pack for some terrible crime. When he descended to the valley, it was only to hunt, and then he moved silent as smoke
through the trees. Yet somehow, Jurek had taken his skin.

That night, the hunter brought musicians to his house. The
townspeople came to marvel at the wolf's hide and Jurek bid
his sister rise from her place by the fire so that he could lay the
horrible patchwork cloak over her shoulders. The villagers
pointed to one fur after another, and Jurek obliged them with
the story of how he'd brought down Illarion, the white bear of
the north, then of his capture of the two golden lynxes who
made up the sleeves. He even described catching the seven little
kits who had given up their tails for the cloak's grand collar.
With every word Jurek spoke, his sister's chin sank lower, until
she was staring at the floor.

Koja watched the hunter go outside and cut the head from
the wolf's hide, and as the villagers danced and drank, Jurek's
sister sat and sewed, adding a hood to her horrible cloak. When
one of the musicians banged his drum, her needle slipped. She
winced and drew her finger to her lips.

What's a bit more blood? thought Koja. The cloak might as
well be soaked red with it.

∽

"Sofiya is the answer," Koja told the animals the next day. "Jurek must be using some magic or trickery, and his sister will know of it."

"But why would she tell us his secrets?" asked Red Badger.

"She fears him. They barely speak, and she takes care to keep her distance."

"And each night she bolts her bedroom door," trilled the nightingale, "against her own brother. There's trouble there."

Sofiya was only permitted to leave the house every few days to visit the old widows' home on the other side of the valley. She carried a basket or sometimes pulled a sled piled high with furs and food bound up in woolen blankets. Always she wore the horrible cloak, and as Koja watched her slogging along, he was reminded of a pilgrim going to do her penance.

For the first mile, Sofiya kept a steady pace and stayed to the path. But when she reached a small clearing, far from the outskirts of town and deep with the quiet of snow, she stopped. She slumped down on a fallen tree trunk, put her face in her hands, and wept.

The fox felt suddenly ashamed to be watching her, but he also knew this was an opportunity. He hopped silently onto the other end of the tree trunk and said, "Why do you cry, girl?"

Sofiya gasped. Her eyes were red, her pale skin blotchy, but despite this and her gruesome wolf hood, she was still lovely. She looked around, her even teeth worrying the flesh of her lip. "You should leave this place, fox," she said. "You are not safe here."

"I haven't been safe since I slipped squalling from my mother's womb."

She shook her head. "You don't understand. My brother—"

"What would he want with me? I'm too scrawny to eat and too ugly to wear."

Sofiya smiled slightly. "Your coat is a bit patchy, but you're not so bad as all that."

"No?" said the fox. "Shall I travel to Os Alta to have my portrait painted?"

"What does a fox know of the capital?"

"I visited once," said Koja, for he sensed she might enjoy a story. "I was the Queen's personal guest. She tied a blue ribbon around my neck and I slept upon a velvet cushion every night."

The girl laughed, her tears forgotten. "Did you, now?"

"I was quite the fashion. All the courtiers dyed their hair red and cut holes in their clothes, hoping to emulate my patchy coat."

"I see," said the girl. "So why leave the comforts of the Grand Palace and come to these cold woods?"

"I made enemies."

"The Queen's poodle grew jealous?"

"The King was offended by my overlarge ears."

"A dangerous thing," she said. "With such big ears, who knows what gossip you might hear."

This time Koja laughed, pleased that the girl showed some wit when she wasn't locked up with a brute.

Sofiya's smile faltered. She shot to her feet and picked up her basket, hurrying back down the path. But before she disappeared from view, she paused and said, "Thank you for making me laugh, fox. I hope I will not find you here again."

Later that night, Lula fluffed her wings in frustration. "You learned nothing! All you did was flirt."

"It was a beginning, little bird," said Koja. "Best to move slowly." Then he lunged at her, jaws snapping.

The nightingale shrieked and fluttered up into the high branches as Red Badger laughed.

"See?" said the fox. "We must take care with shy creatures."

⁓

The next time Sofiya ventured out to the widows' home, the fox followed her once more. Again, she sat down in the clearing and again she wept.

Koja hopped up on the fallen tree. "Tell me, Sofiya, why do you cry?"

"You're still here, fox? Don't you know my brother is near? He will catch you eventually."

"What would your brother want with a yellow-eyed bag of bones and fleas?"

Sofiya gave a small smile. "Yellow is an ugly color," she admitted. "With such big eyes, I think you see too much."

"Will you not tell me what troubles you?"

She didn't answer. Instead she reached into her basket and took out a wedge of cheese. "Are you hungry?"

The fox licked his chops. He'd waited all morning for the girl to leave her brother's house and had missed his breakfast. But he knew better than to take food from the hand of a human, even if the hand was soft and white. When he did not move, the girl shrugged and took a bite of it herself.

"What of the hungry widows?" asked Koja.

"Let them starve," she said with some fire, and shoved another piece of cheese into her mouth.

"Why do you stay with him?" asked Koja. "You're pretty enough to catch a husband."

"Pretty enough?" said the girl. "Would I be better served by yellow eyes and too large ears?"

"Then you would be plagued by suitors."

Koja hoped she might laugh again, but instead Sofiya sighed, a mournful sound that the wind picked up and carried into the gray slate sky. "We move from town to town," she said. "In Balakirev I almost had a sweetheart. My brother was not pleased. I keep hoping he will find a bride or allow me to marry, but I do not think he will."

Her eyes filled with tears once more.

"Come now," said the fox. "Let there be no more crying. I have spent my life finding my way out of traps. Surely I can help you escape your brother."

"Just because you escape one trap, doesn't mean you will escape the next."

So Koja told her how he'd outsmarted his mother, the hounds, and even Ivan Gostov.

"You are a clever fox," she conceded when he was done.

"No," Koja said, "I am the cleverest. And that will make all the difference. Now tell me of your brother."

Sofiya glanced up at the sun. It was long past noon.

"Tomorrow," she said. "When I return."

She left the wedge of cheese on the fallen tree, and once she was gone, Koja sniffed it carefully. He looked right and left, then gobbled it down in one bite and did not spare a thought for the poor hungry widows.

⌒

Koja knew he had to be especially cautious now if he hoped to loosen Sofiya's tongue. He knew what it was to be caught in a trap. Sofiya had lived that way a long while, and a lesser creature might choose to live in fear rather than grasp at freedom. So the next day he waited at the clearing for her to return from the widows' home, but kept out of sight. Finally, she came trundling over the hill, dragging her heavy sled behind her, the wool blankets bound with twine, the heavy runners sinking into the snow. When she reached the clearing, she hesitated. "Fox?" she said softly. "Koja?"

Only then, when she had called for him, did he appear.

Sofiya gave a tremulous smile. She sank down on the fallen tree and told the fox of her brother.

Jurek was a late riser, but regular in his prayers. He bathed in ice-cold water and ate six eggs for breakfast every morning. Some days he went to the tavern, others he cleaned hides. And sometimes he simply seemed to disappear.

"Think very carefully," said Koja. "Does your brother have any treasured objects? An icon he always carries? A charm, even a piece of clothing he never travels without?"

Sofiya considered this. "He has a little pouch he wears on his watch fob. An old woman gave it to him years ago, after he saved her from drowning. We were just children, but even then, Jurek was bigger than all the other boys. When she fell into the Sokol, he dove in after and dragged her back up its banks."

"Is it dear to him?"

"He never removes it and he sleeps with it cradled in his palm."

"She must have been a witch," said Koja. "That charm is what allows him to enter the forest so silently, to leave no tracks and make no sound. You will get it from him."

Sofiya's face paled. "No," she said. "No, I cannot. For all his snoring, my brother sleeps lightly and if he were to discover me in his chamber—" She shuddered.

"Meet me here again in three days' time," said Koja, "and I will have an answer for you."

Sofiya stood and dusted the snow from her horrible cloak. When she looked at the fox, her eyes were grave. "Do not ask too much of me," she said softly.

Koja took a step closer to her. "I will free you from this trap," he said. "Without his charm, your brother will have to make his living like an ordinary man. He will have to stay in one place and you will find yourself a sweetheart."

She wrapped the cables of her sled around her hand. "Maybe," Sofiya said. "But first I must find my courage."

❧

It took a day and a half for Koja to reach the marshes where a patch of dropwort grew. He was careful digging the little plants up. The roots were deadly. The leaves would be enough to manage Jurek.

By the time he returned to his own woods, the animals were in an uproar. The boar, Tatya, had gone missing, along with her three piglets. The next afternoon their bodies were spitted and cooking on a cheery bonfire in the town square. Red Badger and his family were packing up to leave, and they weren't the only ones.

"He leaves no tracks!" cried the badger. "His rifle makes

no sound! He is not natural, fox, and your clever mind is no match for him."

"Stay," said Koja. "He is a man, not a monster, and once I have robbed him of his magic, we will be able to see him coming. The wood will be safe once more."

Badger did not look happy. He promised to wait a little while longer, but he did not let his children stray from the burrow.

✑

"Boil them down," Koja told Sofiya when he met her in the clearing to give her the dropwort leaves. "Then add the water to his wine and he'll sleep like the dead. You can take the charm from him unhindered, just leave something useless in its place."

"You're sure of this?"

"Do this small thing and you will be free."

"But what will become of me?"

"I will bring you chickens from Tupolev's farm and kindling to keep you warm. We will burn the horrible cloak together."

"It hardly seems possible."

Koja darted forward and nudged her trembling hand once with his muzzle, then slipped back into the wood. "Freedom is a burden, but you will learn to bear it. Meet me tomorrow and all will be well."

Despite his brave words, Koja spent the night pacing his den. Jurek was a big man. What if the dropwort was not enough? What if he woke when Sofiya tried to take his precious charm? And what if they were successful? Once Jurek lost the witch's protection, the forest would be safe and Sofiya would be free. Would she leave then? Go back to her sweetheart in Balakirev? Or might he persuade his friend to stay?

Koja got to the clearing early the next day. He padded over the cold ground. The wind had a blade's edge and the branches were bare. If the hunter kept preying upon the animals, they would not survive the season. The woods of Polvost would be emptied.

Then Sofiya's shape appeared in the distance. He was tempted to run to meet her, but he made himself wait. When he saw her pink cheeks and that she was grinning beneath the hood of her horrible cloak, his heart leapt.

"Well?" he asked as she entered the clearing, quiet on her feet as always. With her hem brushing the path behind her, it was almost as if she left no tracks.

"Come," she said, eyes twinkling. "Sit down beside me."

She spread a woolen blanket on the fallen tree and opened her basket. She unpacked another wedge of the delicious cheese, a loaf of black bread, a jar of mushrooms, and a gooseberry tart glazed in honey. Then she held out her closed fist. Koja bumped it with his nose. She uncurled her fingers.

In her palm lay a tiny cloth bundle, bound with blue twine and a piece of bone. It smelled of something rotten.

Koja released a breath. "I feared he might wake," he said at last.

She shook her head. "He was still asleep when I left him this morning."

They opened the charm and looked through it: a small gold button, dried herbs, and ashes. Whatever magic might have worked inside it was invisible to their eyes.

"Fox, do you really believe this is what gave him his power?"

Koja batted the remains of the charm away. "Well, it wasn't his wits."

Sofiya smiled and pulled a jug of wine from the basket. She poured some for herself and then filled a little tin dish for Koja to lap up. They ate the cheese and the bread and all of the gooseberry tart.

"Snow is coming," Sofiya said as she gazed into the gray sky.

"Will you go back to Balakirev?"

"There is nothing for me there," Sofiya said.

"Then you will stay to see the snow."

"Long enough for that." Sofiya poured more wine into the dish. "Now, fox, tell me again how you outsmarted the hounds."

So Koja told the tale of the foolish hounds and asked Sofiya what wishes she might make, and at some point, his eyes began to droop. The fox fell asleep with his head in the girl's lap, happy for the first time since he'd gazed upon the world with his too-clever eyes.

⁓

He woke to Sofiya's knife at his belly, to the nudge of the blade as it began to wiggle beneath his skin. When he tried to scramble away, he found his paws were bound.

"Why?" he gasped as Sofiya worked the knife in deeper.

"Because I am a hunter," she said with a shrug.

Koja moaned. "I wanted to help you."

"You always do," murmured Sofiya. "Few can resist the sight of a pretty girl crying."

A lesser creature might have begged for his life, given in to the relentless spill of his blood on the snow, but Koja struggled

to think. It was hard. His clever mind was muddled with dropwort.

"Your brother—"

"My brother is a fool who can barely stand to be in the same
room with me. But his greed is greater than his fear. So he stays
and drinks away his terror, and while you are all watching him
and his gun, and talking of witches, I make my way through
the woods."

Could it be true? Had it been Jurek who kept his distance,
who drowned his fear in bottles of *kvas*, who stayed away from
his sister as much as he could? Had it been Sofiya who had
brought the gray wolf home and Jurek who had filled their
house with people so he wouldn't have to be alone with her?
Like Koja, the villagers had credited Jurek with the kill. They'd
praised him, demanded stories that weren't rightfully his. Had
he offered up the wolf's head as some kind of balm to his sister's pride?

Sofiya's silent knife sank deeper. She had no need for clumsy
bows or noisy rifles. Koja whimpered his pain.

"You are clever," she said thoughtfully as she started to peel
the pelt from his back. "Did you never notice the sled?"

Koja clawed at his thoughts, looking for sense. Sofiya had
sometimes trailed a sled behind her to carry food to the widows' home. He remembered now that it had also been heavy
when she had returned. What horrors had she hidden beneath
those woolen blankets?

Koja tested his bonds. He tried to rattle his drugged mind
from its stupor.

"It is always the same trap," she said gently. "You longed for
conversation. The bear craved jokes. The gray wolf missed

music. The boar just wanted someone to tell her troubles to. The trap is loneliness, and none of us escapes it. Not even me."

"I am a magic fox . . ." he rasped.

"Your coat is sad and patchy. I will use it for a lining. I will keep it close to my heart."

Koja reached for the words that had always served him, the wit that had been his tether and his guide. His clever tongue would not oblige. He moaned as his life bled into the snowbank to water the fallen tree. Then, hopeless and dying, Koja did what he had never done before. He cried out, and high in the branches of her birch tree, the nightingale heard.

Lula came flying and when she saw what Sofiya had done, she set upon her, pecking at her eyes. Sofiya screamed and slashed at the little bird with her knife. But Lula did not relent.

⁋

It took two days for Sofiya to stumble from the woods, blind and near starving. In time, her brother found a more modest house and set himself up as a woodcutter—work to which he was well suited. His new bride was troubled by his sister's mad ramblings of foxes and wolves. With little regret, Lev Jurek sent Sofiya to live at the widows' home. They took her in, mindful of the charity she'd once shown them. But though she'd brought them food, she'd never offered kind words or company. She'd never bothered to make them her friends, and soon, their gratitude exhausted, the old women grumbled over the care Sofiya required and left her to huddle by the fire in her horrible cloak.

As for Koja, his fur never sat quite right again. He took more care in his dealings with humans, even the foolish farmer

Tupolev. The other animals took greater care with Koja, too. They teased him less, and when they visited the fox and Lula, they never said an unkind word about the way his coat bunched at his neck.

The fox and the nightingale made a quiet life together. A lesser creature might have held Koja's mistakes against him, might have mocked him for his pride. But Lula was not only clever. She was wise.